Dear [...]

Many thanks!

May you enjoy your

journey through

Transylvania!

With gratitude!

[signature]

♡

W9-CPY-327

· THE WEAVERS CHRONICLES ·

THE GOD'S CHAIR

E. C. VARGA

EMTC Publishing | Calgary, Alberta, Canada

THE WEAVERS CHRONICLES
Book One
The God's Chair

© 2018 E.C. Varga

Published by:
EMTC Publishing
Calgary, Alberta, Canada
www.TheWeavers.website

All rights reserved. No part of this book may be reproduced or transmitted in any form or by any means, electronic or mechanical, including pho-tocopying, recording, or by any information storage and retrieval system, without permission in writing from the publisher, except for the inclusion of brief quotations in a review.

Book design by TLC Graphics, *www.TLCGraphics.com*
Cover Design: Tamara Dever; Interior Design: Erin Stark

Spider web image © Depositphotos.com/ihor_seamless

ISBN: 978-0-9937096-0-9

Printed in Canada

I give thanks to the Lord, for he is good;
his love endures forever.

—1 CHRONICLES 17:34

∞

To my husband, thank you.
Transylvania, your homeland, is truly beautiful
and has enough mystery to fill the pages of thousands of books,
starting with this one…and thank you for believing
I could write because "my greeting cards were novels."

∞

Contents

ഗ്ലൗ

When spider webs unite,
they can tie up a lion.

—ETHIOPIAN PROVERB

✺

When Weavers' webs unite,
they can tie up a dragon.

—TRANSYLVANIAN PROVERB

✺

Brothers

It was hot—way too hot! Any normal person would have passed out by now. Any normal person would have escaped this heat long ago and made a mad dash to the nearest source of relief, like a bathtub full of ice. It has to be said that any normal person wouldn't have even been here at all.

But Mike wasn't normal and he knew it. He knew exactly where he was. He was in a vast underground labyrinth, dimly lit by thousands of torches that lined many broad, tall passageways sparkling with a rainbow of colours from the millions of diamonds and gems embedded in the rock. Everywhere small mounds burst with toxic steam, creating a fatal atmosphere for any normal human. The ground burnt your feet, the heat emanating from the tall rock walls so intense it could scorch you from several feet away. A large underground lake, scattered with small islands, gurgled and popped continuously...like a boiling pot of water. Not a single crevice of sanctuary existed, not for humans anyway.

This shouldn't have been a place for Mike either—yet it was. He felt as connected to this place as twins might to one another or even steel to a magnet. He tried to rationalize that this wasn't possible—he should have passed out by now, been burned to death, gone up in flames—but here he was.

It was always the same…walking the familiar passage that would just about lead him to the chamber he knew so well yet had never seen. He was breathing and walking as usual, as if his entire body was heat resistant. It was definitely hot, that he *could* feel, but it was soothing warmth, like a hot bath or the heat of the tropical sun on his back.

He was close to the chamber now. He couldn't see it in the dimly lit corridor, but he knew without a doubt that he was. Whether he wanted to be here or not, it was as if his very soul was being pulled towards the chamber by invisible rope—he was the steel ball rolling unwillingly towards the massive powerful magnet behind the chamber wall.

Only a few feet away now…he held his breath in anticipation of what he would encounter—what would happen next? He took the next step carefully, exactly as he had done so many times before; for years he had made it this far, maybe this time he would make it one step farther. Maybe this time he would make it all the way. He had wasted many hours of his young life wondering what that chamber contained. At times the thought was all-consuming and he couldn't, try as he might, think about anything else. Whatever it was, it belonged to him, solely, like a member of his body, and it could be claimed by no other.

Taking a deep breath, he raised his foot slowly to take the next step, the step that never happens. His heart was pounding so hard he could hear it in his head, his breathing quickening in anticipation. His foot suspended in mid-step, he froze momentarily, waiting….

Would he make it one step farther this time, or would it…?

Swoosh!

It came from behind, it always did, a great gust of hot wind, nearly knocking him off his feet. The vice then closed in around his body, powerful and gentle, never hurting him. He experienced a rush of exhilaration, even though it had happened the same way every time, as he was lifted high into the air. Higher and faster he was being pulled towards the opening at the top of the cave that from the ground appeared as a tiny hole, a pinprick in the landscape. As he soared towards it, the hole grew larger and larger. The path from ground to opening was full of obstacles: large chunks of rock jutted out into his path, small boulders fell as he travelled higher. He had no control of his movements and was at the mercy of what was pulling him. As they negotiated the treacherous path towards the opening, he was whipped side to side.

Suddenly he was out, being gently placed onto solid ground. He should have been frustrated beyond belief, and he was, to a degree—he had been so close! But he was too euphoric to think about it now, as adrenalin coursed through him. He had known it would happen this way, but that didn't change how he felt every time. The flight out of the cave was thrilling and in his heart he knew that his friend, his *brother*, had come exactly at the right time. But, as much as he wanted to know what lay in that chamber and that it belonged to him, he also knew that he was not ready.

Now, exhilarated yet cautious, Mike grasped his brother's long scaly neck and swung himself up onto his back. This action came naturally to him and his movements were executed with ease. He steadied himself, his arms still wrapped tightly around his brother's neck, and whispered a genuine "Thank you" in his ear.

"You shouldn't have been down there! You're not ready yet!" his brother scolded as he got poised to fly, but Mike knew he wasn't really angry, he knew that his brother cherished their time together as much as he did.

"Now, let's get out of here!" Mike shouted, tightening his grip.

The dragon needed no convincing. Before Mike had even finished his command, his brother had stepped forward off the cliff on which they had been standing and dove into the air. They disappeared into thick clouds and all that could be heard were Mike's shouts of joy. This was his favourite part. It felt so real, he felt so alive! Just when it looked like they were careening to their death below came the bursts of air that hit Mike on both sides and the whooping sound of his brother's huge wings as they worked to lift them both up. Higher and higher they went, bursting up through the clouds, then gradually levelling off...

Everything above the clouds was peaceful. It was morning and Mike marvelled as the sun rose, bright rays catching the wispy ends of cloud as heat evaporated the thick cloud cover, creating striking rainbows. He was only a teenage boy, but even *he* could appreciate the glory of what he was seeing. It took his breath away.

There was no breeze except that which came from his brother's wings. Like so many times before, he took this peaceful moment to reflect on his brother. He wasn't sure how he knew they were brothers. They hadn't grown up together, no one had told him that they were, and they certainly weren't alike; in fact they weren't even the same species. Despite this, there was a bond so powerful between them that he just knew, like twins separated at birth who knew their other half even if they'd never met.

Now, a screech so loud and terrible coming from behind him tore through the sky and ripped Mike from his thoughts. Instinctively, his brother dove through the thick clouds below. Mike turned to see what had caused the noise, making the hairs on the back of his neck stand on end. He had only a split second before they were engulfed in wet cloud cover, and all he could see was that the sky had filled with fire behind him.

"*W-what was that?*" Mike shouted over the sound of his brother's beating wings, his voice quivering with terror.

"You are not ready for this yet. Not yet! I will get us out of this!" his brother shouted back, talking more to himself than Mike.

There came another screech, this time seeming farther away, but the effect was the same—it made Mike's skin crawl and it felt as though his heart had stopped beating several minutes before. He gripped his brother's neck tighter.

"What do you mean by, *I am not ready for this yet?* What *exactly* is following us and *why?*" he demanded, but it was futile asking; he knew he wouldn't get an answer, he never did.

Mike sensed his brother's alarm. He hated this part, hated that he could do nothing to take the fear away. No matter how many times they had been here together, it would always be the same. They would always be helpless against their pursuer. Mike willed it to be different. *Just once,* he thought, *just once…please* be different! It wasn't. As usual, he received no reply, so he asked the same question he always did—full of fear and feeling frantic.

"What was…?"

Before he could finish, he was cut off.

"*Shh*! We have to be quiet. *It* is listening."

He knew the silence would come and also the feeling that came with it. Whatever it was that was pursuing them seemed to be capable of emitting a sense of dread so powerful it curdled both Mike's and his brother's blood. Mike could feel the dragon twitching beneath him. He knew what was coming next, yet the feeling of shock and terror would be the same as it had been so many times before. He could do nothing to stop it, nothing to stop any of this, he never could. He wanted to scream, he wanted it to end, wanted to never feel this afraid ever again, wanted to never feel his brother's fear ever again. But he didn't scream and he couldn't end it; he just let it play out the way he always did. He let his brother prepare, then, on cue…*It* came….

As quiet, fast and dead-on accurate as an eagle zooming down onto its prey, *It* was there, right on top of them, giant razor-sharp claws as clear and strong as diamonds, stretching out ready to grab them and tear them apart. Mike knew he would avert this first attempt and yet it still seemed instinctive and as new as ever as he swerved to the right, clinging to his brother's neck and yelling for him to hang on as the creature also banked to the right. They dove through the cloud cover at a speed Mike had never known he possessed but yet had expected—just as before.

The brothers continued their fast descent, their pursuer only seconds behind. Again, Mike was aghast at how fast his brother was, and so agile and prepared. Yet he enjoyed the rush of pride he always felt at this point, and he delighted in the feeling of hope that followed. Even though he knew what came next, it would still be unexpected, it would still shatter his world and his heart would break so completely that he would never be the same again.

His brother's course was taking them into the mountain range below, to the caves. Mike knew exactly the one to which his brother was aiming. The mountain range below was the Carpathian Mountains, which Mike had researched after the first time this had happened. The landscape was committed to his memory now.

He promised himself that one day, when he was old enough, he would go back there—he would be reunited with his brother.

They were nearly there now, but still several hundred feet above the tip of the nearest mountain top. Just seconds behind, their pursuer was getting too close, but they needed to slow down otherwise their momentum would send them crashing into the mountainside. Spreading his vast, glorious wings, the dragon slowed, just enough. Mike knew the cave they were heading for and sensed the diversion his brother was intending to create, but another attacker swooped up towards them, catching his brother off guard. A familiar despair filled Mike. To avoid a collision, they came to a complete stop and attempted a sharp bank to the left. The movements were too sudden for Mike and he lost his grip.

Everything that followed happened so quickly, exactly the same as it always did, and yet that never did anything to prepare Mike or change the outcome. As he hurtled through the sky, screaming, reaching out for his brother, the mountain tops sped towards him. He watched help-lessly, full of the terror that came with certain death as their giant pursuer wrapped its massive claws around his brother's body. The diversion created by the second attacker had put the dragon right into the monster's path—there was no escape. In a final act of tyranny, *It* stared right at Mike with blazing eyes as it plummeted towards its death, sinking massive teeth into his brother's neck, then releasing him from its grip and letting him fall to the ground—dead.

Mike's heart shattered. He screamed and screamed as he watched his brother fall. He wanted this to end, wanted it to change, he didn't want this to be real! Filled with rage, he looked back up at *It*, screaming and cursing him to death when he realised the killer was directly above him. *It* expelled a deafening roar of triumph as *It* wrapped its claws around Mike, a mere second before he would have hit the mountain top....

Screaming, Mike bolted upright in his bed, his heart pounding, tears pouring down his face, his body shaking uncontrollably and soaked with sweat. He slowly forced his eyes open and saw that he was in his own bed. Doubtful that he was seeing right, he felt around himself, frantically grabbing at the sheets and his own body, checking his arms for any signs of injury made by his pursuer's claws. Noth-ing!—not even a tiny scratch. The clock on his bedside table read 3:33 a.m. Relief flooded his body as he realised that it had only been a dream—it happened the same way every time and on the same day every year.

"Well, another year older. Happy sixteenth birthday, Mike," he said to himself quietly.

He continued to sit in the dark a while longer, like he always did, running the details of the dream over and over in his mind, committing them to memory and mourning the loss of his brother, who seemed to only exist in his dreams.

Breakfast and Brandy

The upsetting night made for a rough start that morning. Mike went through his morning routine, his movements mechanical as his mind wandered through last night's dream. A feeling of melancholy hung over him—he was used to this after the dream as well. He knew none of it was real, but a heavy burden weighed on his heart as if it had all really happened.

But now, as he entered his small kitchen he was greeted by the delicious smell of bacon and eggs. His father, who was busy pouring waffle batter and hadn't noticed him enter, had made it a birthday tradition that on the years when he remembered it was Mike's birthday (a condition we'll discuss later) he made him his favourite breakfast. Mike backed up and peeked around the corner to watch his father unnoticed. The birthday breakfast was a good sign. It meant today would be a normal day.

Mike's father was a kind man. Standing at five feet eleven, he had a good physique, lean but solid, and he didn't look to be in his forties. He was handsome as far as Mike could tell, at least judging by the number of single, and not so single, ladies in the neighborhood who went out of their way to speak to him on the rare occasions he went out. His father had a difficult time with simple tasks such as grocery shopping, banking, etc., and Mike had always accompanied him on those trips.

It was a mortifying experience watching as ladies made a great fuss of him. Usually they wore way too much make-up, giggled way too much, drooled way too much and exposed way too much body! Mike was sure there were some visual images he would never be able to erase from his mind. On occasion, ladies would include him in all the fuss too, pinching his cheeks with unnaturally soft, waxy manicured hands with bright false nails too long to do anything with. Their over-Botoxed, pouting, siren-red lips invaded his personal space as they commented on how handsome he was and how he looked "just like his daddy!" Those were the days when Mike wanted to scrub his eyeballs out with bleach. His father was never rude, but Mike could see he was uncomfortable, and he often felt in awe of how cleverly his father could wriggle his way out of their talon-like grips without offending them. His father's kind eyes and thick Hungarian accent gave him a vampire-like advantage that seemed to work magic.

More often than not, though, Mike saw confusion and a heavy sadness in his father's eyes. When Mike was age two, he and his parents had been victims of a random attack back home in Transylvania (Romania) where he was born. His father had suffered several severe blows to the head, which had left him severely paranoid with a sporadic memory. Mike's mother had been killed in the attack and, to make the situation so much worse, the attackers, who were never apprehended, took her body. Somewhere in Transylvania is a grave marked with the name Linnea Weaver, an empty grave. Since the attack, neither Mike nor his father had ever been back.

Mike had no recall of these events and his father's memory of what happened afterwards was sketchy at best, but he told Mike that he decided to leave Transylvania and come to North America for their safety. Mike knew the rest: they had moved from city to city every couple of years since. His father said all the moves were for his health, and that each move brought the promise of better health care and his memory being restored, but Mike suspected that it had more to do with his paranoia than anything else.

Each move always was preceded by a visit from Mike's Uncle Laszlo, the only relative he had ever met. Laszlo was his father's first cousin and only friend. He only came every couple of years and within a few days after his visit Mike would be told that they were moving again. He hated the upheaval, but had to admit that his uncle's visits had a profound effect on his father's clarity. For a month or so after each visit he was normal—well, almost.

As much as Mike enjoyed his uncle's company, he really didn't want to see him too soon. He didn't want to move anymore. He knew the moves were for his father's health, which had been the focus of most of his life, but Mike felt isolated and trapped. He knew there was more out there for him. He felt guilty for thinking this, but he knew it was true.

This morning, Mike continued to watch his father, who was whistling as he placed a large plate of fresh, steaming hot waffles on the table. He looked up when his son finally decided to enter the kitchen, and greeted him with a warm smile and birthday wishes.

"Happy birthday, my son, happy birthday—I prepared all the things you like!"

He hugged Mike and pulled out a chair for him, beckoning him to sit down to the breakfast feast. A fresh wave of guilt passed over Mike. He couldn't quite meet his father's gaze as he thanked him for all he had done, but his appreciation was genuine.

"Thank you, Apa (Papa). Everything looks great! Let's dig in!"

His father was an inch from sitting in the chair when he suddenly jumped up.

"Wait! I forgot something!"

He left the kitchen and went into the dining room. Mike could hear him pulling things in and out of the china cabinet, mumbling.

"Now, where did I put the good stuff?"

He rummaged a moment longer, then appeared back in the kitchen, holding two shot glasses in one hand, a bottle of clear liquid in the other and a triumphant smile on his face.

"What the…?" Mike gave his father a stern look. "Is that what I think it is?"

His father simply smiled and began to pour out the clear liquid.

"Oh, oh, oh no…no, no, no, Apa, I have school today! Everyone will be able to smell it on my breath!"

"Ah!" His father dismissed Mike's concern with a wave of his hand. "You're a big boy now, bigger than me. This…," he pointed to the small, innocent-looking shot glass, "this is nothing. It's…*mouthwash*!" he said, smiling innocently as he handed Mike his glass.

Palinka, silva palinka—looked like water, tasted like gasoline on fire! Back home most people made their own. Plum, sour cherry, pear, there were all kinds. You could drink it before a meal, after a meal, to celebrate, to drown

your sorrows, to settle the nerves or stomach; it was probably the cure for the common cold! No matter, Mike was
sure he'd never be "man" enough to drink it without choking. His father had been kind and had only filled his glass
halfway. He was so sincere in his offer and Mike knew there
was tradition laced in there, so, with as genuine a smile as
he could muster, he lifted his glass to his father's, toasted
his birthday and drank the fiery liquid down.

It was exactly as awful as Mike expected it to be and he
downed his entire glass of orange juice to quench the burn
in his throat.

"*Ugh*! That...was...great!" Mike lied. Both of them
burst out laughing.

Hanna

"Thanks for breakfast, Apa!"

Mike shoved a handful of mints into his mouth and waved goodbye to his father as he made his way to the bus stop. Not wanting to miss the school bus, Mike ran the entire distance to the stop and made it just as the bus pulled up. Out of breath and coughing from nearly having choked on the mouthful of mints, he took his usual seat near the back of the bus. His mouth burned and, finally swallowing the last mint, the thought that he may have taken a few too many at once crossed his mind.

Mike's stop was only the second of several stops the bus made and only a few kids were on the bus. Four others got on at the same stop as Mike: Darren, a good friend of his and fellow wrestler, who was already snoring in the seat behind Mike; Samuel, another good friend, who had mumbled a quick but friendly hi as Mike had climbed on and then quickly turned his attention back to his text book—the same thing he did every morning; Steven, a quiet boy, who had recently transferred to their school and seemed to prefer books to people, but had a knack for wrestling, so Mike knew him; and last, but definitely not least, was Hanna, *the* most beautiful girl he had ever laid eyes on. She had moved to Calgary eight months ago and lived in the same neighbourhood as Mike.

Hanna had been the one who had approached Mike first, catching him completely off guard that first day. Mike had moved to Calgary in the fall, a year before Hanna arrived. He had established a small group of friends with whom he hung out at school, but the bus ride home had always been him alone and all the way at the back. Mike had preferred it that way; he had never socialized much outside school, and certainly never had any friends over because of his father's condition. It was too complicated to explain. He didn't really even understand it himself.

Hanna had sat by herself at the front of the bus for the first few days. At school she kept to herself and barely spoke in class.

Mike had tried to make "accidental" eye contact with her a few times without much success. The one time it worked, he was sure his face turned the brightest shade of red imaginable. After that failed attempt, he settled to just observing her from a distance. He'd watch how she floated down the hallways at school, how perfectly she chewed her food at lunch, how melodic her voice was the few times she spoke (like a choir of angels!) and how many other boys adopted a zombie-like trance when she walked by. Only a couple of days later Mike had noticed Andrew, a grade twelver, speaking to Hanna in the lunch lineup. He was an honour student, nominated as school valedictorian, was captain of the football team and, according to ninety-eight percent of the female population, he was "hot." He had it all and *he* had spoken to Hanna. Mike had to make a move fast or he might lose her to a cliché.

The last lesson of the day, social studies, was one of his favourites and he had always received honours in this class.

Usually Mike never struggled to pay attention, but today he barely heard a word his teacher said; instead he had spent the entire time rehearsing what he would say to Hanna. By the end of the class he had decided that, "Hey!" and a nod of his head as he casually passed her seat on the bus was the best approach and the one least likely to draw attention to himself should Hanna choose not to even acknowledge him. That thought made his stomach twist with anxiety.

The bell rang and Mike jumped out of his seat and ran outside to his locker. He quickly grabbed his backpack, slammed his locker shut, startling the girl whose locker was beside his and, ignoring the glare from her, made his way to the bus before he lost his nerve. He stepped onto the bus, clearing his throat a little as a last preparation, his stomach lurching unnaturally, only to find that Hanna wasn't there yet. All that rehearsing and he had forgotten to consider that he needed to let her get on the bus first.

Other kids were piling onto the bus now and Mike was going to have to move. Frustrated, he walked to the back of the bus and slumped down onto his seat, sinking down as low as he could. Feeling very foolish, he closed his eyes and shut the world out, allowing himself to wallow in a little self-pity. He had barely begun to feel sorry for himself when he felt someone sit down next to him. Irritated that his moment of misery had been interrupted by someone who would choose today of all days to occupy the spot he considered to be solely his, he opened his eyes, preparing to make his irritation clear to this rude individual, when the sound of angels descended upon him.

"Hey, are you all right?"

She had only spoken five words, but they were words he would never forget, ever! Mike was sure he couldn't appear more shocked than he was at that moment. There beside him, on *his* seat, sat Hanna.

"What…ya…uh umm…" He cleared his throat of the frog inside it and pulled himself up from his slumped position. "I'm great…um, I mean I'm fine. How are you?"

Internally he smacked himself on the head. Had he just really said that? Hanna giggled, causing his face to turn scarlet. She put her hand out and introduced herself.

"I'm Hanna."

Mechanically, as if his hand had a mind of its own, he extended it and wrapped his fingers around hers.

"I'm Mike," he said in a daze as they shook hands.

"Do you mind if I sit here?" she asked shyly.

"Of course…I mean no…I mean…" He paused and tried to regain his composure, which was difficult—her beautiful green eyes were looking into his. He tried again. "I mean, yes, of course you can."

"Great, thanks!" She smiled with relief, pointing to her seat at the front of the bus. "Someone took my usual seat," she added.

Mike turned his head slightly, making sure to keep at least one eye on Hanna—he still couldn't believe his luck. There, sitting in the seat that had unofficially belonged to Hanna, was a boy whom Mike had never seen before, but he had the sudden urge to thank him profusely! He turned his attention back to Hanna, who was smiling at him. She looked so beautiful and perfect sitting beside him.

At first he was afraid that he wasn't capable of normal speech, but as the bus ride began, so did the conversation.

It was the same the next morning on the bus and the afternoon and every day since. Mike would never forget that day. It was permanently imprinted on his heart. He was eternally grateful to the boy who had sat in her seat that day. Mike had never seen him on their bus again, not even at school, so Hanna's seat once again became available, but she never sat there again. That was Mike's favourite part of the memory.

Feelings

Now, on his birthday, Mike sat alone on the bus. It rarely happened, but today Hanna would not be there. He had been looking forward to seeing her today of all days; he thought of it as his birthday present to himself just to be beside her for the ride to school. As soon as the bus pulled away he remembered her mentioning an early morning appointment, so she'd see him at the library, where they often met during spare classes. Only a couple of hours; that's not so bad, he thought to himself then drifted into a half-sleep....

To his great relief, Hanna was waiting for him at their usual table in the library, just as she had promised. Mike's day improved substantially from that point on. His lunch hour wrestling match was stellar; not only did he win, but Hanna was there to witness his triumph. The rest of the day went as well as grade eleven could, and soon Mike was boarding the bus once again for the ride home.

"Excellent wrestling match, dude!"

"You made record time today, Mikey!"

The compliments came thick and fast with a full-on whack to the middle back—meant as pure encouragement, of course. Mike slid over on the school bus seat to make room as his extremely tall and broad friend, Darren, flung himself onto it, pinning Mike between himself and the window.

"Thanks, Darren, and my back thanks you too! Just for the record, in case I never mentioned this, my name's not Mikey or dude! Mike will do."

Darren was quick to notice that Hanna had just taken a sudden interest in the boys' conversation. Sensing that this was the reason for Mike's odd reaction to being called Mikey, Darren chose to use the situation to Mike's full advantage, after all, what were good friends for?

"Riigghht!" he drawled, winking at Mike. "Yo! Hanna, did you catch Mikey's...I mean, *Mike* would love to tell you all about it. Hey Mike, isn't that what you were just sayin'?" Darren asked, simultaneously winking and nudging him in the ribs.

"Uh, yeah, thanks Darren!" Mike said, glaring at him as he jumped out of the seat and pulled Hanna across the aisle onto their seat.

Hanna landed with a small shriek, quickly composed herself and smiled warmly at Mike.

"Hey Mike—Darren is right, you really were *awesome* at today's match."

"You came to watch?" Mike asked, trying to act casual as if he hadn't noticed her there.

"I *always* come to watch," Hanna replied, flashing him another famously Hanna, warm smile. "Someone's got to be there to cheer you on!"

"Yeah, you're right," he replied. "Darren's not the cutest of cheerleaders!"

They both laughed and the two of them talked for the remainder of the bus ride. Mike never tired of watching her as she spoke. Her smile made his heart skip a beat, and when she looked at him her dark green eyes seemed to look right through to his soul. He couldn't help noticing things like her hair; it was the most beautiful colour of strawberry blonde. Were boys even supposed to know what strawberry blonde looked like? Her voice, as soft as angels, he loved listening to her speak—it seemed to calm his very being. When they were together it seemed as if they were in their own world, like a magical force field that existed only around them. Mike gave his head a little shake—*where did these thoughts come from?* He felt like his mind was turning into a sappy romantic novel. Thank goodness his friends couldn't read his thoughts!

His mind drifted to other thoughts as Hanna carried on talking. Memories of his dream last night surfaced again, leaving him feeling melancholy. His father's condition also presented itself at the same time. Mike knew he wasn't getting better, even if this morning's breakfast seemed perfectly normal. Mike knew better—it was only getting worse. Thoughts of moving away slowly permeated his other thoughts, jostling for position—front and centre. That changed his feeling from melancholy to frustration.

Mike had moved almost every two years since he was three and he should be used to it by now, he thought, but this time things seemed different. Maybe it was his age. Maybe it was his father's deteriorating condition, or maybe it was that he was tired of moving from place to place and he longed to feel something different. Maybe it was just Hanna. Whatever the reason, his ties with the friends he had made at Memorial High School were definitely stronger. He was sixteen now, so he hoped that would give him a little more say in the matter of moving again. Deep down he knew his father wasn't improving, so staying put might be helpful to him. *Who am I kidding?* he thought. His father was going to need more than Mike's help and an occasional visit from Uncle Magic to help him. He tried not to think about it, but he really hoped that this time they would stay. He enjoyed the new feelings he was experiencing.

The bus came to its first stop, jolting Mike back to reality. Hanna was already gathering her bags together to get off.

"Hey, daydreamer, you ready to get off?" she asked, winking at Mike, making the process of standing twice as hard for him.

He was sure she had magical powers too! With a wink of an eye she could make him go weak in the knees. He smiled back at her.

"Guess I'm a little sore from today's wrestling match."

This was the busiest bus stop. The bus driver waited patiently for the droves of kids to exit the bus then, with a goodbye wave, shut the door. Everyone dissipated into their groups or wandered off by themselves, taking the many different paths to their homes. Shouts of "Later!" and "See ya!" were heard.

Darren, Hanna, Mike and a few of Mike's other friends walked the first couple of blocks home together. Although Mike and Hanna walked side by side, they both carried on conversations with the others, knowing that the last part of their journey home would leave them alone with one another. It was getting harder for Mike to hide the feelings he had for Hanna. His friends managed to do an excellent job of embarrassing him on a daily basis in front of her, so he guessed they knew. She hadn't run away screaming in the opposite direction yet, so Mike was going to take that as a good sign.

Calgary was the city where Mike and his father lived now. It was one of the largest cities they had lived in thus far. They blended in well and were able to live peacefully and quietly in their small community. Like so many other big cities in the western world, you could live in the same neighbourhood for years and never really get to know your neighbours. Most of their moves throughout Canada and the United States were for that very reason. Mike's father preferred it that way—you don't bother your neighbours and they don't bother you. Mike, however, would have preferred to know a few members of his community better—Hanna's family in particular.

Their group was nearing the end of the block where they would part ways. Mike's hopes that their departure from the group would go silently for a change were dashed when Darren, his *former* best mate, broke into a chorus of:

"Mike and Hanna sittin' in a tree, *k i s s i n g*. First comes love..." and so on.

Darren's level of maturity could only be rivalled by that of a five year old. Mike tried to hide his embarrassment and came back with a quick response.

"You'd think that after all these years someone might come up with something better than that!"

This remark only managed to open the floor to the rest of the group and their comments.

"We all know you like her, Mikey!"

"Mikey, when are ya gonna ask Hanna to marry you?"

"Don't do anything I wouldn't do!"

Mike grabbed Hanna by the hand.

"Come on, let's get out of here! These guys could go on forever!"

They made a dash around the corner and into the lane behind the houses. This wasn't their regular route, but Mike was willing to go anywhere, just as long as it was away from his friends! When they were out of sight and earshot, they slowed to a walk. Taking a moment to catch their breath, Mike spoke apologetically.

"Sorry about that!"

"You don't have to be sorry," said Hanna, giggling a little. "You and your friends make me laugh."

"Well, they have the opposite effect on me," he said sarcastically, trying not to look Hanna in the eyes, which just made her giggle even more.

The colour in Mike's cheeks doubled as they walked in silence for a few moments. *She hasn't let go of my hand,* Mike thought. Afraid that Hanna might make the same observation and pull away, Mike tried to keep up the appearance of being calm. Inside though, his heart rate had tripled, small beads of perspiration began to form on his brow and he had suddenly lost the ability to speak. He had heard friends make comments about "sweaty palms" and was seriously debating whether or not to pull his hand away before that happened to him. She would never want to hold his hand again! He was focusing all his will on having dry palms that he didn't even notice the strange look Hanna was giving him, until she spoke.

"Are you all right, Mike? You suddenly got so quiet."

Mike barely had a chance to be embarrassed, let alone reply, when she tightened her grip on his hand a little and turned to him.

"You've had another dream, haven't you?" she asked apprehensively. "It's…it's your birthday today, right?" she said, pausing for a moment then blurting out, "and you look like you received the *weight of the world* as a birthday gift…."

Her cheeks flushed pink as she said it. Mike looked at her standing there, her hands in his, biting her lip and swaying on her tippy toes, playfully avoiding his gaze. *She knows me so well*, he thought. Mike lost the ability to speak momentarily. He had no idea how much time had passed since she had asked her question, until she waved her hand in front of his face to gain his attention.

"*Helloooo!*" she exclaimed, blushing a little.

The only other person whom Mike had confided in about his dreams was his father, but Mike was sure he forgot the dreams from year to year, despite the deeply concerned looks he gave Mike anytime his son mentioned them. Eventually Mike had just stopped telling him. To this very moment, he didn't know why he had told Hanna. There was no reasonable explanation. He thought she was simply amazing and had qualities about her that he just couldn't put into words, but he was still amazed that the words had even come out of his mouth that day he'd told her his dreams. Something had told him that she was *the* only one who would understand.

Still holding her hands in his, he looked into those dark green eyes and spoke quietly.

"Yeah, it was exactly the same one as last year."

Uncle Laszlo

They arrived at the point where they usually split up, going to their own homes. He had no intention of doing anything different today; however, she was still holding his hand, she hadn't thought he was crazy and… well, there was no "and." He simply wanted to savour this moment as long as he could, so he decided that he would walk her home first.

Their conversation turned to the day's events. Hanna was giving a minute by minute account of the "friendly competition turned vicious" volleyball game in gym class as they passed by Mike's house. He looked up, as one would naturally do when passing your own home, and noticed that the curtains were drawn in the den. That in itself wasn't entirely strange, but the outline of two figures cast upon the curtains by the light in the room was.

"Oh no…" he said in despair, interrupting Hanna.

"Hey—you OK?" she asked.

"What?" Mike whipped his head back to face her, realizing that he must have spoken out loud. "Oh, yeah," he said, smiling weakly. She wasn't convinced and gave him a look that said so. He caved in easily and gave a sigh of defeat. "Actually, I'm not."

"What is it, Mike, what's wrong?"

She was so genuinely concerned for him that Mike cringed at what he was about to say.

"Hanna…," he started.

"Yes?"

"I think my uncle is visiting…." He felt like such a schmuck. "He only comes when there's bad news," he said, knowing it sounded so lame.

"Oh Mike, that's terrible—you should go in and see if it's him."

Was it possible for her to be more beautiful *and* kind? He was going weak at the knees.

"I'm sorry, Hanna. I wanted to walk you home and I was…well, I was really enjoying our talk and all…."

His voice trailed off; he couldn't make anything sound right. Two minutes ago everything had seemed perfect and now the possible threat of his uncle being the second figure behind the curtain had changed everything.

"I enjoyed myself too," Hanna replied shyly, "but you really should go and make sure that your dad is alright. You can walk me home tomorrow…and the next day!" she added playfully with a wink.

She was a saint…seriously!

"Thanks, Hanna, *really*… I feel bad (worse than she could imagine, because unless that was a stranger in his home, which *never* happened, it was most definitely his uncle and *his appearance* usually preceded *their disappearance*), can I call you later?"

"I'd love that!" She smiled warmly, gave his hand a squeeze then let go, turned slowly, but before walking away she put her hand up to her ear in the shape of a phone. "Don't forget to call me," she said, and left him with one more gorgeous smile.

"I won't," Mike said, with a smile, lingering a moment,

watching her as she walked away, then with a sigh he turned and walked slowly up to his front door.

He opened the door and stepped into the small hallway. His heart sank. There was an odd looking pair of heavy black boots on the floor and a long, dark trench coat hung neatly above them. He decided right then not to announce his arrival. He yanked at his shoes and considered hurling them clear across the room. He was mad. His uncle's arrival couldn't have been more poorly timed. Under different circumstances Mike was sure he might like his uncle, spend some quality time with him, toss a football around even, but that would be under "normal" circumstances. His visits, the few that he had honoured them with, were anything but normal, so no uncle-nephew bond was going to happen today.

Quietly he walked down the hallway towards the den, where he was sure they were plotting his swift removal from paradise. The closer he drew, the clearer he could hear their hushed voices. He stopped and strained his ears to see if he could pick up some of what they were saying. He couldn't make out much; it was too quiet and the words they spoke, although usually in Hungarian, sounded different. But what they were saying was puzzling. Maybe they talked quietly because they knew he was there. If this was the case then he should make his presence known, but he didn't feel like it, he didn't want to speak to them at all right now—he wasn't ready for it. He continued quietly down the hallway, intending to find solitude in his room, when suddenly he was aware of several flashes of light coming from under the den door.

"*What the…?*"

Mike was startled. He covered his mouth immediately, realizing that he had spoken out loud. What are they doing in there? he wondered. Finding out would mean he'd have to engage in conversation, so he left it, resigning himself to the thought that every visit from Uncle Laszlo was strange, so why should this be any different? Mike hurried down the hallway to his room. He made it just as his father peered through the den doorway, his face white, calling out in a panic-stricken voice.

"Who's there? Michael, is that you? Michael? Are you home?"

The terror in his father's voice drove him out of hiding in his room.

"Hey, Apa," he said, trying to act casually.

"When did you get home? How long have you been here?"

His father pelted him with questions as Mike played dumb and hoped it would work. Obviously, whatever his father and uncle were up to was for them to know and none of his business, at least not yet.

"I just got home."

"I heard a noise in the hallway! Were you eavesdropping?" his father interrupted.

"Uh, yeah, I mean *no*! Yes, I was in the hallway on my way to my room and I, uh…stubbed my toe!" he replied, flustered and confused with his father's behaviour. "Are you all right?"

His father stared at him suspiciously for a moment, then his look softened to one of what Mike could only describe as pity.

"Yes, I'm fine. Your Uncle Laszlo is here."

Mike made a concentrated effort to look happy, but at the mention of his uncle and the prospect of having to move away made it almost impossible. His father's look of sympathy let Mike know that his attempt at happiness had failed. Mike sighed, took a deep breath and responded with an attempt at humour.

"I thought I saw his broomstick parked outside!"

"Michael, you need to come into my office; we need to talk," his father said, smiling feebly.

Every muscle in Mike's body tightened, he closed his eyes and shook his head.

"No, Apa, not this time! *I won't go!*"

With that he stormed past his father, ignored his uncle sitting in the den, tore his jacket off its hook, charged through the front doorway and slammed the door behind him. He could hear his father calling out to him.

"Michael, come back. You need to come back! I can explain!"

"Eet's OK, he'll be back. I'll take care of eet," Uncle Laszlo tried reassuring him.

Hearing those words, Mike thought: *Not this time.* And what did his uncle mean by, "I'll take care of it"? With this thought Mike picked up the pace and started a slow run down the block, instinctively turning towards Hanna's house, all the while unaware that his uncle was only a few steps behind him.

Ever Feel Like You're Being Watched?

Breathing hard, Mike stopped. He hadn't realised how fast he was running until now, when breathing in was actually hurting his chest. He held his chest while trying to take in deep slow breaths. He looked down the block and he could see Hanna's house at the end. He had never been inside, but he had walked her home many times.

He wasn't really sure why he had chosen to go to her. He was painfully aware of his feelings for her, especially at the thought of not seeing her again. Anger and frustration welled up inside him again. Why? Why now, and why again? He didn't understand. For so many years he had tried to, but the older he got the more he didn't or *wouldn't*. That was definitely the case this time.

He sat down on a bench at a nearby bus stop. His head between his hands, he thought over what he had heard in his father's den. Why had his uncle been so insistent on them having to leave now? Had he understood him correctly when he'd overheard that *they* know where we are—and who were *they*? What difference did it make if anyone knew where they were? In the past when they had moved, although it always seemed to be sudden and closely following a visit from his uncle, he had always understood that it had been for his father's health, something to do with better doctors or health care facilities. Come to think of it though, his father's condition never seemed to improve, it just seemed to get worse. Shortly after each move his father would have more clarity, but it never lasted very long. When Mike was younger he would ask his uncle what had been wrong with his father and why wasn't he getting better. His uncle would always say it was a curse, and if he couldn't find a cure for him his memory would all but disappear. When he visited, he explained that he had brought special medicine for Mike's father, but it would only last for a while.

Yet many of those times were the best ones Mike could recall. His father was very involved with him, not distant like he usually was now. As a child he could remember him telling him stories and teaching him all sorts of fun things. He was a very creative man. The stories he told were always about dragons and magic. It was so realistic to Mike, like they were in another world together, casting spells and fighting dragons! Loads of fun for a child, but when Mike got older the fantasy of it wore off. Sometimes his father still tried to tell him the stories, but he struggled with the details and, often, couldn't get too far in the telling when he would suddenly stop and have to ask Mike what it was that they had been talking about. Mike never wanted to disrespect him and he knew a lot of it was because his father was ill, so he'd let him tell as much as he could. It didn't matter to Mike if he didn't tell the whole story, he just wanted to relive the feeling of those special moments. After he finished the stories he would always ask him to come out to a soccer game or watch him compete in track and field or wrestling. His father would withdraw and become silent. Mike would come home the next day from school to find him sitting in his office staring blankly out through the window.

Now, over and over again the events of the afternoon and the bits of his father's and uncle's conversation he'd heard whirled around in his head. And that bright light he'd seen under the door. As much as he tried he just couldn't make any sense of it. It became exhausting and he grew tired. He hadn't realised how much time had passed until another of the many buses that had passed him by this time pulled to a stop. The door to the bus opened and instead of people exiting the bus, the driver called out to him.

"Hey, kid, everything all right? This is the third time I've driven by on my route and every time I've stopped, you're here."

Mike looked up at the bus driver. The colour in his cheeks gave his embarrassment away. He didn't really know what to say, so he mumbled a feeble response.

"I'm fine, thanks."

He turned his gaze away, hoping that the bus driver would take the hint that he could drive on to the next stop. Mike could feel the driver staring at him, but just when he thought he'd never leave and he was sure that if he stared at his shoes any longer he'd burn holes in them, he heard the bus door closing.

"It's gettin' dark out, kid. I wouldn't stay out here for long. People bin seein' strange things in the neighbourhood! You'd best be gettin' on home!"

With that the doors closed and the bus drove away. *What is with everyone today?* Mike wondered as he watched the red rear lights of the bus decreasing. "Seeing strange things?" he repeated the bus driver's words to himself. Well, he had certainly seen and heard a few strange things that afternoon at home, but the way the bus driver had said it made the hairs on the back of his neck stand up! Feeling sufficiently creeped out, he looked over at Hanna's house and whispered to himself.

"Don't be such a chicken! Just get over there!"

As he headed towards her house he tried hard not to think about the driver's words. He must not have been trying very hard though because he jumped at every little sound. Feeling foolish, he stopped for a moment and leaned against a nearby street lamp, trying to gather his wits. The light helped to calm his nerves. He quickly scanned the area and the coast was clear, so he moved towards Hanna's house again, but just as he did so there was a loud rustle in the hedge bordering the front lawn of the house he was passing. Mike jumped back so far that his back landed against the car parked on the road. The impact of his body against the car set the alarm off immediately, causing Mike to jump back towards the bushes. He would never admit this later, but it's possible he had even let out a shriek!

Ready to bolt in any direction just to get out of there, he made the move to get up. As he did so he heard the front door of the house open. A man, clearly upset at his car alarm having been set off, came down the pathway towards the bushes where Mike had landed. Really not wanting to, for fear of what was in the bushes, but having no choice, Mike pushed himself into the undergrowth as far and as quietly as he could. Scared, scratched up and feeling completely foolish, Mike sat perfectly still hardly daring to breathe. The owner of the car approached, Mike praying that darkness and the thick branches hid him well enough. The owner turned the alarm off with the push of a button on his key ring and stood there silently scanning the street for the culprit responsible. After what seemed like hours to Mike, who was beginning to feel quite cramped, the man shouted into the darkness.

"I know you're out there! Whoever you are you just stay away from my property! Ya hear? Next time I'm callin' the cops! This might be workin' on other people around here, but ya ain't scarin' me!"

Mike wasn't sure, but he thought he heard the smallest amount of fear in the man's voice. He heard him walk away, cursing under his breath. He didn't want to make a move until he was back in his house, doors shut and lights out. He sat and waited and as he did so the hairs on the back of his neck stood to attention and a new wave of fear enveloped him—he noticed a set of huge shining eyes staring at him and froze! He wasn't sure what those eyes belonged to, but he was sure they didn't want him in those bushes anymore than he wanted to be there. Frozen to the spot, and positive that the eyes were moving closer to him, he heard the joyful sound of the front door closing. He didn't think twice! Mike bolted out of those bushes as fast as he could, heading straight down the street. He didn't want to look back, he just ran.

Going against every fibre in his body, his head—almost as if it was independent of his body—turned around and looked towards the bushes. There, standing on the pavement like it owned it, right beside the car was a huge, fat alley cat. Mike came to a complete stop, laughed at himself and enjoyed the great wave of relief that washed over him.

Shaking off the last of the fear, he continued on to Hanna's house. He got to the edge of her pathway and stopped. The house was in complete darkness. The only light was coming from the doorbell. He looked at the time on his cell phone, thinking that it was too early for everyone to be asleep, although…sunset was still early at this time of year which gave one the feeling that it was later than it actually was—it was only seven thirty.

Maybe they had to go out, Mike thought. He ran across the lawn and ducked under Hanna's bedroom window, at least he hoped it was hers. She had previously indicated that that was her bedroom. He picked up a twig from the ground and gently tapped on her window three times, murmuring:

"Please be home."

He waited a few moments. No response. He tried again. As he waited he realised how silly he must look, waving a twig and talking to himself. It was just like playing magic with his father when he was still a kid. Still no answer, so he thought he'd give it one more shot, only this time without the murmuring. He rapped a little louder three more times. After a couple of minutes he decided that nobody was home. Disappointed, he ran back across the lawn, took one last look at the house, hoping to see some indication that someone was inside, then turned and started back home.

"*Great!*" he exclaimed in frustration.

He had wanted to talk to her so badly, get everything off his mind. He wasn't really sure when or if a move was really going to have to happen, but he knew that he didn't want to go without being able to see her one last time.

"*I hate this!*" he shouted out loud.

"I know," came a voice from behind him.

Legendary

Mike whipped around to see who had answered him. He half-expected to see his father standing there, but it was Uncle Laszlo, who approached him and placed his hand on his nephew's shoulder.

"I know how disappointed you are, Mike. I know dat dis vuz da last ting you vanted (I know that this was the last thing you wanted)." His Hungarian accent was terribly thick.

Mike pulled his shoulder away from his uncle's grip, feeling very angry.

"Did you follow me?"

"Yes," his uncle replied simply.

"Why?" asked Mike. "I *am* old enough to be out on my own, you know. In fact, I'm sixteen now, and I won't have to move anymore. I can live where I want to!"

"I know."

He didn't seem bothered that Mike was angry with him. Actually he was looking quite sympathetically at him, which threw Mike off a little, but he didn't back down all the way.

"Why can't you just come to visit like other people's relatives do? And why are you the only one who ever comes to visit us? Don't we have any other relatives?" he asked in exasperation.

His uncle took a few steps past Mike, turned around to face him and placed both his hands on Mike's shoulders.

"I know dat dis eez hard for you. I vill explain everyting, but not here. Now vee must go, and quvickly!"

Nothing in Mike wanted to go, but something about the way his uncle was acting told him not to argue. Silently, with a nod of his head, he complied. As they ran, his uncle constantly seemed to be scanning their surroundings and at one point grabbed Mike by the arm and pulled him between two houses into a small lane that led to the neighbourhood playground. Once there, Mike was shoved behind a small climbing wall and his uncle motioned with his index finger to his lips to be silent, the other hand hovering over his pocket as if he was preparing to draw a gun if the moment called for it. Mike did as he was told, but he could not escape the feeling that his uncle had lost his marbles. Their stay behind the climbing wall was brief, and before Mike knew it he was being pulled up and silently motioned to move forwards quickly. They cleared the park and without incident ran the rest of the way.

When they were, what Mike assumed, safely at home, he turned on his uncle.

"What the heck was that all about? What is *wrong* with everyone today?"

Before his uncle had a chance to answer, Mike's father rushed into the hallway.

"Michael! Laszlo! You're all right?"

The last bit sounded more like a question than joyful relief.

"Yes, vee are OK, but dey know vee are close. Dey vere looking for him, dey knew he vuz out, but vee lost dem at da park."

Mike's father and uncle exchanged grave looks as Mike just stood there completely baffled and exasperated by their conversation.

"Could someone *please* explain what is going on? Why is someone looking for me, and *who* are *they*?"

Mike's uncle took him by the arm gently and led him to the den, where he motioned for him to sit. Mike did so. His father sat right beside him and patted him gently on the back. He looked at his son with what Mike could only describe as an attempt at comfort mixed with *hold onto your seat!* Mike looked back at his father with thanks in his eyes, but in his mind all he could think was that his father and uncle must have had too many shots of the old palinka!

Uncle Laszlo sat down opposite them, took a deep breath and looked Mike directly in the eyes.

"Dere are many tings vee need to tell you, Mike, and many tings you vill not understand. I ask only dat you listen vell and keep an open mind. Please understand dat vee have kept it from you for your safety—and your fazer's."

Mike tried to prepare himself, but he was just so confused and they were acting so strangely, it made it difficult for him to be sincere in his efforts.

"Please just tell me! This is all just too weird!"

Mike's father suggested that he should be the one to explain to his son. Laszlo nodded his head in silent agreement. His father turned to him, cleared his throat and stared into his eyes for a moment before he spoke. Clearly this was not easy for his father to say, whatever *it* was, but by this point they had built up the suspense so much Mike thought that he would burst at any minute, and it was not going to be pretty. As if his father could read Mike's mind he finally spoke.

"Michael, we are going home."

The den was wrapped in silence for a few moments as both men gave him time to absorb that comment. Mike already knew that a move was likely, which made him frustrated and disappointed enough, but the keyword in his father's statement was "home."

"*Home…*" Mike said slowly, "what do you mean by *home*?"

The indicator on Mike's patience metre was quickly inching to the 'cautious—may explode' setting. His father hurriedly put his hands over Mike's, as if to keep him from leaping out of his chair.

"Hear us out, Michael! We are…. no, it is *time* to go home," he said emphatically. "We cannot stay here or any other place any longer—it is time."

His father spoke with such clarity that Mike knew this topic wasn't debatable, which only served to anger him more.

"Why?" he simply asked, exhausted now by the afternoon's events.

"Mike, I know you overheard us talking dis afternoon in da den," Laszlo said calmly.

Mike didn't even try to deny it.

"You must be curious as to vat happened in dere, yes?"

Mike nodded, wondering where this would lead.

"It vuz *magic*, Mike! At least dat is vat de common people call it, but for your fazer, me, you and da rest of your family, eet eez our vay of life!" his uncle stated enthusiastically.

"*Maagic. Rrriight!*" Mike drawled, barely able to keep a straight face and came back to his original assumption that palinka was at the root of this absurd behavior. *Maybe they drank the whole bottle and then hid the evidence,* he thought to himself. He leaned in close to this father's face and sniffed suspiciously. He pulled his face back, a little surprised that there wasn't even a hint of the sharp smell of fermented fruit. His father gave him an odd look.

"Mike!" His uncle raised his voice a little, not in anger, but with conviction. 'Dis eez all going to seem strange and unbelievable to you, I know. Vee should not have let you forget—eet vuz a mistake." He looked at his nephew with sympathy. 'You—make no mistake—your fazer and I have not been drinking too much palinka, huh?"

Who was he kidding—*of course* they had been drinking too much palinka! They gave Mike a moment to absorb this news. He wasn't even sure what his next question should be, so he started slowly.

"So…are you telling me that *I…you…*the *rest* of my *family* can do *magic?*"

"Yes," his father and uncle replied simultaneously, the look on their faces so sincere, which unnerved Mike.

"Is this some kind of cruel birthday joke?" he asked.

He was completely unimpressed. Mike's father lowered his head in disappointment. His uncle sighed, shook his head, stood up from his chair and walked over to the window, rubbing his forehead. After a couple of thoughtful moments, he turned around and faced Mike and his father. Holding his chin between his index finger and thumb, like all good thinkers, he squinted his eyes and slightly looked away from them, almost as if looking for a question he had misplaced somewhere in the room.

"Home eez in Transylvania, a small town called Segesvar. Dere are ozser vizards, bad ones, who have been searching for you and your fazer for many years. To tell you *vy* vould take much time dat vee do not have right now, so I'll give you dis…. Not only are you a vizard—you are also *da* vizard. Your birth was foretold and vee, all of our kind, need you to come home."

"Whoa—you really *have* lost it!" was all Mike could manage, thinking they had reached a point of being beyond ridiculous!

"I vill explain everyting to you in time." Uncle Laszlo sighed, knowing that he had failed in his attempt to clarify the matter. "Regardless of what you believe right now, vee are leaving dis place tomorrow. Your family—your *people* are vaiting for you to return. Dere are tings dat only you can do and no ozser. Zsose who are after you seek to take from you vat they cannot have. Foolish beasts…. They know *nozsing*!"

His uncle was temporarily sidetracked in anger and continued to rant for a moment longer about things that his nephew couldn't understand. Mike looked back and forth between his father and uncle to see if either of them would finally crack and give up the charade.

"*Mike!*" Laszlo blurted out, causing Mike to jump a little in his seat.

"Yes!" he said, giving his uncle his full attention.

"You haven't eaten."

"No…I guess I haven't, why?"

"No matter," his uncle snapped, waving the thought away with his hand.

Mike sat frozen to the spot, staring, stunned, straight ahead. He couldn't believe his eyes! There, right in front of where he and his father sat, appeared a small table with three plates heaped with food—really appetising food. His stomach rumbled.

"Where…where did that all come from?" Mike shrieked, leaping out of his chair.

"You don't like eet?" his uncle challenged. "I can make eet all go avay eef you like?" he questioned, teasing him.

"No! No!" Mike exclaimed, holding his hand up to stop his uncle. "This is *unbelievable*! I don't get it! How…?"

"Dis eez nuting, Mike," his uncle interrupted. "*Dis* sustains you. Eet's child's play. Dat's how you say eet here, no?"

He took a few steps closer to Mike, bent down on one knee, took his hands in one of his and slapped his other hand down on his nephew's shoulder. Staring intently into his eyes, he spoke.

"Mike, vut *you* are capable of—vut *you* vere born to do—vill be legendary! You are an incredibly powerful boy! You do not know eet now and none of dis seems real, I know, but you vill see!" He stood up abruptly. "First vee must get you and your fazer home," he began again, with the same passion. "Vee need to restore your fazer's memory, completely. Vee do not have much time. It has taken me so many years to find da cure for your fazer." His tone was desperate and sad. "Now, after all deez years I have found eet! But it cannot be done vitout you, Mike!"

Mike sat in silence. He had absolutely no idea how to respond, so instead, he did what growing boys do best—he ate. While he did so, he thought about what had happened to the sixteen-year-old boy who had woken up in bed that morning. He had attended a perfectly boring day at school then had a magical walk home with the girl of his dreams. His greatest undertaking was growing, eating and quiet nights in doing homework and taking care of his ailing father. Hormones and puberty were difficult enough, but being *legendary*? Mike rubbed his head, unconsciously searching for a lump or wound—maybe he had taken a blow to the head in that afternoon's wrestling match and he was imagining all this; he did have the strangest dreams.

But this food tasted so good and the smells were wonderful. *You don't dream this*, he thought. He took the end of the fork and poked at his arm with it, expelling a cry of pain, which was real and the situation was crazy.

"Son, what on earth are you doing?" his father shouted, nearly leaping from his seat, his son's sanity a clear concern. "Perhaps this was bit too much, Laszlo," he said, exchanging a seriously concerned look with him.

"Clearly," was all Laszlo managed to say.

They sat in silence watching Mike as he continued to eat, both expecting another worrying episode.

"*Legendary…*" Mike said, laughing to himself, shaking his head as he chowed down.

He had no idea how his uncle had made a table full of food appear, or how bad the blow to his head must have been, but for now all he wanted to do was eat, go to sleep and pretend that none of this had happened. That's exactly what he decided to do, so he left both men sitting silently, looking completely perplexed.

Gone Without a Goodbye

The morning came early for Mike. He awoke with a start. He had been dreaming about witches, wizards, magic and dragons—anything and everything to do with magic.

Shortly before he awoke he dreamed that he was fighting another group of wizards, who were after something he supposedly had. He didn't know what it was they wanted, but in his dream they were willing to kill him for it. All the while the fight was continuing, he could hear sirens in the background. He looked around to see if they were coming for them and realised that the fight was taking place in the neighbourhood park where he and his uncle had hidden earlier that night for real. Spells were flying back and forth, and Mike could remember hoping that no one from the neighbourhood could hear or see what was going on. How would he explain this to them? How could he keep them safe?

The sirens were louder now, sounding very close. Mike turned to see a convoy of fire trucks passing the park. He looked around in panic, trying to determine the destination of the vehicles. His heart stopped when he saw a home nearby engulfed in flames. It was right where Hanna's house was in reality. Fearing that it really was her home, he left the fight and made a dash for Hanna's house. He hadn't made it out of the park and to the street when one of the opposing wizards appeared before him, as though he had materialised out of thin air, and struck Mike down with a spell. Mike crashed to the ground in agony…or so he imagined, after all it was just a dream.

As he lay there clutching his chest, he looked over at the wizard who had struck him. The wizard's back was turned, so picking up his wand, which had fallen to the ground, he aimed it with the intention of striking back. Just as he did so, the opposing wizard turned around. The spell was cast. It had left his wand and was heading directly for the other wizard. Mike could do nothing to stop it now as he realised that the opposing wizard was *Hanna*!

That last dreadful thought awakened him.

Mike sat on the edge of his bed, rubbing the back of his neck, playing the last scene of his dream over and over again. He glanced at the clock, it was 7 a.m. The house was quiet, his uncle and father still sleeping. A small plan started to form in his mind.

Mike got ready for school as quietly as possible. Now that he knew his uncle had a sixth sense for what he was doing, he was careful not to make the slightest sound. He was also painfully aware of the fact that this was probably a stunt that wouldn't go over well with his father or uncle. It's just Hanna, Mike thought to himself—he'd be back before they even woke up. Whether or not she believed him, Mike was sure she wouldn't tell anyone—she'd probably just go through life remembering the poor boy who went insane at the age of sixteen.

Within fifteen minutes Mike was ready and sneaking out through his bedroom window. It was a small jump to the ground. Mike had done this many times before after he and his father had gone to bed for the night. Sometimes he just needed to get out and clear his head with a brisk walk in the quiet of night. He successfully executed his jump out of the window and made a dash for his and Hanna's regular meeting spot. They'd meet there every day and walk to the bus together. Secretly it was Mike's favourite time of the day.

He arrived there with five minutes to spare. He got his breath and started the conversation in his head. With the moment of her arrival nearing, how *exactly* was he going to explain this to her? There was no doubt in Mike's mind that she was an understanding individual; she had never made him feel awkward about his dad's condition. She never laughed at him when he talked about his reoccurring dreams. Come to think of it, now that he had a moment to think about it, she was usually the one who brought up the subject.

This is good, Mike thought. She might not think I am a total freak. He paced back and forth on the same spot, trying to find more reasons why Hanna should accept him knowing magic was perfectly normal. Let's see, he started…she comes to all my games. She sits with me at lunch and on the bus every day. We walk home together. She held my hand….

At that memory, Mike stared off into the distance and gave a heavy sigh. Snapping back to reality he returned to his thoughts. On the other hand, she's only known me for two months. She knows we have moved a lot, but doesn't know why—*I* don't even know why! She knows my dad is ill and a little strange…and that I have weird dreams about dragons…*and,* so far, she has never invited me over.

"Oh man!" Mike covered his face with his hands. "I can't do this! She's gonna think I'm nuts! There's no way she'll believe me!"

"Believe what?"

Mike jumped two feet in the air.

"W-wha…? W-who?" he stuttered.

Kyle, a classmate, had appeared out of nowhere, causing Mike to swallow his heart whole!

"Who are you talkin' to, Mike?" Kyle asked curiously, a small hint of sarcasm in his voice.

"Ahhh…no one! Just…you know…just hangin'. You, who are *you* talkin' to?" Mike asked, thinking that he had cleverly turned the tables.

Kyle looked around the area where they were standing with confusion in his eyes, then back at Mike.

"I'm, uh…talkin' to *you,* Mike. Hey, you OK, man?"

"Yeah, fine," Mike answered, knowing full well he sounded like a complete idiot.

They stood there in awkward silence for a couple of moments, not looking at each other. Finally Mike broke the silence.

"You waiting for someone?"

His friend Kyle stared at him like he was observing a tiny bug trapped inside a small glass cage for his next science project.

"I'm, uh, waiting for Sean. You know Sean? We meet here every day and walk to the bus stop with you and Hanna?"

Kyle made every sentence like a question, giving the full impression that he thought Mike was slightly challenged this morning.

"Oh…ya." Mike uttered.

Kyle turned his head and tried to look his friend directly in the eyes.

"You haven't heard what happened to Hanna's house last night, have you?"

Suddenly extremely interested in anything Kyle might have to say, Mike snapped his head around and stared at him.

"What? What happened?"

"I can't believe you don't know, man! Everyone heard it last night!"

He looked at Mike, expecting to see some acknowledgment of what he was saying, but there was none. Mike just stared back at him waiting to hear what it was that involved Hanna he had missed. Why did his friend keep looking at him like he had missed the space shuttle being launched from the neighbourhood park?

"You mean you never heard the explosion, the fire, the fire trucks, the sirens? Unless you slept somewhere else last night there is no way you could have missed all that!"

Mike, recalling his dream, stood there speechless. Thoughts whirled around in his head like a tornado. He grabbed Kyle by the arm and asked him, with more urgency than he had cared to reveal, what had happened to Hanna, was everyone all right, did anyone get hurt? His friend pulled his arm away from Mike's deathly grip and, rubbing his arm in the same spot, replied, only this time he didn't try to hide the amusement in his voice.

"Everyone's OK, Mike. My dad says that no one was home when it happened. He was part of the fire crew that was called out to the scene. He only came home this morning, having worked on containing the fire all night. He said he'd never seen anything like it; the explosion should have taken out the whole block, but only Hanna's house was affected. It was like the fire was stuck to her house. They had to use special chemicals to put it out, water just seemed to make it worse. When they interviewed the neighbours, an old lady said that she had seen Hanna and her family leave in a taxi just an hour or so before the explosion, and she was sure they had loaded a few suitcases."

Mike was in a daze. He stood dumbstruck for a moment as he tried to process what he had just heard, hoping beyond hope that the last twenty-four hours of his life had been just a really bad dream and that he'd wake up any minute and lead a delightfully *normal* day. Mechanically he thanked his friend, waved to him mumbling that he would see him later, and carried on to the bus stop.

He knew his chances were slim and this was pushing his father's orders, but he just had to see if Hanna was at school. He just couldn't leave without saying goodbye and seeing first-hand that she was really okay. He arrived at the bus stop and, in between morning greetings from his friends, he kept a keen eye out for Hanna. There was talk from the neighbourhood kids about the events of the previous evening and, of course, much speculation as to who, what, when, where, why and how it all went down. Had she said something about it yesterday on their walk home from the bus stop? He couldn't recall. She had seemed perfectly fine. He was sure she had even said, "See you tomorrow, Mike."

Disappointment and fear grew inside him as every minute passed without her appearing. Mechanically he got on the bus, sat in their usual spot, endured the noisy ride to school and contemplated every different scenario of what could have possibly happened last night. It had struck him as odd that he had dreamt the fire, the sirens and Hanna! Why would she go without saying goodbye? How was he going to let her know where he was and that he'd be back as soon as he could?

Naturally he hadn't told his father or uncle his intentions of coming back here as soon as he was legally able. He figured he would go and humour them for a while. If he really had family, he would love to get to know them, but, like all things that seem too good to be true, he was having doubts about all this magic stuff. He knew he couldn't explain what had happened last night, and he really wanted to believe that it was all real, but it was hard, really hard, to convince yourself that you can do magic and in another world your return was greatly anticipated and needed. Mike wasn't even sure that in *this* world his own teachers knew his name.

The bus pulled up to the school, the kids filed out and dispersed in every direction. Mike headed straight for the library where he met Hanna every day. Hoping with everything in his heart that he would find her sitting there reading, waiting for him to arrive, he entered the library. It took him but a few seconds to reach their usual spot—she wasn't there. He sat in the library until the first bell went, still no Hanna. Reluctantly, Mike dragged himself to his first class, knowing his father and uncle would be awake and wondering where he had gone, but he had to give it a try.

Mike sat down in his usual spot and waited. Five minutes passed, then ten, then twenty. He couldn't wait any longer. He was already in huge trouble. His uncle and father had warned him against leaving the house without them again now that the "*other* wizards" knew they were close. Frustrated, angry, sad and confused, he stood up from his desk and excused himself from the classroom. He made a quick stop at his locker and took out his wrestling items, a few ribbons and medals, and, most important of all, a photo of Hanna. How was he going to get hold of her now? How was he going to be able to explain why he had suddenly gone without saying goodbye or why he had to leave? I guess that is what the Internet is for, he thought, but it would just seem so impersonal; however, it would have to do. He had her cell number as well, and then it dawned on him he could call her quickly.

Kicking himself for not thinking of it sooner, he hurriedly left the school and dialled her number. The phone rang once, twice, three times, four times—no answer. No matter, he could at least leave her a message. A familiar voice came on the line.

The cellular number you have dialled is not in service.

"What?" Mike exclaimed.

He tried again; maybe he had misdialled. Over and over again he dialled her number he knew by heart. It wasn't possible to misdial ten times. Feeling utterly defeated and sadder than he ever thought he could, he boarded the next bus and headed home. Life was so miserable right now that the wrath of his father and uncle seemed like lighthearted fun.

When the bus pulled up at Mike's stop, he exited and bumped right into his uncle.

"*Oh*…great!"

Uncle Laszlo's look was so stern that a lecture wasn't even necessary. Mike was fully aware he had pushed it too far, but thought he'd offer up an "it was for a girl" excuse in the vain hope of appealing to his uncle's memories of young love. It didn't work. His uncle only glared at him harder.

The short walk home was silent. When they arrived, his father, looking equally as disappointed, handed Mike some luggage.

"These are yours. Since you weren't here we packed for you. You have five minutes to check your room over and then we must go."

Wow! We have to leave already? Stunned, Mike went inside the house, down the hall and into his room. There was only one thing he wanted and that was a scrapbook of pictures he had kept and had added to over the past nine years or so. It was a collection of pictures, notes, letters and clippings, all of his best memories since they had started moving. He placed it carefully into his carry-on bag, took one last look at his room and walked out to meet his father and uncle.

Mike and his father climbed into the car while Uncle Laszlo went back up to the house and from the car they could see a series of small flashes coming from the interior. A minute or two later he returned, entered the car and spoke to Mike's father.

"Eet eez done."

"What's done?" Mike asked, risking being yelled at.

"Dey can't know you have been here, Mike," his uncle replied. "I had to erase any evidence of you and your fazer having lived here."

"Oh," was all Mike could say.

Just like that, his existence was made non-existent. *Kind of like the house going up in flames*, he thought. Just like Hanna's house. One minute it was there, the next, gone.

He didn't know what to feel. He just watched as all the familiar places flashed by outside as they sped along.

"Don't worry," he mumbled quietly. "I'll be back as soon as I am seventeen."

He shut his eyes and tried not to feel anything, at least not until they arrived at the airport.

Patience Is a Virtue

No one said a word during the ride to the airport. Uncle Laszlo and Mike's father kept a keen eye open for anything suspicious, at least that's what Mike imagined. They just kept looking from window to mirror to side mirror or towards the back of the car, then they gave each other the all-clear with a look.

The silence gave Mike an opportunity to reflect peacefully; however, all he was able to think about was how much he was going to miss this place, especially Hanna. Feelings of anger and frustration rose in him again. Where *was* Hanna? He thought about the day before, when everything in his life was still relatively normal or at least routine. They had had such a good walk home together. Hanna hadn't given any indication that she was going away. When they had parted, she had said she would see him tomorrow. Something must have come up, like a family emergency, for Hanna to leave without a word, he thought, trying to find some comfort. Yeah, that must be it. That would explain why her family was seen leaving last night and possibly why she had no time to call him.

When they had spoken of family she had always indicated that, other than her parents and two older brothers, she had no family in Canada. That would explain her cellphone not being in range. The only way to say goodbye would have to be via email. He'd try to call her again in a few days if Uncle Laszlo allowed him to make contact. He looked up to find that his uncle was staring at him through the rear-view mirror with a look that made Mike certain that he had read his mind. OK, OK! Mike thought to himself, directing his inner words to his uncle on the off chance that he *could* read his mind. I'll just think about wrestling or dragons! To Mike's surprise his uncle had turned his gaze away from him and, he couldn't be a hundred percent sure, but it looked as though he was smiling. *Really? I guess anything is possible now.*

He leaned his head against the window again and let his mind drift to the dream from the previous night. To wake up from his dreams felt like saying goodbye to a brother or a best friend and not knowing when you might see them again. Well, this situation feels the same, Mike thought, expelling a sarcastic laugh.

Before he had a chance to reminisce further, his father interrupted his reflection.

"We're here!" he exclaimed, appearing to be excited and nervous.

As they unloaded their suitcases from the car and piled everything onto a luggage cart, Mike couldn't help but feel some happiness for his father. It must be exciting for him to be going back home after so many years. Although he had never discussed it with Mike, when Mike asked about his past or family, his father would just become quiet and unresponsive. Mike could just tell that this trip home was highly anticipated by his dad and uncle, for that reason.

Once inside the airport, Mike felt some excitement himself. The hustle and bustle of the large airport made it difficult to dwell on hard feelings. There was too much happening all around them and too much to see. The last time he had been here was when they had moved to Calgary. They had arrived late and he could only remember feeling tired and exasperated by the move. He hadn't taken notice of it before, but this airport was huge. There wasn't anything you couldn't do, from dining near the space shuttle to relaxing at an oxygen bar. Anything and everything was available somewhere to buy, even dinosaur fossils or gigantic polished trilobite fossils that stood two feet high. Who would want to pack that in their luggage, he didn't know, he just knew that you could buy it among many other strange and wonderful things, like a beautiful and expensive horse's saddle. This was Calgary, Heart of the New West, and you never knew, even at the airport, when you might need something like a saddle!

They continued on to their check-in desk, amused at some of the things they saw, and Mike could feel that the mood for everyone had lightened up a little. He smiled to himself as he felt a bit of the morning trouble slipping away. He truly had felt bad for disobeying his dad and uncle, and was glad to see that they were also looking much happier.

It wasn't long before they found themselves through security and the duty-free area and patiently waiting to have their row called for boarding. Within a few minutes of waiting, their row had been called and before he knew it they were sitting side by side, with Mike directly by the window, just how he liked it.

As the plane ascended into the sky Mike watched the place to which he had grown most attached begin to grow smaller and smaller—the downtown melting into the many suburban areas surrounding it, then the city itself becoming a dark patch in the giant quilt that made up the landscape of the surrounding prairies. Each field a different shade of yellow, green and gold tilled with perfect lines— until he couldn't see it anymore. He wondered how long it would be until he could come back for good. He glanced over at his father and uncle, both already dozing off. That looked like a great idea to Mike. No one had slept well the night before and they had a long flight with a stopover in London ahead of them, so Mike pulled his cap down over his eyes and promptly fell asleep.

The flight from Calgary to London was uneventful. All three of them slept most of the way with a few interruptions for dinner, breakfast and teatime. The arrival in London came faster than Mike had imagined. From there they would collect their luggage, stay one night in London and make their way to the London Luton Airport, where they would catch a smaller flight to Transylvania. Uncle Laszlo had arranged everything, having recently experienced London before, so they let him lead the way.

It was dark outside when they finally left the airport. The air was thick with humidity and pollution, and the temperature was a lot milder than it was in Calgary. There was still a lot of traffic and people on the streets, and things seemed noisy to Mike, but he liked it. It was a different kind of energy and it seemed familiar to him.

Uncle Laszlo hailed a taxi for them and once inside he explained that they had some family in London, an aunt and uncle, but to err on the side of caution they would not try to contact them now, but rather stay in a hotel. It was best for them, especially Mike, if they passed through England unnoticed. Wow! Even here he had family—an aunt and uncle—from whose side of the family? Did they have kids? How old would they be? Mike's uncle must have been aware of the hundreds of questions he would have! He was secretly beginning to believe that his uncle might have worked as a torturer in some past profession!

The taxi ride felt really long to Mike, considering the short distance they actually travelled, and also jerky. Maybe it was the smaller cars, the windier roads or the fact that everyone drove on the opposite side of the street and about three times faster than anyone in North America, but it was definitely *not* relaxing! They arrived at the hotel, checked in quickly and proceeded to their room. Much to Mike's dismay, they were going to share a room with three beds instead of separate rooms—for his safety...again.

They could smell the wonderful aroma of breakfast being prepared in the pub off the lobby of the hotel and all agreed that, as it was 7 a.m. here, they were hungry. After eating what Mike decided was one of the heartiest breakfasts ever, the three of them made their way back to the room. His father and Laszlo agreed to take shifts and watch the hotel and room for any suspicious *wizardry* activity, while Mike was allowed to do anything he wanted, as long as it was in the room.

"Seriously?" Mike exclaimed. What was he supposed to do for the whole day? "This is London! There are so many cool things we could see and do!"

"Sorry, Michael, not this time. I will bring you here again," said his father.

With a heavy sigh, Mike flung himself down onto a lounging chair, grabbed a magazine from the side table and jerked open the pages, almost tearing it in two, showing his dissatisfaction with every move. His uncle looked over at him and spoke with as much compassion as he could muster for his dramatic nephew.

"Mike, I know dis doesn't make sense and eet doesn't seem fair to you, but dis eez about keeping you alive! Ozser vizards have…." He paused for a moment, pondering the consequences of finishing his sentence, decided, then began again. "Ozser vizards have killed before…over you!"

"I didn't ask for this!"

"Mike, dis vill all make sense tomorrow ven vee get to Segesvar. You'll see. You'll take da train to Luton Airport and from dere eet eez only a couple of hours, and by tomorrow night you and your fazer vill be home again! I vill stay vit you today and get you to da train station late dis afternoon. From dere, you two are on your own. Sumvun vill be at da airport in Segesvar to collect you."

"Why aren't you coming with us, and how are you getting there before us?" Mike questioned, his curiosity rising.

"You two vill be safe once you are on da train. I must get to Segesvar before you and prepare for your arrival. The ozser vizards vill be expecting you to travel vit me, my vay, vizard style, *first class!*" he exclaimed, raising one eyebrow.

Mike knew his uncle was trying to appeal to the North American in him, with his hand actions and lingo, but it just didn't suit him. Mike managed to keep a straight face and not laugh at him.

"Will I learn to travel *wizard style?*" he asked, putting his fingers up in quotation marks.

"Yes, you vill vhen vee have you safe and sound back home."

That comment sent Mike's imagination free and he spent the next hour thinking up all sorts of possibilities. The best he could come up with was being beamed from one place to the next, like something out of an old sci-fi movie. At one point in his imaginative search, he glanced over at his uncle, only to see him laughing quietly to himself, looking at Mike!

"Well, you'll just have to show me then, won't you?" he asked defensively, glaring his uncle down.

"You have no idea, Mike, you have no idea!" he replied, chuckling and continuing to laugh a little while longer.

Mike was not amused. There wasn't much he could get past his Uncle Laszlo, he could see that now. He wondered if every wizard had a special power unique to them or if they all had the same powers. If they did each have their own exclusive skill, what was *his*? As he sat and thought about this, he chose not to look over in his uncle's direction, refusing to be his afternoon entertainment....

⌒ﮞﮞﮞﮞ◡

Before Mike knew it he was being shaken awake by his father.

"Michael, it's time to go."

Mike lifted himself out of the large wing chair in which he had apparently fallen asleep. The jetlag must have taken its toll on him while his mind wandered earlier with thoughts of magic and wizardry. His father handed him a mug of something hot.

"Here, drink this. It will help with the jetlag and wake you up."

Mike looked at it sceptically, but took it anyway.

"What is it?" he asked.

"Tea," said his uncle, "made from frogs' eyes and cats' claws."

Both men burst into laughter. Scowling, Mike drank it in one go and handed the cup back to his father.

"Are you two done making fun of me yet? For the record, that drink was *disgusting*!" he added, making a wry face as they continued to laugh uproariously.

As promised, Uncle Laszlo accompanied them to the train station. He gave Mike and his father careful instructions about what they needed to do from this point and explained that a trusted family friend, Attila, would be waiting for them at the airport in Marosvasarhely. As Alexander went for a luggage trolley, Laszlo pulled Mike closer.

"You *must* keep an eye out for your fazer too, Michael. He seems to have more clarity, but it von't last much longer and hees magic eez not strong...."

"What can I do?" Mike interrupted.

"You can do more dan you know. Take dis."

He handed him a leather pouch. Mike opened the small pouch and looked inside. What he saw looked like marbles, so he took one out to examine it.

"*Cool!*" he exclaimed with awe.

A white mist swirled around inside the marble, looking like a miniature galaxy. He looked at his uncle questioningly.

"Eef you tink you are being followed, you and Alexander eat one immediately; eet vill help. Dey are a little bitter, I find, but have a nice aftertaste—dey're great for freshening your breath too." He winked at Mike. "Your fazer's coming, just put eet away for now. He von't understand vy I haven't entrusted eet to heem. He eez already losing hees clarity, look."

He pointed towards Alexander, who was now returning with an arm full of magazines and no luggage trolley. Mike looked at his uncle and smiled.

"Now that's the Apa I'm used to!"

Mike was referring to the many times his father had set off to do one thing, forgot midway what he needed and returned with something completely different. As a result, grocery shopping, banking etc., were often Mike's responsibility.

It took a bit of effort to get onto the train and into their private compartment, but once there, Alexander settled down with his magazine assortment and Mike waved goodbye to his uncle through the window.

Trains in Europe run punctually, so it wasn't long before it set out. The ride to the smaller airport was just over a couple of hours. It was a silent ride, as the two of them didn't often speak, even at home. The silence was never uncomfortable, being simply how Mike had grown up. The train arrived in the smaller airport with little time to spare. Not being familiar with the airport made it difficult for them to find their way to the check-in counter. Feeling very out of place, Mike and his father inched along patiently while being bumped and knocked around by the million other people trying to get to the front of the queue. Mike never knew he was claustrophobic until now. He took a deep breath and tried to focus on the goal ahead—the check-in clerk. That didn't help, as she was currently reprimanding a very frazzled customer for asking her to hurry things along.

After what seemed like hours, they reached the desk, checked their luggage, had their tickets printed and found themselves sprinting to get to customs. The line there was even more disheartening! There must have been a thousand people, a thousand very impatient, late and angry people, ahead of them. Looking down at his watch, Mike took note of the time.

"We are cutting it really close, Apa. I hope this line moves faster than I imagine it will."

"Me too, Michael, me too," his father said, showing signs of frustration.

Maybe he doesn't like crowded places either, Mike thought as a wave of heat passed over him and his heart rate sped up. Expending every last bit of his, and everyone else's, patience, Mike suffered in the long line and eventually he and his father made it through, only with minutes to spare as they passed into the next corridor.

Mike was beginning to doubt that the committee responsible for the design and efficiency of the airport knew what it was doing. Carry-on bags in hand, they ran down to their gate with the rest of the frantic passengers. They arrived with literally only seconds to spare, along with what looked like the entire passenger manifest. Once through the boarding gate they made their way to the tarmac where they would board the plane. Assigned seating wasn't a luxury this airline offered and with this in mind, Mike grabbed his father by the hand and began a sprint to the boarding stairs. Everyone else had the same idea and suddenly Mike felt like he was running the last hundred metres of a marathon.

Once on the plane, they quickly found seats, stored their carry-ons and slumped into their seats.

"Finally!" Mike exclaimed with an exhausted sigh.

"Ya...finally!" repeated Mike's father, with a clear tone of irritation.

"Well, on the bright side, at least we made it," said Mike encouragingly.

"Hmpf...bright side!" mumbled Mike's father, staring out through the window, mocking Mike's attempt at encouragement.

Whatever! Mike thought, knowing that at this point, any attempt to lighten the mood would end badly for him. It was best to let him simmer down at his own pace. He prepared himself for the silent treatment he knew was coming, grabbed a magazine from the pouch in front of him and tried to get comfortable in his seat as his cellphone rang. Surprised, he dug around in his carry-on bag at his feet and pulled out the phone. He was shocked to see Uncle Laszlo's smiling face on the caller ID screen with the number 1-800-GET-HELP written underneath. Stunned, he answered the phone.

"Hello?"

"Hallo, Michael, eetz your Uncle Laszlo here. I just vanted to see eef everyting eez going according to plan."

Something in his uncle's voice made Mike believe that he was fully aware of what was going on.

"Ah...hey, wow, perfect timing! The plane is just about to take off from the airport from *hell*," he answered sarcastically.

Mike's father turned his attention from the window to his son.

"Is that Laszlo?" he asked, trying to reach for the phone.

Mike covered the speaker on the phone and hissed out a frustrated *yes*, all the while trying to avoid his father's grasping hand.

"Here, give me the phone! I'll talk to Laszlo."

Mike, desperate to make his father calm down, gave up the battle and handed the phone to him. He felt like telling him to chill out, but knew that the disrespect would only anger him further and bring on an hour-long lecture that Mike was sure would make his head explode at this point.

Despite the troubles they encountered getting onto the plane, the flight went well. They landed in no time and began filing off the plane. Mike's mood shifted to anticipation. He realised he couldn't wait to see his family.

"Family!" he whispered to himself, genuinely feeling excited.

Luckily for the two, things at this airport moved at top speed. The family friend, Attila, waiting for them recognised Mike's father immediately. He embraced them both with tears in his eyes saying how wonderful it was to see them and that they had waited a long time for them. Mike wasn't sure what he meant by that, but was moved by his genuine affection and joy.

Aside from being warm and tired, the ride home was as wonderful as Mike could have ever imagined. His father looked so happy, and asked question after question about this, that and everything in between. Attila answered every question with equal enthusiasm.

The journey was long, but Mike was determined to enjoy every second of it.

10

Family!

The winding roads didn't seem to want to end, and although his stomach and head were arguing with him, Mike couldn't help but notice how beautiful and picturesque the countryside had become. They had already passed through some of the quaintest little towns and villages he had ever seen where cows, chickens, ducks and geese lined the dirt roads, giving way to the cars and then continuing to make their way to the surrounding fields or farmyards. Most of the houses were small and simple in design. Almost every home, although squashed close to one another, served as a farm as well and had been in the family for many years.

Some of the properties were dressed with the most beautifully carved and intricately designed wood gates, some bearing the year in which they were erected. For every village thirty or forty homes lined either side of the street. Large telephone and electricity poles were spaced evenly along the roads and were topped with gigantic stork nests. Occasionally Attila had to swerve or stop to avoid colliding with the horse-drawn carriages that many villagers still drove. Mike had to admit that as foreign as everything looked, somehow it was all familiar too, and in a small way he also felt that he belonged. It was a good feeling.

It had been a long drive with a couple of pit-stops in between when Attila pointed out the valley ahead of them.

"We are coming up to your family's village."

Mike sat up a little straighter in his seat and craned his neck to see through the front windscreen. He noticed his father do the same, as though this was the first time for him too. Mike wondered how much his father remembered and what kind of an emotional effect seeing his family would have on him. Back home, or at least what used to be home, anytime Mike attempted to bring up the subject of family or the past, his father would simply shut down. Like a mannequin in a department store window, he looked real, but was lifeless. It wouldn't last long, but it was always upsetting. Except for Uncle Laszlo, he had no one he could talk to about family and his heritage, and unfortunately his uncle operated on a need-to-know basis only. Apparently, until now there wasn't much that Mike needed to know.

He realized that there was only ever one person he had ever felt comfortable talking to, and that was Hanna. That thought brought back the recent past and a heavy feeling settled in his chest, like it had done so often in the last couple of days. He had to find a way to get a hold of her! It seemed doubtful that there would be any modern technology in the village, but then again, this was a village full of wizards and his uncle *had* mysteriously contacted him on the plane. That little bit of hope perked him up. Even though it had only been two days, he missed Hanna's smile, her laugh, the way she could comfort him with just a look in her eyes. She was his best friend and two days without her were two days too many. He just had to remind himself that this move was only temporary. He would do whatever it was that his family needed him to do, it couldn't possibly be that important—for after all, he was just a teenager, with no skill set that he could imagine would be that useful—and then he would get back home to Hanna.

A comment from his father jolted his mind back to the present.

"It looks exactly the same. I can't believe it! After all these years, it hasn't changed," Alexander said breathlessly.

Mike was in a daze. The village looked like something straight out of *Grimm's Fairy Tales*. In fact he wouldn't have been at all surprised to see Snow White and the seven dwarves or Little Red Riding Hood appear around the next corner or maybe working in the fields.

At first glance, he thought, the village had all the same characteristics as the hundred or so others they had passed on the way there, and maybe the difference wasn't so much in how it appeared, but rather how it made you feel. To a non-magical person it would just be quaint and charming, and he and his dad might leave feeling as though they had just spent time in an enchanted village. Yet Mike began to feel as if he was being drawn in, more than a visitor, more like the guest of honour at a great banquet being held to celebrate his return. He had an overwhelming sensation of familiarity. And if everything his father and uncle had told him were true, and it was beginning to feel like it had been true, then Mike had spent much of his childhood right here, in this village, with the people he was about to meet.

Mike took a moment to imagine himself as a child running through the streets, playing with cousins or visiting relatives...and what it might have been like walking the cows home and tending to the farm. There was bound to be something here that he would remember—he would still have some memories, right? There had to be. According to his father, they had left here when Mike was three. He had often had memories of his father playing magical games with him before he started school. Could it be that some of these memories were from *here* and not any of the other homes in which he had lived? But why did he only ever have memories of his father being with him and no one else? If he tried hard enough, could he remember his mother? Questions began to whirl around in his head. And, what would his relatives think of him if he didn't recognise them? Would they understand him? Had Uncle Laszlo been keeping them up to date on how the Weavers were doing?

"Michael! *We're here!*"

Mike was torn from his thoughts by the sound of his father's excited voice. He looked through the window to where his father was pointing. There, at the end of a long dirt road, was a quaint and simple house. Ducks and chickens scurried about as the car advanced slowly down a dusty road towards the house. A couple of barns with cows lined one side of the road and small green hills, scattered with flower beds and topped with plum, apple and cherry trees, lined the other. Here and there were small wooden shacks filled to bursting with dried corncobs.

He saw two large pear trees that stood like giants in front of the house creating a canopy of shade, no doubt a welcome relief for the inhabitants on hot dry summer days. A home-made wooden swing hung from one tree near a well topped with a small roof, from which a bucket hung for extracting water. Under the two pear trees was a pergola that spanned the distance between the house and what looked like a smaller house beside it. A long wooden table with equally long benches, a huge concrete pad and several small stairways leading here and there in every direction from the house were also under the canopy of the trees. And, standing on top of the concrete pad, filling every square inch of it, was a large group of people all smiling and waving at them.

"Who are all those people?" Mike asked, unable to hide the amazement in his voice.

"Your *family*!" Attila exclaimed excitedly. "They have been waiting for your return for a long time. This is a very special day for them!"

He turned around and smiled comfortingly at Mike, sensing his anxiety. Mike smiled feebly in return. He knew that Attila was trying to help and he was grateful for it. In just the short time he had known him he felt that Attila was a very loyal friend to his family. He also was silently thankful to his Uncle Laszlo for sending Attila to fetch them from the airport.

Attila stopped the car directly in front of the huge crowd now moving en masse towards them. Mike decided the best thing to do was stay behind his father; after all, he would remember them before Mike ever would, right? His father got out of the car first, which shocked Mike because he had been so silent throughout the whole ride, and Mike hadn't been sure what he was thinking or feeling. As Attila came around the side of the car, Mike climbed out and used the opportunity to sneak in behind both of them.

His father stood still for a moment, as if welded to the spot, and stared at the crowd of family before him. Mike wasn't sure if his father was happy, nervous or just trying to remember who all these people were.

"Apa, are you OK?" he asked, placing his hand on his father's shoulder. There was no response.

And now, screams of joy and delight at seeing their long-lost relatives were coming from the family moving towards them, some with smiles, some with open arms.

"Apa?" Mike asked nervously, shaking his father's shoulder a little.

He turned slightly towards his son and patted his hand, never taking his eyes off the crowd.

"Yes…yes, yes, I am fine." As if in a daze he began to move, grabbing Mike's hand and pulling him forwards slowly. When Mike was beside him his father leaned towards him and spoke softly, "Michael, this is your family!"

He squeezed Mike's hand, then looked straight into his eyes, his own eyes suddenly full of remorse. "I am so sorry that I had to keep you from them for so long."

The pain in his father's eyes and voice were too much to bear. He wished his father didn't feel that way.

"Apa, it's all right, just…just…don't leave my side yet, OK?"

He smiled at his father, trying not to look like a nervous five year old.

"I won't if you won't," he replied with a grin.

They both laughed quietly to each other and turned to face the excited crowd, now gathered directly in front of them….

⁂

During the next hour of his life, all Mike could remember was a lot of hugging, kissing, crying, laughing, crying again, hugging again and being pulled and pushed from relative to relative. They all exclaimed how they could not believe how grown up he was. Mike tried to explain in broken Hungarian, which only brought more shrieks of delight and more crying, that it had been thirteen years and how sorry he was that he didn't remember anyone. All the while he tried not to lose his father and made a great effort to ignore Uncle Laszlo, who suddenly had appeared and was enjoying the spectacle and making sure that Mike knew it. When Mike finally reached him, he glared at his uncle a little, who looked down at him and laughed, bringing him into a one-armed embrace, the other hand being occupied by a shot glass of palinka.

"Vell, how vuz dat?"

"A little heads-up would have been nice," Mike responded sarcastically.

His uncle laughed out loud.

"Dere vould have been no fun een dat!" He tipped the glass in Mike's direction. "Velcome home, Mike!" he exclaimed, shot the palinka down, grabbed Mike by the shoulder and led him away from the crowd. "Come, I vill show you vere you and your fazer's rooms are."

Happy to have a few minutes away, Mike gladly followed him. He looked back quickly to ensure that his father was all right and was relieved to see him laughing and toasting with a couple of his cousins. At least he thought that's who they were. It was hard to know after meeting so many people at once.

When they entered the room, Mike was pleased to see that it only had one bed in it. He meant no offense to his father, but he was happy for the privacy. It was a small room with the bed, a wall full of shelves and books to fill them. There was a ceramic tile oven opposite the bed with two wing chairs separated by a small round table. The remaining walls were decorated with colorful tapestries and paintings. Mike felt very welcome and comfortable, so he sat down, put his head back and let out a huge sigh of relief. Having not adjusted to the time change, it felt good to sit for a moment and not be rushed to get back up yet.

Uncle Laszlo sat in the seat across from Mike. He looked at his nephew with a serious expression on his face.

"Mike, I vant you to know dat I am very proud of you; you did a great job getting you and your fazer here and keeping yourselves safe. I know dat dis move eez not an easy one for you and vee have thrown a lot of surprises your vay. Dere eez so much more to tell you, but for tonight you just take some time to get to know your family and get some rest."

Mike looked at his uncle, surprised at the praise he had received.

"Uh…thanks, Uncle Laszlo."

His uncle smiled and started to get up, but as he did so he turned to his nephew.

"I know you'd razer rest, but dere are a few more family members to meet. Come, I'll introduce you."

Mike took a deep breath and got up out of the very comfortable chair. He heard a tiny clink coming from his pocket and suddenly remembered that he still had the small satchel of mystical marbles his uncle had given him. He pulled it out of his pocket.

'Hey, Uncle Laszlo, before we go I should give these back to you," he said, holding it up for his uncle to see.

"Ah yes, da in-a-pinch travel pearls!"

"The *what?*"

"In-a-pinch travel pearls," his uncle repeated.

"What exactly do these do? You told me to use them if we found ourselves in trouble."

"Yes, yes, deez are most handy vhen you find yourself *in-a-pinch*, so to speak. Dey are da wonderful creation of your Uncle Bernard, you haven't met him yet, he's from your mozser's side. Had you found yourself in trouble you vould have simply svallowed one like I instructed and da next ting you knew, you vould have found yourself here. Eet eez a bit of a rough ride, not da nicest way to travel, I got sick the first couple of times I tried, and da landing can be a bit bumpy, but uddervise eet vorks vonderfully vell!"

"You mean all that grief in getting here could have been avoided simply by swallowing this?" Mike asked, staring at him in disbelief, his voice rising a little towards the end of the question.

"Yes. I did not tell you how simple eet vould be because vee don't alvays need magic to find a vay out," he explained, picking up on Mike's irritation. "Let your instincts guide you. You are very powerful, Mike, even vizsout your magic," he stated, slapping Mike on the shoulder and making for the door.

My magic, Mike thought, then drew in a deep breath to calm himself before he followed his uncle. It was hard to be so aggravated and have deep respect for someone at the same time. He was taken to an outdoor kitchen that they entered through a beaded curtain. The room was full of relatives, younger relatives that he had not met earlier. He didn't have a moment to feel awkward, as his uncle began introducing everyone to him. He made his way around the room meeting cousin after cousin. Even though his father had never talked about it, Mike had always suspected that he had some family and had often guessed as to the number of unknown relations he had, but this was better than he had ever hoped for. The majority of those he was introduced to were boys of a similar age. There were a few girls, most either much younger or much older than Mike, except one, Eva, the daughter of Janus, who was the son of Anna, his father's aunt, all of whom lived on the farm where they were gathered today. Eva had just turned fifteen, a year younger than Mike.

Laszlo had begun to pour palinka into several small, handmade ceramic cups for the older cousins when something bolted through the beaded curtain, knocking Mike off his feet and onto the floor. He shook his head a little from the surprise of falling and looked up to see one of his cousins, hand stretched out to help him up, suddenly suffer the same fate when what appeared to be a pig rammed him square in the back of the knees. Mike jumped up and grabbed his cousin's outstretched hand to keep him from falling as well. It took but a second, when suddenly several of his cousins and his uncle were casting spells all over the room trying to stop the pig, which was now running around everyone's feet under the table and doing a good job of avoiding the spells. A couple of unlucky boys were hit by the spells instead, causing their legs to freeze momentarily.

Angry words were being exchanged between cousins when something else came bursting through the curtain. Mike had only a second to glance behind him to see that it was a girl, a very angry girl, who was holding a smaller boy in her arms and two wands in one of her hands, which the boy in her arms was desperately reaching and screaming for. The pig suddenly dashed out from under the table right in front of him. Not thinking, Mike lunged at the animal, and both he and the pig fell to the kitchen floor with a crash. Still not thinking, just doing, Mike managed to pin the pig down using one arm and his legs, all the while keeping a firm hold on the pig's squealing wriggling body.

It took Mike a couple of seconds to realize that other than the pig's squeals, the room had gone silent, but then clapping and hoots of congratulations filled the room. Feeling very awkward and wondering just how long he might have to hold the pig down, he turned his head around uncomfortably towards his uncle to plead for help. But at that moment the girl who had walked in with the screaming boy spoke to him in Hungarian.

"Are you Michael?"

Struggling to hold the pig down and through clenched teeth he answered that he was. She turned to the screaming boy in her arms and demanded that he apologize to Mike. The small boy's first thought was to scream louder in defiance, but one look from her and he changed his mind. A tiny squeak of an apology left his mouth. Satisfied enough, and with one quick movement of her wand, she stunned the pig then held out her hand to Mike and helped him up.

"I am Elizabeth, Laszlo's daughter, and this little disaster is Tibi, also a cousin of yours. I am sorry about the pig… Tibi is just learning to use his wand and he thinks the farm animals are his to torment. My father tells me you are an excellent wrestler and from what I just witnessed I'd say he was right. Good job on the pig."

Mike stood and brushed himself off. "Ahhh…thank you, nice to meet you—both, and good job on the pig yourself," he said.

They both looked down at the animal as it lay paralysed at his feet, and laughed. Tibi began wriggling in Elizabeth's arms, reminding her that he was still captive. Leaving Mike with his many cousins, who were slapping him on the back, congratulating him on his excellent capture, she turned on her heel and reprimanded her father. Laszlo, who was now looking quite embarrassed, led his daughter and Tibi outside to avoid any further humiliation. Mike waved goodbye to his uncle with mock sympathy. If it was possible to have a favourite cousin among the many he had met in the last hour—Elizabeth was the one.

Mike's success with capturing the pig was reason enough for his cousins to have a toast in his honour. A few of the older ones decided that several toasts were in order. Mike just sat back and enjoyed his new family. Knowing that his father was now in good hands he was able to relax and get to know his relatives. At first he wasn't sure about communicating, although his father spoke Hungarian with him often. It was a pleasant surprise and a relief to find that most of them could speak some English. It was so easy being there among them all; he couldn't believe how naturally it came to him.

Elizabeth returned to their group after a short while, minus Tibi, and sat down next to Mike. She expressed how delighted she was that he and his father had returned. She had grown up hearing about Mike and his father, and that the day they returned would be cause for all witches and wizards to rejoice. Mike chuckled at that comment and asked if saving his cousins from the wild pig was his destiny. They both laughed at that and continued to talk until they were all called to dinner.

Elizabeth was fourteen, soon to be fifteen. She was tall for her age, slim with long skinny legs. She had a kind face, huge blue eyes that seemed to look right through you and a head full of long, frizzy blonde hair. Mike imagined that this is what someone with long straight hair might look like after they had stuck their finger in a light socket. Her display earlier with her father assured Mike of her strong personality. He noticed during his visit with her and all his other cousins that she wasn't one to back down easily and had a way of questioning you that made you feel compelled to be honest. She was a *no BS* kind of girl and Mike liked that about her. Although surrounded by a family he never knew he had—all of whom were accomplished witches and wizards—in an environment where one could feel very intimidated, Elizabeth, and all his cousins for that fact, made him feel right at home, like he had always belonged. It was not what he had expected.

Before long his Aunt Anna, the owner of the farm, came in to announce that dinner was ready, motioning for Mike to follow her.

"I have a special seat for you and your father."

She squeezed his hand tightly as she said this and Mike was quite certain that her eyes were brimming with fresh tears. For fear of making her cry, something all his aunts were good at, he was discovering, he simply smiled back and followed her.

When they arrived at the dinner table Mike could not believe his eyes. Another long wooden pergola, this one covered in grapevines, stood overhead and the table was long enough to hold sixty people at least. To his surprise the table was packed full! It was going to be hard remembering who everyone was. Down the length of the table in the centre were dishes brimming with food of all kinds. Some Mike recognised and many more he didn't, but every bit of it looked and smelled mouth-wateringly delicious, making him realise how hungry he was. Huge fruit trees hung over the pergola and ornately crafted dishes decorated the table. There were flowers of all kinds and colours, which looked like they had been woven together into long braids that ran along plates and glasses, and in and out of the heaped plates of food.

Mike's aunt, who was now wiping her eyes, sat him down right in the middle of one side of the table next to his father, who also looked as if he had been crying. Mike politely thanked his aunt and sat down in his chair. He scanned the table with all its food and guests, and suddenly felt quite intimidated.

As soon as he was seated his father took him in a one-armed embrace. "Isn't it wonderful, Michael? Everybody here is our family! Isn't it good to be home?"

Mike looked at his father, who was now dangerously on the verge of crying again, so he smiled to reassure him. He returned his embrace, telling him everything was great. He didn't add that he really wanted to know why on earth everyone was crying if this was supposed to be such a happy occasion. Instead he just patted his father affectionately on the back.

"It's OK, Apa, it's OK...why don't we enjoy some of this food that smells so wonderful? I am starving!"

They both turned their attention back to the table, only to find everyone had cups full of wine and shot glasses full of…you guessed it, palinka! Laszlo was standing across the table from them, drink in hand, proposing a toast to their health and of gratitude for their safe return home. To Mike specifically, a toast to his long anticipated return and his strength and courage to embrace his future, his calling, a foretelling from long ago, and may he be well protected from his enemies!

Mike, who up until this point was still in awe of the cups and glasses that had miraculously filled themselves, and wished he hadn't missed seeing it happen, suddenly tuned in to what his uncle was saying. What had he just heard him say? Before he even had a chance to ask his father, everyone stood and the clinking glasses and shouts of "To your health!" began. Those near him were patting him on the back and toasting his courage and strength. He looked across the table at his uncle and made a mental note to corner him later and ask him what that was all about. The toasting came to an end and everyone sat down to find their soup bowls filled and their dinner plates full of a variety of dishes from which wafted the most wonderful aromas! Again, Mike had missed it, but the grumbling in his stomach told him it was time to stop questioning and eat.

For hours, it seemed, everyone ate, drank, laughed—and cried, of course, usually in that order—and celebrated Mike and his father returning home. To Mike's amazement he was able to keep up with the questions and genuine interest that his *new* family had in him. He found that he remembered much more Hungarian than he had thought and was able to communicate with everyone.

Early on in the dinner, Elizabeth had seated herself between Mike and his father. At first she spoke with Alexander and told him of the early memories she had of him and how happy she was that he was back. Mike sensed the deep respect that she held for his father and was impressed when she brought up memories of Alexander's wife, Mike's mother. At first he thought that his father would shut down and leave the table, but Elizabeth seemed to have a similar effect on him, very much like on her father, Uncle Laszlo. Mike listened intently as she spoke of his mother. Even though her memories were few and she had been very young when Alexander and Mike disappeared—another question he had for his uncle—she was able to recall her beauty, kindness and the unique gifts she had as a witch. Apparently one of Elizabeth's fondest memories was one where Mike's mother , Linnea, would make the flowers dance to cheer her up when she was upset, which had apparently happened often and still did. Mike sat mesmerized by her story, and as she told it that memory came flooding back to him. He remembered! In his mind's eye he could see his mother as clear as if she were standing in front of him.

Mike stood up from his chair very suddenly and excused himself from the table. Oh, no! Now *he* was in danger of crying! He quickly made his way to the house as if to use the bathroom, but as soon as he was out of sight he ducked around the corner and walked up into a small group of fruit trees and bushes behind the house. He sat down among the shrubs, hiding himself from any passers-by. He had grown up so secluded, so isolated from family members that he had never shared these thoughts or moments with anyone. When he thought about his mother, those were his own, very private thoughts, and hearing about her from some-one else had caught him off guard. He stayed where he was a little while longer enjoying the new memory. When he felt that he would no longer spontaneously burst into tears at the mention of her he took a deep breath and made his way back to the table.

Hoping that his sudden departure hadn't been noticed, he returned and sat down as if nothing had happened. The instant he did so, Elizabeth turned to him.

"I am so sorry if my talking about your mother upset you. It's just that I didn't think I would ever get the chance to let your father and you know how much your family meant to me. No one was sure if you would ever return to your home."

Mike was contemplating whether or not he should get up and run away! Instead, he did his best to look nonchalant.

"Oh, *that*; I just needed some fresh air, that's all. Not used to having shots with dinner, you know."

"Oh, sure," she said. 'I guess you and your dad aren't used to large family gatherings anymore."

"Exactly!" Mike replied, happy that she hadn't made a big deal out of it.

He had the distinct feeling that she knew he was lying and, again, found himself in admiration of her ability not to push the matter. He prepared himself mentally for any other surprises, but none came. As it was, the rest of the evening passed without incident and soon everyone was saying their goodbyes and goodnights. Every relative hugged him and Alexander, and praised them for their brave return before they left, promising to see them again for breakfast.

Finally, after saying goodnight to Elizabeth and Laszlo, who were the last to leave, Mike and his father were escorted by his aunt to their rooms to retire for the night.

"Good night, Apa," Mike said as he hugged his father.

"Good night to you too, Michael, may you sleep well."

With that they parted and went into their respective rooms.

11

The Girl
in the Flowers

Sleep did not come right away. Mike sat slumped on the bed, staring into nothingness. What the heck just happened? The last couple of days had been a whirlwind of information, some of which he had no idea how he was going to process. As crazy as it had all been, however, he had to admit that he felt very drawn to this place. There was a warmth about his relatives that was familiar to him. He felt a wonderful comfort in knowing that he had a family beyond just himself, his father and Uncle Laszlo.

The village where his family lived was beautiful. Their home was warm and comforting, full of noise, something to which he certainly wasn't accustomed. He loved his father deeply, but had to admit that they led a very quiet life. The mood in their house was often dark and melancholy, his father's passive behaviour leaving a lot of the thinking and doing up to Mike. Here the bond between his cousins, aunts and uncles was wonderful to him—a real family.

As he sat and mulled over the happenings of the day, he began to look around the room. Everything was so different. Hard work and great care had gone into every detail of the room, actually the whole house. There were intricate tapestries hanging on every wall. Some were fabulous landscapes of rolling hills and lush greenery surrounding small villages.

Others were of people, perhaps ancestors (he'd make a note to ask tomorrow, he had so many questions already), others had a mystical feel to them, swirls of colours moving across the tapestry like a child had wiped his hands through the hues of an evening sunset scattered with stars, and yet there still seemed to be form to it, a purpose.

"Just like everything else in this place. It doesn't make sense," Mike whispered to himself.

He expelled an exasperated sigh followed by a huge yawn. Just then he noticed a steaming cup of tea on the bedside table. He didn't usually drink tea, but right now it seemed to be exactly what he wanted. The timing of its appearance couldn't have been more perfect. As he sipped the welcoming drink he began to notice a wonderful sense of calm and tranquillity wash over him. His eyes were getting heavier and his thoughts began to change from the overwhelming day he had just had to the beauty of the landscape, the dark rolling hills and the clear black sky painted with an infinite number of stars. It all seemed to form a frame around this quaint little village that he now knew as home. He felt safe, provided for, loved, much like he imagined a comforting hug from his mother might have felt.

What *is* in this tea? Who left it here for me? It must have been Anna Nani. Very strange, he thought. From the first moment she had laid eyes on him he felt as if she knew what he wanted or what he was thinking even before he did. He hadn't had thoughts like these in years. As vulnerable as it would have normally made him feel, he had to admit that, this time, he was okay, as though it was allowed. He didn't feel the need to quickly shove his feelings back, deep down to the bottom of his heart, for fear of being found out. His aunt had probably brewed up some special concoction or cast some spell over him, who knows? After all, she is a witch! I am a wizard! None of it made sense, yet it explained so much that it made perfect sense! He hoped beyond hope that tomorrow things wouldn't seem so crazy. He sure had a lot of questions, and somebody had better be willing to answer every single one!

Mike let his thoughts drift to warm feelings of relaxation once more, snuggled himself further into the thick duvet on his bed and before he knew it those thoughts turned into dreams and one of the best nights of sleep he would ever remember having…

<hr />

"*Mike? Mike?*"

Mike stirred in bed. Did somebody just call him? He lay still for a moment and listened carefully, then it came again.

"*Mike…? Mike…?*"

The voice was very soft, but he could definitely hear someone calling his name. It sounded so far away though. Maybe it was coming from outside. Should he get up? The house was silent, and it was still dark outside.

"*Mike…? Mike…?*"

The soft voice came again. This time he could make out that it was a child's voice, actually it sounded like a young girl. It was familiar to him, but he couldn't place it. Maybe it was one of his many new cousins, but they didn't speak English, so they wouldn't be calling him Mike.

He lay there for a moment staring up at the ceiling, straining to hear the voice again. *The sky sure is beautiful here*, he thought. He was positive he could see every star in the universe. With a start he bolted upright in his bed!

"Stars, why do I see stars?" It suddenly occurred to him that he was not in his room, but outside—in his bed! "What the…?"

Was this some kind of magical trick his relatives were playing on him—some kind of bizarre initiation into wizardry? Very, very carefully he turned his head to see what was around him. He was definitely outside. His heart was pounding so hard it was almost deafening to his ears. He tried taking deep breaths to calm himself, hearing his PE teacher repeating these words during their yoga lesson: "Deep breaths, children—in through the nose, out through the mouth," or was it in through the mouth and out through the nose? This wasn't helping. His breathing was doing nothing to control the pounding beat of his heart! He swore under his breath.

"OK, Mike, *think*!" He concentrated, his eyes closed tightly. "This is probably just a dream," he whispered, keeping his eyes closed and lying back down, determined to fall back asleep or get out of this dream anyway.

Just as he was about to open his eyes to prove to himself that he was only dreaming he heard it again…

"*Mike…? Open your eyes.*"

The voice was so familiar to him. He had to see who it was.

"Who's there? Where are you?" he questioned, his voice shaking as he called out into the darkness.

No reply.…

He called out again and still no answer. He decided to leave the safety of his bed. The voice hadn't sounded threatening, in fact, when he thought about it again, he didn't actually feel intimidated in any way. If it wasn't for the darkness he might be perfectly brave. He waited to see if his eyes would adjust to the darkness and he soon found that what he was actually looking at was a forest, a very dense, dark forest.

"Geez!" he exclaimed with a sigh. "This is creepy!"

This is something right out of a fairy tale, he thought. Dark forests with huge trees that loomed down over you, the branches stretching out to you like the contorted limbs of some creature of the night out to ensnare lonely travellers who have by error stumbled into the forbidden forest! He shook his head as if to clear it of these thoughts. This witch and wizardry stuff was really getting to him.

All right, Mike, suck it up, you can do this, he thought. And then, as if on cue, a little light shone through the dense canopy above and revealed the forest floor covered in beautiful white flowers.

"Trilliums!" Mike whispered, surprised that he knew what he was seeing. He had never seen this kind of flower before. Each one looked like a soldier, standing tall and strong, with broad green leaves covering the forest floor, much like lily pads do on a pond, topped with an equally large flower that bloomed with only three white petals.

"Trilliums," he whispered again, not knowing how he knew, but he was sure of it.

Mike gingerly stepped out of his bed and tiptoed through the thick flowers, not wanting to damage them—they stood so proud. The flowers began to stir, so he retracted his foot quickly and sat down carefully! Holding his knees close to his chest with his feet well out of reach of the forest floor, he cautiously peered over his knees to see what was happening. He couldn't believe what he saw next. The flowers were parting and creating a long clear path for him. He stood and walked down the path slowly, one foot in front of the other, waited a moment and when nothing dramatic happened he felt safe to continue. He moved forwards and executed every step ninja-like, so as not to disturb any flowers. The light was still shining through the branches above onto the forest floor, almost exactly where the path was being made. He thought it all very odd, but hey, it was just a dream, right?

The soft call of his name came again. He strained to make out from which direction it was coming and followed the path, which seemed to have shifted with his movements. He mused over the flowers' behaviour and thought that if this was what magic was going to be like, he might just like it. He stopped for a moment and observed the pathway ahead, concluding that he would continue on the trail the flowers had made for him; they seemed to know where he needed to go.

He hadn't walked far when a figure in the short distance became clear. He stopped dead in his tracks. Before he had a chance to consider if the figure was the source of the soft voice, it called out once more, only this time it called out, *Mihaly*, his full Hungarian name, and with such genuine happiness and excitement. Mike stared at the figure ahead, feeling compelled to respond with the same familiarity, but other than the voice, he had no clue of its identity. He raised his hand and gave a meek wave. It waved back enthusiastically. He decided to move closer to at least determine the gender, although he was pretty sure it was a girl.

With his hand in the air waving, to indicate he was coming closer but that the figure was to stay right where it was, he walked forwards until he could make out that it was indeed a girl.

"Hi," he said, still waving.

That's where his side of the conversation ended. He wanted to say so much more—*who are you, where am I, why does your voice sound so familiar to me, is this a dream, are you real, is this magic?* W-where was his voice, and why wasn't he using it?

Without thinking he continued to move closer to her, and when he could make out her face he stopped. She wore a hooded cape, but when he was close enough she removed the hood.

"*Hi,*" she said, as if it was a foreign word to her.

She had an accent. Mike didn't respond—he just stood there staring at her. Not only did her voice have a familiarity to it, but her face did too! She was younger than him, at least by a couple of years. Her face was soft and there was a wonderful kindness in her eyes, which looked like emeralds. The sun that peeked through from above caught her eyes sparkling playfully, and she beckoned for him to follow her. He took a step forwards to do so when someone or something grasped his shoulder and shook him.

Feeling more than a little startled he whipped around to see what had grabbed his shoulder, but found nobody and nothing there, just the dark forest with the tall gloomy trees swaying in the wind. He must have brushed past a branch. He shook himself once all over to rid himself of the creepy feeling that had suddenly enveloped him and turned back to follow the girl. To his astonishment and unexpected disappointment, she had disappeared!

"Hey! Where are you?" he called out. Only silence was returned, so he tried again. "Hello? Hello? Please come back; I have so many questions! Who are you?"

"*Breakfast*," came her soft voice from far away.

"*What?*" he shouted into the empty forest.

Had he heard that right? Did she say *breakfast*? Feeling certain that he had misunderstood her answer, he asked again.

"*Who* are you?"

"*Breakfast!*" she shouted; only this time it wasn't her voice.

It sounded like a boy. Startled, Mike spun around to see who else was there with him—no one. The entire forest had gone black again and he could feel the trilliums closing in around his feet. Without hesitation, he bolted back in the direction he had come. Barely able to see the forest floor, the regard he had had for these majestic soldier-like flowers had all but disappeared with the sudden rush of fear he felt!

"*Breakfast, breakfast!*" the little boy sang, giggling.

He felt his fear gauge spike through the top! This was something straight out of a horror movie!

"*Breakfast, breakfast!*" the boy continued to sing.

Just when Mike thought he would never reach his bed, he saw the vague outline of it just a few metres ahead.

"Oh! Thank good—"

Whack!

Mike felt himself being flung down hard onto the forest floor where he lay, the wind knocked out of him. He tried to get up and realised that whatever had hit him was still on top of him! Keeping his eyes shut tight he felt around for a stick, anything to protect himself! Maybe he should have been groping around for eggs and bacon! The voice was still singing for breakfast! A frightening thought occurred to him—perhaps *he* was breakfast! He groped around in vain, but found nothing, in fact the forest floor was soft, very soft, like blanket-and-pillow soft. He opened his eyes to find his would-be assailant wasn't the vicious starving creature he had thought, but his little cousin sitting on him.

"Breakfast, breakfast!" he was singing to wake up his new cousin, singing with sheer delight at using apparently the only English word he knew.

Mike, now feeling very foolish, bewildered—and hungry—was snuggled down in the safety and comfort of his bed! His little cousin shrieked with delight at the sight of Mike opening his eyes, and jumped off him. His twin brother giggled at his brother's antics, pointing at the door with a look of *'you are in huge trouble!'* Mike's attacker looked towards the bedroom door to find his mother standing there, anger written all over her face. Mike just lay there amused by the whole situation.

He was alone now. He could hear his cousins outside, pleading their innocence in Hungarian and apparently losing the battle with their mother. His mind very quickly transported him back to his dream. He couldn't get the girl and her familiar voice out of his head. Where would she have led him if he had followed? He knew that it didn't make sense. You never follow a stranger, yet he had been ready to follow her, no questions asked. He felt as if he had known her forever, like he had his father.

He lay there a moment longer pondering the meaning of his dream, when his stomach growled loudly in annoyance at him still being in bed. He sat up and stretched his body out. Considering the night's events, he felt incredibly rested. A small surge of excitement coursed through his body. What was he going to learn about today? He could barely wait to tell his father about the dream!

A Hidden Meaning

After what seemed like an hour of getting ready for the day, longer than Mike had ever taken to get ready before, he sat down next to his father at the once again beautifully adorned table. In Hungarian, he wished everyone a good morning. His Anna Nani asked him how he had slept. By the look in her eyes, Mike was sure she knew he had had an excellent sleep and he was also sure, now, that she was the one who had left him the tea.

"It was the best sleep I can ever remember having, thank you."

"It must be the good country air," she said, winking at him.

Mike laughed to himself. He hadn't had too much interaction with his aunt yet, but she seemed like a very kind and clever person. He liked that. To look at her, there was nothing elaborate: she looked and dressed much like most of the older women…a black shirt and skirt, and a black scarf over her hair—very simple—in fact, everything here seemed basic in its way.

There was a well from which they drew their water, an outhouse, no car except the one in which they had arrived. The huge garden was weeded by hand, the cows were milked every day by them, and if you had chicken for dinner it came from the many that wandered around free. Judging by the sudden cry of a chicken that had just been beheaded, Mike was pretty sure that they didn't use magic to kill and prepare the evening meals. Although they did have a bathroom with running water, a toilet and tub, it was separate from the home and he guessed that it was only used by visitors from the city and baths for the little ones.

Mike was brought back to reality by the sound of his uncle's laughter. He looked at him only to realize that he was laughing at him. Mike looked at him questioningly.

"What?"

"Are you alvays dis serious at breakfast?" his uncle asked. "You should eat, den tink," he added.

Mike looked at him and faked a smile, hoping for something witty to come to mind, but just as he opened his mouth to reply, his stomach gave a loud grumble that could be heard by all. Embarrassed, he looked down at his stomach, rubbing it in an attempt to make it stop. His uncle was laughing again and just as Mike looked up to glare at him, his father turned to him.

"Here, Michael, try some of these eggs, they are the best you'll ever have."

He pushed a plate full of scrambled eggs with pieces of fried sausage, onion and yellow peppers towards him and as he did so, Elizabeth joined them at the table.

"Shame on you, Apa!" she scolded. "Pay no attention to my father," she said, turning to Mike, "he's using his wit to compensate for his hunger. You see even wizards need to diet," she added, winking at him.

Laszlo grumbled a little under his breath just as Anna Nani placed a bowl of fruit in fresh yoghurt in front of him. Mike laughed and dug into the fabulous breakfast before him.

After breakfast, Mike, his father, Laszlo and Elizabeth went for a walk. His father had insisted that Mike get to know the village and his surroundings, and it would also give his father a chance to recover some memories. Mike was only too happy to comply.

As they walked, Mike took the opportunity to tell them about his dream. Both his father and uncle put it down to Anna Nani's famous tea, but Mike noticed his father's worried look.

"What is it, Apa? Something's on your mind, I can tell by that look."

"I don't know. I...I just feel as though it has a hidden meaning." He shrugged his shoulders. "But I don't know what."

Elizabeth, who had been listening to the conversation intently, looked up at her father, who she could tell was avoiding her gaze.

"Apa, does the dream remind you of something?" she asked.

Laszlo turned his gaze towards his daughter. He knew that she knew him too well and that she wasn't likely to be quiet about it until he gave her an answer.

"Dere are large fields filled with deez white flowers everyvhere. Dey are very common. You probably saw several such fields driving in from da airport...vee should continue on; dere eez much more to learn before lunch."

He abruptly turned back towards the path they had been following. Elizabeth knew her father well enough to know that he was holding back, but also knew she shouldn't press him for more. He would have good reason for not sharing the information.

Uncle Laszlo changed the subject and was now explaining to Mike how important it was that no one, outside of the family, with very few exceptions, learn that Mike and Alexander had returned...yet. There would be a time for that soon enough.

"So what *exactly* does that mean?" Mike asked—a slight edge to his voice and wondering why *exactly* they had returned now if no one was to know of their existence, *and*... how on *earth* a family of their size was going to keep this quiet.

Laszlo had picked up on the edge in Mike's voice and answered with an air of patience one might exercise on a three-year-old who responds to everything with 'Why?'

"Ven ve left Calgary, I explained to you dat sumvun eez after you—yes? He looked at Mike and Mike gave a quick nod in acknowledgement. Although the family knew they were back, all were sworn to secrecy. Mike asked his uncle how he could be sure that everyone would stay quiet, even the little ones. His uncle told him that everyone knew how important his return was and that they had been living with this secret for a very long time.

Other than the children old enough to attend the Wizard and Dragon Training Academy, rarely did any of them go into the city and hadn't since the day Mike and his father had disappeared. Many feared they would be targets, so they chose to live in smaller towns and villages among the Non-wow's. His uncle was the Weaver family's last residing member on the wizard's council, but only attended meetings when necessary. The other members were residents of Bodon, a small piece of land that had belonged to the Weaver family for hundreds of years. It had always been protected by magic and could not be seen or entered by anyone outside the family.

Mike asked his uncle why he and Elizabeth risked going to Segesvar if the family was such a target—and what was the wizard council anyway?

Laszlo explained that there were thirteen towers in Segesvar, one for each of the founding families of magic in Transylvania. The thirteen families had come together and formed a council, Segesvar and their family towers. Each tower was preserved and protected by both powerful magic, specific to that family alone, and by a "family" dragon. The towers served as homes and sanctuaries for their families. No one from another family could enter the home without invitation from a family member, and even that could only be achieved by powerful magic known only to that family. This was done so that no one family could become more powerful than the next and rise to power over all. Unless a family died out completely, their tower could never be taken from them, for only when the last family member died did the magic protecting the house also die. Even then the fate of that tower had to be decided by the council.

Yet, over time, as is always the case with mankind, certain families had grown tired of the old ways and the boundaries set for their protection by their founding fathers, and had become greedy, desiring power…one family in particular. Mike's uncle never explained which family, telling him it was a long story for another day.

Uncle Laszlo continued explaining to Mike the importance of every family having representatives on the council. Although they knew wizards and witches existed elsewhere in the world, the wizard council remained anonymous and isolated from the rest of the wizard world, a duty that the first members of the council took upon themselves and they had always been successful. Transylvania was home to the only vampires, werewolves and dragons in the universe. Trolls, elves and dwarves also inhabited Transylvania, but were known to also exist in other parts of the eastern world.

With some families wanting to rise to power, it was important that there be at least one or more representatives from every family to vote for or against changes to their laws. The Weaver family was one of the largest and most powerful families, and Mike's father, his Uncle Laszlo, and a few other uncles had always been on the council, but with all of the Weavers having fled, there was no one left to represent the family. After Alexander's family was attacked, Laszlo took it upon himself to find those responsible. He surmised that the best way to accomplish this was to remain on the council. He did not attend often, but just enough to show that the Weaver family was still present and accounted for.

Wow! This was surreal. Mike felt like he had just had a history lesson on someone else's family, a family from a very bad fairy tale! A wizard council, magical towers, his family's magical village, dragons, trolls, werewolves and vampires! And again he wondered, what was so important about him and his parents that warranted the attack that killed his mother and sent his father and him into exile? Who had attacked them? In thirteen years had no one figured it out?

Mike stopped walking and sat down on a nearby rock. He looked overwhelmed, which had not gone unnoticed by Elizabeth.

"Apa," she said to her father, "I think Mike has heard enough for now, don't you?"

She motioned to Mike sitting on the rock. Her father looked over at him and saw a very young and exhausted boy. There was still so much more he needed to know and learn, and Laszlo knew that he didn't have much time to accomplish it, but his daughter was right—for today it was enough. He looked over at Alexander, who had walked a little farther ahead to a small river that ran along the path. He had found a large willow that hung over the water and had taken refuge in the shade it provided. He too looked tired. This concerned Laszlo even more than Mike's exhaustion, for he knew his nephew was young and strong, much stronger than even he knew, but Alexander…the spells that had been cast on him all those years ago, and all the time that had passed since then, were only now working against him.

Laszlo knew what he needed to do, but he was afraid Mike and Alexander weren't ready for it.

Elizabeth walked over to her father and took his hands in hers.

"Apa, didn't you say that the next and only opportunity for Alexander Bacsi to regain his memory was on the first full moon of the summer?" she asked, almost as if she was reading his mind.

"Yes," he replied absent-mindedly, still pondering his cousin's condition.

"Well…?" She waved her hand across her father's face to break his stare. Startled and annoyed, he turned his gaze on her.

"Vell…?" he echoed.

"*Apa!*" she exclaimed, throwing her hands up in the air in exasperation. "That's less than six weeks away!"

Seeing that he had pushed his daughter to the brink of an explosion, which wasn't difficult, he softened his gaze and spoke calmly.

"My dear daughter, I know. Eet's just dat—"

"We must go then!" she interrupted. "They'll be fine. Mike is very strong, you know he is, and he will learn quickly—it's in his blood. I know you are afraid for Alexander Basci, but he was once very powerful too. It will work! Mike will need his father! He can't be who he is destined to be without Alexander Basci!"

As usual, his daughter was right. So often she was the voice of reason for him. He looked down at her, squeezing her hands in his.

"You are right! Eet eez time, but first vee eat!"

He smiled at her and kissed her forehead as she released her hands, waved her wand about her head, spoke a quiet spell and with a wink said: "I'll be right back!"

There was the sound of a small crack and she had gone. Mike glanced up from the rock he was sitting on and looked over at his uncle.

"What was that?" He had heard the crack and now noticed that Elizabeth was no longer there. "Where is Elizabeth?" he asked, momentarily forgetting all the other questions that were whirling about in his head.

"She's gone to bring us lunch. Come on, let us go join your fazer over by da river. He has picked an ideal place to relax and eat."

Mike was stunned, but happy at the mention of food.

"How did she—?"

"*Magic!*" his uncle cut in, smiling.

Mike was disappointed that he had missed seeing how Elizabeth had disappeared. He kept missing all the magic, it seemed.

"Will I learn to do that too?"

"Yes, Mike, yes, and so much more." There was another sudden crack in the air. "Oh! Dere she eez!"

Mike jumped at the sound and turned to look where his uncle was pointing. There was Elizabeth, standing not three feet behind them, beaming from ear to ear and holding a large basket of food. Mike stepped towards her and offered to carry the basket.

"That was fast!" he exclaimed.

Elizabeth laughed as they walked towards the tree.

"As soon as you have a wand, I'll teach you how to do that."

Mike smiled and thought to himself how many times a spell like that would have come in handy in his lifetime, like when he was late for school or avoiding Ronald Moody, a boy who had bullied him for the entire third grade. That had been the year that Mike realised wrestling was the sport for him.

They all sat down under the giant willow tree. Alexander was delighted at having lunch by the river, and was able to recall a few memories of passing afternoons by the river with Laszlo when they were still young. Mike listened intently to the stories as he always did, because they were so few and far between. Eventually Laszlo and Alexander engaged each other in conversations of the past, helped along by a shot or two of palinka and ice cold beers to combat the heat of the afternoon.

Mike and Elizabeth went down to the river and swam in the shallows, all the while Elizabeth happily answering any questions Mike had for her and vice versa. Mike could not remember ever being in any place that had made him feel so at home.

What Do Wrestling and Wizards Have in Common?

The next couple of weeks passed quickly for Mike. Most days were spent getting to know his huge family, always accompanied by his father and Laszlo. From the amount of information his uncle would dump on him daily, Mike gathered that he was attempting to make up for the thirteen years of wizarding life that he had missed: the family history; the history of wizards and witches, dragons and other magical creatures; how Bodon came to be and the importance of it for their specific family; the thirteen founding families of wizardry; the importance of keeping Mike and his father's arrival quiet and on and on. He was grateful for it and cherished the time getting to know the family he never knew he had, but he was accustomed to spending his days with his friends at school, which oddly enough he missed. There had been those few precious moments after school, his favourite time of day, when he would walk home with Hanna. He missed *that* the most.

Mike's father enjoyed each visit thoroughly, along with the copious amounts of food and drink. Even though he wavered in and out of clear memory, sometimes speaking of the past like it had happened yesterday and other times having no recollection of where he was and why, everyone was sympathetic to their situation and delighted that Alexander had returned home with his son. The culture was different here from anywhere Mike had been with his father. There was an unconditional devotion they had for one another, like the prodigal son; it didn't seem to matter where you were or what you had done, they were just happy that you were home. The only difference was, this prodigal son had left without wanting to do so.

As much as Mike enjoyed the days, he really looked forward to the evenings; Elizabeth, Mike, Arpi, Feri and a few other cousins spent most evenings down by the river. The days were so hot that one could barely wait to jump into the cool clean water.

Arpi was a year younger than Elizabeth, and Feri would be sixteen next month, nearly the same age as Mike. They were the children of Laszlo's younger brother, Zsolt. They had a sister too, but she was only ten. On occasion, after much assurance from his two sons that they would keep all four eyes on her at all times, Zsolt would allow her and a few of the younger cousins to join them down by the river to escape the sweltering heat. Mike was happy about this, as he relished every chance to get to know his family...and they were a lot of fun.

Mike had so much more in common with his cousins than he could ever have imagined, and strong friendships were formed fast. No matter where he lived and how many times he and his father had to move, he'd always had friends, some relationships stronger than others, but the opportunities to make lasting bonds were few. Evenings had been spent caring for his father, he didn't like to leave him alone on weekends and social media was out of the question. Laszlo had always made it very clear that the cut had to be clean every time they relocated.

On two occasions, as with the last move to Calgary, Laszlo himself didn't even know that they were moving. He had arrived for one of his routine visits, had worked his magic on Alexander—Mike fully expecting to have to move the next day—then stayed for a couple of days and left. Mike was shocked and pleased to find that he hadn't come to warn them and suggest the next destination. A week later, Mike had just left school at the end of the day and was making his way to the bus when he spotted a taxi parked across the street. His father climbed out and was waving him over. Mike knew immediately what was coming, so despite his father's urgency, he turned back, told his friends he wouldn't be taking the bus and said goodbye to them and the bus driver, a jovial man. He was a retired grandfather of fifteen grandchildren, in need of something to do in his "spare time," and Mike had become very fond of him. His father, who was thinking remarkably clearly for once, had arranged everything.

⌀〰⌀

After much relentless persuading from Elizabeth one day, Laszlo had agreed that he would take Mike back to Seges-var and let him see his home, the Weaver's tower. It was the equivalent of gaining access to the archives in the Vatican or being allowed to roam the Pentagon freely. The president's chair—take a seat! At least that is what his uncle had said. Mike was sure Uncle Laszlo was overreacting completely, judging by the number of times Elizabeth rolled her eyes at her father's dramatics, but he played along with everything.

So that he'd be allowed to go, Mike agreed to *anything* his uncle asked; he could throw him into a Little Bo Peep costume and ask him to herd a flock of sheep all the way there, if he thought that would help. Thankfully, Mike's pride had been spared and it hadn't come to that. When Laszlo Basci finally consented, Mike had to contain his desire to leap into the air and yell "*Yes!*" at the top of his lungs.

The next day Laszlo announced he was going into town for a council meeting with the WWF. Hearing that, Mike had just about choked on another one of Anna Nani's fine Hungarian meals. WWF? They told him that was the name the council members had given themselves—The Witch and Wizard Federation. Other than his own father, Mike knew no one at the table would catch the humour in this name…which also stood for the World Wrestling Federation. Moreover, his attempt to explain the unique wrestling style of the WWF only brought forth many questions: Why would anyone fake wrestling? If it's fake, why do they get paid? Who is dumb enough to watch fake wrestling? Had *Mike* ever watched fake wrestling? Was that the kind of wrestling club he belonged to and, if it was, why didn't he just take an acting class instead? Why do they dress in costumes that reveal the very contours of their bodies, which no one should ever have to see? If it's meant to intimidate, it's not working, so why hasn't someone told them that? Lastly, in good American fashion, why aren't the families of these *actors* suing their sons for bringing shame onto their families? Mike made a note to keep his comments about other North American wording similarities to himself the next time.

After the assault of questions died down, Mike posed his own questions. It was obvious that respect was a one-way street, so he chose the higher road and did not show his amusement at their *very* serious responses. Apparently it had been months since Laszlo's last attendance at their monthly WWF meetings. Over the years and in between Laszlo's frequent trips in search of Mike and his father or information that would lead him closer to the answers they had all been searching for, Laszlo would attend these meetings as the Weaver family representative. The time for the Weaver family to make its comeback was upon them.

A couple other families also held powerful seats on the WWF, one being the Taylors, whose family tower was right beside the Weavers'. They had been long-standing friends of the Weavers and the families felt a strong alliance to one another, as both their towers stood watch over the only other gate into the city. Mike tried to picture this. Laszlo explained that the Taylors had two children—a son, Sandor, who was seventeen (he thought Mike would have got on well with him), and a daughter, Aniko, who was sixteen and apparently quite beautiful (Laszlo thought Mike would have got on very well with her too!). No way, Mike thought to himself. His heart belonged to one girl only and that was Hanna, and all this talk of close friends and family ties only made him miss her more!

"Dey left over half a year ago to stay vis family in Austria, udervise I vould have introduced dem to you already. I am certain dat dey vill return soon. I vuz hoping dat der fazer,

Dani, vould have been back. I hope to see heem at da meeting tomorrow night. Maybe dey have returned." Laszlo looked at Alexander with a warm smile. "Dani vill be very happy to know dat you are finally home. He has missed you all deez years and has helped me as often as he could."

A look of worry and concern washed over Alexander's face as Laszlo said this, and he shook his head.

"He shouldn't have done that. I didn't ask anyone to get involved, not even you, Laszlo... You risked your life for us. Who knows what the consequences will be! Laszlo, please don't tell h—"

Before he could finish his plea, Laszlo cut him off. "Alexander..., Dani vuz...eez your best friend, so he vould have done eet even eef you told heem not to!

Alexander's expression softened.

"He always was a good friend. I hope he and his family have returned and are safe now." He looked at Mike and gripped his hand. "When it is safe, we will visit with them."

Mike smiled at his father, thinking how good it was to see him so happy. It was strange to think of his father being any different from how he had been for most of Mike's life, but he had always wondered why he never made or mentioned any friends. Of course, now he was beginning to understand why, and it made him feel awful inside that his father had been forced to leave everything and everyone behind. He was silently thankful that his father's memory was so poor most of the time. It can't have been easy for him losing his wife to an unexpected attack, not being able to remember who attacked her and why, being magically cast away from his family and friends for thirteen years and raising a small child full of questions that he was unable to answer because a good chunk of his memory had been erased…and constantly having to move around for fear of being found. Mike hoped that his father's best friend, Dani, had really returned. Even though he knew that just being with the family had helped his father and himself tremendously, nothing could replace a best friend. That was a feeling Mike was all too familiar with, and just thinking about it made him miss Hanna more than ever.

Mike had missed the last couple of minutes of what his uncle was saying about the topic of tomorrow's council meeting, his full attention had been with thoughts of Hanna and what had happened to her. In the flurry of activity over the last few weeks and the overload of information he had received, not to mention the new supersize family he had to get to know, he hadn't had much time to think. He couldn't have even sent a text message or email because there was no service out here and not one relative owned a computer.

He had always wondered what it would feel like living off the grid, but he had to admit it *was* peaceful, except on days like today, when he really wanted nothing more than to get a hold of Hanna and find out where she was and what had happened. Had she returned to her home after the fire and found that he had left? Was she angry that he had not said goodbye? Had she even come back, and why hadn't she tried to contact *him*? Maybe she didn't miss him… Maybe he had misread her friendship, their holding hands, how she always made sure she sat beside him on the bus, the long walks home together, the awkward silences, the way she laughed at all his jokes, the intense heat and the desire to kiss her every time she stood next to him.

Mike let out a long sigh. Laszlo, hearing it across the table, stopped in the middle of what he had been saying and questioned his dreamy-eyed nephew.

"Are vee keeping you avake, Mike?"

"What? Yes... I m-mean...n-no," Mike responded, startled. "Well...I am a little tired. It's been a long day, that's all, s-sorry."

Everyone at the table was laughing now, some more openly than others. Elizabeth was giving him a glare that told him she didn't believe a word of what he had just stuttered out. He returned her look with a sweet smile, silently thanking her for laughing so unnecessarily loudly. The laughter died down and his uncle continued where he had left off.

Mike made a concerted effort to put Hanna temporarily at the back of his mind and focus on what Uncle Laszlo was saying, but that proved much harder than he had imagined; every thought was a memory of their time together and how it was prematurely cut short so "cruelly" by his father and uncle. Thankfully the longing to see Segesvar, the place that he had called home for the first three years of his life, was so strong that he was successful in prioritising his thoughts and showing his uncle how interested he really was in what he was saying.

When he finally tuned in he caught something about a large Gypsy caravan that was passing through Segesvar. Although they were a common sight in most wizarding towns, they were known for their associations with the "less-than-savoury" members of the wizard world. This particular caravan was much larger than usual and Laszlo suspected that they too were interested in the outcome of tomorrow's council meeting.

The next hot topic of discussion was the seven-year Dragon Egg Hunt (this was the second time Mike had to suppress his laughter as the scene of small excited children being released into a vast field on a sunny Easter morning, squealing with excitement when they found the brightly coloured eggs half their size, nearly stumbling under the weight of them, flashed through his mind). But he pricked his ears up almost immediately just at the mere mention of dragons. He listened very politely, for the number of times he had dreamed about dragons and the many times he awoke swearing it had all been so real, the thought that their existence *was* real, made him almost giddy with excitement.

Mike could remember as a young child the stories his father told him about a particular dragon, making it sound as if the dragon was his best friend, which to him was ridiculous, knowing that his father's condition wasn't "quite right," so he learned to take the stories with a pinch of salt. He still loved the stories though and sometimes, even now, when he would have his reoccurring dream, he would wake with the hope that his father's stories held some truth.

Hanna slowly crept to the forefront of his mind once more that day; he remembered she was the only person he had ever talked to about his dreams and she hadn't even laughed at him when he admitted that his father used to tell him dragon stories. He still didn't know what it was that made her so easy to confide in, but without even realising it he would just begin to blab freely. It was as if his mouth had a will of its own.

He could remember how embarrassed he had been the first time he ever spoke of dragons. He wished he could travel back in time and stop himself from opening his mouth, but after he started talking about dragons, she had said something that he would never forget. "You know, Mike, I have had dreams about dragons too." This was said without a hint of sarcasm in her voice, in fact her voice was distant and dreamy. "Sometimes they seem so real. Wouldn't it be great if they really were?"

"Dere have been deaths een da past two egg hunts…" his uncle was saying.

Mike tuned back in immediately to hear what his uncle had said. Had he just heard that correctly?

"What did you just say, Uncle Laszlo?" Mike asked, hoping he had not heard right.

"Really, Mike, have you listened to anyting I have been saying?" his uncle asked in mock disapproval.

"Of course I have—every word (he lied), it's just, you said *two deaths*. How dangerous can an *egg* hunt be?" Mike questioned, not really being clued in.

"Vell, very dangerous vhen you are hunting for *dragons'* eggs."

He looked at his nephew seriously, not fully understanding why Mike was having difficulty understanding. Mike laughed a little.

"You don't *really* hunt for dragons' eggs, though, do you?" Mike asked with a giggle. "I mean, it's just a metaphor for something greater, a moral lesson for the kids, right? Teach them right from wrong or how to deal with the dangers out in the real world, right?"

He looked around the table from person to person, searching for an ally. There were none, just a chorus of laughter. Humiliated, Mike began to realize that he was pure entertainment for his new family.

"Apa, you're so mean!" cried an indignant Elizabeth. Ignoring any reply her father may have had for her, she turned to Mike to explain. "Maybe you were too young to remember the dragons, but they are the reason that the TFF, the Thirteen Founding Families of magic, made their home here. You see, Transylvania is where the first dragon originated. Dragons are ill-tempered and greedy, they don't live well together and many die in a territorial fight. The TFF are the only wizards who know how to train a dragon. They get the egg just before it's ready to hatch, then it's raised by the family that claimed it. The dragon will remain loyal to that family until death. Trouble is, female dragons only lay eggs every seven years and even though wizards have great power over the dragons, when protecting her eggs the female dragon is a force to be reckoned with, becoming smarter with every hunt. Only a few wizards are selected each hunt, but they have to be skilled in dragon training."

"Oh!" was all Mike could manage.

As Elizabeth spoke, bits of vivid images from an all-too-familiar dream flashed through his mind. He was more confused than ever, but admittedly he was thrilled at the prospect of seeing a real dragon. In his dreams, flying felt so natural, so easy…was it possible that he was really destined to fly? He looked over at his father, wondering if he had any memory of these hunts, but the blank look on his face told him he didn't. He took a moment longer to mull over this new information and decided that, whether it was really the way Elizabeth described it or not, he wanted it to be real.

"Cool!" he exclaimed, nodding with acceptance.

Uncle Laszlo gave an approving smile, Elizabeth beamed and his father looked worried. Spurred on by the news of the hunt, Mike listened intently for the remainder of the evening, asking as many questions as his family would answer.

Sleep was difficult that night. Images of what a real dragon might be like ran through his head and when he finally nodded off he dreamed of dragons' eggs.

In the dream, he was flying through the sky in the clutches of an angry female dragon that was warding off the attacks of several young wizards. He felt a jolt, like an electrical shock, as they cast their spells. He was yelling at them, telling them to hit the dragon, not him, but his cries were futile; they could neither see nor hear him, for he was inside the egg....

14

Guilty

It was still dark outside in the small village. Witch, wizard and animal alike were quiet. Sleep had been cut short by restless dreams and the desire to see his birthplace, so Mike had hiked in the dark to the top one of the tallest hills that bordered the quaint village of Bodon. He sat atop a large boulder wedged into the crest of the hill.

Heavy thoughts preyed on his mind as he looked over the village that was now his home. It felt strange to say it at first, but as each day passed he felt more and more drawn to this place and less attached to his last home. He tried to convince himself that it was only natural to be fond of your birthplace, but up until a month ago he had been a normal kid with a normal life and normal dreams for the future, and now…well, who knew what was to come? He was an entirely different person now, and the transition from normal to a "fictional character" had been sudden and surreal. Admittedly, many things made more sense to him now and the knowledge of his heritage did a lot for his ego, but if he put too much thought into it, like he was doing now, it all became confusing and overwhelming again.

No matter how much he liked his new life, it didn't include Hanna or any of his other good friends. A wave of guilt washed over him, as it had done so many times in the last few weeks, when he realised that, other than Hanna, he hadn't given much thought to his friends—he hadn't said goodbye to them either. He felt as though he had swallowed a bowling ball, which sat heavily in the pit of his stomach, when thoughts of what they—everyone—must have thought about his abrupt departure. Not that he considered himself in such high regard; it was just a really crappy thing to do to your friends, the first *real* friends he had ever had.

He pulled his cell phone out of his pocket, knowing it was useless; he hadn't even gotten so much as one bar, even up here. Scrolling through the thread of unanswered texts to Hanna, frustrated and lonely, he typed one last time:

Where r u?

A lone rooster call came from the village below, pulling Mike from his thoughts. The bright morning sun peeked over the hills sending thin rays of light over the village. His aunt would be awake soon, preparing breakfast and tending to the animals. She could probably take care of the entire farm with a wave of her wand and yet, every day, she was up at the crack of dawn and ran her farm just like any other farmer would. He got up from the rock he was sitting on and started down the hill. He wanted to make it back before anyone else woke up. He was sure that his uncle would revoke his offer to let him see the city if he knew that Mike had dared to walk about unaccompanied, so he picked up his pace and ran back to the farm.

Everything and everyone was peaceful as Mike came up to the back of the house. Breathing a big sigh of relief, he made his way around the side of the house where he had snuck out through his bedroom window a couple of hours ago. He had left it slightly ajar to make re-entry easier. Slowly he pulled the window open and looked through the gap; his father was still fast asleep. He climbed in quickly without making a sound, crawled back under the covers and was just settling in when he heard the creak of his aunt's bedroom door. That was close!

~~~~~

Within the hour, the house was buzzing with the sounds of morning. His great aunt and uncle were tending to the calls of hungry animals, his younger cousins were chasing each other plus ducks, chickens and any other free-roaming animals about the farm. He could hear Anna in the kitchen preparing breakfast, scolding her children through the open window for tormenting the chickens.

Mike entered the kitchen, greeted Anna and began pulling dishes from the cupboards. He had learned that his offers of help would be refused, as he was a guest, so he politely ignored her protests and began setting the table. Once again he was so hungry, having already been awake for several hours, that he would do anything to make breakfast come sooner this morning. It was only a matter of minutes before everyone was seated and passing around plates of food. As he chowed down, Mike was sure that if he had eaten breakfasts like this back home he would have stayed awake through every class.

After breakfast Laszlo and Elizabeth came by. Laszlo pulled the two aside to go over the final plan for the day's excursion. He had taken on his most authoritative voice and was speaking very slowly—Mike was sure this was for his benefit, but he refrained from rolling his eyes and getting caught...he couldn't risk losing this opportunity to see his home. Instead he gave his uncle his full attention, nodding his head in agreement with everything he said. Elizabeth, on the other hand, was rolling her eyes at him freely, knowing that her father wouldn't notice, making it very difficult for Mike not to laugh when he glanced over at her.

The plan was simple: that afternoon, Laszlo would take Mike and Elizabeth to Segesvar. Laszlo and Elizabeth could enter through the main gate of the city, but Mike would have to enter through a tunnel from the outer wall that led right into their family tower. Mike would have some time to himself to tour the tower alone while Elizabeth and Laszlo ran errands. When it was time for Laszlo to make his way to the WWF meeting, Elizabeth was to go to the tower, meet up with Mike, the two would exit the city through the tunnel and return to the village before sunset. Everything was great except one thing—his father wasn't coming.

"Uncle Laszlo, why isn't my father coming?" he asked, feeling a little hurt.

"Mike…" Laszlo started, 'eet eez too soon. I am afraid dat da memories dere are too much. Eet will only set heem back. His good friend, Dani, will come here to visit heem. He has vanted to see heem since hees return a few veeks ago. Dey vere best friends and he has missed heem all these years."

Mike trusted his uncle's judgment, but he had to admit that he had been looking forward to having his father there with him. Mike shrugged, trying not to show how much it bothered him.

"OK."

"Very good," Laszlo said empathetically, 've vill leave at 3 p.m."

15

A Friend in Dark Places

Mike thought 3 p.m. would never arrive. He was already waiting at the end of the long dusty road that led up to the farm when Elizabeth and his uncle arrived.

"Excited?" Elizabeth asked with a giggle.

"Yes," he said defiantly, adding, "*totally*!"

There was no need to go back up to the house. Zsolt, Laszlo's brother, had already left with Mike's father to meet with his long-time friend, Dani. Sensing that it would seem like unnecessary cruelty to Mike if he delayed their excursion even the slightest, Laszlo pointed in the direction they should start.

"Shall vee?" he said, smiling.

Mike didn't hesitate, starting down the road straight away, giving his pockets a final check. Laszlo had given him another small satchel of "in-a-pinch-pearls" just in case, and Mike had also brought his phone. Although useless as a means of communication, it worked well as a camera and Mike intended on taking as many pictures as he could.

It was a short distance to the edge of the village and in the fifteen minutes it had taken them to get there, Laszlo had repeated the plan ten times! Mike was relieved, and by the look on Elizabeth's face, she was too, when he stopped and announced that they had made it to the departure point. Mike looked around and noticed that there was no mode of transportation. It occurred to him that he had no idea where Segesvar was in relation to their village or how they would get there. Before he had a chance to ask, Laszlo answered as he pulled a small satchel from the inside of his leather trench coat, it looked suspiciously like the satchel he had given Mike earlier.

"Dere are many vays vee can get to Segesvar easily and quvickly, but today vee need to travel safely and undetected. Take one ball out and have eet ready to go."

Elizabeth already had hers in her hand. Mike quickly grabbed one and held it out for Laszlo to see.

"Good," Laszlo said. "Now, *gently* put eet between your back teeth, but *do not* bite before I say so."

His uncle held his breath and a small bead of sweat ran down the side of his face as Mike placed the tiny ball between his teeth. Mike was sure it was overkill, but chose to remain silent and obedient; after all, this was his first time. To humour his uncle, he opened his mouth and pointed to the "unbitten" marble. Laszlo expelled a sigh of relief and resumed natural breathing. With the back of his sleeve he wiped the sweat from his forehead and proceeded to grab their hands, motioning for Elizabeth and Mike to do the same.

"OK, vhen I say *now!* I vant you to bite down on da marble and picture our destination, vhich vill be behind da courtyard of the Tailor's tower." He looked at Elizabeth and she nodded her head in understanding. "Mike, you von't be able to picture our destination, so just tink *Tailor*, nozsing else, hold on tight to our hands and don't let go!"

Mike nodded his head in agreement, musing at the coincidence—when hadn't he thought of Taylor? It was Hanna's last name!

Laszlo placed his marble into his mouth, grasped their hands tightly and, looking at them both, exclaimed:

"*Now!*"

With the name Taylor repeating in his mind, Mike bit down hard on the marble. A cold bitter fluid filled his mouth and ran down his throat, causing him to gag. As he forced the disgusting liquid down, he felt himself lifting off the ground. Feeling suddenly very insecure and still wanting to throw up, he looked at Elizabeth for reassurance as they ascended higher. He had just managed to catch her attention when she squeezed his hand hard. Suddenly they began to spin so fast Mike felt as though he was on an out-of-control g-force ride at an amusement park. Faster and faster they spun and Mike felt his hands slipping out of theirs.

"Hold on, Mike, *hold on!*" Laszlo yelled, but it was too late.

Mike's hands slipped away then, all in a split second, and Laszlo and Elizabeth screamed:

"*Think Tailor!*"

His short life flashed before his eyes and suddenly, as if a giant vacuum had come up behind him pulling his stomach through his back, he was sucked backwards into darkness.

"*Taylor, Taylor, Taylor!*" Mike screamed over and over again as his body was pulled through the darkness at the speed of light.

Only a few seconds had passed when suddenly some unseen force whipped his body around, making him feel like his back had been hit by a train moving at top speed.

Not that either direction was enjoyable to travel in, but if he was *forced* to make a choice, moving forwards would be the one; at least this way he could see what was coming.

Unexpectedly it appeared—a pinprick of light in the far distance. Second by second it grew as Mike careened towards it at lightning speed. He could make out that it was an opening, a portal, and it looked exactly like all the portals he had ever seen—in movies. He almost laughed, but he realised that in a second, literally, he was going to fly through it. He shut his eyes and began to scream.

"Aaaahhhhhh!"

Pfoowp!

Like a tennis ball shot out of its automatic dispenser, Mike flew through the opening, screaming. Eyes glued shut, he braced himself for an impact he was sure would flatten him. A few seconds passed and nothing happened, then he realised he wasn't moving anymore. Several possibilities of what had just taken place flashed through his mind, but the dominant one was that he had died instantly upon impact and was now floating in Heaven.

He slowly opened his eyes. The first thing he became aware of was that he was going to be sick. The second was that he wasn't floating in Heaven, in fact he was on solid grassy ground, keeled over and vomiting, and he was sure that when you got to Heaven you would feel overwhelming joy, not the urge to be sick. He used a nearby tree to pull himself up. His legs were weak and shaky, and his head was still spinning. He was sure he had just thrown up everything from as far back as three weeks ago. No sooner had he stood when...

Pfoowp!

Laszlo and Elizabeth flew through a hole in mid-air, then, just like that, came to a complete stop and were standing beside him. Elizabeth immediately ran to Mike's side.

"Mike! Are you OK?" she asked, while Laszlo let out a big sigh of relief.

"Tank God you made eet!" Looking at Mike seriously, he began an arsenal of questions.

"Vy did you let go? I told you not to let go! Do you know how hard eet vould be to find you? You could have ended up anyvhere! You could have ended up stuck in da vorm hole—*forever!* Mike, your fazer vould never have forgiven me!" He stopped for a moment and inhaled deeply, shaking his head in confusion. "Mike, how…how *did* you get here?"

Mike stared at his uncle for a moment.

"I did what you told me to do; I thought *Taylor*…I'm fine by the way, thanks for asking!" he ended dryly.

Elizabeth gave her father a stern look. Taking the hint, he walked over to Mike's side, placing one hand on his shoulder.

"I'm sorry, Mike. Dat must have been a horrifying experience for you. Are you OK?"

"Yeah, sure wait… *No!*" he added, turning on his uncle. "You could have *warned* me!"

"Yes, Mike," his uncle admitted, not wanting to aggravate his nephew's apparent irritation, for fear of being heard by the many guards that continually patrolled the perimeter…not to mention the dragons, which had a keen sense of hearing. "I really should have varned you."

"That really sucked, you know!" Mike exclaimed in frustration, still using the tree to hold himself up, but a small smile started at the corners of his mouth. "But man, am I ever happy to see you guys!"

"*You're* happy?" Relief and joy flooded Elizabeth's face. "Mike, we thought you had gone forever! How did you know this place was our destination?"

"I didn't. I told you, I just kept repeating *Taylor* over and over again. It was the last thing I heard you say before I was sucked through space," he said, gripping his stomach with his hands as he said the last part.

"I don't understand...."

"Neizser do I!" Laszlo interjected, looking as confused as Mike about the whole thing.

"I'm just so happy you're here!" Elizabeth finished, grabbing Mike and pulling him into a hug.

After Elizabeth had loosened her grip, she and her father helped Mike to stand properly. Laszlo made him chew on some small bitter leaves that he plucked from a nearby bush, saying it would settle his stomach. After Mike had forced the bitter leaves down, he looked at his uncle and cousin, who seemed to be feeling perfectly fine after their stint through space.

"Seriously, is there no better way to travel than this?" he asked dryly, pointing to where the opening of the worm hole had been.

"Well...dragons, but they're a little obvious," Elizabeth answered.

"Ha, ha!" he laughed sarcastically, sensing the amusement in her voice.

"Don't worry, Mike, you'll get used to it," Elizabeth assured him, smiling brightly.

"No way," Mike mumbled under his breath. "So...where are we again?"

Laszlo pointed towards a tall brick wall covered in vines.

"Vee are behind da courtyard of da Tailor tower."

The wall towered above them, thick mossy patches covering the parts shaded by huge oak trees, which seemed to surround them. At the base of the wall and running the length of it, were the most beautiful rose bushes Mike had ever seen or smelled. Each bush was a different colour or variety of rose, the branches hanging heavy with them and the air was filled with the fresh intoxicating scent. Behind them stood a grove of fruit trees thick with sweet smelling blossoms, the ground was scattered with a rainbow of wild flowers, and fields of corn and wheat spread out behind them blending with the lush green rolling hills, scattered with vineyards that surrounded the valley in which they stood.

The feelings of nausea were replaced with those of excitement as Mike remembered why they had come. He knew the Weaver family tower was close by. He looked at his uncle.

"So...where's the tunnel?" he asked, finding it difficult to suppress his delight.

Laszlo smiled and beckoned them to come towards him, then pointed towards the forest behind them.

"Come, dis vay."

They walked quietly and carefully. The forest was thick with old trees—oaks, beeches, firs and spruces—huge trunks and gnarled branches that seemed to reach out for them, surrounding them. Very little light made it through the canopy of dense foliage. If there was a path they were following, Mike couldn't see it. The ground was covered with layer upon layer of decomposing leaves. They hadn't been walking long when Mike looked back to where they had entered the forest—a cold shiver ran down his spine. The edge of the forest had completely vanished and all that lay behind them was the darkness and the eerie outline of the trees, which had now taken on a monstrous look. He quickened his pace a little and came up beside Elizabeth. Before she had a chance to comment on his wimpish behaviour, he spoke first.

"This place is freakin' me out!"

"You've got that right! The sooner we get this done, the better," she replied, throwing Mike right off guard.

He had expected bravery and sarcasm from his cousin, but got fear and no comfort whatsoever. Still, it felt better to be walking beside her than behind her.

Within a few minutes they came to a small clearing. Laszlo motioned for them to come to where he was standing a couple of metres ahead. His uncle was facing a row of tall shrubs that bordered one side of the clearing. When they were standing beside him he pointed towards the shrubs.

"Dis eez eet."

Mike looked at the undergrowth and wondered what part of *this is it* was *it*, because all he could see were bushes. Laszlo, noticing Mike's questioning look, untangled the shrubs from one another, revealing what looked like the ruins or the remnants of an old town wall. It had to have been there for hundreds of years. Whatever its original height, it was down to about three feet now and not much wider. One side of the wall tapered down like steps. Thick moss and a variety of fungi covered most of the remaining rock and brick. Mike's uncle gave him an exasperated look.

"Dis is vhere you vill enter."

Mike stepped towards the wall, examined it closely, then turned to his uncle with a doubtful look.

"How exactly do I enter?"

Laszlo expelled a long sigh.

"Elizabeth?" He motioned for her to come forward, and she did as her father asked. "Now, vatch vut I do so you'll be able to do da same ven you leave da tunnel togezser—you *must* leave togezser. Mike, eef you are alone in da tunnel you vill not be able to open da door from the inside vizsout a vand."

"A wand!" Mike nodded his head in acknowledgment.

"Once the spell is cast on da door eet vill only remain open just long enough to get inside. Follow da tunnel. Dere vill be a vall at da end dat has da Weaver family crest on eet, all you need to do eez place your hand on da crest and speak your full name—eet only opens for a Weaver. Vunce you are true dat door, follow da vinding staircase. At da top you vill come to a mirror, simply place your hand on eet, speak your full name again and pass zsrough...."

Laszlo paused for a long moment, beginning to doubt whether this really was a good idea. Maybe he was placing too much responsibility on his nephew—the repercussions of Mike being seen could be devastating. On the other hand, he *had* brought him this far—if he denied Mike this opportunity today, he knew his nephew was clever enough to find his way back here on his own, and that was a risk Laszlo couldn't afford to take.

Mike stared at his uncle, waiting for him to finish his dramatic long pause. An awkward silence began. He looked at Elizabeth, asking with his eyes what was wrong with her father. She just shrugged her shoulders and her facial expression told him she had no idea.

"Uncle Laszlo…." Mike began.

"OK! No time to vaste!" his uncle interrupted, suddenly having sprung back to life, causing both Mike and Elizabeth to jump. "Come, come!" he exclaimed, beckoning them impatiently.

At this point Mike was certain that he'd never understand his uncle, and Laszlo was certain it was useless appealing to a teenage boy. Elizabeth knelt down in front of the small wall, her wand ready.

"All right, Apa, show me the spell."

"Place da tip of your vand anyvhere on da vall and write…," he began to say as he knelt beside his daughter, then stopped and turned to Mike. "Mike, are you ready?"

"Yeah, as ready as I can be," he replied, as if trying to convince himself.

"OK, kneel down here beside Elizabeth and be ready to enter vhen da door opens. Oh—and here eez a flashlight…." He fumbled in his pocket and pulled out a small flashlight, handing it to Mike. "Ozservise you von't see a ting in dere," he finished casually.

Mike took the flashlight and instinctively turned it on and off a couple of times. His uncle gave him a disdainful look.

"As eef I vould give you one dat doesn't verk!"

"Just making sure…," Mike mumbled, his voice trailing off.

With a sigh, Laszlo turned his attention back to Elizabeth.

"Again—place da tip of your vand on da vall and vrite da word *ajto*. All lower case," he added hurriedly, catching Elizabeth before she began the spell. "Ready?" he asked Mike, who gave a quick nod in reply. "Begin," he instructed Elizabeth, watching every movement of her wand to ensure that it was correct.

At the last stroke of her wand, several bricks in the centre of the small wall disappeared, leaving behind a crude opening. An overpowering earthy smell emitted from the tunnel. Waving the stench aside, Mike leaned forwards and peered inside. It was completely black. He swallowed hard and looked back at Elizabeth and Laszlo, who gave him a look that told him to hurry up, so he got his flashlight ready and crawled through the opening cautiously.

He had barely made it into the tunnel when he saw the small amount of light shining from the opening disappear, just as though a candle had been snuffed out. The sudden intense darkness and the cold dank air made the hairs on the back of his neck stand on end. He whipped the flashlight from his side and had it on and out in front of him as if he was drawing a gun. It took a moment for his eyes to adjust. The beam was powerful and Mike could see quite far into the tunnel, which was long and narrow, rather like it had been dug out by a giant mole. The ground was cold and damp with roots sticking out everywhere, even on the side walls and ceiling. It looked barely big enough for Mike to crawl through. The paranoid relative who created this escape tunnel was either really short and skinny or didn't feel that a quick getaway would ever be necessary.

Mike started crawling forward carefully. It took him several minutes to make it to the bend, and once around the corner he could see that there was another long stretch before he would reach yet another bend—it went on like this for the next fifteen minutes. Scratched, cold and wanting a breath of fresh air, he stopped and shone the light as far down the tunnel as it would reach. Again it shone only as far as the next bend. He started the slow crawl forwards again, wondering if secretly his uncle enjoyed pushing his patience.

He was a few feet from the next bend when a root from the ceiling caught the back collar of his shirt. Cursing under his breath, he yanked the root away, but he hadn't progressed even another inch when his foot was caught on another root. Frustrated, he pulled his foot hard, freeing it from the root, but in the meantime other roots were catching in his hair.

"*Aaargh!*" Mike shouted in frustration, brushing madly at the clinging roots in his hair and anywhere else they were catching.

Thinking that he was free at last, he made to move ahead when a root grabbed his arm. At first he thought he had caught his arm on *it*, but as he attempted to pull his arm away he saw that *it* was wrapping itself around his arm as if it was intentional. His first feeling was amusement mixed with annoyance. He pulled at the root, which he noted had a surprisingly tight grip, freeing his arm and commenting out loud, more to justify the actions of the root and calm any thoughts of a potential threat.

"Magic roots? It *is* a tunnel made by a *magician* after all!"

No sooner had the words left his mouth then another root began wrapping itself around Mike's left calf. Twisting himself as best the cramped tunnel would allow, he reached down and grabbed the root, yanking it until he was free. A couple more times he freed himself from the grip of other roots that attempted to wrap themselves around his limbs, slowing Mike down to a near standstill. Sweat now running down his face, he stayed still for a moment, not sure of his next move. *Are these pesky roots a temporary problem or just the beginning of more to come?* The tight quarters of the tunnel and the lack of fresh air only made matters worse. Mike wiped his brow in frustration, yelling as he slammed his hand back to the ground.

"Uncle Laszlo! Did you forget to tell me something!?"

Mike knew it wouldn't accomplish anything, but it felt good to shout. Naturally, there was no reply. Mike gave a heavy sigh and decided to move on, but as he attempted to lift his hand he realised it was stuck—yet another root had wrapped itself around his wrist.

"*Get—off—you—creepy—irritating—root!*" Mike growled as he tried to free his hand. "What the…? No way!"

Surprised that he was unable to free himself, he tried again, only with more force—it was no use. He went to reach with his free hand to pry the root off, shocked that he couldn't move that hand either. He watched dumbfounded as roots emerged from the walls around him—reaching out like gnarled bony hands, grabbing any part of him with which they could make contact. The thought of being stuck in the tunnel, not knowing how long it would be before someone came to look for him, caused a sudden surge of panic. Mike wrestled frantically against the roots, but his efforts were futile—he was no match for their strength. As they wound themselves around his body, they just became thicker and tighter. There was nothing he could do but observe his fate in horror as the roots squeezed him so tightly that even breathing was becoming difficult.

None of it made any sense. Did everyone who passed through this tunnel experience this? Was there a counter spell? Did his uncle not know about this? Why was this tunnel even here? Who, other than a Weaver family member, would even know about this tunnel?

Confused and scared, Mike began yelling commands at the roots, in the hope that he might say the right thing—a counter curse perhaps—but that was likely to be futile, as he had no wand, not even a free hand to wave about.

"Roots—*be gone!*"

Nothing....

"*Disappear, roots!*"

Still nothing...maybe if he tried it in Hungarian.

"*Engedjel te atkozott gyoker!*"

Nothing....

"*Tungyel!*"

Again nothing. Maybe if he asked nicely?

"*Please roots—please, please go away!*"

Nothing worked. He lay there completely still, wrapped up like a mummy, in roots. He wanted to cry, but that would require too much breathing and, although the roots had stopped moving, their grip was still intense.

It suddenly occurred to him that he would run out of air soon, and even if someone came looking for him he'd be dead before they found him. No sooner had he had this morbid thought, when he felt the dirt beneath him begin to shift. Defeated by his thoughts of dying in the tunnel, he had no energy left to try to determine whether this was a good sign or not. It wasn't. The ground started rumbling like a mini-earthquake reserved for just this little portion of the tunnel, and as it rumbled Mike could feel the ground begin to give way right beneath him. Earth began to gather around his body, higher and higher. The roots began to move again, but this time they were pulling at him. He was sinking and the roots were pulling him down into the abyss beneath.

"What the...! No way! *No* way! No, no, no, no, *no!*"
Mike shouted. He was going to be swallowed up by the
ground—buried alive—there would be no trace of him
left. No one would ever know what had happened to him.
"This *isn't* happening! *No way is this happening!*" he yelled,
wrestling against the deathly grip of the roots with all the
strength he could muster.

Nothing helped, and as he sank deeper into the chasm,
anger gave way to pleading. All but his face and the tips of
his feet were visible as he cried out.

"Not like *this*... Dear God, please don't let me go like
this. Please, *please help me!*"

He watched as the tips of his feet disappeared into the
ground.

"Help...help...*help*! Laszlo? Elizabeth? *Pleeaassee, someone...anyone...!*"

Mike's last word was cut short as bits of dirt began to fill
his throat...

16

The Flowers Told Me

"Tante Beska! Tante Beska!" a young girl yelled as she ran through a field of wild flowers, holding her long skirt high at her sides so as not to hinder her pace…*"Tante Beska!"*

A woman stood up from behind a wall of young sunflowers she had been tending.

"Dear one, what *is* the matter?" she asked gently, in response to the young girl's cries.

Breathless, the girl stopped short, nearly slamming into the woman.

"Tante Beska! He's in trouble! We need to help him! There are roots… They're enchanted… He's in a tunnel… They're pulling him into… We have to help him, *now*!"

"Dear one," the woman said soothingly as she pulled the girl in for a hug. "Calmly now; who needs our help and where is this person?"

She looked down at the young girl, who was taking deep breaths, trying to calm down. Despite her beautiful youthful features, striking eyes that seemed to change colour with her surroundings and long hair that fell playfully past her shoulders in every shade of blonde possible, all she could see was an old woman carrying the weight of the world on her shoulders. The young girl looked up into the woman's kind eyes. Long tresses of soft grey hair hung down on either side of the woman's face, held back by a single band that encircled her head like a crown. Her face, although aged, had a look of youthfulness about it, but now it was etched with concern.

The young girl started again with more urgency.

"It's him—*The One!*" she exclaimed with pleading in her eyes. "He's trapped in a tunnel just outside Segesvar! I don't know why he's there... he shouldn't be, but, Tante Beska, there are roots, horribly big roots, and the roots...." She gripped the older woman's arms tightly and stared into her eyes, her own eyes as large as saucers, a storm of colours swirling in them, as would often happen when she was scared or terribly upset. "The roots—they're going to kill him...! They're pulling him into the earth!" she cried, now tugging at Tante Beska's arms.

"*We've got to help—right now!* He's running out of time! We might already be too late... Oh, Tante Beska...," The young girl turned to her aunt, her large stormy eyes brimming with tears, "what if we are too late?"

The dam burst as tears streamed down her face freely.

"Dear one...," Her aunt knelt down beside her, cradling the young girl's head against her shoulder. "We aren't too late—*look!*" She pointed to the largest tree on her property; a giant willow that stood thirty feet high, its canopy spanning an incredible fifty feet. "It's Vardtrad, the sacred tree, we will find the answer there."

The young girl practically sprinted the short distance to the enormous tree—she had to duck to get under its thick protective canopy—and ran straight for the trunk and wrapped her small arms around its enormous girth as far as she could, which wasn't very far!

"Vardtrad, Vardtrad, you must help *The One*. He is trapped in a tunnel near Segesvar and the roots... oh, the roots are *killing* him! I don't understand why!" she cried, clinging to the tree for dear life.

The enormous tree made a deep groaning sound as if waking from a deep sleep, sending waves rippling through all the branches. Tante Beska was now standing beside the young girl who, sobbing silently, communicated her pleas with the great tree. She took one of her small hands in hers and held it tight. She stretched her other hand flat against the trunk of the tree and motioned for the young girl to do the same. Tiny fresh green vines began to emerge from the tree, wrapping themselves around their hands, tickling when they began to coil around the fingers. The young girl could feel energy flowing through her hand almost like a pulse. Her hand began to glow red, not unlike when you place a flashlight on the palm of your hand and you see the light shine through to the other side. Fascinated, she watched as her hand continued to pulse and illuminate. She didn't have to say anything to the tree; it was as if it could draw the necessary information from her hands alone.

After a moment the small bright green vines retracted themselves from their hands and disappeared back into the tree, taking with them the red glow of energy. Reluctantly, the young girl withdrew her hand from the tree.

"That's *it*?" she asked quietly, staring down at her empty hands.

She looked up at her aunt, hoping that she would give an explanation or tell her the next step, but with a compassionate smile on her face all her aunt said was:

"It's out of our hands now. We have done all that we can do from here."

"*What?*" the young girl exclaimed, disappointment filling her eyes. "How will we know if he's OK? How do we even know if we made it in time? He's *The One,* he *has* to be OK—he *needs* to stay alive! Tante Beska, there's got to be more…."

The young girl's words were cut short as a small twig covered in tiny, white beautiful aromatic flowers landed in her empty hands. She stared down at her hands and then back up to her aunt, who smiled down at her and gently stroked her hair.

"White heather—the tree has answered your request—this flower symbolizes protection and requests granted. You did well, dear one, he is safe."

A smile of pure relief and joy spread across the young girl's face as she jumped up and embraced her aunt, tears of joy streaming down her cheeks.

They left the canopy of the tree and as they were walking back towards their home, a quaint but quirky and ill-proportioned cabin that looked as if it would topple at the first sign of wind, Tante Beska asked the young girl how it was that she knew the boy was in danger and where he was. The young girl, who was now humming a bright tune and had been skipping instead of walking since they left the tree, replied simply:

"The flowers told me."

17

An Ancestor's Prophecy

"Help! Help! Somebody please, anybody, *anything*, *help!*"

Mike had kept his head elevated as long as he could to stop the dirt from filling his mouth, nose and eyes, but now it was too late… this was it; the dirt was at the corners of his mouth. He shut his mouth to keep the dirt from filling it up. He could still breathe through his nose, but he was sure that he didn't have more than a minute. A minute, he thought. Only one minute—what can I do in one minute? *Nothing!* That's what he could do in one minute, which was now more like thirty seconds—*absolutely nothing!* Not even his life was flashing before his eyes, like he'd heard others say as they faced peril. I can't even have *that?* I get to just lie here helplessly and wait for death to come?

He was numb, he couldn't even cry anymore as the dirt was less than an inch from filling his nose and eyes. *Though I walk through the valley of the shadow of death…. More like, I crawl through the tunnel of death,* he thought sarcastically. *I will fear no evil, for thou art with me….* Mike suddenly stopped thinking as a cool breeze passed over his face and with it he was sure he heard someone whispering.

"*Leave him be, he bears the mark… leave him be!*"

Mike pushed his face up just a little more, trying to clear his ears of dirt. Afraid that fear and despair were making him feel and hear things that really weren't there, he stopped breathing for a moment and strained his ears. He counted the seconds:

"Twenty, twenty-one, twenty-two…."

When he reached thirty, despair set in again and he was convinced he had just wanted the voices to be real. *Oh, just take me, already*, he wanted to shout, instead he screamed as loud as he could while keeping his mouth shut. Seconds after his restrained temper tantrum, he felt it again, only this time more strange—a gust of wind wafted over his face.

"Go back to your trees or I will cut you from them, then you shall surely die. He is the bearer of the mark, leave him be!"

It wasn't a distinct voice, it was as if the wind itself was speaking, but this time Mike was sure he had heard it. He was sure he had heard *bearer of the mark, leave him be!* He wanted to give a shout of joy, but his mouth was still covered in dirt.

Almost immediately the roots lessened their suffocating grip on Mike, giving him a chance to lift his head enough to shake the dirt pile from his face. Immensely relieved to be able to breathe through his mouth again, he felt the urge to speak.

"You heard him…it, whatever—*leave me be!*"

The ground beneath him began to shift and rumble as the roots pulled Mike's body from his dirt grave. As he ascended, a cliché image of Dracula rising from his coffin crossed Mike's mind. A cold shiver ran down his spine and he started yelling at the roots, the dirt and anyone else who might be listening, for he had no clue who or what had saved him from the killer roots and the carnivorous dirt.

"All right, get off me… Get—off—me—before—I…."
He struggled against the roots, which were beginning to
recede, as he contemplated how he might end his threat.
"Before I…." Still unable to form a clever ending, he pulled
frantically at anything he could get his hands on. "Before
I, I…before I bloody freak out! That's right…before I *completely… bloody… freak…out!*"

With each word he ripped at the remaining roots. He
quickly patted down his body, searching for any stragglers
that he could take his vengeance out on, but found none.
Not wanting to stay one second longer, he felt around for
the flashlight, found it, turned it on and before he could
convince himself to chicken out, he scanned the entire tunnel around him. He didn't know why the roots had done
what they had and he didn't know what stopped them from
doing what they were going to do—he just knew he wanted
out of the tunnel immediately!

He didn't think twice, not even once, but just crawled
ahead through the tunnel as fast as he could go (a crawling sprint, if you will). Every bump on the ground or root
protruding from the tunnel wall, which may have brushed
him as he hurried past, drove Mike to move faster, then
suddenly there was a wall. Mike had been moving so fast
that he hadn't noticed it until he crashed into it.

"Grrrrrr!" Mike growled as he rubbed his forehead.
"What the…? *What now?*" he screamed in exasperation.
He rubbed his eyes, then reaching forwards with his
hand, he felt the bricks on the wall in front of him. "The
wall…!"

He felt the wall with both hands, his eyes now fully
adjusted to the dark. Then he looked up and saw the

Weaver's family crest above him. Realizing that he could stand, he practically jumped up and hugged the wall.

"*The wall*," he whispered, expelling a huge sigh of relief.

He took a deep breath and wasted no time; he wanted out of the tunnel as soon as possible. He placed his hand on the crest and spoke.

"Michael Weaver!"

Before he had a chance to take his hand away, the entire wall before him disappeared. Amazed and relieved that his tunnel journey was coming to an end, he took a couple of steps forwards, quickly clearing the threshold of the wall, not sure how quickly it might rematerialise. He stood for a moment and took in the narrow stone staircase. It was dark; medieval-looking torches lined the winding stairwell. Mike looked back to where the wall had been before taking the first step, and to his surprise the wall was back. Shaking his head, he began the ascent up the long stairwell. The stairs wound on for some time and Mike began to wonder just how far underground he had been.

He made it up the last few steps and came to a small landing. Letting the burn in his thighs subside, he stopped to look around. There was very little light, but what he could make out were the two walls on either side of him and the wall in front, but no mirror.

"Seriously?" he said, letting out an exasperated sigh. "It's got to be around here somewhere...," he mumbled to himself as he leaned in close to the walls.

Running his hands over the bricks in the wall, he searched for something, anything that might be out of place, not that he would know what to do even if it was—no wand and no clue. Feeling very ordinary, and with a little less enthusiasm, he continued running his hands over the bricks on the wall to his left. After a few moments of feeling every crevice, he moved on to the wall in the middle. He had to move in much closer to see any detail on this wall. He could see bricks, but they appeared to have less depth than the other walls, almost as if they had been painted. Curious, he leaned forwards and reached out his hand to touch the surface. As his fingers touched the faux brick, a silver liquid began to fill in from the edges of the wall moving towards the centre, closing around Mike's fingers where they were still touching the wall. He pulled them away quickly before the liquid made contact with his fingers. He watched as the silver liquid filled in completely and transformed into a solid wall of glass! He stared, fascinated, as a frame began to take form around the mirror's edge—tiny branches, intricately weaving themselves up the sides and over the top of the mirror.

"*Cool,*" Mike whispered in complete awe.

He took a moment to admire the woven branches (he was a Weaver after all). On closer examination he could see that there were shapes twisted into the intertwined branches. He looked closer still and could see they were actual dragon shapes—dragons of many different kinds! As he looked them all over, one in particular caught his eye, so he shone his flashlight at it to get a better look. He gasped. The resemblance that it bore to the dragon in his dreams was remarkable: the body, wings, tail, everything right down to the eyes, were the same! Mike ran his finger from the top of the dragon's head all the way to the tip of the tail. As he released his finger, the dragon turned its face towards Mike, gave a small screech and flew away.

"*Awesome!*" Mike breathed.

Just like a child in the toy aisle of a major department store, who can't resist pressing the "try me" button on the most annoying talking toy of the year, he touched as many dragons as he could and watched with wonder as they all flew away. He turned his attention back to the mirror and decided that it was time to do what he had come here for. He wasn't sure how much time he had lost while being buried alive and he wanted as much time as possible to see his home and Segesvar. Placing his hand on the glass he spoke his full name loudly.

"*Michael Weaver.*"

He felt the glass giving way under his hand and watched in amazement as his hand went through the mirror as easily as if he had reached into water. Like anyone would (well, anyone who's had to put their hand through a mirror, that is), he drew his hand back out quickly and looked over it curiously. He wasn't sure what he might see on it, but suspected that you couldn't just put your hand through a mirror and not have *any* consequences, but as it was, there was no visible change to his hand. Just to be sure, he tried putting his hand through and back again. Again he saw no change and decided that he should just get this over with.

"On three—one, two…*three!*"

He held his breath, shut his eyes and took a large step. He stood for a moment, eyes shut, waving his hands around in front of him and felt nothing, just emptiness. Hesitantly, he opened one eye and then the other, half-expecting to see the mirror still in front of him—it wasn't. He was standing on a balcony in a large round stairwell. The balcony ran along the wall completing a full circle. The railing was made of stone and each spindle was carved to look like woven vines closing around a thick stone pillar. An image of roots wrapping around his body flashed through his mind sending shivers down his spine.

Several sets of stairs led off this floor either going up or down and running in all directions, each one leading to other circular landings similar to the one on which Mike was standing. The wall behind him, where the mirror hung, was made of large stone bricks, and a thin dark blue rug ran beneath his feet around the entire landing. Opposite Mike were three arched doorways with heavy-looking wooden doors. Large paintings hung on the walls between the doors. Without looking, he knew that the wall that ran behind him was a mirror image of what was across from him, and that to the right of him hung a large empty tapestry that ran the entire height of the tower.

Mike walked towards the tapestry, running his hand over the smooth surface of the railing when a familiar feeling hit him. The closer he drew to the tapestry, the more familiar everything became. He looked at each door as he walked past and *knew* what lay behind them, but the images weren't entirely clear; they were blurry, almost like his memories were shrouded in fog. The clarity didn't really matter, for instinctively he knew what he was remembering. In a daze he continued towards the massive tapestry. From the top downwards it passed behind each balcony on each floor. It hung heavily, as its length was several floors long and it spanned nearly a third of the wall. As far as Mike could tell (perhaps this foresight came naturally to him, the Weaver that he was), it was made of intricately woven linen. He reached out and touched the material—not out of curiosity, for he knew what would happen once he felt it—and from the point where his finger touched, hundreds of tiny spiders appeared spreading out from his finger, busily weaving fine gold and silver threads into the linen. First twigs, then branches leading to bigger branches, then a trunk, which was woven with shiny threads of copper and deep browns of varying shades. The spiders moved quickly as if moving in fast-forward.

Mike watched in awe as the large tree took shape. He looked down as far as he could see and saw that faces and names were appearing at the tips of each small branch. It was a family tree! The Weaver Family Tree.

Weaver! Spiders! Until this moment, he had never thought about the connection between his name and these superior weavers of the animal kingdom. Now, instinctively he searched for his own family. He looked the tapestry up and down, surprised to see that his family was one floor down.

It took him several tries to navigate the stairwells, though. Every time he thought he had found the correct one leading to the floor below, he ended up on a different floor. Eventually he figured out what the pattern was—two floors up, three down, and one up again—and made it to the floor below him. Here was a picture of his father's face staring straight ahead and right beside him was his mother.

Mike leaned in closer. She looked like a stranger and yet his mind began to fill with perfect images of her face from the past. He was overcome by a sudden sadness; he had never had the chance to grow up with her in his life; he didn't even know what it was like to have a mother. He had never known any of his friends long enough to know their parents very well, let alone their mothers, so it was hard to imagine what he had missed and it's not like his father hadn't done the best he could, but he still felt an emptiness that he realised now only a mother could fill.

He reached out and touched her face, which to his surprise came to "life." Her face turned towards him and gave him a warm smile. It caught him off guard and he felt his eyes tear up. He lingered for a moment longer, trying to memorize her face then slowly took his finger away. At that point her face turned slightly away and resumed its blank look. Mike wiped his eyes and took a deep breath, turning his attention to the picture next to his mother's—the face of a small child with a head full of blond hair and a bright toothy grin—it was *him*. Mike had never seen pictures of himself as a child. He smiled; he had to admit he had been pretty cute. He glanced at the other faces on that part of the tapestry, and many of them were the aunts, uncles and cousins he had recently gotten to know.

He couldn't help but smile now; only a month ago he was the only child of a father with a severe memory problem and the nephew of an annoying and paranoid uncle. Now he was part of a family that was bigger than he could ever have imagined. Up until this moment, unconsciously, Mike had maintained that his coming to Transylvania was temporary, just a really long vacation. Up until this moment, all that he had learned about himself, his family and the world, was fascinating, but surreal, just as though at any moment he was going to wake from a dream and go back to the "normal" life he knew before. He was home now and he knew it. Every fibre of his being knew that this was where he needed to be—where he wanted to be.

Mike made his way down each staircase, full of curiosity now and wanting to see the whole tapestry. He came to one particularly odd-looking individual—an old man with frazzled hair like a mad scientist who had lived who knows how long ago, but judging from his attire it was a long, long time. His name on the plaque said Boldizsar. That suits him, Mike thought to himself. Mike placed his finger on his great ancestor's face, and the face turned towards him. Mike was expecting a nice warm smile, like he had received from his mother's picture, instead the old face was sombre, and Boldizsar began to speak.

"Great Dragon Rider—the one who bears the mark. Born to the Weaver and spirit of the Dragon, the mark is the key…this is your burden."

Mike tore his finger away from the face and stumbled backwards. What did he mean by key…and Dragon Spirit…and burden?! He looked back at the face of his great ancestor, which had now gone silent and was again staring blankly at nothing. A shiver ran down Mike's spine and instinctively he put his hand over the birthmark on his back. Before coming here, the mark had never meant much of anything to him, but now it had been forced to the forefront of his thoughts. He remembered that he had even been forbidden by the family to remove his shirt in front of anyone. He gave his head a shake and tried to shove the gnawing thoughts to the back of his mind. *Quit worrying,* he told himself.

Now would probably be a good time to see the rest of the tower, he thought. He was already on the main floor and, with one last look at the tapestry, he turned and made his way to the first doorway on his left. It was an arched entrance with two massive wooden doors. Where the two doors joined was the Weaver's family crest, each door having half the crest carved into it. Mike placed a hand on each large iron handle and pulled as hard as he could. Once the doors were open he saw that he was looking into a vast towering library. Thousands of books lined the two walls on either side of him. The wall in between, the one he was facing, was actually a massive stained glass window that went from floor to ceiling. Unlike the others, the room seemed new and unfamiliar to him and he didn't feel he had much memory of it, but being particularly fond of reading, he felt he could have spent a month there and not even made a dent in the vast number of stories sitting on those shelves.

As difficult as it was, he closed the doors to the library knowing that he didn't have much time before Elizabeth would be back and he would have to leave this wonderful place. Across the foyer to the right of the staircase was another large doorway, also displaying the Weaver family crest. Mike heaved on those two great wooden doors, revealing a huge banquet hall. Judging by its enormous size, he was certain his entire family could fit into it…and that was exactly what it was meant for.

He stepped inside, taking in the grand setting of the room. Two long, rustic wooden tables ran the length of the room and a large stone fireplace centred the wall opposite the doors. Thick, black wooden beams lined the walls in patterns of squares that reminded him of a home straight from the Black Forest. High above the tables hung seven large metal chandeliers with thick candles. Large bright windows cast stretching patterns of sunlight across the stone floor. Mike couldn't think of a grander setting for a feast or party, but when was the last time it was used for such an event? The thought of it made him feel slightly jealous that he hadn't been around for the last thirteen years.

He decided to continue on to the next floor, hastily exploring room after room, some bringing back vague memories while others didn't seem familiar at all. The rooms for families to stay in were the ones that felt most familiar. He was standing in such a room when he noticed that the curtains had been pulled to the side—which was odd, he thought, since the windows had been covered in all the other rooms. Mike knew that going near any of the windows was a bad idea, but the urge to glance out was too strong to resist. From where he was standing he decided he couldn't be seen anyway, so what harm could come from just taking a peek?

From the height he was at, he could see the tops of old buildings and another tower almost directly beside the Weaver tower. He wondered who that one belonged to— had his uncle told him? He knew that each family of the thirteen founding families of magic had a tower that represented their trade. He sat for a moment just listening, imagining what wonders the streets below held. Suddenly he heard what sounded like a group of kids laughing and talking in another language. He wanted to look out so badly, but responsibility won out over curiosity and he let the group pass by without giving in to temptation. Not a moment later he heard the familiar sound of another group of teens, mainly girls, he guessed, as there was a lot of giggling, and even though they were conversing in another language he could tell the girls were teasing one another. Someone must have said something very funny because the group suddenly burst into laughter. One girl's laugh seemed to stand out from all the others, making Mike quickly turn his attention back to the window. This was a wonderful laugh, reminding him so much of Hanna's laughter, and although he knew she couldn't be here, he looked nonetheless, carefully examining each face with a false hope that he would find Hanna there. By this time, however, the group was too far away down the lane for him to make out anyone clearly and they were in a cluster…but he heard that familiar laughter again as one girl chided another.

"Maria, you're terrible!" he heard. He *knew* that voice—it *was* Hanna's, or someone who sounded exactly like her! Hearing it was beautiful and like a slap in the face all at the same time. Was he ever going to be able to get her off his mind? He knew she was miles away—or should have been, he actually had no clue as to her whereabouts. He slumped down against the wall now feeling miserable, trying to stop thinking about her; she had left *him* and he lived in a different world now—one that had no Hanna, only magic, prophesies and the fate of his kind, which had been placed strategically on his shoulders. He wished back then he had told her how he felt about her, there had been many opportunities, but he had let them slip through his fingers—now he would never get that chance.

While his heart broke into a million pieces and fell to the pit of his stomach, an irrational idea was forming in his mind—he would go outside! He just had to hear the sound of that girl's voice again. He knew it would just make him long to see Hanna more, and if his uncle were to find out he would most likely kill him, but it felt like the right thing to do.

18

Gypsies, Grunts and a Girl

Mike jumped up, left the room and hurried down several flights of steps until he reached the main floor. He considered using the front door, but quickly decided it was a bad idea, too much exposure; he needed another exit. There has to be another way to get out, he thought, frantically searching the entire main floor. The last room he entered was a massive kitchen and even though he had been through there just twenty minutes earlier he hadn't noticed the door to what he presumed was the cellar.

He hurriedly opened the door. A long, narrow dimly lit stairwell lay before him. Without hesitating he ran down the flight of stone steps. It was definitely a cellar; the air was damp and smelled musty, the only source of light coming from the torches that hung on the stone walls. For a moment he stood at the bottom of the steps contemplating in which direction to proceed; left, right, back up the stairs? He looked both left and right, but one dimly lit, seemingly endless, long passageway was no better than the other, and he was losing time and patience.

"Oh, *come on!*" he shouted impatiently.

His shout echoed through the passageways, bouncing off the stone walls, creating a "surround sound" effect. Being a young man of a generation where graphics, special effects and sound quality ranked higher than physical appearance, he took a moment to appreciate the sound.

"Cool!" he stated, very impressed.

Without another thought, Mike turned to the right and hurried along the passageway, which turned out to be shorter than it had appeared. It was simply a long bend that continually veered to the left. He passed several doors on either side, but he got the feeling that none of them was an exit. It seemed to him that he had gone almost half-circle when he finally came upon an entryway that had no door. The light from the room stretched into the passageway beckoning him to enter, and he accepted, grateful for the light and the hope that it was a way out.

Mike passed through the arched entrance.

"*Wow!*" he exclaimed in awe.

He wasn't standing in a room but in a massive tunnel, at least a hundred wooden barrels lining each side of the stone walls. The floor was smooth flat stones just like tiles. There were torches along the walls and candles sitting in stout wine bottles—which were barely visible beneath layers of dripping wax. Each was set atop every third barrel or so, illuminating the tunnel. On every barrel, just above the tap, was the Weaver Coat of Arms burned into the wood.

Mike could see that the tunnel led to another room, so, as fascinating as everything was, he hurried through with the hope that he would come across an exit.

This room was small, but bright and cheerful with circular, crudely carved walls. To his right were four old barrels placed on end, each topped with a candle and a small white cloth. To his left, barrels serving as the base of a small counter supported a large slab of oddly shaped aged wood, the counter top. The wall behind the counter was a stack of wine casks, all on end, taps forward and ready to pour for thirsty samplers. The deep imprints in the bar stools left "behind," literally, by many patrons suggested that this place had been around for a *very* long time.

Then Mike noticed what looked like a small doorway in the corner hidden between two of the walls.

"What the heck, I might as well give it a try," he said out loud, walking towards it.

It was a small door, probably to a storage area, but the sheer desire of wanting to get outside made him open it nonetheless. To his surprise it revealed a dark shallow flight of steps leading up to another door and, so excited at the prospect of having found an exit, without a second thought and taking two steps at a time, he flew up the steps. He didn't take a moment to catch his breath or consider his next step, he reached out and pulled the handle, opening the door slightly. He peeked through the crack and to his great delight there was sunlight and fresh air—finally!

"*Yes!*" he whispered triumphantly.

He took a moment to assess his new surroundings—before him was a short arched tunnel leading to a narrow walkway lined with tall bushes and towering trees.

He knew that he was breaking all the rules and that the consequences of his actions meant certain wrath from Laszlo, which may or may not involve—but was not restricted to—being thrown into the dungeon, only being able to resurface when they had need of him to save the world. But, he wasn't going to be *completely* irresponsible!

He pulled the hood of his sweater, now covered in mud and torn at the back where the roots had grabbed at him, over his head, providing some concealment for his face. Feeling proud of himself for remembering this bit of espionage, he drew in a deep breath, opened the door fully and stepped out. He shut the door quietly behind him and made his way through the short tunnel—giving no thought to how he might re-enter the tower on his return.

Within seconds Mike found himself at the arched entrance with only the narrow stone walkway and the row of hedges facing him. Carefully he scanned in both directions and decided that there was no one around to notice him. He stepped onto the walkway, turned left and gingerly made his way towards the cobblestone lane in front of the tower where he had seen the teenagers. In a few seconds he had made it to the intersection where the walkway and the cobblestone lane converged. He stayed close to the wall, being careful not to be seen as he made a quick scan of the lane. Only one man, far down the lane—and I am not going in that direction anyway, he thought.

Pulling his hood down further over his head he stepped into the lane and ahead saw the wider street that the girls had taken. It appeared to lead into the centre of the town, so he took a few steps, thinking that if anyone saw him he would look completely out of place. As he continued walking he became much more confident, however, and soon decided, heck, no one would give him a second glance.

The group of girls he'd seen earlier of course were long gone. He decided to follow the street sounds to a busier avenue ahead. He had almost made it there when a couple of older men and a woman came out of nowhere, turned onto the street and headed towards him. Mike lowered his eyes to the ground, tugged on the hood to keep it close to his face and tried to look as much of a dark moody teenager as he could, hoping it was the acceptable look for teenagers here as much as it was back home. The three people walked past him taking no notice, and Mike expelled a huge sigh of relief.

Reaching an intersection, he peered left and right, quickly ran across then continued on his way, slouching, face hidden, hood pulled down. He could see the cross street was had a lot of shops and was full of people, and with every step his insides lurched. At the next intersection, he stopped for a moment, not quite stepping out onto the street. He casually glanced in both directions; turning right would take him up a hill that looked like it ended with a long narrow passageway that led to an even steeper hill. To the left was a street lined with little shops and pubs, ending in what looked like the town square—that had to be where the majority of the noise was coming from, he thought. He made an executive decision and decided the girls had gone towards the market square.

A surge of adrenaline coursed through him as he walked, feeling like he was committing a major crime and getting away with it—well, in a sense he was, according to the "law of his uncle." He pushed that thought to the back of his head, knowing that responsibility would convince him to turn around and retrace his steps. Making sure to keep his face hidden he continued walking with the crowd.

He forced himself to walk past many fascinating magic shops, knowing if he went in he'd run out of time. They looked so interesting, full of oddities, nothing like back home. Until now, the world of magic for him had only existed in movies and books, but here the magical world or trade in those movies and books really did exist.

He couldn't help lingering just for a moment, looking through the display window of one store that caught his eye. The sign above was written in Hungarian, but he knew what it said—*Dragon Riders*. There were many racks and shelves of cycling suits, jackets, boots and accessories…some more like riding suits and then again others made of leather. The items that caught his eye the most were straps to go across the shoulders and chest, holsters, swords, belts and knife sheaths for boots, wrist belts and thigh holsters. Throughout the small store Mike could see several mannequins fitted out in a variety of dragon-riding attire. These particularly caught his eye. As shoppers passed the mannequins they would strike various poses, some drew a sword from their back, others pretending to be a jockey, swinging from side to side as if riding an invisible dragon. Mike assumed it was to demonstrate the aerodynamics of the suit, but it was strange and fascinating at the same time. It was obviously as commonplace to find dragon-riding clothes here as it was to see the latest equestrian wear back home.

The layout of the store was very similar with ladies', men's and children's sections. There was even a sale rack located at the back with a sign hovering above the rack in mid-air with the words, *Get Last Year's Fashion up to 50% off* printed in bold flashing red. Mike caught himself debating which of the various styles made for more practical dragon riding. He gave himself a mental slap; if his friends back home knew what he was doing right now he thought they would dump him in the nearest garbage bin! The sound of laughter pulled his attention away from the store and as he walked away, as unbelievable as everything seemed, he promised himself that at the first opportunity he would come back and walk the streets of this town freely, and this store would be the first place he would visit.

Mike hurried to the centre of the town, the market square, as lingering at the *Dragon Riders* store had cost him precious time. Keeping his head down, on reaching the market square he was stunned at the number of people hurrying and bustling about. Like New York City, he guessed—yet, it looked exactly as Mike had always imagined an outdoor market would have been one hundred years ago: kiosks, tables, carts and even caravans set up everywhere. Small tents covered tables stacked high with fresh vegetables and fruits. There were jewellers, metal smiths and more leather retailers than Mike had ever seen. He saw tables full of fresh fish and various meats, baked goods and even souvenir stands.

Dazed, Mike quickly scanned the crowd but it was useless; there were just too many people and too much going on. A small fire of hope died inside him. What was I thinking? he thought, scolding himself, for he knew it had been a ridiculous notion that he had really heard Hanna. The feeling of hope was replaced with the reality of guilt. Mike had heard the expression so many times in his life, "What a man won't do for a woman," and, in his case, he may have done this only to spend the next year of his life jailed by his uncle.

The toll of church bells ringing out for 4 o'clock pulled him back to reality, making him realise he had little more than forty-five minutes before he was supposed to meet

Elizabeth back at the tower. Still fascinated by what he saw around him, it didn't take much for him to decide to stay and look around the shops, after all it wasn't every day he got to visit a magical marketplace, and seeing as this was his first time, he felt he owed it to himself. *You've already come this far, so what's a few more minutes?*

Mike ambled through all the wares, being careful not to linger at any table too long. He reached the far side of the market and found himself in front of a caravan that was tucked into the corner. This mysterious, almost hidden caravan had the strangest things for sale, like rabbits' feet, dried herbs and strange-looking meats that he didn't recognise, which were hanging from a valance over a small door that led into the back of the caravan. He also saw brightly coloured scarves and flowers, gold and silver jewels mixed in with used household odds and ends. There was even a small table that had used electronics of all sorts on it.

Do wizards even use electronics? he thought, but then he remembered his uncle had a cellphone and so did some of his other cousins. Oddly enough, though, no used cellphones could be seen on the table. It all gave Mike the creeps, so he decided the sooner he left this place the better.

Mike was definitely short on time and realised he had better get back to the tower. The less Elizabeth knew the better, for he did not know if she would tell her father, although Uncle Laszlo would know she was keeping something from him and it wouldn't be fair for Mike to put her in that position. He liked and respected Elizabeth well.

He had turned to walk back to the tower when he came face to face with a beautiful woman. She was stunning; she had dark olive skin and long black hair that fell in curly tresses over her shoulders and down to the middle of her back. She wore long, delicate gold earrings that reminded Mike of bygone times and a long, brightly coloured floral skirt that touched the ground. Her soft white blouse was tied at the waist, from which gold chains hung loosely, and gold bangles adorned her wrists. Her eyes were dark and mysterious, and seemed to be able to look straight through Mike. Mike realised he was staring, and he was sure his cheeks had blushed the colour of red roses as she looked at him. He quickly apologised for nearly knocking her over and made to continue on his way back to the tower when she grabbed his hand and turned his palm upwards towards her.

"Hmmm...such an interesting lifeline, I have to insist you have your palm read," she said in a sultry voice.

A strange feeling filled Mike's head. He didn't remember saying the words, but he must have agreed because she took him by the hand and before he knew it he was sitting down at a small table behind the caravan. Sitting opposite him, she spoke, and he felt like he was in a dream. She was insisting that he remove his hood.

"Such a handsome young man, you shouldn't be hiding your face underneath that hood. Here, let me see your face."

Before Mike knew it, his hood was removed and he was staring back into her mysterious eyes.

"Now, let me see your hands." She took both his hands and turned them, palms facing upwards. "Hmm...how very fascinating."

"What is it you see?" Mike asked, never thinking that in his lifetime he would ever take palmistry seriously.

She captivated him with those eyes as she smiled at him.

"I see many great challenges in the future for you."

'What challenges, what kind of challenges?"
She lowered her head and scrutinised his palm once more.
"Ah yes, *very* interesting."
"What kind of challenges?" Mike repeated.
Without answering, she turned her eyes back to his palm.
"*Very* interesting," she repeated, more to herself than Mike. She looked up at him and without taking her eyes away, she asked playfully, "I haven't seen you here before, are you new to the town? Such a handsome boy like you I would never forget."

Mike felt the heat in his cheeks intensify and at the same time he was at a complete loss for words. It suddenly occurred to him that that leaving the tower had been a bad idea, a very bad idea. Something in the way she was looking at him had set this thought in motion. *What was I thinking?* he scolded himself mentally. Had he really thought he was going to get away with nobody seeing him? He got up from the chair, turned his head away and mumbled:

"Ah…thanks, I've gotta go."

No sooner had he stood up to leave when he came face to face with another woman, hideous in comparison with the beautiful lady who had read his palm. Her face was old; Mike was certain he had never seen that many wrinkles before. But worse, his eyes were forced upon her beard of long, scraggly sparse hair hanging from her chin. Mike's stomach turned over in disgust. She was dressed the same as the first woman, but there was definitely no feeling of hypnotism when he looked into her eyes. He'd never seen anything like her before. Her nose was as crooked as Mike imagined a real witch's would be and in it was a large hoop. Suddenly, she grasped his hand.

"What are you doing, young man, why in such a rush? My beautiful daughter has read your palm for you," she cackled.

"Thanks, yeah it was g-great, b-but I've really gotta go. I'm l-late…," he stuttered, trying to get around the lady, who was surprisingly light on her feet.

No matter how he moved to the left or right she blocked his way. He backed away from her instead, thinking he could make his getaway that way.

"There is no rush. Stay, stay for a while, come and see…."

She took him by the hand, wanting to lead him back to the caravan door. It was at this point Mike *knew* that something was very wrong. He tore his hand from her grip.

"I've gotta go, thanks, but *no thanks!*"

When he thought it was finally clear for him to go, male twins appeared out of nowhere and barred his way. They were gigantic!

"Where are you going?" The less intelligent looking, of the two mumbled. He spoke Hungarian but not a dialect Mike recognised. Mudder asked you to stay. It would be rude not to honour her request," they said simultaneously, walking towards Mike.

They reached out their arms to grab him one on either side, but they were heavy-handed and Mike was younger, sharper and stealthier in comparison. He ducked down just as they reached out for him and ran underneath their arms. He was fast and had nearly made it out from behind the caravan when another man, who looked identical to the twins, stood in his path and grabbed -triplets… great! Mike's momentum put him right into the man's strong grip on his arms, but he didn't want to struggle and cause a scene because that would have drawn attention to himself and the Gypsies. Uncertain of what to do, he initiated some of his wrestling tactics and momentarily managed to free himself from the man's vice-like hold, but at that moment the twins returned and Mike knew there was no way he could escape all three of them.

What was the use of being the wizard if you couldn't use magic, especially in moments of great need? Mike had noticed that none of them had used magic on him, just pure brawn, but that had proved enough, seeing as he couldn't use any magic. The triplets made a circle around Mike, his mind racing with thoughts of what they wanted with him. He couldn't understand the sudden interest, or maybe they just did this on a regular basis? Fear and adrenaline coursing through his body, he was considering his next step when he suddenly lunged forwards going for an opening between two of them. The attempt was unsuccessful, as they had anticipated his move and Mike knew then that he had lost the element of surprise, not sure if he'd ever had it.

The three had a firm grip on Mike now and he was being roughly escorted back behind the caravan. Completely panicked at this point, he couldn't care less if he caught the attention of the entire market; he knew that something very bad was about to happen if he didn't get away from the Gypsies. He struggled harder, throwing punches where ever he could.

"*Hey*! Let *go* of me! What do you want with me? I'm nobody of interest," he shouted. Mike's efforts were futile. He may have been a skilled wrestler, but he was no match for these three ruffians. "*Let go of me!*" Mike yelled, twisting with each word, trying to break the deathly grip of the one triplet clone holding him.

"*Hey!*" Mike heard someone shout. "*Put him down!*"

Before Mike had a chance to see the owner of the angry voice, he felt the triplet holding him stumble forwards as if he'd been shot in the back. Releasing his grip on Mike he fell to the ground stunned. Mike watched as clone number three writhed in pain, large, nasty-looking red welts appearing all over his body. Something flashed past Mike's head and he saw another clone drop to the ground like a boulder wrapped up in a tightly woven potato sack, unable to move his arms or legs. Another flash of light and the final clone fell to the ground in the same manner. No loyalty here then, Mike thought as he saw the two ladies take off down an alleyway as fast as they could, the younger one clearly making better progress than her hideous mother.

"Mike!"

He turned his head at the shout of his name—he *knew* that voice, he'd know it anywhere, but somehow his eyes couldn't convince his brain that what he was seeing was real.

"Mike…" she said again.

"*Hanna?*"

Mike heard himself say her name, but couldn't believe his eyes.

"What are you doing here, Mike?"

"What am *I* doing here? What are you…?"

Mike started his question, but before he had a chance to finish he heard another familiar voice.

"Mike, *what* are you doing out here?"

It was the same question, but definitely a different tone. Elizabeth came storming towards him, giving him a nasty glare. She pointed her wand at the two women running in the distance nearing the end of the alleyway and with a look of *don't worry about it, I've got this one*, raised it and cast a spell. The two ladies dropped to the ground wrapped in the potato sacks, like the two clones.

"I'll take care of the rest," Elizabeth said, and with a swish of her wand the two ladies were lifted off the ground and floated over to where they were standing. She proceeded to place her wand on both of their foreheads and whispered, "*Expelled!*" A small wisp of smoke escaped from their foreheads like a match being blown out, like a candle being snuffed out.

Mike was speechless for a moment, not sure what his next word or action should be. Elizabeth and spells. And then, *Hanna*? Here? Before he had a chance to gather his wits, Elizabeth turned on him, glaring.

"What are you doing out here? Apa is going to kill you."

Mike had no response. He knew there was nothing he could say that was going to sound logical to Elizabeth, so he just shrugged his shoulders and turned to look back at Hanna.

"Oh, Mike!" she cried, running over and giving him a hug. "I can't believe you're here!"

This was a moment Mike had only imagined in his wildest dreams—Hanna throwing herself at him. What more could he have asked for? Feelings of confusion and frustration mixed in with elation made his cheeks flush crimson. Hanna stepped back, releasing her grip on him. Mike didn't think it was possible but he had forgotten how beautiful she was.

"I…I don't get it," he blurted out. "I don't understand— how are you here, where did you go? I'm so confused. Did you know that I was a wiz…? Wait!" He observed the wand in her hand. He met her eyes, his as wide as saucers.

Knowing his words were going to sound foreign, he spoke his next question slowly. "Are you a…a witch?" The look in her eyes was all the answer he needed. 'No way… you can do magic?" He was stunned.

Elizabeth, who had been looking on, was clearly surprised. 'I knew that you two knew each other," she said, "but I had no idea that you were a couple!"

"Oh no, I mean, it's not like that—I mean…," both Mike and Hanna blurted out at the same time.

"Are you sure?" Elizabeth giggled. Mike and Hanna looked at each other— the color in their cheeks growing noticeably darker— then looked away quickly.

Elizabeth gave Mike a knowing look then turned "Elizabeth serious" once again. "Seriously Mike, what are you doing out here?" Mike gathered that she didn't really want an answer— just the opportunity to scold, and so he let her continue. "You have a lot of explaining to do and obviously you two have a lot to talk about. Let's get you back…my dad is going to put you in jail until you're 21, you know that, don't you? Come on…." She turned to go and grabbed Mike's hand, catching him unawares. If it was possible for his face to go a deeper shade of red—it did. He yanked his hand out of hers and made his best attempt to recover himself.

"Alright! I can… manage on my own." He grumbled. He stole a quick glance at Hanna. She wasn't laughing at him, as he suspected she might— no, to his surprise, she was scowling at Elizabeth. His heart gave a tremendous leap. He had so many questions for Hanna but decided against asking any until they were back at the tower…where they might have a chance to be alone…might.

And the lecture continued…

"Mike, do you realize how many people might have seen you out here? Do you know how dangerous this was? How did you even get here and why did you even leave the tower? My dad is going to kill you!" This last comment she threw out in every other sentence as she continued to question and scold Mike…all the way back to the tower.

"I get it," Mike said finally when she had taken a moment to breathe. Hanna had remained silent the whole way. The thought of what she might be thinking of him, just now, made him cringe. They had arrived at the tower and Elizabeth stopped them.

"What door did you leave the tower from?" she asked.

Mike pointed towards the cellar door—he was afraid to speak. She turned to Mike and said, "The door's not open!"

Finding his tongue and getting his courage back, Mike replied, "Why would I leave the door open?"

"Well, how were you going to get back in?" she asked, sounding exactly like a school teacher he'd once had.

"Umm…," was all he could manage.

Elizabeth continued fuming, and Mike decided he'd better diffuse her rage…and fast. He picked a twig off the ground and with a swish and flick said, "Alohomora!"

Elizabeth was clearly not amused, he ventured an explanation: "You know—it's the spell Harry Potter used to open up doors." That got no response, so he continued, "…the boy wizard?… who went to Hogwarts?… school of magic?… the boy who lived…?"

"The *what…who*?! Never mind! We've got to get in. Here." She reached up to the top of the door, running her hand along the sill until she finally found what she was looking for—a key. She shot him a scolding look, then quickly unlocked the door, replacing the key in its hiding spot. Then she stepped across the threshold, turned to Hanna and said, "Hanna Taylor, welcome to our tower."

Taylor? Eyebrows raised, he gave her a questioning look.

Elizabeth sighed with exasperation, "Only a Weaver family member can enter their family tower; anyone else has to be invited in."

"Oh."

When they were finally inside, Elizabeth turned and laid into him, "Okay, Mike you've got some serious explaining to do. Why did you leave? You were warned. You knew how dangerous it would be if somebody saw you!"

"Nobody recognised me, I had my hood pulled over my head and kept my face to the ground," he growled.

"Yes, well, those Gypsies at the caravan saw you and they *are* dangerous, Mike. Maybe they can't perform magic like wizards can, but they have their ways of drawing people in. Unsuspecting people like *you*." She jabbed a scolding finger at him. Mike made a mental note to never look a beautiful Gypsy woman in the eyes again.

Elizabeth continued, "…and dealing with the Gypsies is never a good thing but *provoking them to anger* is even worse! Do you know how lucky you are that we were there!?"

"I didn't *do* anything, okay?" He threw his hands up and turned away. He was getting tired of being told what to do and to watch every move he made, *especially* in front of Hanna. He still couldn't believe she was here. He turned back and drew a long, slow breath. "Look…," he started, "all I know is that one minute I was walking away and the next minute a pretty…," he glanced quickly over at Hanna, who raised her eyebrows at him.

"Uh umm…." He cleared his throat and continued. "A Gypsy woman asked me if I wanted my palm read. I remember saying no, but somehow I ended up at the table. She started reading my palm and then I got up to bolt, but this hideous woman—she looked like an old witch…" maybe that wasn't a choice description considering his audience…"uh, umm… never mind— and out of nowhere her three Goons arrived and jumped me!"

"Did she *say* anything to you? Tell me *exactly* what she said when she read your palm," Elizabeth asked urgently.

"She said that she…," man, this was embarrassing, "that she saw many challenges ahead."

"Anything else, Mike, was there anything else she said…?" Elizabeth pressed.

Mike was really starting to get irritated now. "Look," he barked, "she didn't say anything important,…so there!" he ended lamely.

"Are you kidding? *Everything* they say is important," Elizabeth shrieked.

"What does it matter? She wouldn't know who I was anyways and besides—you did something to alter their memory. I know you did. I saw smoke coming out of their foreheads. That's what it was, wasn't it?"

"Well…yes," she admitted reluctantly, a little taken aback that Mike had caught on to that spell, but still feeling indignant enough to defend herself. She blurted out, "But, Mike, that's not the point!"

At that Hanna gave a smile to Mike that made his heart melt. Unfortunately, it had a different effect on Elizabeth, who's face was taking on the look of an angry ogre. With as much composure as an ogre can manage, she drew in a long breath through her nose, turned back to Mike and asked, "Mike—why did you leave the tower in the first place? I mean— what on earth made you think that that would be a good idea?!"

"I didn't think that it would be a *good* idea— I didn't think that it would be a bad idea! I didn't think...I mean I thought...." He shut his eyes tightly and took a deep breath in through his nose and back out, and tried again, "I *thought* I saw Hanna...*that's* why I left." He could barely meet Elizabeth's eyes and he didn't dare look at Hanna, though he could feel her gaze on him.

"What?! Mike, why would you risk....?" Mike and Hanna both gave her a sharp look. "Oh!" she managed, as the lightbulb clicked on. There was a moment of awkward silence, then Elizabeth turned abruptly on her heel and mumbled something to the effect of..."I'll be back in a few minutes."

Finally, alone, both of them stood awkwardly, staring at their feet. Mike had been dying to have a moment alone with Hanna and had a thousand questions, but, now that it was here, he couldn't manage a single syllable. Hanna too was silent.

After what seemed like an eternity, both started talking at the same time.

"Mike..."

"Hanna..."

"You go first."

"No you go first."

"Hanna I...where did...what happened? Oh, Hanna, I

am so confused. You were there one day and then you were gone…and, and now you're here and you're a…a…."

"A witch. Yes." she interrupted. She took a deep breath and blurted out, "I know this is a big surprise…and I never meant to lie to you."

"You knew who I was all along?" He asked, hurt evident in his voice.

"Yes—but Mike…"

"So…." He shut his eyes again, trying to steady himself against this new revelation. "You knew who I was and *what* I was—*am*—and you didn't tell me because…?"

"I…I wasn't allowed," she said, looking apologetic. "I wasn't even supposed to have any contact with you," she added feebly.

"What? Why *not?!*" Mike blurted—now feeling confused *and* hurt.

She took a step toward him and reached for his hand, "Mike, please!"

"Please *what?!*" He jerked his hand away from hers and turned away.

She continued, "I do know who you are, I always did, but I wasn't your friend just because of that! My father and your father were…*are*…best friends. No one knew what had happened to you that night, when…when your family was attacked. No one even knew if you were…well…if you were alive! Your whole family had to go into hiding and my father tried to keep in touch but after a while your uncle felt that my father was putting himself and his family in too much danger. For a few years, it stayed that way. But then one day Laszlo came to see my father. He told him that he knew that you and your father were alive and that he knew where you were. It was getting harder for Laszlo Basci to do this on his own—he couldn't be here looking for your attackers and be with you—keeping you safe. My father insisted that Laci Bacsi let him help and before I knew it we were on a plane to Florida. Mike—"

"Florida?!" Mike interrupted. "What do you mean, *Florida*? We lived there five years ago! You mean to tell me that you have known about me for five years?!"

"Of course I have, Mike…everyone knows about you…I mean, everyone *knows* the prophecy about your family." The look in Mike's eyes told Hanna that this last piece of information wasn't as helpful as she had hoped.

She tried again, speaking faster, anticipating an explosion at any moment. "Look, Mike, it's true that we knew of the prophecy…but when we first moved all we knew was that we were on the way to Florida and that we weren't allowed to use magic under any circumstances. We were home-schooled and barely made friends with anyone. No one ever told us that we were there to watch over you. We weren't even told about your family!" It was working. Slowly the look of shock was leaving his eyes.

"Mike…" She reached out tentatively for his hand, this time he didn't pull away—and cautiously took a step closer. She spoke softly, toying with his hand, suddenly having difficulty meeting his eyes. "Mike—when I met you at school, I didn't know who you were…it wasn't until after… Oh, Mike—you mean everything to me…it crushed me not to be able to tell you, I wanted to tell you so badly and I never wanted *this* to happen. But I would have put you in so much danger, Mike, you've got to understand…and I would never have been able to forgive myself."

But…all *he* knew was that she was holding his hands and he couldn't possibly imagine feeling better than he did at this moment.

Hanna stared into his eyes, but couldn't read the expression on his face. She felt desperate at the thought that he didn't believe her—and why should he? She knew how it looked and how it sounded. She hung her head and her hand slipped out of his. "Mike, I just don't know how to make you understand, how to make you believe me!" Tears were falling freely down her cheeks. Embarrassed, she turned her face away, briskly wiping the tears. Mike felt like he had been punched in the stomach. But then, all the hurt and confusion he had been feeling fell away with every tear that rolled down her cheeks. He took a step closer.

"Please don't cry," he said softly. He placed his hand under her chin, lifting her face gently. "Hanna," he said, wiping the tears, then brushing her hair away from her face. She looked up and met his gaze. At that, Mike forgot the world around him. He forgot what had happened and what danger he might be in. He only knew that at this moment her piercing green eyes still wet with tears glistened like precious jewels and captivated every bit of his being.

"I believe you," he whispered as he drew her closer to him, with exceptional tenderness he took her face in his hands. Holding her gaze, he bent his head slowly to hers. His heart was pounding so hard against his chest that he was sure she could hear it. He closed his eyes to steady himself and then his lips met hers. And the world fell away. All that remained was Mike and Hanna. Time was no longer relevant…he wanted to stay this way forever and so did she. Having never truly kissed a girl, Mike was worried that his lack of experience would be seriously obvious or that perhaps Hanna didn't feel the same way about him as he clearly did for her, but all doubt was erased the moment their lips touched— Hanna wrapped her arms around his neck and returned his kiss with equal longing.

It seemed an eternity when, finally, breathless, they drew apart and yet Mike felt instantly cheated of time when the kiss ended. There was a moment of awkward silence— both feeling bashful and yet unable to part from one another. Finally Mike spoke. "I've wanted to do that since the first time I saw you." He was having difficulty meeting her eyes. Doubt began to surface again and a knot was beginning to form in his stomach.

"So did I." Hanna spoke softly. The knot left as quickly as it had come and Mike was filled with pure elation.

"I want very much to do that again—may I? He felt foolish but didn't want to assume anything. He wanted everything to remain feeling as perfect as it did at this moment.

"Yes." Hanna blushed tremendously but all Mike could think was that it made her that much more beautiful. Without hesitation he bent his head to hers as she pulled herself to her full height to meet his lips. Again, Mike lost all sense of time…

"Mike!" We need to go!" It was as if someone had run their nails down the chalkboard of Mike's paradise…Elizabeth was back.

Elizabeth came around the corner and stopped short when she saw them together. They quickly stepped apart, looking surprised and a bit guilty. Hanna whispered, "Oh, I forgot she was still here."

Mike could not tear his gaze from Hanna's face. But there stood Elizabeth, having seen them kissing, and he knew the spell was broken. Looking down at Hanna, he heard Elizabeth complain, "Time to go. My father will know you left the tower. Let's go."

Hanna whispered, "When can I see you again, Mike?"

Ignoring Elizabeth, Mike replied with alacrity, "As soon as possible!" Hanna giggled, causing Mike to blush yet again.

"How can we stay in touch?" Mike asked.

"I'd say call me, but using our cell phones wouldn't be a great idea…if my dad found out…who knows what he'd do," Hanna said sheepishly. She was silent for a moment concentrating. "I'll send a message to Elizabeth." She looked over at Elizabeth, who, to Mike's surprise, was blushing slightly, but nodded her head in agreement and smiled.

Then Elizabeth added, "Oh man, we are so dead!" and she gave Mike a hurry-it-along look.

Mike thought, I don't care if they put me under house arrest until my seventeenth birthday, I don't even care about that trip back through the tunnel…all I care about is Hanna.

He realized later that he had forgotten to tell Elizabeth about the prophecy he'd heard, but was so happy to find out that she hadn't said anything to her father and uncle about that wild day. Mike floated off to bed that night, saying goodnight with a smile…which his family assumed was due to his having a good outing that day. And in a way, it was.

19

Type O

The streets of Segesvar were quiet that night—everything was still and the stifling humidity left behind from the scorching hot day hung heavily in the air. Darkness had fallen over the small town and the bright moon shone into the quiet streets and alleyways, casting eerie shadows on the walls.

The faint tap of a hard-soled shoe hitting the cobblestone street was the only sound as a lone figure could be seen walking through a narrow lane. He wore a black trench coat, and was shielding his face with its high collar. He stayed in the shadows close to the walls. The narrow lane he walked led to the market square. Once there he paused for a moment and scanned his surroundings, then, certain that he was alone and with no watchful eyes on him, he made a quick dash towards the long dark stairwell that led to the cemetery.

Once inside the tunnelled stairwell, the dark figure quickly leapt up the steps until he reached the first landing. There he stopped and turned to face the wall of the tunnel to his left. A faint blue glow radiated from the tunnel wall, then suddenly the wizard disappeared from sight.

The other side of that tunnel wall was equally as still and dark, but there was also a distinct feeling of dread in the air as if a malicious evil lurked around every corner. Despite being a wizard and more than capable of defending himself, the feeling made him shiver.

"*Welcome.*"

The sinister greeting came from the shadows, making a chill run down the wizard's spine. A man cloaked in black appeared before him. His skin was pale, his hair was black and his eyes void of any colour except for the dark, blood-red pupils. The wizard figure gave a start.

"Must you do that? You knew I was coming!" he said sharply.

"You're early," the cloaked man drawled maliciously. "Silly little fly—you shouldn't fly into the spider's web without warning." He drew close to the wizard and smelled him, inhaling deeply. "You have brought a tasty gift?"

"Yes, naturally," said the figure, horrified as he always was by the cloaked man's behaviour. He drew the left side of his trench coat open slightly and revealed a long flat sac filled with blood. "Type O, just as requested," he added.

The cloaked man was rubbing his hands in anticipation, and the bearer of the blood was sure he could see saliva from the corner of his mouth glistening in the moonlight. He quickly drew his trench coat back around himself.

"For Vitaros only—you know he doesn't like to share. Now please, if you will, take me to him. The less time I spend here, the better off I'll be."

There was a hint of disgust in his tone. Although he knew he was superior to this *creature* in every way, it didn't stop the uneasy feeling that came every time he was in its presence. Everyone knew you couldn't trust a vampire; it was in their nature. They were the demons that walked the earth by night and hid in the dark places by day. Created by darkness, in the darkness they would remain. Unfortunately, he needed them and they needed him; in fact they would prove to be quite useful to him if all went according to plan.

He remembered back to the time when they had first approached him. He had been so repulsed by them with their sickly pale skin, soulless eyes and obvious insatiable thirst. They did nothing to hide their desire to make a meal of you and to suck you dry of every drop of blood until there was nothing left of you but your pale, cold dead body. Few people survived a vampire attack. Contrary to popular belief, people don't turn into a vampire just from a bite. Most die. A person's soul has to be very dark to survive a bite and in those cases they welcome the transition into vampire. The vast majority of people have a good soul, therefore, they are not able to make the transition because their soul is unwilling.

The vampire led the way down a long dark passageway into a dimly lit corridor lined with many small glass cells, each containing one single tomb. Tombs began to open as they passed each cell, the scent of fresh blood waking the vampires from their deathly sleep. So strong was the aroma that it was as if he had set off a fire alarm in each cell. Not one vampire dared to come out, for they were no match for a wizard, and this particular one was their only hope of strength and freedom once again. They moaned and cried like starving inmates as he walked on, and it sickened the wizard to see them in such a pathetic state.

⟲

More than a thousand years ago the vampires had been free and powerful. They held most of Eastern Europe in a deadly grip of fear; they were what nightmares were made of—the bogeyman that came in the night and stole the young. While they fed on human blood they remained strong, but it was a short-lived reign; humans, wizards, wolves and later werewolves waged a war against the vampires that took several years to win. In the end they had reduced the vampire population to little more than a hundred, keeping their thirst and strength at bay with chicken blood. Those same hundred now stood in their cells behind their glass doors watching the wizard as he passed by.

The passageway came to a dead end. A large concrete wall stood before them. Directly in front of them, about midway down the wall, an image of a hideous demon with tall horns twisting up from its face was carved into the concrete. The image was stained in black, but the eyes shone blood red. The vampire escort placed his hand on the image and a deep rumble echoed through the corridor as a massive piece of the wall slid along the floor revealing a door that opened into a dimly lit room.

"*Enter*," a voice came from the darkness.

Only the wizard entered. The vampire escort seemed to know his place and bowed humbly as the wizard passed through the doorway. The moment he was inside, the heavy door shut behind him with a loud boom.

The room was simple. There was a beautifully carved open coffin made out of wood and lined with dark red silk. A large chair, or rather a throne, was in the centre of the cold room and intricately designed wooden side tables were positioned on either side of the throne, each supporting a large candelabrum, the only light in the room. A tall cloaked figure sat in the chair, his features hidden in the shadows, for which the wizard was thankful; he had always found his features particularly hideous.

"Good evening, my friend." He spoke darkly. "I trust that Viktor treated you well?"

"Yes, Vitaros, I had no trouble getting here and I see you did as I requested; everyone fed before my arrival?" the wizard asked, seeking confirmation.

"Yes, of course. You were in no danger," the vampire replied sadistically; then with a hint of resentment he added, "You know we are weak from the years of chicken blood you feed us. We are not a threat to... *your* kind."

"Yes indeed, you're not. It is rather pathetic really that without human blood you are powerless and weak."

He withdrew the sac of blood from under his coat and held it up for Vitaros to see. The vampire swiftly stood up from his chair, rushed forwards and reached out his large boney hand, snatching at it greedily. The wizard pulled the sac of blood out of his reach, taunting him.

"Uh-ahh—I need my answer first," he scolded.

Vitaros bared his teeth and hissed at the wizard.

"You treat us like dogs!" he snapped, but stepped back submissively. "We were once powerful and ruled over man— they feared us! They trembled and cowered in the night, powerless while we feasted!"

"And you will again. Tell me that the transformation can be done and I will personally lead your first attack," the wizard said, holding the bag out of reach, waiting for the vampire's answer.

"It can be done," he said, almost reluctantly.

"You are sure?"

The wizard wanted to know that it wasn't just the promise of fresh blood that was motivating the vampire's reply.

"Yes, *yes!*" Vitaros exclaimed with annoyance. "It has never been done, as you know, but the same rule applies to wizards as humans: your soul only needs to be dark enough. I think we can be sure yours is," he added sarcastically.

"I will want it done soon!" he snapped, carelessly throwing the sac of blood towards Vitaros, who grabbed it greedily and sank his teeth into it.

Blood squirted everywhere as he devoured the contents of the sac. He ate with the same hunger and vigour as a man who has gone for weeks without food.

"The boy will be seventeen in a year and our army must be ready before then," the wizard continued, ignoring Vitaros's animal-like behaviour. "By the next full moon…yes, that will be perfect! I will send more blood. I expect you'll be strong enough by then?" he questioned, turning his attention back to Vitaros, who had finished drinking.

The vampire was wiping the last drop of blood from his chin as he stepped closer to the wizard.

"Yes indeed, I will be strong enough again," he replied, smiling cruelly.

Seeing his face more clearly now, the wizard already noticed the change in Vitaros's features; his face was no longer as demonic as it had been before and it was taking on the features of a handsome man.

"And you will keep your end of the bargain?"

"Yes." A demonic smile crossed the wizard's face. "I will have my army and you will have your freedom."

A Couple of Extra Wands

Morning came quickly. Mike, his father, Laszlo and Elizabeth walked through the dark village quietly. They had all agreed that it would be best to leave in the early hours of the morning so as not to have to answer any unnecessary questions. Mike looked at his watch. It was 3 a.m. He was happy to see that they had started their journey on time. According to Laszlo, many of the farmers would be getting up soon, so they had to keep to their schedule. There was an occasional yawn, but otherwise no one spoke.

Every day for the last week, Laszlo and Elizabeth had shown Mike from where they would be departing the village, and taught him the necessary spell to pass through yet another tunnel for safe passage as well as the enchantments that kept the village hidden. It was the same spell he had spoken into the tunnel that led him to Segesvar, two events from which he was still reeling!

He still couldn't believe that he had run into Hanna, and here of all places! Nor did he understand it all yet, but that didn't matter so much right now. All that mattered to him was that she was near. All the questions he had had and all the worry wondering what had happened to her and her family, where they had gone, how he was going to find her and how he was going to explain that he was a wizard—all that was okay now. Knowing that she was safe and she would miss him made the length of this journey seem that much more bearable. He already couldn't wait to see her again.

Mike must have had a starry look in his eyes because Elizabeth was quietly giggling. He looked at her, and she grabbed her heart and batted her eyelashes at him, pretending to swoon. He cleared his throat and tried to look serious, but it didn't work; he knew she wasn't being mean, it wasn't in her nature. He smiled at her. Since his chance meeting with Hanna in Segesvar (which neither his father or uncle had found out about), Mike had met with Hanna a couple of times, yesterday evening being the second. Uncle Laszlo, with a grin that said "I am so clever", has finally introduced Mike to Dani, his father's best friend, and Aniko (Hungarian for Hanna), his daughter. Mike was stunned, relieved and grateful, but had an ever-growning suspicion that his uncle's sole purpose for living was to pick on him.

Mike didn't mind the teasing; he knew that Elizabeth understood what Hanna meant to him. She had become one of his best friends and she herself had eyes for someone, a boy from her school she had told Mike about. He was from a family whose loyalties to the council were in question, so she never mentioned him to her father. She said she wouldn't until his family was cleared and found to be loyal again. Her father had put the last thirteen years of his life into finding those responsible for the attack on Mike's family, so she couldn't bear to tell him about the boy.

Mike had to admit to himself that he was envious of Elizabeth and his cousins. As ironic as it seemed, because any boy his age would love to be in his shoes—no school, no work, spend your days learning magic—*he* would love to be at school every day! He missed being around his friends and especially Hanna—he missed the wrestling club, he missed the bus ride home, he missed being just plain Mike, no one important. He tried not to think about it too much; the thought of being away from Hanna for the next couple of weeks depressed him enough.

Yet he was excited about this journey and, if he had understood his uncle correctly, the hidden dwarf city to where they were travelling would teach him a lot. Laszlo was going to find a way to, hopefully, regain Alexander's memory for good, a thought that delighted Mike. He now understood that his father had not always been this way, but Mike had never known him to be any different. Several times over the last couple of weeks, Laszlo had told his nephew that *if* this worked, they would know who the attackers had been the night that Alexander had disappeared with Mike—*and* what really happened to his mother, something that was enormously important to both Mike and his father. Nonetheless, Mike could not deny how much he already missed Hanna.

Like he so often did, he had drifted off so far with his thoughts that it took a smack on the arm from Elizabeth to bring him back to the task at hand.

"*Ow!*" he exclaimed. "What the—?"

"We are almost there!" she replied with a smile.

Mike looked ahead and saw the thick hedge that concealed a magically encrypted tunnel that would take them out of Bodon and to a small dirt road, one that nobody travelled. Laszlo's cousin, Attila, the same one who had picked them up from the airport and brought them to

Bodon, would be waiting with the car to take them to the train station. As they approached the hedge two figures materialised out of the shadows. Mike stopped and put one arm out across Elizabeth to stop her, but she continued to move forwards, smiling back at Mike as she did so.

"It's Zsolt Bacsi and Arpi," she whispered to Mike.

Mike continued on, cautiously at first, but soon realised there was no need for caution. He wasn't sure why his uncle and cousin were there, but he was very happy to see them. They all greeted one another with handshakes and hugs. Still wondering why they were there, Mike asked Arpi as they were shaking hands. "So…have you guys just come to say goodbye this early in the morning or couldn't you sleep?"

"*Sleep*? No, I was too excited," Arpi replied, laughing. He noticed Mike was confused. "We are joining you, thought you might need a couple of extra wands," he explained.

A rush of relief washed over Mike; until now he hadn't realised how anxious he actually was.

"That's great!" he shouted, with more enthusiasm than he expected. Clearing his throat, he attempted to regain some composure. "I mean, of course, the more wands the better."

"It will be an honour to help you and Alexander Bacsi. I am sure that if they could, the whole family would join you on your journey today," Arpi said, his tone serious.

Mike didn't know what to say to that; this was new territory for him. He felt so grateful to his new family and yet so afraid that he would let them down. It was best not to think about it too much, he found. And yet…it was impossible to believe that he was more than just plain Mike.

"Speaking of family, where is Feri?" Mike asked, diverting the attention from him to someone else.

"He really wanted to come, but Apa told him he's too young for such a dangerous mission."

This comment brought Mike back to the reality of what they were embarking on, and he had been warned of the dangers of where they were going. The forests, especially those of the Carpathian Mountains, were home to many creatures. Most were harmless woodland animals like black bears, deer, elk, rabbits, squirrels and chipmunks. Even coyotes and foxes were often seen, but they did not fall into the unsavoury category of the creatures he had been warned about. No... he might be "lucky" to encounter creatures he only thought existed in Hollywood movies, like the *lycan*, better known as the werewolf, as well as trolls—not the small ones who live under the bridge either...apparently that branch of the troll family only lived in Germany. And, last but not least, goblins!

Except for the obvious reasons, saving his father's memory and trying to find a lead to his family's attacker, he really couldn't see any reason to even embark on such a journey. Thinking was becoming exhausting again, so he pushed his thoughts to the back of his mind.

"I'm glad your father said no to Feri. I am not too sure I want to go myself," he said, whispering the last part quickly.

Arpi gave him a quick reassuring pat on the back.

"It's my first time too. I'm glad that there are more of us."

Their conversation came to an end as their fathers motioned for them to pass through the hidden gate. As they exited on the other side they could see Attila parked a little way down the dirt road and once everyone had joined them they made their way to the van and piled in.

The sun was slowly making an appearance and everyone was properly awake now, so the ride to the train station was much noisier than the walk to the hidden gate. Mike was glad of the distraction from his thoughts and joined in with small conversations here and there. The ride wasn't long and before he knew it, they were pulling up to the small train station.

Mike wasn't sure what he had expected, but definitely something bigger. There were many other passengers waiting to board the train, which surprised him again. Uncle Laszlo explained that the station was much like a bus stop Mike was used to; people used the trains to get to and from the villages and towns in which they worked. Right now it was "rush hour" for them and that would explain the number of people waiting. Mike remembered his father and Laszlo discussing the timing of the journey to the mountains; they had purposely wanted to go unnoticed, so the crowds helped.

They purchased their tickets and within ten minutes the train arrived. They boarded, but seating was difficult as it was already so full, but—again—this would work to their advantage. They sat in smaller groups—the kids in one compartment, the adults in another. Elizabeth said it was still early in the day for the school kids to be on the train heading for school, but it wasn't uncommon for groups of them to travel earlier when they rode. The train ride would be about an hour and a half, so the kids took advantage of this and slept while the adults quietly discussed their strategy, everyone voicing their opinion on the matter. Mike was sure that there had been a disagreement between the men more than once. He just smiled and dozed off again, for he had come to know this behaviour as normal for groups of Hungarian men.

Once again, sleep was fleeting. Mike awoke to find that the view had changed dramatically; they were now surrounded by mountains on all sides. The scenery was, as he had found so often in Transylvania, breathtaking. He had always loved the Rocky Mountains of Canada too. He found that the mountains here appeared smaller, but were covered in far more lush greenery than the Rockies, or at least the Rockies on the Alberta side. Here the rails seemed to wind endlessly upwards around the mountains.

They stopped in the town of Deda Bistra and got off the train. According to his father, the walk to their ultimate destination, a mountain called The God's Chair, was approximately an hour away by foot. They started their trek immediately. There weren't many people who had alighted from the train at Deda Bistra and there were even fewer people out hiking this early in the morning. They found a footpath immediately outside the small town and were soon alone.

After walking for only about twenty minutes, Laszlo announced that they should stop for a mid-morning break. It had been a long time since their very early breakfast, so the break was welcome as was the good food that had been prepared for them by Anna Nani. She really had a talent for cooking, not forgetting the "special" teas, Mike discovered. She had brewed another one of her magical pots of tea the evening before to help Mike and the rest of the group get a good sleep and calm their excitement.

Mike stopped in mid-chew and suddenly wondered if his father was afraid—he hadn't even thought to ask. A ball of guilt began to form in the pit of his stomach, making it difficult for him to swallow. He choked a little and his cousin Arpi gave him a concerned look. Mike attempted a smile in return and motioned that he needed a drink. His cousin had obviously misunderstood and passed him palinka instead of water. Mike, in his haste to clear the lodged food from his throat, took a huge swig and swallowed before he even realised what it was. Coughing and sputtering he glared at his cousin and spoke as politely as he could muster, given the circumstances.

"Does *anyone* in this country drink water? How is palinka supposed to help anyone when they are choking?"

Arpi burst out laughing. Confused, Mike just continued to glare at his cousin.

"*What?*" he asked.

"You were choking? You looked nervous and scared to me, so I thought you might need a drink. You know, to calm your nerves!"

By now, everyone in the group had bent an ear to their conversation and they were laughing along with the two boys. Mike noticed how hard his father was laughing and decided not to ask him if he was afraid or not. He was just happy to see him happy. Maybe he was worrying over nothing, he told himself.

The break over, the men looked again at the map before returning to the trail. By Laszlo's and Alexander's calculations, they should reach their destination by early evening. Tonight was going to be a full moon and they would need it to reveal the location of the city of dwarves.

It was very strange to Mike to think about the purpose of today's hike, in fact even though he had already seen so many things he never imagined he ever would, the whole thing seemed so far-fetched—a secret fellowship of wizards, travelling the dark and forbidden forests of the Carpathian Mountains where legends of werewolves and other mystical creatures were said to live. The light of the full moon would reveal the way to an ancient dwarf city where enlightenment and the path to yet another magical destination awaited!

The God's Chair was said to be the home of a small fountain, which, if incantations are said correctly and you drink from it at the exact time that Mars is in line with Venus, a lost memory can be restored! Okay...maybe Mars didn't have to be in line with Venus, but the rest did sound pretty "out there." Mike was sure of one thing: if wizardry didn't work out for him, he was definitely going to write a book! He kept his mind occupied for the next couple of hours thinking about titles and characters for his story.

Werewolves 101

The afternoon seemed to drag. It was hot and everyone was in need of a rest and hydration. They could hear the sound of a river nearby and made their way towards it. A couple of minutes off the pathway and they were all enjoying the cold and refreshing taste of the mountain water. A few metres farther up the river the water was coming down what looked like long shallow steps, the water pooling on each step. They took advantage of the calm water in the shallow pools and waded in it until they felt the heat of the afternoon sun dissipate. They had a quick bite to eat after that, not lingering long as they had to keep to the schedule. Mike and his two cousins were quite certain that the men had underestimated their memory of this journey from younger, more vibrant days.

"Why don't we just use magic to get there?" Mike asked Elizabeth as he pulled out of his pocket the little marbles that his uncle had given him for emergency travel. "I've got these and I have enough for everyone. Why not just use them?"

Elizabeth gave a start when she saw what he had pulled from his pocket.

"*Put those away!*" she hissed, putting her hands over his to hide them and pushing them back towards him.

"Huh? What did I miss? We *are* wizards, aren't we? Have I broken some bizarre and insanely difficult-to-understand law of the wizarding world?" Mike asked, having a difficult time containing his annoyance.

Elizabeth softened a little. She had to remind herself that many things were still new and unknown to him.

"Sorry, really, I didn't mean to be so harsh."

Mike's irritation subsided, knowing her apology was sincere.

"I can't believe my father didn't tell you. I think he forgets, like me, that you didn't grow up in this world." Elizabeth leaned closer to him and whispered. "There are very dangerous creatures that roam these forests. Apa mentioned them, yes?"

Mike nodded in reply.

"Well, here is the full story," Elizabeth began… "These dangerous but magical creatures can sense when magic is being used by others, especially when it's within their territory…and they are some of the few creatures that can. Just think of them as normal-looking wolves, with an additional characteristic—they also can *smell* the magic being used, so the less we draw attention to ourselves the better. They rarely attack humans, but wizards, well…let's just say they don't like us very much…yes, that includes you. The dwarves, on the other hand, live in harmony with the werewolves, but these wolves know the dwarves are powerful enough to eradicate their entire wolf population. Historically, however, the dwarves have respected the wolves' existence and have given them these forests to live in peacefully. The wolves agreed to this arrangement, for they know their limitations, such as attacks by humans.

"In return for their freedom," Elizabeth continued, "they protect the dwarves and their ancient city. It has worked that way for many centuries and very few wizards have ever found the city. However, I have to say, the wizards haven't always had the respect for the dwarves that they should. Dwarves possess a very ancient and strong magic that makes them a powerful adversary to werewolf and wizard alike. They also are the only ones who can make wands, delivering each and every wand personally to the witch or wizard that it's personalized for. Furthermore, werewolves were created by wizards to help protect against and fight the vampires. The legend of werewolves began two thousand years ago when a wizard and a wolf became good friends. There was a time when wizards had a deeper respect for the werewolves. Initially they were our *companions*, much like humans have a relationship with their dogs, but they aren't simply 'wolves.'

"Now the vampires are a different story. We never have lived in harmony with vampires…actually that is very difficult to do. Vampires are evil beings and are impossible to satisfy. They thirst for blood and an immortal existence—little else satisfies them. The Western world has romanticized the vampire, but make no mistake, they were born from evil and that is what courses through their veins.

"No one knows why, but vampires have always feared these woods. Knowing this, we drove them here from our villages many times, and few ever returned from the forest," she continued.

"A bit more about our background…the wizard Halldorr, who came from a coastal village by the North Sea in Norway, had travelled far, searching for other wizarding communities. It took him many years to travel through Europe and finally here to Transylvania, but when he arrived he fell in love with the mountains and the landscape so much that he chose to stay. His purpose was to find and connect with other wizards of the world, so it didn't take him long to befriend many of the elder wizards of this area. They were happy to learn of the culture and skill of their wizarding brothers in other parts, and soon learned that the wizards from Halldorr's tribe possessed the unique skill of communicating with nature and animals. They connected with animals via thought, not words, and used emotion to communicate with nature.

"Halldorr spent much of his time wandering the mountains and forests, the very forests into which we drove the vampires so many times over the years. The morning after a particularly bad vampire attack, Halldorr meant to enter the forest and see what it could tell him of the vampires that had been driven in there the night before. He hadn't gone far when he heard the cry of a wolf nearby. He felt that the wolf was in pain and found him lying next to the river beside two very dead vampires, who looked as if their throats had been torn out. The morning sun had not penetrated the forest's canopy yet, so the bodies of the vampires had not burned. As Halldorr drew closer to the injured wolf his presence was suddenly acknowledged by what looked like the rest of the pack. They were protecting their dying leader.

"Halldorr sensed their hesitation and used his magic to extend his thoughts to them and the injured wolf, letting them know that he could help. They let him approach and allowed him to come close to Aato (Noble Wolf), the name Halldorr gave the wolf. After seeing the damage done to Aato by the vampires, Halldorr was not sure what he *could* do. Magic would only work to mend the wounds, but nothing could change the poison that flowed through Aato's veins. The vampires had bitten him several times and the poison would soon kill him or worse, turn him into a beast, an animal the shape and mind of which are mutilated by the vampire poison. There aren't many of these types of beasts because most don't survive the transformation, but if they do, they are the *most* hideous and loathsome creatures that walk the earth and they become slaves to their masters' bidding. They are killing machines and devour everything in their path, but they have ten times the strength they used to have. They are the stuff of *real* nightmares!

"And so, knowing his options were small," Elizabeth continued, "Aato now chose to put his trust in Halldorr and communicated to him that a blood transfusion could work. Every member of the pack was willing to do this for their leader—share their blood. There was a catch; it could not be wolf's blood, it had to be given willingly by a *man*. That night, it's said, the pack howled in agony and disgust so loudly that all the neighbouring villages heard it. Man's blood was strong enough to stop death and, mixed with the wolf's blood, it would transform the wolf forever. The wolf would have the physical ability of man, like walking on two legs, it would have the power of reasoning and the emotions of man, but the strength of ten wolves," she added. "Wolves are a very pure species and they saw man's emotions as a weakness, despite what the blood could do for them. It would be a disgrace to any wolf to mix their blood with that of a weaker species.

"Halldorr saw no reason not to oblige Aato with the transfusion, but there was another catch. The transfusion could only be done through a wolf's bite. They had to wait until Aato's thirst for blood was unbearable and then he would bite Halldorr and drink his blood until he felt it consume him. Naturally, Halldorr was less than enthusiastic about it once he heard what the process involved. For one, he might not survive the bite. A wolf bite wasn't what he had bargained for and there was a good chance that Aato would not be able to control himself after the bite, and end up turning on him and killing him. It was a lot to consider for both Halldorr and Aato. Neither was bound to one another, but both knew the alternative. The change from wolf to beast had to be stopped.

"Neither said a word to the other. Halldorr simply lay down beside Aato with his wand at the ready—that much he could direct. If Aato lost control afterwards, Halldorr would simply have to kill him, which seemed to be understood, as none of the pack protested. The bite had been to the thigh, Halldorr bore the scar to the end of his days, but it did not take long for the transformation to begin. Aato was able to control himself and stopped as soon as he felt the wizard's blood flowing through his veins. Using a little magic, Halldorr sealed his wound quickly, just enough so he could run if necessary.

"Holding his wand ever at the ready, he pulled himself up and stood back as the transformation occurred. Aato howled and writhed as his body began to change. Growling and whimpering, the pack backed away slowly, not understanding or approving, and fearful of the change that was taking place. Almost as fast as it started, it ended. With a whimper, Aato collapsed onto the rocks and lay motionless. Halldorr hadn't realised it until then that he had been holding his breath throughout the entire transformation. He exhaled a huge breath and very slowly, on his hands and knees, crawled over to where Aato lay.

"Fur and blood were everywhere. Halldorr stared at him, amazed by his size. It seemed impossible, but Aato was almost twice the size he had been before. He still had the appearance of a wolf, but the wizard could see by the way he lay there that his hind legs had lengthened and had taken on a more humanistic look. His front paws had the appearance of fingers with massive razor-sharp claws. His fur had changed from its original blond colour to the deepest black Halldorr could ever remember seeing. Around his head the fur had the appearance of hair. The sheer size of his body was almost frightening to observe; Halldorr guessed that he was at least nine feet tall with the build of five of the strongest men he had ever seen. He wasn't sure if he wanted him to wake, but wake he did and with such a howl that Halldorr and the remaining pack cowered in fear, Halldorr covering his ears fearing deafness. The wolves from the pack were rubbing their ears on the ground, trying to bury their heads.

"It finally stopped and when Halldorr and the rest of the pack felt brave enough to look up they saw Aato standing on his hind legs and glaring down at them all with the most surprising eyes that looked like pools of liquid silver. Shocked at the changes in their leader, the pack slowly approached growling and barking at him. Halldorr sensed that this would not be a good time to linger, so he quietly slipped back into the woods and, with a touch of magic, returned home as fast as he could.

"Fearing what retribution there might be, Halldorr refused to leave the safety of his small cabin. The bite in his leg was difficult to heal, even with magic. He was weak and would need to leave his cabin eventually, but every night he could hear Aato's lonely howl. He knew it was him, he could feel it in his soul. Aato kept far enough away so that Halldorr could not communicate with him, which only served to make the wizard feel as if he was always being watched. He knew that Aato was travelling alone, but he wasn't sure if the pack had left him or vice versa. He feared that perhaps, in his anger, Aato might have killed the entire pack, but a few nights later that worry was laid to rest when he heard the remaining pack join in with Aato's howling. They were calling to him, he knew it. As each night passed the howling came closer and closer until Halldorr couldn't take it anymore and he left the safety of the cabin to meet the creature he had created.

"He didn't have to go far. He had barely made it to the edge of the river, just a mile from his cabin, when he heard Aato speaking.

"*I am here.*"

"Halldorr stopped dead in his tracks and turned slowly to face Aato, who stood directly behind him as mighty and dark as Halldorr remembered him. Afraid to, but he did it anyway, he looked up into those silver eyes expecting to be struck down by the sight of them or turned to stone, he wasn't sure. What he didn't expect to see was the compassion in those eyes when he finally did look up.

"'My dear Halldorr—thank you!' Aato said.

"Shocked, Halldorr stumbled backwards, feeling very unsteady and extremely unlike a wizard, as though all his skill had suddenly left him! Aato gave a loud laugh sounding more like a bark than anything else, and reached out to steady his friend.

"'The change from wolf to wolf-man was a little more than I bargained for,' he said. 'I left the pack, as I could see that they could not accept what I had become. Three nights ago I heard the pack fighting, so I hastened back to them as I had not gone very far, and when I got there I saw that the vampires that had attacked us that night you found me were back, twice as many this time. A fire was ignited in me, something I had never felt before—I jumped in without thinking! I tore through them like they were crippled prey—those I didn't kill, fled. Unknown to anyone, we have always guarded these forests and protected the humans and wizards that border the area, and now I pledge that until my last day I and any of my kin will be your warriors against those bloodsuckers! Where or when you need us we will come. I am indebted to you for my life.'

"Touched by Aato's gratitude, Halldorr asked him to recount the events he could remember, it being obvious to both of them where this would lead. Halldorr went to the wizard council with news of the events and, after much convincing that it was safe, a group of elders accompanied Halldorr to the forest, where they had the honour of meeting Aato. Hesitant, but amazed that such a thing could be accomplished they accepted Aato's pledge of allegiance.

"Shortly after this meeting the vampires attacked in numbers, the likes of which they had never envisaged. Halldorr and several other wizards fought alongside the wolves and Aato. There were wounded, as in any battle, wolf and wizard alike, but only three of the wolves had been bitten. So effective was Aato in killing off large numbers of the bloodsuckers, and so impressed were the wizards with his abilities that three of the elder wizards from the council stepped forwards, willing to aid in the transformation, one of them being Daniel, the president of the WWF at the time. The wolves agreed, as none wanted the alternative. However, a witch was necessary as one of those bitten wolves was a female. Only one witch sprang to everyone's mind—Eva, the wife of Daniel, a powerful witch with a kind heart. Upon hearing the request and seeing the outcome of the battle she came forward willingly.

"That female wolf, named Ylva, recovered and became Aato's mate. Their pups, born as werewolves and just as Aato had promised, became warriors against warriors and served to protect wizard and human alike from the vampires. So it should have continued, but unfortunately later generations of werewolves, who only knew Aato as a legend, did not feel the need to fulfill his promise and felt that they deserved more respect than they were being given. Halldorr had passed on and his friendship and bond with the werewolves was no longer honoured; it was now merely a folktale. The wizard population saw the werewolves as slaves, dogs if you will, and the werewolves felt superior and far more powerful than they were given credit for. The animosity from both sides caused an irreparable rift that has lasted until this day. The werewolves still hunt the vampires and protect the woods, and they would probably steer clear of a human, but a wizard? Well…let's just say, it's best to keep yourself unknown in these parts," Elizabeth finished.

Shivers ran down Mike's spine. He felt as if Elizabeth had just read him a story from *Grimm's Fairy Tales*, not the Disney version—the original one full of darkness, strange creatures and someone's untimely death! Glancing nervously over his shoulder into a dark patch of trees they had just passed, he thanked Elizabeth for the explanation and asked her if she knew any light-hearted tales she might want to share. The three of them laughed together as they continued the climb up the mountainside.

Things that Howl
in the Night

Slowly the sun was beginning to set and the travellers were starting to feel the effects of the day's long journey. The afternoon had passed without incident and they had made good time, so they all agreed to have a quick refreshing break before the last leg of the journey. Laszlo mentioned to his nephew that he hoped the cabin was still where he remembered it to be, but there was a small chance that it may have been relocated or, more likely, he simply wouldn't be able to find it.

Everyone except Mike, who had never been there before, huddled together to consult the map. Mike took this time to walk down to the river a kilometre away to refresh himself. Kneeling down at the water's edge, he cupped his hands, splashed his face a few times and drank until he felt hydrated. The water was good, so good in fact he felt like he could run a marathon! Whatever the name of the river, he would now call it the Red Bull River. He smiled to himself as he jumped up and began to retrace his steps to the others.

He hadn't taken three steps before coming to a sudden stop. Was that a growl he'd heard? Beginning to panic, he scanned the area around him quickly—he saw nothing. He put his hand to his ear and listened intently. Did I really hear something growling or was it just Elizabeth's graphic account of the werewolf that is messing with my mind? he thought. But he remained frozen to the spot for several more minutes, too afraid to move, trying to convince himself that it was nothing...but the "chicken" in him was winning the battle. The embarrassment of being so scared was just the push he needed to get back to the others. Even though the braver part of him won, he still felt that sprinting back would be the better choice of travel.

Mike was in mid-sprint and could almost see the others when it came again—now louder, a deep menacing growl! This time there was no denying it, so he didn't stop to look, he just ran faster. Fuelled by the river's water he covered the distance between him and the others in what felt like the speed of light!

"*Run!*" he shouted. "There's something in the trees! It's right behind me, *run!*"

Without hesitating, the others got up and ran after Mike, who in his panic simply motioned for them to get up as he zipped by them still shouting:

"*Run!*"

"What did you see, Michael?" his father asked breathlessly, having caught up with him first and running beside him.

"*See?* I didn't see anything! I *heard* something and by the sound of its growl, it's huge!"

Mike motioned with his arms spread as far apart as they could go, showing the imagined size of whatever had growled at him.

"*Michael!*" his father exclaimed, stopping dead in his tracks.

"*Apa!*" Mike turned to his father, full of panic. "What are you doing? *Run!*"

By now the others had caught up with them, and had slowly come to a standstill.

"Why are we stopping? Is it gone, whatever it is that we are running from?" Arpi asked, gasping for breath.

Mike put his hands over his face as he groaned in exasperation.

"Look, guys, I don't think it's a good idea to linger. Whatever it was that growled at me down by the river, made every hair on the back of my neck stand up! There is something out there and *I* don't want to meet it, so come on, let's just get out of here!"

Thinking the others could see the logic in his suggestion, he turned to run.

"Mike! *Wait!*" Elizabeth yelled after him.

He turned around, surprised to see that they were all still standing there.

"*Guys?*" he yelled questioningly. "What are you doing?"

Alexander and Laszlo walked towards Mike. His father placed his hand on his son's shoulder. Mike noticed the look in his eyes, the same look he always gave him when he was sure Mike was overreacting, but he didn't want to make him feel stupid. Mike looked at his father and sighed heavily.

"Apa, I know what you're going to say. Please don't. Just *don't.*" He put his hand up as if to stop his father talking. "There *is* something out there and it's not friendly!" He looked at everyone, pleading with his eyes. "Now can we please get out of here? *Please!*"

"I think my story of the werewolf might have scared Mike a little," Elizabeth stated quietly, looking at Mike with sympathy in her eyes.

Laszlo glared down at his daughter disapprovingly.

"Sorry, Apa, but he really needed to know," she pleaded.

"Oh, come on, are you being serious?" Mike asked, losing his patience. "It's *not* the story! I mean, it doesn't help knowing it and it did freak me out, but *this* is not in my head!" Flustered, he looked up at everyone and seeing that he hadn't been very convincing, he shouted at them in a final attempt. "*Please*! I know what I heard and I am not sticking around!"

With that statement he turned and started to walk away. He knew no one was following. He didn't want to beg and he didn't know what else to say to convince them. Whatever was out there hadn't put in an appearance, so doubt crept up on him slowly. Painfully aware that all eyes were on him and not wanting to admit that he may have overreacted, he stood with his back to them. His father spoke first.

"Michael…come back. We'll do a quick search of the area, but we need to be on our way. The sun will soon set and then…well, then we *really* need to be careful."

"OK," Mike said, hanging his head in defeat.

"Whatever might be out there seems to be gone now," his father said, smiling.

"You're probably right…uh, *Apa!*" he suddenly yelled.

Mike turned around and leapt forwards, knocking his father to the ground and rolling him out of the way, just as a huge wolf sprang up behind him. He heard the creature land with a heavy thud right where he had just been standing. Mike scrambled to his feet, pulling his father up with him, ready to bolt in any direction possible, when he heard a second growl behind him. His heart, which had been pounding so furiously that his chest hurt, came to a complete stop. So menacing was the growl that it made every hair on the back of his neck stand to attention.

Nothing, not even the horror story Elizabeth had just finished telling him not an hour ago, could have adequately prepared Mike for what stood in front of him—not a wolf, but a huge, angry, ten out of ten in ugly *werewolf*! Mike wasn't about to turn around to confirm if there was another one behind him, although he was quite certain there was.

Laszlo, Zsolt, Arpi and Elizabeth were huddled together in a circle with their backs to each other, each with their wands at the ready. Calmly, Laszlo told Mike and his father to slowly back away from the werewolf behind them and make their way to the centre of the ring they had formed. Without hesitation, the two did as was suggested as Alexander spoke quietly to Mike.

"Don't make eye contact, just walk ahead of me and keep your eyes down."

Mike, whose heartbeat hadn't returned yet, bent his head down and spoke quietly out of the side of his mouth.

"Apa...?"

Alexander placed his hand on Mike's shoulder.

"It's OK, Michael, I am scared too."

Mike placed his hand over his father's and didn't let go until they were with the others. Only seconds had passed since the first werewolf appeared and yet it seemed like hours. Everything was moving in slow motion and then one of *them* spoke, causing Mike and Elizabeth to jump.

"What do we have *here*?" one hissed.

"Smells like a pack of pathetic wizards to me," hissed the other.

They then made a sound that Mike could only assume was laughter, but coming from them it sounded like maniacal barking, a lot like hyenas would sound, but with deeper voices.

"Looks like they're lost, too," the bigger one hissed, smirking.

He stepped forwards, causing the huddled group to step back. It was obvious to them that their huge adversary was enjoying the intimidation, a thought that turned Mike's stomach. He was so scared at this point that he wasn't sure if he was even breathing. He already knew that his heart had stopped beating a few minutes ago.

The werewolf who was addressing them spoke again, only this time he wasn't mocking them, he was angry.

"What is your business here? To what do we owe the pleasure of *your kind* here?" he demanded, emphasising *your kind* with disgust.

Wow! Mike thought to himself. Elizabeth wasn't kidding; they really don't like *our kind*. Alexander stepped forwards first. Immediately the werewolf lunged at him with a fierce growl in an attempt to put him back in his place. To Mike's amazement, his father didn't even flinch, in fact he took another step closer and spoke.

"Our business is our own. Our journey is time-sensitive and this is an unnecessary delay. We are unarmed; we are no threat to you or the forest," he said.

Everyone was holding their breath in anticipation of the werewolf's reply. He simply stared them all down, holding a continuous low growl. Mike could feel Arpi shaking next to him. He looked over at him and thought that he resembled a ticking time bomb that was ready to go off at any moment. The way he held his wand reminded Mike of a loaded gun in a small child's hands—unpredictable! Mike reached his hand out and lowered Arpi's wand, shaking his head in disagreement. Arpi lowered it a bit, but the look in his eyes never changed. Mike was sure that the werewolf had caught their exchange because he suddenly looked right at Mike and sniffed the air.

"No threat, huh?"

He growled at Alexander as he drew closer to Mike, continuously sniffing like a dog that's caught the scent of its prey in the air. He came right up to Mike and Arpi, bent his huge body down and, bringing his nose directly in front of Arpi's face, sniffed and growled.

"Your friend is right; put the wand away before you hurt yourself."

The chorus of hideous laughter that followed his comment sounded distinctly as though there were more than two. Mike and the others looked around them and realised that two more werewolves had come up to join them.

"Great!" Mike groaned under his breath.

The large werewolf turned his attention from Arpi to Mike and laughed in his face, causing Mike to stumble backwards, landing on his rear. This sent another chorus of laughter through the air. Alexander ran to Mike's aid, but before he could reach his hand out to help him up, the werewolf's hand came up and planted itself firmly on Alexander's chest, stopping him in his tracks.

"This one's interesting; he doesn't carry the same stench as the rest of you!" he said, spitting out the last words in disgust.

Everyone who had a wand drew it; Elizabeth's and Laszlo's were pointed at the werewolf standing over Mike; Arpi's and Zsolt's were pointed at two others. The pack growled in reply. This is getting out of hand quickly, Mike thought to himself. He couldn't fathom the outcome, but he was sure that it wouldn't be pretty, most likely someone would get hurt and he definitely couldn't let that happen! *How exactly do I do that?* he thought. His only real skill was wrestling, he had no wand and even if he did, his magic was still in its early stages. First things first; he looked over at his father.

"It's OK, I'm OK."

With as much confidence as he could fake, he jumped up, brushed himself off to give himself a moment to regain his composure, then took a bold step towards the wretched creature in front of him. As best he could he looked him straight in the eye, which wasn't difficult as the werewolf had already lowered himself to Mike's level. Mike could feel the heat of the creature's breath on his face, the smell so bad it was stinging his eyes. Wow! It was going to be hard not to comment on that! After wiping his eyes, he held his hands open, raising his arms up to either side of his shoulders.

"No wand, no threat, absolutely nothing interesting about me or our business here," he said.

Mike stood his ground as the werewolf, who was staring so intently at him that his head began to hurt, spoke.

"I think that we can all agree that you *look* pathetic…"

Another round of hideous laughter.

"Yet…your smell…it's interesting…"

The werewolf put his nose right up to Mike's neck and sniffed slowly. Mike was frozen to the spot. He was so repulsed by this that every part of his being wanted to throw the creature as far from him as wizardly possible! He was sure the werewolf knew it too. What was so interesting about *his* smell anyway? *Seriously?* To his surprise, the wretched creature pulled away from him.

"*Ash!*" he shouted. "He smells of *ash!*"

He stumbled backwards away from Mike as though he couldn't get away from him fast enough. The other three backed away too, muttering and scanning the sky in panic.

"What kind of devilry is this!?" the big one barked at Mike, still moving farther away.

Finding their behaviour and comments odd, Mike turned his head towards his shoulder and sniffed.

"*Ash?*" he enquired, turning to the others. "I don't smell of ash."

None of them knew what to say and just shrugged their shoulders in response. Whatever the significance of ash was to the werewolves, they were all just relieved that the smell of it was working to their advantage.

"Alexander, Mike, Elizabeth, go ahead of us...*run!*" Laszlo shouted.

He was the first to take advantage of the werewolves' strange distraction. Knowing that neither Alexander nor Mike had wands, they were the likely choice to continue on.

"Alexander, you can find eet. You vill remember where it is. You must get dere before da moon eez too high! Go, *now!*"

Wasting no time, Alexander grabbed Mike and Elizabeth by their arms and pulled them with him. Surprisingly, they made it through two of the smaller werewolves without any difficulty; they were still frantically scanning the sky. They hadn't gone too far when they heard the first spell being cast, then a loud yelp from one of the werewolves, then another spell and yelp. The sounds were so much more powerful and violent than Mike had ever imagined they would be. He glanced back; the forest was lit up with bursts of blue, green and yellow every time a spell was cast. He could still hear the yelping and shouting from both parties. Mesmerized by it all, he stopped, watched and listened, trying to make sense of what was happening. He bent down, resting his hands on his knees, trying to catch his breath, but it was so loud in his head he held his breath for a moment, closed his eyes and listened carefully.

"Michael! What are you doing?" His father had noticed that Mike had stopped, so he turned on the spot and ran back to his son. "Why have you stopped? Are you hurt? What happened?"

"Dad…?" Not opening his eyes or moving from where he was he put his hand up to stop the questions. 'I'm all right. Nothing's wrong…except…we aren't over there helping!" He was standing now and gestured violently with his arm, pointing to where the two parties were battling it out. "Why are we running? We should be helping!"

Alexander placed his hands on his son's shoulders, and looking towards the ground and, shaking his head, let out a big sigh.

"Michael…," He raised his head and looked his son in the eyes. "I know you want to help. So do I, but without wands we would be of no use. Werewolves are extremely powerful creatures."

"*Exactly!*" Mike shouted in exasperation. "All the more reason why we should be helping! Just because we don't have wands doesn't mean we aren't wizards! There must be something we can do!"

"I want to help too, Michael, but there's more to it than that. Someone has to make it to the cabin before the moon is too high, otherwise we won't find it. Without the cabin we cannot find the dwarves. Today is our only chance, otherwise our journey will have been fruitless!" Alexander sighed heavily again. "Do you understand, Michael?"

Mike could see that his father was completely spent.

"Yeah…I get it. It's just…."

"I know, son," Alexander interrupted, "I'm scared too." He pulled Mike in for a fatherly hug. "Try not to worry; Laszlo and Zsolt know what they are doing. They are powerful wiz…."

"Apa?" Mike backed away to look at his father, but his father pulled him back again and began to smell his hair! "Apa! What the…?" Mike was struggling to back away, but his father's grip was still stronger than his. "*What are you doing?*" he shouted as he continued to struggle.

Without any warning, his father stepped back and let go, sending Mike flying backwards. For the second time that evening, he stood up and brushed the dirt and leaves from his trousers. Trying not to sound as angry and humiliated as he was, he spoke very carefully.

"Apa…w-what was *that*?" he asked, pointing to his hair on the last word.

Alexander answered, not really speaking to Mike directly. "You smell like ash…."

"*What?*" Mike exclaimed.

"You smell like ash," his father repeated courteously, then he started to pace, one hand supporting his forehead in deep concentration, muttering to himself. "I know that smell. I know that smell, but from where?"

The fighting was getting worse. Mike looked from his father to where the trees were alight with flashes of colour, then back to him, sure that he had lapsed into temporary insanity.

"*Apa!* Now is not the time for reminiscing! Things are getting really bad over there!"

Ignoring his son, Alexander continued pacing, muttering to himself.

Mike shouted one more time in frustration. No reply.

"Mike, what are you two doing?" a very breathless and highly annoyed Elizabeth asked.

"*What...?*"

Mike spun around to see Elizabeth standing there, bent over trying to catch her breath and glaring at them like they had lost their minds. Straightening up she stomped towards him and asked again, equally as annoyed as the first time.

"What are you two doing here? You just left me! Mike, we don't have much time! Now, let's go!"

"I can't," Mike replied.

"*What?*" she screamed through clenched teeth, smacking him in the arm as she spoke.

All Mike could do was point at his father, who was still pacing, muttering and holding his head. Elizabeth looked at her uncle, lingered for a moment to take it in and then stared back at Mike mouthing, *what the?*

"I have no idea," Mike replied, rubbing his forehead. "He says I smell like ash and now I can't get him to move. He just keeps pacing and muttering to himself."

"*Ash? Seriously?*" she yelled, clearly unimpressed. She looked at Mike pleading, "Mike, we've got to go! We have to get out of here, *now!*"

He looked her straight in the eyes, with equal pleading.

"I know him. When he gets like this, there's nothing I can do to change it. He's like a dog with a bone; he won't let go for anything! Either we go on without him or I stay here and you carry on without us."

"What? *No!*" she exclaimed. "Look, Mike, I don't think you understand how important this is! We won't get this chance again for a very long time! My dad, *your uncle*, has sacrificed everything to get us this far! We can't stop now! I'm sorry; we just don't have time to wait. There must be something you can do?"

"Believe me, *I know* how frustrating this is!" He was feeling defensive now. "I know what needs to be done, but I am telling you that my father wouldn't be doing this unless it was something important! I'm not leaving him!"

Mike pulled himself up to his full height and glared down at Elizabeth. She had nothing to say, which was remarkable for her. Feeling defeated and speechless, two feelings she wasn't familiar with, she mumbled 'Fine!" and turned to walk away. She had only taken a few steps when she turned back and gave one final plea.

"Mike, *pllleeeaaassseee!*"

He couldn't help but be amused. Pleading did not come naturally to her and here she was trying her very best. Quickly wiping the smile off his face he turned to face her.

"You know I can't."

His sympathy was sincere and she knew it too. Mike sensed that her humility wouldn't last long and the fight was sure to get out of hand soon if something wasn't done. He looked over at his father, still pacing and muttering, and noticed that the fight between the werewolves and his relatives had become more deadly. It looked as if the treeline was on fire, there were so many spells being cast, making Mike's anxiety return.

"Apa, please don't worry about what I smell like, we really have to go! Why is it so important anyway?"

His father stopped pacing and looked up at him.

"I don't know, but I do know that it is important," he said, returning to his pacing.

Elizabeth's moment of humility ended abruptly.

"*Aargh!* Why do you have to be so difficult? I can't go ahead without you and your father. *My* father would kill me!"

The sound of Elizabeth's voice actually tore through his ears and caused a piercing pain in his head. It was worse than hearing nails scratching down a chalkboard. Between his father mumbling on about ash, her stubbornness and the very real threat of a gruesome death at the hands of creatures that had only existed in fairy tales up until a few hours ago, he was sure that this was the closest he had ever come to insanity—and her voice was the last straw. Mike wanted to scream until he couldn't scream anymore.

Instead he took a deep breath and tried one more time. "Elizabeth, *please!*" he shouted as he turned to face her. "You're so stubborn! Just let it g—" he cut his last word short.

With her arm stretched out in front of her, wand in hand, Elizabeth was pointing directly at Mike and advancing quickly.

"What the…? What is your problem?" Mike yelled at her, his hands held up in defense, backing away from her—this was too much, she had gone too far.

"*Mike…!*" she yelled, still advancing.

"*Elizabeth!*" he yelled back, interrupting her. He was really mad now. Walking towards her with equal vigour, he threw his hands up in exasperation and repeated, "What is your problem? Put the wand d—!"

She didn't let him finish his sentence, lifting her wand higher and shouting.

"Mike! *Down!*"

Without hesitation, Elizabeth cast her spell and everything happened simultaneously and so quickly. Mike dove out of the way just in time and could feel the heat of the spell burn his cheek as the bolt of energy whizzed past his face. In mid-dive Mike searched frantically for his father, hoping he was out of harm's way. What he actually saw didn't register until a few moments later—his father was searching the sky shouting happily.

"*Dragon*! Michael, you smell like a *dragon*! Michael…?"

Just then his father must have seen what had transpired with Elizabeth and he ran towards his son shouting his name frantically, shouting for Mike to get down. Like a cougar going in for the kill, his father suddenly crouched down and sprang towards Mike with a power he did not know his father possessed. Mike braced himself for the impact of his father landing on him, but it never happened, instead he sailed clear over him. Mike, watching him in awe, craning his neck up and over to see where he would land, suddenly understood that neither Elizabeth's spell nor his father's giant leap were intended for him. There, only a couple of feet behind him were two werewolves, one dead with smoke rising out of what used to be its chest and the other pinned face down into the ground by Mike's father, but *not* dead—not dead!

"*Apa!*" Mike shrieked, jumping towards his father to help.

He spotted two more running towards them at full speed. He realized how quickly everything was getting out of control, when a blast like a building exploding sounded behind him. The power of the blast sent him, his father and the werewolf his father had pinned down, hurtling through the air. The three of them landed hard on the ground several feet away, before rolling to a stop. Mike heard the distinct crunching of bones breaking, followed by a sensation of heat, then a searing pain through his left thigh. He had landed on something that he was sure was the werewolf, which was writhing in pain beneath him. His eyes, blurred by the pain in his leg, scanned the surrounding area for his father and the source of the blast. He located him and relief flooded his body when he then saw his father coming towards him, appearing to be unhurt.

Mike heard a pain-filled cry from under him, followed by the tearing of flesh, *his flesh*! He cried out in pain as the werewolf lashed out at him, nearly severing his arm with its claws. Adrenaline coursed through his body at a rate he was sure should stop his heart, but he turned on the werewolf, letting the searing pain of every movement fuel his actions. In an instant he had turned himself over, pinned down the weakened werewolf's arms with both legs, taken a firm grip of the creature's head and, in one violent jerk, twisted until he felt the sickening snap of its neck vibrating in his hands.

He slid limply off the dead body, his own body still working off the adrenaline, oblivious to his broken leg and shredded arm. Lying on his side, he began to wretch violently. By now his father had reached Mike, lifted him under his arms and dragged him away from the two dead wolves. He gently lay him down in between a row of nearby shrubs. Placing his hands on his son's chest he ordered him not to move and told him that everything was going to be okay as his dragon was there—then he had gone.

Mike lay there, stunned. His ears were ringing, his heart still pounding so hard his chest hurt, listening. All he could hear was chaos, and he tried hard to focus in on voices, his father's voice especially. The ringing in his ears, probably from the blast, made it difficult, but in the distance he could hear Elizabeth screaming. It didn't sound as if she was in pain though, more like commands. Good, she's all right, he thought. Laszlo was shouting what Mike thought were spells because each shout was followed by a bang, like a gunshot. Good, he's all right. He desperately continued trying to hear his father. Where was he? Why can't I hear him?

Without warning, there was another blast, farther away this time, but violent enough that the ground beneath him shook and rumbled so hard it pushed Mike over and into the bush beside him. He cried out—the pain in his leg was blinding. He swayed in and out of consciousness, trying desperately not to pass out. He knew that passing out would bring relief, but he still hadn't homed in on his father's voice in the chaos and he was afraid that another blast might come and finish him for good. Finding enough strength to turn his head to the side, he began retching violently again, not even caring that he could feel the warm liquid seeping down his neck and soaking the ground beneath his shoulders. Gasping for air between bouts of vomiting, he felt the distinct burning of smoke every time he inhaled. He registered that something was on fire, but what and how close? He listened intently for the sound of crackling nearby and felt for the heat that a fire would bring if it were close—nothing. Very carefully and making all attempts not to pass out or vomit, he propped himself up a little on his good arm and craned his neck to see something, any sign at all of where the smoke was originating. Mike had barely lifted his head when he heard it—the voice for which he had been searching.

"*Anaroth!*" his father was yelling.

The way he was shouting let Mike know that he wasn't hurt or in danger, in fact he sounded happy, really happy, the kind of happy you express when you run into someone you haven't seen in years! Worry filled Mike instantly. *He's lost it! Who do you suddenly run into in the middle of a wizard-werewolf bloodbath, in a secluded part of a forest in the desolate Carpathian Mountains, who would make you so happy?*

The thought of his father alone in the chaos, having gone slightly mad, was all Mike needed to decide that he had to get up and get to him. Magic would be the easy solution, but he hadn't learnt much and still no wand. Feeling helpless and a little sorrier for himself than he would admit later, he screamed out in frustration. Tearing as much grass as he could with his hands he flung it at the trees looming over him. The result was pitiful at best; nothing but the dry grass falling back into his face. If he just had something to lean on or to pull himself up with, he would try to get to his father. He searched his immediate area as far as he could reach, but found nothing, so figuring he would not be found, he decided to do the only thing he could.

"*Apa! Apa!*" he yelled, "*Come back! Please come back!*"

As he had figured, there was no reply, not from his father or anyone else. The anger in him heightened to an uncontrollable level. There was nothing for it; he simply let the words fly from his mouth like a bullet from a gun.

"*Apa! Get back here, now! I can't see you and I can't get up to come and get you! Leave the stupid fight and the stupid werewolves and stop calling out stupid names of stupid people who aren't in this stupid place!*"

Expending every last bit of air in him, he slumped his head into the ground. Just then a powerful wind passed through the trees above, causing them to bend to the point where Mike was sure they'd snap. The wind subsided as fast as it had arrived and the trees swayed gently back to their upright positions. Mike had instinctively crossed his arms over his face, and was slowly moving them away when it came again. First there was a loud *swoosh* and then came the wind. Like a storm it whipped through the trees, bending them beyond what Mike was sure they could bear, but again, nothing but a shower of leaves fell to the forest floor. So confused as to what was happening, Mike continued to keep his arms crossed over his face while he tried to figure out this latest development.

Two more times the wind passed through the trees above Mike and then he figured it out—something, something very large, was flying over him! Just thinking it made him feel stupid, because it was just so unbelievable, but then, so was everything else that had happened today. What was it his father had said to him a few moments ago? He lay there wondering, staring up through the branches where he could see the dark sky and a few scattered stars. He knew darn well what he had said; he was just having difficulty accepting it. Let's not kid ourselves; when someone says everything will be okay because his dragon is here, you need to question the validity of the statement. Deep down, Mike knew what he had heard was right, and even if his father hadn't told him, he knew with every fibre of his being that a dragon was exactly what was flying over the trees!

It wasn't that his father had said *his dragon* that told Mike that this dragon was on their side, it was his heart and mind that had. He felt connected to it. A familiar feeling began to take hold of him. His dreams! It was just like his dreams! They always felt so real and this felt so much like them! His dream world and this current reality were colliding and becoming one within him! Overjoyed at this sudden turn of events, he shouted out:

"*Apa, I get it!* The ash, the dragon...*I get it!*" Fuelled by this new knowledge, he decided it was time to try and get back out there. He couldn't believe the relief he felt at knowing that there was a dragon flying overhead! "This is seriously messed up!" he mumbled to himself.

Once more he felt around in the bushes and grass nearby for something to help get him back onto his feet, but he couldn't stop the smile that was slowly spreading across his face. He was close to losing his patience with the useless shrubbery around him, when he felt another strong gust of wind pass through the trees, but this time there was no dragon—he knew he would sense it if there were. The wind was forcing the trees to the point of cracking then...they split, directly above Mike. He barely had time to prepare for falling debris, or worse still, an entire tree, when, one after another, two branches fell and hit him on the head.

"*Seriously!*" he yelled at the trees, the wind, anyone who would listen. "You have the entire forest floor to fall on and you land directly on my head!" he added, throwing one arm up in frustration. He sat staring up at the canopy, which had stopped moving as if waiting for an answer. Naturally there was no reply, but a strange and highly unlikely thought came to him. "Wait a second…they had the *whole* forest floor and they landed *right on me!*" he repeated to himself, out loud.

Mike reached for the two branches that had landed on him and put them on his lap. *I can't believe it! Of course, why not, right? I mean where else could this happen?*

He held the two branches up with his good arm, laughing in amazement; both were exactly the same long length, both were perfectly straight and ended at the top in the shape of a 'Y', and right where you'd expect to be able to place your hands for support was, of course, a small stump of a branch. Like home-made crutches! There was no need to double check the length; something told him that they were the perfect fit.

Slowly, painfully, he moved himself up onto one knee, being careful to keep his other leg lying straight back, then, grabbing both crutches, he placed one into each arm pit, gripped the smaller stump for support, took a deep breath and attempted to pull himself up. Shooting pain coursed through his body from the wound in his arm. He didn't have the strength to get all the way up and felt himself falling backwards. Instinctively he held onto the crutches, much like you would grab a railing if you had slipped on a flight of stairs, but he knew it was in vain; the crutches weren't stationary. Preparing for more searing pain, once again he yelled out, but the dramatic moment passed and he realised that the crutches never moved! He gripped one and shook it hard—nothing, not a single movement. It was as solid as a tree!

"OK, I get it, you're magical. Let's see what else you can do." Not knowing the proper incantation he blurted out, "*Lift me u—*"

Without letting him finish, both branches began to grow, slowly lifting Mike to the standing position. As with just about everything these days, he stood amazed for just a moment, trying to take in the wonder and absurdity of what had just happened.

"Telepathic crutches, cool," he mumbled, smiling to himself.

Feeling bold once again, he took his first step forwards and the shooting pain from his injured arm told him that he wasn't going anywhere no matter how magical the crutches. I wonder if I can telepathically conjure up bandages and some morphine, he joked to himself, trying to ignore the feeling of wanting to pass out. No sooner had he spoken the words than a vine began to spiral its way up the branch and over his arm. Mike watched in amazement, wondering if this was a good or bad thing. When the vine reached the gashes in Mike's arm, thick, broad rubbery leaves began to grow and place themselves directly onto the wounds. Once the injured area was covered, the leaves began to wilt and as they did so they secreted a syrupy substance that on contact gave relief and cooled the skin. Mike was so relieved that he watched in pure fascination the remainder of the vines working.

Once the secreting had ended, the wilted leaves clung to his skin like a Band-Aid and gently shrunk, pulling the gaping cuts closed. Mike reached with his other hand and touched the leaves once they had stopped shrinking and pulling. He was amazed; they felt like skin and the pain was almost non-existent. At this point the vine shrivelled and fell away from his arm and crutch, leaving just the leaves behind.

Not knowing whether he was responsible for everything that had happened or someone else, he decided to say thank you out loud anyway.

"*Thank you!*"

A gentle breeze blew past his ear and as soft as a whisper he heard:

"You're welcome."

Cabin in the Woods

With the aid of his "magic crutches," Mike made it to the clearing faster than he could have dreamed. Time passed by in a flash, and he felt completely removed from the scene before him, watching as if from afar. Bursts of light from spells being cast revealed moments of chaos scattered across the field. It was hard to tell where anyone was or how close. Small fires were burning everywhere and Mike could see patches of trees ablaze on the opposite side of the clearing. He tried listening for Elizabeth first—it was doubtful that she could be silent at any time. A brief moment passed as he concentrated on her voice. He did hear her briefly, but then it was drowned out by the cries and howls from the werewolves as a huge shadow covered the moonlit sky.

But this time he had no hesitation or fear of what this meant. Mike watched in awe as an enormous dragon swooped down on the werewolves. The creature drew in a deep breath, making the werewolves wild with fear. Mike heard his father and Elizabeth cheering and then complete silence, like the calm before a storm, then the roar of fire as the dragon breathed out, cutting a swath through the field right up to the werewolves, who were running for their lives and howling in terror.

Mike let out a whoop as the dragon flew by, the blazing trail it left behind lighting up the entire area. He scanned the clearing quickly and soon spotted his father, Laszlo and

Elizabeth, who all seemed none the worse for wear. Farther off to his right he spotted a crouching figure. By its size it looked like his Uncle Zsolt. Mike's heart sank as he realised there was another body lying on the ground beside him— it could only be Arpi. Mike attempted an awkward run towards his uncle, shouting his name.

"*Zsolt, Zsolt!*"

"Come! Help me! Quvick! He's been bitten!"

Laszlo made it to him first as he was the closest. By the time the others had reached them, Laszlo and Zsolt had Arpi propped up between them. Elizabeth was the first to react, letting out what sounded like a gasp mixed with choking sobs as she began to cry.

"Oh Arpi, what have they done?"

It looked to Mike as though Arpi had been bitten in the neck and blood was pouring out all down his left side. He felt sick to his stomach.

"W-what did they…? Is he…? Is he g-going to be OK?" Mike stammered, barely wanting to hear the answer for fear of what it might be.

Laszlo and Zsolt seemed to be oblivious to the questions as they carried Arpi straight to Mike's father.

"Alexander, please…tell me…how bad is it?" Zsolt choked out the question, desperation in his voice.

Mike could feel his eyes watering up and was thankful for the dark. Everyone, except Elizabeth, who was crying as quietly as she could, watched in silence as Alexander carefully observed the wound, which Mike could now see was a bite to Arpi's left shoulder. He watched in awe as his father gently spoke to Arpi, keeping him calm as he felt around the wound. Mike remembered back to the times when he had injured himself and how he had insisted that his father care for him, not a doctor. He had healing hands and such clarity and calm in those moments that sometimes Mike had even wished they'd last longer.

Alexander was now asking Arpi several questions that Mike didn't understand. It would be later that he would begin to make sense of them.

"Look into the moon," Alexander said. "Do you have a burning sensation in your eyes? What do we smell like? Is my heart beating fast or slow?"

Most of Arpi's answers came in moans and he was slowly taking on a zombie-like look, with pale skin and colourless eyes. This alarmed Mike and apparently everyone else. Alexander stood up suddenly.

"He's turning! You have to get him home now! Go to Sandor Bacsi in the village. Tell him what's happened. He can help him!"

"I'll never get him home fast enough!" cried Zsolt.

"The marbles, Mike, *give them the marbles!*" Elizabeth piped up suddenly. "Apa! Mike has the marbles you gave him. He won't be able to control his destination even if he comes to, right?" she shrieked.

"Yes, yes, Elizabeth eez right! But vee can!" Zsolt said.

Laszlo turned to Mike, who was already rummaging through his pockets to retrieve the marbles, and his uncle nearly dropped them in his haste to grab them away from Mike. Flustered, he shoved the marbles into Zsolt's hand. "Go! *Now!* Sandor Basci!"

Zsolt popped one into his mouth while simultaneously shoving one into Arpi's and then, in the blink of an eye, they were gone.

Elizabeth immediately turned to Alexander. "He will be OK, won't he?" she asked desperately.

Alexander placed his hand on Elizabeth's shoulders and spoke gently.

"I know how awful it looked...." He turned and looked at Mike, placing a reassuring hand on his shoulder as well, drawing him closer. "He is going to be all right. We are very fortunate that you had the pearls with you, Michael, thank you...and how clever it was of you to remember them and their use, Elizabeth. Those pearls will very likely save Arpi's life."

"Apa always says you are the greatest wizard he's ever known!" Elizabeth exclaimed, nearly knocking her uncle over as she flung her arms around him.

Mike and Laszlo laughed along with Alexander as he tried to steady himself from this unexpected display of emotion. Realizing they were all having a chuckle at her expense, Elizabeth pulled away slightly embarrassed.

"Well, it *is* what you've always said," she mumbled, looking at her father.

"Eet eez true. I have always thought eet and said eet, and I still do," he said, chuckling and slapping Alexander on the shoulder. He looked at his cousin and became serious. "Vee vill get you fixed up, I promise. Dat's vy vee are here." He glanced at the moon. "By da looks of da moon, vee are running short on time and had better get moving!"

The eerie cries of the werewolves filled the air, causing the hairs on Mike's neck to bristle.

"Blast dose wretched volves!" Laszlo shouted. "Let's move!"

Exactly at the same moment, Alexander remembered Mike's injuries and Elizabeth noticed them for the first time.

"Oh my…Mike! What happened to you?"

"Laszlo, *wait!*" Alexander shouted. "Michael is hurt, he can't…." His father turned and looked at him. "Michael, you were so badly hurt…how did you…? Wait, what's this?" He gently touched the leaf wrappings on his son's arm and the vines that were securing his leg. "Michael, how did… *you* do this?" he asked, fascinated.

"I didn't—"

"Your mother…she knew this kind of…," his voice trailed off.

"Knew this kind of *what*, Apa?" Mike asked, desperately wanting to know the answer. His father so rarely spoke of his mother, but Alexander just continued to stare at nature's handiwork.

"*Apa!*" Mike was demanding his father's attention. "Mom knew this kind of *what*?"

Not taking his gaze from Mike's arm, his father replied… "*Magic.*"

∽

The cries of the werewolves were getting closer.

"*Dammit!*" Mike cursed, looking in the direction of the howls. He wanted so badly to know more about his mother, but knew that now was not the time. "Apa, *I* didn't do this. The branches dropped out of the sky, they're magical too, and then I wished for my wounds to be cared for and suddenly vines started creeping up my leg and arm. It all happened without me doing anything."

"It doesn't make sense," Alexander said, shooting a questioning gaze at Laszlo, who shook his head in agreement just as Elizabeth pulled at his arm in a panic.

"Apa! I think we had better try to figure this out later. *Look!*"

Everyone turned to look at where she was pointing. A pack of five werewolves were running towards them at full speed!

"*Ragados Halo!*" Laszlo shouted, pointing his wand directly at the advancing pack.

Just then a sticky, web-like substance appeared and clung to the trees and ground surrounding the pack, trapping them. It seemed to Mike that every movement they made only ensnared them further.

"Nice," Mike whispered, exhaling, making a mental note to learn that spell as soon as he had a wand.

"*Dis vay!*" Laszlo shouted, waving his hand towards the treeline ahead and reaching out to help Mike. "Come, Mike...." He took one arm and placed it around his shoulder, motioning for Alexander to take him by the other arm and hastened awkwardly toward the treeline.

"Wait...the crutches—I can use...." but he was cut short by his uncle.

"This is faster!" he said absently, pulling Mike forward, scanning the forest.

They had only been running for a few minutes when they heard the werewolves behind them again, but they continued to push on, Laszlo and Elizabeth throwing spells in the path of their pursuers.

⌀⟋⟍⟍⟋

Twenty or so minutes had passed and the deeper they travelled into the forest the more difficult it became for the three of them to negotiate the terrain. Trees grew close together, the forest floor was covered with fallen debris and the path ahead seemed to be getting steeper and steeper, or so it felt to Mike, whose wounds were burning fiercely again. He could feel the wolves gaining on them and he didn't want to admit that he was hurting.

"Michael, you need to stop!" his father exclaimed, noticing the grim expression on his son's face. "Laszlo, he needs to rest!"

"Just a little furzser, Michael? Vee are close," Laszlo said, stopping and calling back to him.

As desperately as Mike wanted to stop, he wanted to get away from the werewolves more. "No—I'm fine...really," he said as convincingly as possible. The thought that Elizabeth might confide in Hanna and share this moment of bravery with her fuelled his resolve to press on.

The werewolves had split their group, making it more difficult for the four of them to defend themselves. It also was hard to keep track of where or how close they were. Laszlo had said they were nearby, but how near *are* they, Mike wondered, and where had the dragon gone? Mike had sensed its presence so strongly before and now there was nothing. Maybe his focus on the pain was lessening his ability to feel the dragon, which bothered him more than he could understand at that moment.

"Are we lost?" he blurted out, not wanting it to sound as rude as it probably did. "I think they are gaining on us...."

They *were*.

"No, vee are not lost," Laszlo said, but he didn't sound convincing. "Eet *must* be here," he added, more to himself than anyone else, and it sounded more like a question.

Laszlo and Alexander studied the map closely, mumbling to each other. Elizabeth stood close to Mike, watching for any sign of the wolves. Mike mused to himself, watching his uncle and father poring over the map, turning it this way and that, from this angle to that angle.

"I guess the magical world and its artifacts have yet to be loaded into Google Earth," he quipped.

Elizabeth, who had heard Mike's comment, couldn't help but laugh a little, and Mike gave her a smile.

"I feel pretty useless right now; isn't there anything I can do to help them?" he asked.

"Hey, you're not fooling me; I know you don't want your father to notice, but I can see that you're in a lot of pain. We need to get you to the cabin. I never imagined the werewolves would be this awful!" she replied grimly.

"What good will it do to get to the cabin right now?" Mike asked. "They'd still be able to get in. I'm sure the front door would snap like a twig with their strength! We need a better hiding place, one where they can't smell us!" he suggested, his irritation rising as the pain in his arm and leg escalated.

"Mike, you're *brilliant!*" she squealed, carefully throwing her arms around him, but still making him wince.

"*What?*"

Elizabeth was already running towards her father and Alexander.

"Apa...I can buy you some time, not much, but some. Mike had a great idea, but I need your help!" She grabbed him by the arm and didn't allow him to reply, pulling him several paces away from where they were standing before she explained herself. "We need to isolate our smell from the wolves. They'll always know where we are, even if they don't see us, right? We must create a shield around ourselves and somehow throw off their scent, make them believe we are somewhere else."

Elizabeth was practically vibrating, she was so excited. Laszlo smiled down at his daughter, understanding what needed to be done. Mike's father, who had come to stand next to him while Elizabeth explained her plan, turned to look at his son.

"Your shirt, Mike…we need your shirt."

Mike began to rip his shirt away from the arm that was wounded, his father helping him, as it was difficult and painful to do alone. Alexander held the shirt up and searched for the perfect branch to hang it on, and as he did so Mike could hear him mumbling to himself. "Yes…yes, the shirt will work just fine."

Finally he found the branch he was looking for, hung the torn and bloody shirt over it, jogged back to Mike, grabbed him gently by his good arm and said, "Now, let's get you away from here."

They hobbled their way over to Laszlo and Elizabeth, who had been preparing the spell for the shields. Once there, Alexander stood Mike beside Laszlo and he stood next to Elizabeth. Simultaneously, Laszlo and his daughter chanted the spell as they swirled their wands around them-selves and their respective partners.

"*Pajzs Test!*" they spoke together.

"Michael, you must stay close to me or the shield will not hold. Ready, let's all move together."

As quickly as they all could, they made their way deeper into the trees, making sure to tread quietly, for the shield did not protect them from sight. They found a heavily wooded area where the ground was level and clumps of low-growing, thick bushes, covered in bright red berries, were available to hide behind everywhere. Taking advantage of the perfect terrain for concealment they ducked down behind one of the bushes.

No sooner had they caught their breath than they heard the unmistakable howl of a werewolf, now scorned by his enemy's cunning! That was by far the worst sound Mike had ever heard, making every inch of his skin crawl, and he was sure he heard a small whimper from Elizabeth. They sat as still and as quietly as they could, all the while listening, trying to determine the whereabouts of the werewolves during their search. They are *definitely* thorough, he thought.

It seemed to Mike that they had sat there for at least an hour. He didn't want to ask, for fear of giving away their whereabouts, but had their moment of opportunity slipped away? His uncle had watched the moon almost the entire time and he was sure he had heard him swear under his breath at one point. Just when he thought he couldn't take it anymore, Laszlo urged them all to get up; it was time to make a move. They got up slowly and, making sure to stay close to one another, followed Laszlo as he continued on.

༄

Just then the dragon bore down on the wolves, coming in like a crashing plane. As he passed over the wolves, he rained down fire on them, scorching them and everything else in its path. The travellers covered their ears and turned away as the wolves burned, crying out in agony. Mike had been wrong earlier—*this* was the worst thing he had ever heard or seen. It was enough to make him retch, and retch he did, Elizabeth too.

It was finally over and all that was left behind was a solid path of black at least fifty metres long. Nothing, not a single thing was left to see, except the sickening sight of charred werewolves, burned to death where they stood, like statues carved of charcoal. There was nothing they could do, not one of them, except stand and stare at the horror before them.

Mike felt it again, that pulling feeling on his soul—the dragon was returning! He might have been excited about it before, but now he was scared.

Why would he come back? he thought. The werewolves were all dead as far as Mike could tell. Had some escaped and lived? He didn't think anything could have escaped, and even if they had, they wouldn't be dumb enough to come back, would they? What *was* it then? Forcing himself to think rationally, he realized this may be like the "double tap" rule of the dragon code of killing—always scorch a second time, just in case!

There was no more time to think about it, for Mike could see the dragon coming in again, bearing down just like he had before. Only this time, he was bearing down on *them*, or so it seemed, but Mike was sure he would feel it if the great beast's intentions were ill towards them. Not taking any chances, they all ran for cover as they heard the telltale drawing in of breath before the rain of fire.

Mike and his father were crouched down at the base of a huge tree, his father's arms wrapped around him as if protecting him from an imminent and inescapable explosion. Everything about this situation screamed "doom," but Mike felt no fear and he was sure his father didn't either. They were both incredibly calm. Maybe calm is what you feel when you know death is imminent, Mike wondered to himself.

The time for wondering was over, the rain of fire began. Mike shut his eyes tightly. *This is just like my recurring dream!*

He didn't want to see what would happen next...he would feel it soon enough, he thought. He just prayed it would be fast. He waited, clutching his father with all his might....

Nothing....

Wait...a little heat, but it felt nice against his skin; it took the chill away. That's all. So, was it over? Was he dead? If he was, he was still holding on to his father. That was good. Images of the charcoaled bodies of the werewolves came to mind and his stomach turned. Fearing that it might be true, and without opening his eyes to confirm it, he pressed against his father's back with his hands, searching for anything that felt normal and not burned. The wonderful texture of his jacket was all he felt. Somewhat relieved, he decided to open his eyes to confirm it as the truth. He opened them slowly, one at a time, and relief flooded every part of his body!

We aren't dead—far from it! And, oh wow...

"Apa! Laszlo! Elizabeth!" He shook his father. "Look! I see it!"

He was pointing ahead down the path of flames laid by the dragon, and at the end of the path, there it was, encircled with flames, as if a picture frame of fire had been placed around it—the cabin.

Fireproof

"The dragon…he wasn't trying to kill us…he was helping us! I *knew it!*" Mike exclaimed.

He was so happy he wanted to jump, but instead managed a slightly awkward hop on his good leg, which nearly sent him face-first into the ground had it not been for his father's steadying grip.

"Easy, Michael, let's get you to the cabin without any further injuries," he said, relieved.

Looking over at Laszlo and Elizabeth, who were on the opposite side of the "charcoal path," Mike saw relief on their faces too.

The walk to the cabin was short and the burnt path made it easier for Mike to walk. They managed to make it there just as the frame of fire died out. The cabin would have disappeared completely from sight had Laszlo not spoken the spell he had been instructed to invoke, but Mike could still sense the dragon's presence. He couldn't see him, but his gut feeling told him that the huge creature was there nearby and would not have allowed them to lose sight of the cabin.

"*Thank you!*" Mike shouted into the forest.

Elizabeth, clearly still shaken up by all that had happened, stared at Mike as if he had gone insane. Laszlo, who had been holding her close by his side the whole time, gave her an extra squeeze and spoke in a more gentler tone.

"Vee vould not have found da cabin or have made eet here alive, had eet not been for Ormgard"—dat is the name of dis dragon.

As they approached the door, they were hit by a sudden gust of wind. Almost as fast as it came, it was sucked away from them…then once more, with more force, as they were nearly blown over by another gust. Mike knew, without a shadow of a doubt, it came from the force of Ormgard's enormous wings, lifting him up and into the night sky. They all craned their necks to see beyond the cabin and, in a breathtaking sight, they watched as Ormgard gracefully ascended, seemingly in slow motion, his neck stretching towards the sky, beating his enormous wings—at least a span of forty feet, from clawed tip to clawed tip—and pulling his scaled body up higher with every beat.

Just then, Ormgard let out a screech that made them all cover their ears. It was incredibly loud, but Mike felt it was meant to be pleasant…like saying good-bye. His father confirmed that later, and explained that Ormgard had been wishing them a safe journey.

Laszlo slowly opened the door to the cabin and they all followed closely behind, entering into complete darkness. Mike remembered the stone Hanna had given him that night before he had left on this journey and dug it out of his pocket. He held it up, just as she had shown him, blew on it gently until a crack formed around the centre and proceeded to remove the top half of the rock, revealing a blue crystal set in the centre.

Elizabeth broke his concentration. "Ooh, Mike, where did you get that? Those are really rare." Her eyes widened in awe with every word. "That's a blue moon crystal, really powerful. I only know one person who has one, Han…" Realization dawned on her, then a huge smile slowly crept across her face. "Was that a gift from *Hanna?*" she asked with sugary sweetness in her voice.

Mike could feel all eyes on him. He chose not to answer and prepared to complete the final step. He cleared his throat, looking from side to side.

"Um…do you mind?" he asked awkwardly, hoping they would turn their attention elsewhere, which they did, but not without showing their amusement at this sudden revelation.

Once all eyes were averted, he leaned in close to the rock as if to kiss it, but instead, with his lips barely touching it, he whispered her name:

"Hanna."

The crystal immediately began to glow, becoming brighter and brighter by the second, until it was so bright it lit up the entire cabin, which they could all see now. Laszlo patted Mike on the back.

"Nicely done, Mike, nicely done," he said, winking.

Mike looked over at his father, who had a strange grin on his face.

"Let's find you a place to lie down and get a warm fire started."

Mike was grateful for his father's practicality. He helped him to a sofa positioned in front of a massive fireplace, making Mike comfortable while Laszlo and Elizabeth, busy waving their wands around the room, managed to get a fire started and several kerosene lamps lit. Once there was enough light, Mike replaced the top piece of blue moon crystal and blew gently on it once more, causing it to reseal itself and once again take on the appearance of an ordinary rock.

The sofa was old and dusty, but Mike was too tired to care. He lay there, taking in the details of the cabin, while his father examined his wounds more closely.

The cabin was small, no bigger than a large living room. The fireplace was directly in front of them as they entered; it had an iron tripod standing in it and hanging from the centre of it was a large cast iron pot. Laszlo was removing the pot from the tripod. After he had put it down, he drew a small leather pouch from a hidden pocket in his long trench coat. Mike watched in fascination as he began removing whole carrots, potatoes, onions, a small jar of ground paprika and even a butcher's package of stewing beef from the tiny pouch. As fast as he was removing the ingredients from the pouch, they began slicing and chopping themselves in mid-air and falling into the pot below. Laszlo noticed Mike staring at him.

"Emergency Gulyas kit; every Hungarian should have one, vizard or not!"

He turned his attention back to the pot with a smile and with what Mike could only describe as a look of love. He knew his uncle loved food, well actually he didn't know a Hungarian who didn't, especially a good Gulyas, but this was a small bit of magic he never thought he'd see. He wondered if the "emergency kit" came in a variety of dishes, like maybe, pizza.

Smiling to himself and feeling a whole lot better now, he examined the rest of the tiny cabin. To his left he saw

Elizabeth sitting on a bench at a long, roughly constructed wooden table. Completely unaware that she was being observed, she was mumbling to herself, busily rummaging through her own emergency kit, looking for leaves that Laszlo said would make a good tea to help with Mike's pain. Along the wall behind her was a small run of counter space with a few cupboards and a small wooden stove. Mike could see that a fire had been started there too and that a small cast iron kettle was already beginning to steam. To his right was an old ladder that leaned precariously against a small landing. Mike could see three beds of varying sizes and shapes, made from bulky beams of unfinished wood, possibly lined with what looked like straw—fresh straw.

Elizabeth served him the tea. Mike wasn't sure if the tea or the warmth of the fire, which had turned the tiny cold cabin into cozy warmth, was responsible for his sudden exhaustion, but he could do nothing to stop his eyes from shutting....

His dreams were filled with the events of that day. He relived the entire, long, exhausting horrible journey, only this time he was just a bystander, watching the events unfold before him. Several times he found himself shouting out to his family, warning them of an attack. He watched as the alpha male wolf made his attack on Arpi. The scene was a bit fuzzy, but he was sure it made him physically sick to watch.

Anger now welling up inside him, he took to the air and he was flying. Looking down on the battle and witnessing the violence, the savage attacks from the werewolves, his anger became a calm rage and he had a sudden urge to spit fire. He felt the beat of his wings increase. He was moving faster now, bearing down on the werewolves. He drew in a huge breath and with a cry of rage, let out a stream of fire on his helpless victims below. It sounded like thunder, and he held his ears until it stopped. It was then that he realised he wasn't the dragon, he was *flying the dragon* and he could feel the dragon's emotions.

The dream quickly changed. He felt the dragon being called to the edge of the clearing. The voice he heard was soft and gentle, like that of a little girl. He had heard this voice before. The dragon instantly obeyed the command and Mike suddenly realised where they were. He looked down and right on the edge of the clearing, in a small clump of bushes, he saw *himself*. From his vantage point, he didn't look good, in a lot of pain. Then the girl's voice was calling the dragon again. She was asking him to "help the boy." Once again the dragon obeyed, making several trips back and forth over the treetops, forcing branches to bend to the snapping point. Mike then saw two perfect branches landing on his body below, but before he could get a better look, the dragon was flying back to the battle. He craned his head as far back as he could, and there he swore he could see a trail of trilliums leading away from his body and into the forest. Now he understood where he had heard that girl's voice before. She was the girl in the flowers from the dream! The dream he had experienced the first night after he and his father arrived in Transylvania. He wanted so badly to fly back and follow the flowers, but it was only a dream….

Without warning, in the dream his dragon bucked him off and Mike felt himself falling to the ground, which was getting closer, quickly! He screamed just as he was about to hit, and then…nothing happened, no hit. Instead, he found himself lying in a soft bed of hay, and a feeling of peace and great relief washed over him. It felt so comforting, he didn't want to wake up, but that didn't stop whoever was shaking him, from waking him. Reluctantly, he opened his eyes and saw that the culprit was his father.

"Michael…Michael, it's time to wake up," his father said, gently shaking him.

It took him a few moments to make sense of where he was. His brain seemed to be in a fog that was difficult to navigate, but a sudden shooting pain from his left leg brought him straight through the fog and back to reality. Instinctively he reached to sooth the source of the pain, only to remember, much too late, that his arm was injured too. Eyes shut tightly, he let out a growl of frustration and pain.

Alexander, who had been sitting by his side the entire time, reminded Mike to deep breathe, which helped to calm him down. Very carefully, being fully awake now, he propped himself up. Laszlo had brought him more tea, the same oddly flavoured one that Elizabeth had given him before he fell asleep, and it helped with the pain almost immediately.

Forgetting the pain now, he suddenly became aware of the activities going on around him…the smell of something delicious coming from the pot over the fire, for one. Everything looked much cleaner, which must have been Elizabeth's doing; she liked her surroundings clean and orderly. He wasn't lying on a bed of dust anymore, in fact he wasn't even on the sofa anymore, but on one of the straw-filled beds from the landing above them. It was surprisingly comfortable and warm. He guessed that it had been easier for them to move the bed down than to move him up.

He was curious about how they might have achieved moving him without waking him and was about to ask when he noticed that his uncle was crawling on the floor by the side of the fireplace. He was placing his ear close to the wall, listening carefully as he rapped against the wood. It was such an odd and comical sight, Mike wanted to ask what the purpose of his uncle's floor expedition was, but a loud crack from the fire momentarily diverted his attention. A moment was all it took; he found himself concentrating on the fire, something wasn't right about it. He focused harder, unable to break his gaze if he wanted to, then he saw it as if it was being drawn before his eyes. There, behind the glowing embers in the fireplace was what looked like a small arched door. The outline glowed white hot against the rock wall.

"Uncle, is that what you're looking for?" he asked, fascinated by what he was seeing.

Laszlo pulled his ear away from the wall and looked to where Mike was pointing. At first he could see nothing but the fire and assumed that Elizabeth may have made the healing tea too strong and it was messing with his nephew's vision. He made a mental note that he would have to take time to review the proper tea-making procedure with her again, for this wasn't the first time she had made a tea too strong. The memory of his poor Uncle Janos growing back three extra toes on one of her first attempts to help mend a broken bone made him grimace. He was just about to turn back to his task of knocking and listening when Mike, sensing his uncle hadn't seen what he was seeing, wondered if he might be hallucinating.

"Laszlo Bacsi, did you see it, or am I the only one who sees a glowing doorway in the fire?"

Mike looked around at everyone, waiting for an acknowledgment that they saw it too, thus in turn removing the doubts of sanity he was having. His father was closest to the fire and was the first to acknowledge it.

"Laszlo, he's right, look *there*."

He pointed, drawing his cousin's attention to the blackened bricks on the back wall of the fireplace. Elizabeth too had noticed. The glowing outline of the small arched door was getting stronger, making the image clearer.

"Ooh! I see it too! Look there, Apa!" she shrieked excitedly, pointing and trying to draw her father's attention to it.

"Yes, I see eet!" Laszlo barked, agitation obvious in his voice.

He had been looking at the fire as intently as any of them, and was embarrassed to admit that he had not seen it until everyone was pointing directly at it. A bit ashamed that his first thought had been of his daughter overdoing it on the tea, he softened a little and thanked Mike.

"Vell done. I vouldn't have zsought dat eet vuz in da fire."

Leaning in closer to examine the door, which was shining white hot now, he noticed other lines beginning to take shape following the arch. Slowly each shape burned itself into the top of the door.

"What is that, Laszlo Basci? I'm sure I've seen it before," Mike stated, completely intrigued, struggling to remember where he had seen it, but something told him it was a distant memory.

"Dey are runes. Eet eez very old Hungarian," Laszlo explained.

Mike didn't notice that Laszlo and Alexander exchanged knowing looks at his recollecting the shapes. Laszlo wasn't really surprised that he did, for he had long suspected that much of the ancient magic was ingrained in Mike's memory. He said nothing of it, for fear of overwhelming the lad; he still had so much to learn or rather, remember, and he didn't have much time.

"Few vizards use dis Hungarian anymore and even fewer know how to read eet." Laszlo looked back at Mike, who was limping his way over to the fire, a look of intense curiosity in his eyes, which he couldn't take off the glowing door. "Do you know vat eet says, Mike?" Laszlo added, curious to know if what he suspected about his nephew was true.

"Of course he doesn't, Apa." Elizabeth laughed at her father's ridiculous question. "He's been a wizard for a month, you expect too much!" she scolded, clearly exasperated with her father.

Mike wasn't paying attention, otherwise he might have taken offense at his cousin's obvious lack of faith in his wizarding abilities, for he seemed to be hypnotized by the burning image of the door. Leaning forwards, he reached his hand into the fire.

"*Mike!*" his father and Laszlo shouted in unison, Laszlo reaching out to pull his hand away from the flames.

"Vat are you zsinking?"

Mike resisted their efforts to stop him. The fire had no effect on him, not that he had even noticed, still being in a trance-like state. Laszlo stumbled backwards, jerking his hand away from the intense heat of the fire, fumbling for words as he watched Mike reach through the fire and trace the lines of the runes with his finger. By this time Alexander had taken hold of his son, catching him off guard and grabbing him around the waist, which was not yet immersed in the flames, pulling him out of the fire quickly.

He looked him over for signs of charred skin or clothing, but other than the injuries he had sustained the evening before, which Mike was wincing over, there wasn't even so much as a singed hair.

Alexander was stunned; Mike had been immersed in the fire long enough for anyone to suffer serious burns, but not even his clothing was scorched. A mixture of amazement, relief and anger flooded over him and without warning, he began yelling at Mike, questioning his son's sanity and irresponsible behaviour. He was so completely flustered that it was almost comical to watch—almost.

Mike wasn't sure what possessed him to do what he had done, he wasn't even sure that he had had a choice in the matter, he certainly didn't feel it at the time; deep down he just knew it would be okay to reach through the fire. Interrupting his father in mid-lecture was probably the worst thing he could do right now; it was a cardinal sin and would only provoke another lecture, possibly worse than this one. Respect was *the* virtue, but a nagging feeling that they were running short of time convinced Mike to act.

"I know what the runes say!" he blurted out.

There was nothing but dead silence. His father, who had stopped his rant abruptly, was staring at Mike in amazement—and irritation for being interrupted.

"*What?*" he questioned, stepping towards his son.

Mike couldn't tell whether the question came from his father's need for clarification because he hadn't *heard* him correctly or an obvious disbelief of what he had blurted out. A little more gently this time, Mike repeated, "I know what the runes say."

Everyone was standing around him now. Laszlo and Alexander exchanged looks again, noticed by Mike this time, but what they meant by it he didn't understand. His father turned to Mike, laying his hand on one of his shoulders and spoke gently.

"Michael, what *do* the runes say?"

Mike saw that it had been difficult for his father to ask that question and wondered if he had once had the ability to read the runes before the night they had been driven from their home. Feeling a little crowded, he pulled himself up slightly, cleared his throat and, looking from face to face, spoke with as much confidence as he could muster.

"It says: *Courage may carry you through fire, but the path ahead will reveal your true desire. Friend or foe, your journey's end will show. One ends with breath, another in...death.*" Mike struggled with the last word. "*Wow!* They really don't like wizards, do they? Are you sure this is the only...?"

Mike never finished his question. He turned to find them all staring at him, their expressions a mixture of disbelief and wonder. "I don't know how I knew that!" he exclaimed, answering the unspoken-but-obvious question hanging in the air. "I also don't know how I know this... but we have to hurry, the portal will soon close. I can..." He struggled with the next phrase. They hadn't stopped staring at him and no one had said a single word. He cleared his throat again. "Uh-huh...I can feel it fading away."

Laszlo jumped up immediately and gathered everyone to him. He didn't know for sure how Mike knew; he had a couple of guesses, but he had experienced enough with the dwarves to know not to leave an offered door unopened for too long.

"Mike eez right, vee have to move quvickly! Everyone stand in a circle, vee need to pass zsrough da fire. I vill perform a spell for us all. Stay still."

Mike, who was being held up by his father and Elizabeth, cleared his throat and stepped forwards gingerly.

"Uh-hum…Laszlo Basci?"

His uncle, who had his wand raised in the air, eyes closed and a mere second away from performing the spell, opened his eyes in alarm, completely bothered by the fact that he was being interrupted when he had asked specifically for their silence and cooperation, and Mike had stepped out of the circle, clearly breaking the "stand still" rule he had enforced only seconds before—*and* they were short on time!

"Mike, vat are you doing?" he shouted, vexed to the breaking point.

Mike straightened himself up and limped forwards one more step, taking himself completely out of the circle.

"I don't need the spell. I don't need protection from the fire."

"Michael…," his father started, but Mike cut him off.

"Apa, trust me, I don't need it. The fire had no effect on me earlier. Look!"

He stretched his arm out for his father to examine. There wasn't so much as a singed hair. His father looked up at him, doubt etched on his face.

"Michael, I don't know how to explain this…" he said pointing at Mike's arm, "but you should let your uncle—"

He was interrupted by Laszlo, who placed his hand on Alexander's arm as he spoke in a defeated voice.

"Alexander Bacsi, Mike eez right. I don't fully know how, but I am certain dat he eez. Eet vill be OK."

He motioned for Mike to make his way slowly to the fire and then, before anyone else could interrupt him, he chanted the spell, waving his wand in a circular motion above their heads.

"Weird!" Elizabeth said, fascinated, following her father and uncle towards the fire, where Laszlo and Alexander each took hold of one of Mike's arms and prepared to enter.

On the count of three, Laszlo stepped into the fire. He was completely immersed in flame, but was fully protected by a thin, barely visible blue shield that outlined his body. A small handle on the door, which looked like a twisted branch that had grown out of the brickwork, curved itself up to the latch release and ended in the shape of a poplar leaf. Laszlo reached down, grabbed the handle and pressed his thumb to the leaf-shaped latch release. There was a loud click as he did so. He looked back at the others in acknowledgment, the three of them eagerly waiting for him to pull the door open and wondering how long the "fire protection" spell would last. He hastily turned his attention back to the door. With a huge tug and many creaks and squeaks it began to open. Judging by the sounds and the bits of brick and rubble that fell from the seams, Mike figured that the door hadn't been used by anyone in decades.

As Laszlo heaved on the door, they all heard the sound of rushing air. It was an eerie sound, like on a stormy night when powerful winds find the smallest crack under a door or window that isn't fully secured, or a chimney flue that's been left open and rampage through the room already darkened by the stormy sky outside. The more Laszlo pulled the door open, the stronger the wind became, pulling at the flames in the fire, then just when the door was open as far as it could go, there came a powerful rush of wind that sounded as if it had travelled down a long tunnel, and then a loud crack as it snuffed out the fire like a candle on a birthday cake.

Thankful that they no longer had to walk in the fire, the rest of them proceeded towards the door and one by one, led by Mike, they passed through the doorway. Once on the other side, they stopped and took in their new surroundings.

It was very dark and smelled of earthworms and wet dirt after a good rain. But just then the small amount of light that had come from inside the cabin began to fade.

"Mike, your blue moon stone…" Elizabeth whispered to him, feeling quite unnerved in the dark.

"Oh yeah, the stone," Mike replied, equally as uncomfortable in the pitch-black.

He fumbled around, trying to retrieve the rock from his pocket. Once he had it securely in his hand he began the motions to get it to glow, first blowing on it to reveal the thin glowing line that would separate the bottom from the top, then whispering Hanna's name, which seemed to echo loudly, throwing Elizabeth into a fit of giggles and he was sure he heard his father snicker at him too. The scowl on Mike's face was visible as the stone began to glow brighter and brighter. Elizabeth stopped and quickly apologized, but she really wasn't sorry, and Mike knew it too.

They could now see that they stood in a large tunnel. Three of them could easily stand beside one another and the ceiling was at least another four to five feet above Mike, who was already an impressive six feet two inches. Maybe the werewolves used this tunnel too, Mike thought to himself, sending a shiver down his spine.

The ground was earthy and moist, but scattered earthen stalagmites could be seen along the edges. They were quite tall, confirming Mike's theory on how long the tunnel had been there. The walls and ceiling were stone, with long stalactites hanging down the sides like large pointed teeth, each with the smallest drop of water clinging to the end of it, holding on as long as it could before falling to the top of the stalagmite directly below it. There it would break its form and disperse over the tip and be gone forever; no longer a droplet, but forever a part of the stalagmite.

The tunnel appeared long and winding. Here and there, where it was wider, steaming pools of dark water could be seen along the wall. They weren't very big, some as small as a bath and others like an oversized hot tub. Now Mike understood why the tunnel had had the distinct smell of sulphur since they had entered, why it was perpetually wet everywhere and why there were so many stalactites and stalagmites. There must be a natural spring nearby that was feeding the pools in the tunnel.

The smell and rising steam from each pool were actually inviting to Mike, reminding him of home. While living in Calgary, he had once gone on a school field trip to Banff, a quaint little town nestled in the Rocky Mountains of Alberta. It was one of the most beautiful places he had ever remembered visiting, and not just because Hanna had also been there. Banff was a ski resort town and home to a massive hot spring pool and spa. It had a unique history during the early 1900s of catering to the wealthy who were seeking a Canadian mountain adventure. Some would stay for months at a time in the majestic Banff Springs Hotel, a massive stone structure, much like a castle in Europe, built into the side of a mountain.

Nearby in Banff, Mike recalled, tucked into another mountain at the base of a huge natural spring and one of the longest gondola rides you could take, were hot springs. The massive hot pool, easily accommodating a couple of hundred people at a time, was rustic in design, meant to look as if it were a natural extension of the mountain itself, which it originally was. Over time and gaining in popularity, a spa had been built into the mountain and a small terrace with rock table and chairs had been carved away, which looked down over the mountainside and through the valleys to neighbouring mountains, one of them home to the Banff Springs Hotel.

Not that Mike was in the habit of pondering romantic moments, but that day, soaking outside in the naturally hot waters of the pool, surrounded by mountains, trees and snow as deep as he was tall, in temperatures of minus fifteen degrees Celsius, large snowflakes falling gently and disappearing into the steam, nature just couldn't have been more perfect. Hanna being there hadn't hurt a bit.

Later Mike learned that Transylvania was home to many natural springs as well, many that fed rivers. Scattered throughout the countryside were numerous taps the locals had installed to draw water from the springs. Each spring held a different mix of natural minerals and made claims that each benefitted different ailments ranging from the common cold to multiple sclerosis to diabetes. Signs that had been placed at each well listed the many ailments thought to benefit from its particular mix. It was just one of the many places he wished to visit again with Hanna...

Mike's daydreaming had helped to distract him from the pain and difficulty of walking. After an hour, his father, who had been supporting him since they entered, headed for a large rock, perfectly situated at the base of the wall, like a park bench, and motioned for Mike to sit down.

"We need to rest. Mike's bleeding again. Elizabeth, please hand me your bag."

Mike looked down the tunnel as far as he could see in the dim light while his father tended his wounds and wondered how much farther they had to go and what would greet them on the other side.

"How much farther can this tunnel possibly go?" Elizabeth snapped, echoing his thoughts and causing everyone to jump, her exhaustion and the horror from the previous day's journey beginning to take its toll.

"And why is it that every answer we need requires a long perilous journey?" she finished sarcastically.

Mike thought she had made a good point. Laszlo gave a sympathetic laugh; he knew his daughter and her moods all too well, and chose not to engage fully. Everyone was tired, hungry and shaken by the events of the previous day. She was a tough girl, and that made him very proud, but he wished he could permanently erase the images of yesterday from her young mind.

"I veesh I could tell you, but I don't know," he said sympathetically, patting the rock beside him, asking her to sit down next to him.

It looked as though the tunnel went on and on, none of them sure how far. They sat in silence for a few moments, each taking in their surroundings, looking for a sign, a clue, anything that might lead them to an exit.

Mike's wounds now were painfully reminding him that he wasn't making it to any exit—no matter how close—

any time soon. His father was quietly reminding him to breathe deeply through it. The damp heavy air made it difficult for Mike to take in deep breaths, making him lose his focus and patience. His father could see that Mike was getting agitated—thinking that the pain had become really unbearable, and with only compassion and sympathy for his son's condition, he reminded him again to take slow deep breaths.

"Really take the air in, fill your lungs full. It will help with the pain," he suggested, as if Mike had completely forgotten the purpose of the deep breathing exercises.

"Well, it's not working!" Mike growled in frustration.

"Just try, Michael. Focus. It *will* work," he reassured him calmly, giving his son a sympathetic smile.

Just then, a searing pain shot through Mike's leg. Gripping it in an attempt to stop the agony, he abandoned all his patience and good manners.

"No, Apa, it *won't* work!" he snapped. His defense later, when he was apologizing, was that it was mostly the pain doing the yelling. But right then he yelled, "The air is too thick and damp! I feel like I'm breathing through a wet sponge!"

Alexander was taken aback by his son's sudden outburst and Mike could see the disapproval on his face. He was sure his uncle was displeased as well, but he didn't even bother to look in his direction.

"Michael—" his father began with strained calmness, but was cut off by his son.

"Apa, can't you feel it? *There's no air!*"

Pain and frustration had reached its peak. Mike stood up, gripped his leg and tried to suppress a scream before continuing on in the direction they had been going. Sensing that his son had reached a point where he couldn't be reasoned with, Alexander made no move to stop him. They all watched silently, waiting for Mike to collapse or come to his senses, when he stopped abruptly near a small bend in the pathway and turned back to the group. He was preparing to let them know that the air was even thicker here and that he could see no end in sight.

"It's even worse—"

Suddenly, hit by a gust of fresh air, Mike stopped mid-sentence, instinctively inhaling several deep breaths. He turned back to the group, who by now had realised that something was happening, and were hurrying to catch up.

"Hey, guys—there's fresh air—*I feel fresh air!*" he exclaimed, beckoning them to come quickly. "Hurry, I think we're close to the end!"

Just as they arrived another gust came. Everyone stopped and took a few deep breaths.

"It came from this direction," Mike said, pointing to where the tunnel bent to the right.

Everyone made their way around the bend, each hopeful that a way out would be discovered around the corner.

"What the...?" Mike began.

"It's a dead end!" Elizabeth finished, the disappointment in her voice echoing what everyone was feeling. Instead of an exit, a rock wall lay before them. "It doesn't make sense!" she groaned.

"Elizabeth's right; I don't see any other paths but I know I didn't imagine the fresh air," Mike stated, looking around. He went up to the rock wall and determined to find a way to open it.

Snow Mike and
the Several Dwarves

Sunlight suddenly penetrated the darkness. As the great stone door opened at his touch, Mike was the first to step through cautiously. He gave the all-clear and the others followed him outside.

They were standing on a path that led through a beautiful forest. The pathway was lined with a rainbow of wildflowers. The sun peeked through enormous willow trees, every branch laden with soft white cotton, taking the brightness of the sun and making it glow. Vivid butterflies and enormous dragonflies flickered exotic hues of opal as the sunlight hit their bodies.

There was something else too. Mike could hear the sound of children's laughter fading in and out—carried on the wind. Elizabeth also noticed it and, after searching the air, leaned over and whispered:

"*Fairies!*"

Mike was beginning to wonder if all the fairy tales he had read in his childhood were based on reality. *Well, why not?* he thought. Like a hummingbird, a fairy paused momentarily in front of him and gave a little giggle. He could certainly see why the dwarves wanted to protect this place, but he didn't understand what all the fuss was about and why it was so difficult to get there. Mike did think it odd that they hadn't seen a dwarf yet, but then, what did he know about this world? Was that the bubbling sound of a brook nearby?

Everything seemed perfectly harmless and he was sure no evil could befall someone in this beautiful peaceful place in such a serene setting, yet when he looked at his uncle all he saw was the tense look of anticipation. Laszlo was walking along the path slowly and cautiously, the look on his face almost comical as if anticipating that at any moment something might leap out in front of him.

They hadn't walked very far when all of a sudden Elizabeth froze, causing Mike, who was only a few paces behind her, to run right into her. Elizabeth let out a small shriek.

"What's up?" Mike whispered loudly. Without tearing her gaze from the trees, Elizabeth waved her hand in the vicinity of Mike's face, shushing him. Mike swatted at her hand as if ridding himself of a large flying pest near his face. "*What the?*" And then he heard it too; at first he thought it no more than a gust of wind blowing through the trees or the scurrying movement of some small animals in the brush, but he noticed now that it was building in intensity and unless the animals in the brush had called all their friends, it had to be something bigger...much bigger! But for all his searching, he couldn't see *what* was making the noise.

Suddenly, a large group of short, stout men—the dwarves, Mike guessed—materialized from the trees, as if they had been there the whole time—giving them all quite a start! There must have been more than fifty of them, Mike guessed and they seemed to be extremely unhappy with them.

Then Mike noticed they were eyeing Elizabeth with curiosity and even lecherous looks. Elizabeth gasped and squealed, grabbing Mike to hide behind him. "I thought dwarves were supposed to be kindly and helpful—these don't look anything like the ones from Snow White," Mike whispered out of the corner of his mouth.

"The dwarves from *where*...eek!...never mind!" she hissed as one of the larger, more menacing dwarves stepped closer, and she shrunk even further behind Mike.

"State your business!" the largest of the group said, stepping further forward. He held a particularly vicious looking weapon—one end was a solid-looking hammer and the other end had several large silver spikes about it.

Feeling quite intimidated, Mike and Elizabeth took a couple steps back in unison. Alexander and Laszlo remained where they were, completely unintimidated. The dwarf that had spoken gave them a thorough once over. The look on his face revealed he was not impressed...and also, equally unintimidated. He made a "mmpfh" sound and, smirking, spoke over his shoulder to the rest of the gang behind him..."Gather in, lads—these ones look dangerous to me!" This was said with as much sarcasm as he could possibly manage, causing the lot of them to burst out laughing.

Laszlo, up front with his wand, didn't flinch but the expression on his face showed his irritation. Mike tried to look defiant but with Elizabeth clinging to him, cowering and peeking over his shoulder, all he could muster was a fatherly, "It'll be all right."

Laszlo took a step forwards, staring the head dwarf right in the eye and said, "Vee are here for a wand."

Those who had been snickering went silent. The smile was wiped from the largest dwarf's face.

"Watch it, lad," the largest dwarf ordered, "We do

delivery only. That's how it's always been. We know it and you know it too! Now tell me why yer *really* here or turn around and go back to where you came from!" He tapped his weapon against his other hand as lightly as if it were a spatula, then sneering at them, he suggested—with pleasure, " I can have my hammer escort you out."

This time it was Alexander who stepped forward and stated, quite calmly, "The wand we're after was never delivered."

"Careful, lad—that's a dangerous accusation yer makin'!" A flush of hot red was making its way up the dwarf's short neck. He took a step closer, pointing an accusing finger at Alexander, not quite able to reach his face. Alexander put his hands up in defense, but didn't back away and showed no sign of intimidation. In fact, Mike was sure he saw the corner of his mouth twitch, trying to repress a smile.

"It's not an accusation. It is a fact," Alexander stated simply. The color rising in the dwarf's neck took on a new speed and was closing in on his forehead now. "It-is-the-wand-of-Michael-Weaver," Alexander said quickly, before the steam burst through the top of the dwarf's head. That brought the dwarf up short. He took a step backward, looking more than a little stunned. "How'd you—," he started, then cleared his throat loudly. He regained his composure quickly and drawing himself up to his full height, pointed his finger back into Alexander's face.

"Now look here, let me make this as clear as possible, so's I don't have to say it again: We do *delivery* only! Now I don't know who you think you are, comin' in here, askin' about...."

"I am Alexander, father of Michael, of the Wizard house of Weaver," Alexander cut in quickly, before the dwarf got ahead of himself.

"Well...uh umm—," the dwarf cleared his throat harshly, clearly this new piece of information threw him from his tough act. Once again he tried to regain his composure. "Do you have proof?" he said with a sardonic smile.

Mike's father and Laszlo exchanged a look of agreement and they both reached into their pockets and produced their wands. Mike looked on, fascinated.

The large dwarf gave Alexander a dubious look and plucked the wand from his hand.

"Hofgar!" he called over his shoulder, without taking his eyes off Alexander. "Take the wand an' check it!" A shorter, less grim-looking dwarf, appeared at the large dwarf's side and took the wand.

He held it up, moving it this way and that, scrutinizing every millimeter of it. When he was satisfied with its appearance, he held it in his hand as if weighing it, then ran it under his nose as if it were a cigar.

Mike couldn't fathom what that might have proven but he watched on, fascinated. Finally Hofgar produced his own wand and tapped it gently against the tip of Alexander's wand. An image like a hologram, small but clear, appeared out of the tip of Alexander's wand—it was an image of his face. The hologram spun and as it did so, revealed the Weaver coat of arms.

The large dwarf gave a dissatisfied grunt, "Go back..." he started reluctantly, "and let them know we have...*guests*." The last word came out with extreme difficulty.

Immediately four dwarves dispersed into the forest, each in a different direction and then, just like that, they were gone. It was like they had disintegrated.

The large dwarf then handed the wand back to Mike's father, who reached his hand out to receive it. Instead of relinquishing it, the dwarf hesitated and for a moment they held the wand together. Finally, the large dwarf let go. They stared at each other as Alexander placed the wand back in his jacket pocket. *They look so ridiculous,* thought Mike, who was trying hard not to laugh out loud. Elizabeth's hand tightening on his shoulder helped keep things serious. Clearly her perspective of the situation was different from his.

"We do one thing and one thing only for yeh lot—we craft your wands! We don't take kindly to unexpected visits from your kind. The four of yeh are four too many! I'm doin' yeh a favour and yeh'd do well to remember that," the leader said.

He spoke sternly, and Mike assumed that most of it was meant to intimidate, but it was hard taking seriously someone who had to strain their neck to look at you. The massive hammer he wielded, with ease, helped a little.

"Now, who are the rest of yeh?" he asked as if he was tiring quickly of being hospitable.

"I am Laszlo of da House of Weaver, first cousin to Alexander, and dis…" He pointed at Elizabeth, who was still hiding behind Mike but popped her head up over Mike's shoulder. "Dis eez my daughter, Elizabeth," he said with a sigh. "Elizabeth, come out from behind Mike."

She did as bid and gave her father a meek smile. Laszlo just shook his head. There was a moment of silence. The dwarf looked Mike over carefully, taking in his current physical condition.

"And yeh?"

"He just said who I…" Mike replied, his voice trailing off, pointing at his uncle.

The dwarf was clearly not amused.

"A cheeky one, are yeh?" He took a step closer towards Mike and gave him a bring-it look. "Now, would yeh like to try that again?"

With great difficulty, Mike tried to erase the smile that was still on his face. He felt like he was talking to an animated character from the movies; the dwarf's behaviour, right down to his Scottish accent, was so cliché, and besides, weren't dwarves from Germany?

"Ahem!" He cleared his throat and tried to look as serious as he could. "I am Michael of the House of Weaver, son of Alexander." He extended his hand to the dwarf.

Now it was the dwarf's turn to be amused.

"You can put that away; dwarves don't shake hands."

Mike extended his arms and hobbled towards the dwarf, who stumbled backwards, trying to avoid Mike's embrace. He glared at Mike, clearly taken aback by the attempt to greet him, his cheeks burning crimson.

"Dwarves don't hug either!" he growled.

Laszlo tried to stifle a laugh. Elizabeth let out a frightened squeak as she moved closer to her father, and Alexander had a distant look on his face—it was apparent at the moment that mentally he was somewhere else. Mike put his hands up and hopped back from the dwarf.

"OK, I get it—no contact, no emotion."

"Ahh, yeh are a cheeky one. Well, Michael, of the House of Weaver, you don't look so good; sort of useless really. Got into a fight with a wolf, I imagine?" he asked, a devious and satisfied smile spreading across his face.

"The wolf looks worse than I do," Mike said pointedly, the smile on the dwarf's face vanishing.

"I'm keepin' my eyes on yeh," the large dwarf said, pointing a stubby finger close to Mike's face. "On *all* of yeh," he added as he turned to point at the rest of them, squinting sceptically. He grunted, took a step back and looked them over once more with great disapproval. "*Wizards!*"

He then pulled his wand from his belt and gave it a quick swish in Mike's direction. Mike felt a strange tingling sensation course through his body, starting in his feet and working its way up to the tip of his head. As it passed over his broken leg, he could feel the bones fusing themselves back together and the strength returning. As the wand moved over one of his wounds he could see millions of tiny fibres of muscle and tissue weave themselves together, leaving nothing but a pale scar behind. The wound ended up completely healed. It had all happened so quickly. Mike dropped the crutches, stretching out his leg and arms.

"*Wow!* Hey, thanks!" he said, amazed at what the dwarf had done.

"Well, I can't very well carry yeh now, can I?" the dwarf grumbled. Mike didn't have a chance to respond but he couldn't help but smile.

"Let's get this over with," sighed the dwarf, exasperated. "Now, follow me." He turned and motioned for them to follow, then looked back over his shoulder. "And don't even think about strayin' off the path; the forest dwarves that dwell here don't take kindly to strangers and are likely to greet yeh with an axe!"

Elizabeth gasped.

He glared at Mike out of the corner of his eye. "And wipe that smile from your face!" He faced forwards again, shaking his head, grumbling to himself. "Great dragon rider! Humph!"

Mike turned to Elizabeth, who looked as if she might faint from fear and amazement at any moment. 'I think he likes me," he said, smiling as he inspected his arms and leg as if they were brand new.

Elizabeth stared at Mike with unnaturally wide eyes that made her resemble a Japanese Anime character, insinuating that she thought he had gone insane. Mike simply shrugged his shoulders and carried on. He didn't know what it was about this place, but he felt invigorated and happy. The landscape was so peaceful and serene, and yet everything seemed alive and full of energy.

They walked the rest of the way in silence.

Dwarf Magic

It wasn't long before they came out of the forest and into a clearing that overlooked a wide valley. Mike was enjoying the walk, and now, with his healed leg, he felt like a brand new person. Even his father was smiling and walking taller. There weren't many things that Mike and his father had done together outside their home, but they had always made an effort to hike or camp in the nearby wilderness, he recalled. Mountains, valleys, rivers, lakes, foothills, prairies and canyons—they enjoyed it all. This place was no different.

But Laszlo and Elizabeth had been silent for the entire walk. Laszlo took a practical and cautious approach, but seemed to be enjoying the beauty around him. However, Elizabeth hadn't taken her eyes off the lead dwarf, the look of fright hadn't left her face and the size of her eyes hadn't changed. It was quite possible she hadn't even blinked once, Mike thought.

As they looked around, they saw below them quaint little white houses with chubby red rooftops scattered throughout the valley, some beside a stream and others on the hillside opposite where they were standing. Swirls of puffy white smoke escaped the many small chimneys.

"This is just like the Smurfs, only in red," Mike whispered to Elizabeth.

"Who?" Elizabeth snapped loudly.

Mike's comment had broken Elizabeth's trance-like state and she was clearly irritated to be back.

"The Smurfs... You know, those little blue... Oh, *forget it!*"

Mike was beginning to understand that the ability to leave the dwarves' habitat had been reserved for a select few such as himself and Elizabeth's family.

"Right, this is as far as yeh go."

The low boom of the large dwarf's voice tore Elizabeth's attention from Mike.

"*What?*" she snapped, her cheeks immediately flushing a deep red, the look of fear returning to her face.

"No one, and I *mean* no one, gets to know the way into the mountain," the dwarf continued, undaunted. "You'll have to go another way...."

Laszlo reached into his pocket and produced a handful of marbles.

"Oh, no yeh don't," said the dwarf, shaking his finger at Laszlo as though scolding a small child. "No wizard magic!"

Laszlo did not argue, and placed the marbles back into his pocket.

"Vat kind of magic, den?" Laszlo asked.

A devious smile crossed the dwarf's face.

"*Dwarf* magic."

They gave each other questioning looks, except Elizabeth.

Noting her look, the dwarf said, "Don't get your knickers in a twist—I'm only goin' to put yeh to sleep. It'll only be for a few moments." The dwarf almost sounded disappointed.

"Right, then—put out your hands."

Each of them put a hand out, palm up. The large dwarf tapped each palm lightly with his wand. A few seconds passed and nothing happened. They all exchanged curious looks, and that was the last thing Mike remembered.

Grumpy

"Wakey-wakey, Sunshine!"

Someone was lightly slapping Mike's cheeks. He opened his eyes to see the large dwarf smiling a deviously satisfied smile. He was already familiar with that look and he barely knew the dwarf.

"I'm not even going to ask," said Mike, allowing his eyes to adjust to the light, or lack of it, in the room in which he was sitting. He wondered where the others were.

"Oh, *come on*. Would yeh ruin me fun?"

"You don't strike me as the kind of dwarf who likes to have fun unless it's at the expense of others," Mike snapped.

"True, especially at *your* expense," he said, the devious smile surfacing once more. "Now, we're goin' to have to find out if yeh are who yeh say yeh are."

"*What*? You saw Alexander's wand…it showed who we were!"

"Not good enough. Give us a hand and we'll just give a wee poke in your finger—there, just like that," he said as he stabbed the tip of Mike's finger with a smaller wand.

"*Ow!*" Mike was sure he had *poked* a little harder than was necessary. "What do you mean you need to prove I am who I say I am?" he mumbled, sucking the tip of his finger.

"Well, we can't just give a wand to the first person who walks through the door sayin' he is Michael Weaver, can we now?" He said it as if it should be obvious information. "Give me your other hand." He reached to grab Mike's hand, but Mike pulled it away defensively. "Oh *come on*, do yeh mean to tell me that the *Great Dragon Rider* is afraid of a little blood?" he asked, howling with laughter.

"Everyone's afraid of something!" Mike said defensively, pulling his hand farther away from the dwarf. "Aren't *you* afraid of anything?"

"Laddie, the only thing I'm afraid of is that the one they call the Great Dragon Rider, the hope for our future, won't man up before his seventeenth birthday! Now give me your hand."

"Very funny!" said Mike, not amused, and he really wasn't. He had to agree with the dwarf that he wasn't sure if he would ever be man enough to do what was being expected of him. "So, how is taking my blood going to help you prove that I am who I say I am—do you do DNA testing or something?" Mike asked, trying to change the subject.

"Close," replied the dwarf without looking up.

He was examining the blood as it filled the tip of the wand, a strange wand indeed. It looked to be made of wood, but the top inch of it was made of glass fashioned in the same shape as the wood. It had only been a pinprick of blood, but the glass portion looked as though it was completely full. Mike examined the tip of his finger where the blood had been taken; he felt violated. He gave a shudder and turned his attention back to the dwarf.

"Don't you just have a stack of wands lying around?"

"Let me explain something, lad," the dwarf said. "Wands are not mass produced, like chairs or pencils," he began. "Each one is handcrafted by the dwarves, made from the wood of the oldest oak trees in the forest. A thin tube is hollowed out of the middle down the length of the wand and then filled with the purest silver— mined by the dwarves, of course," he stated, sounding for all the world like a school teacher. "Each wand is then personalized, hand carved with a wizard's family crest.

"Moreover, each family has an oak tree of its own. Many hundreds of years ago each family planted a seedling for an oak tree, then dripped their blood over the seedling to forever implant their DNA into it. This way, ensuring that every time a new member of the family was born, the tree would grow a special branch…for the purpose of the wand. The dwarves harvest the branches and then craft the wands. A courier dwarf then delivers the wand personally to the family," he continued, "so, in answer to yer question, no, we don't have a stack of wands lying around!"

Mike, feeling a little sheepish, began to look around the room, which looked like a lab. He noticed a sign over the only door into the room. It read: "The pure heart will not be touched by the flame." *That's curious,* but he kept the thought to himself. He could see they were definitely underground, but how far down he couldn't be sure. The walls were constructed of rock and dirt and held in place by large planks of wood as was the ceiling. Torches mounted on the walls gave the room sufficient light. Mike got the feeling he was in an underground mine. Mike noticed that every few metres where planks should have been, solid rock jutted out at the foot of the wall and gradually tapered near the top, where it was nearly flush with the planks.

At waist height—dwarf waist height—were small basins that had been carved out of the rock itself and, from where

Mike was sitting, it looked as though a narrow hose or tap protruded from the rock directly into each basin. A symbol was carved into the rock above each tap. The one closest to Mike, on the right, had an anvil with a hammer laying across it; the next had a shield made of copper with a sword laying across it; the next, an image of a fish. Mike stopped and counted all the symbols around the room—thirteen, just as he suspected.

Then he turned his attention back to the dwarf, who was busy working over a basin across the room. Curious, he walked over to him and looked over his shoulder, which wasn't difficult, as he stood nearly a foot and a half taller than the dwarf.

"So…what *are* you doing with my blood anyway?"

"Well, first we're goin' to let the tree tell us if yeh are indeed a Weaver," he replied in a manner of a teacher, keeping his attention on the task at hand.

He placed the tip of the wand in the basin, which was full of water. The blood drained from the wand into the clear water. Mike watched, fascinated as the thick, dark blood sunk to the bottom of the basin as quickly as if it were a pebble. It pooled at the bottom while the rest of the water remained crystal clear. What he had thought was a tap or hose protruding from the wall was actually a root. It wasn't very big, maybe the width of his finger. The end of the root sat at the bottom of the basin where the blood had pooled.

"What's that going to do?" Mike asked next as he moved to the other side of the basin, leaning down, eyes fixed on the pebble of blood.

"Well, why don't we just watch *quietly* and see?" the dwarf replied sarcastically, sighing with growing irritation.

Mike gave him a sardonic smile and turned his attention back to the basin. Suddenly, the root-like tube sucked the droplet of blood into it. Not a hint of the thick red blood remained in the clear water. Mike's jaw dropped.

Impatient to see what would happen next, he looked up quickly and blurted out his next question…"Now what?" sounding like a four-year-old. After that, he quickly returned his gaze to the basin so he wouldn't miss what would happen next.

The dwarf rolled his eyes at Mike's impatient questions, and replied, "When I said, watch *quietly* and see, was I not speaking a form of English that you can understand?"

Not wanting to give the dwarf the satisfaction of knowing he felt belittled by the remark, Mike drew in a long, slow breath, considering how to respond.

The dwarf took his silence as a victory, none-the-less. Smiling to himself, he replied, "If ye are *indeed* who ye say ye are…," he paused, looking up at Mike, as if expecting him to suddenly confess that he, indeed, was *not* Michael Weaver.

Mike replied with a blank stare.

"Hmpf! As I was sayin—*if* ye are truly Michael Weaver, the root will return the blood to the basin as it was. If yer *not* Michael Weaver…" a small but satisfied smile began to form, "… the blood will turn the water black as night!"

Conscious that the dwarf was waiting to see the effect these words had on him, Mike took a step back and stumbled.

"Are ye nervous, lad?" The large dwarf's belly shook from laughter.

Head down and eyes closed, Mike let out another sigh. He now knew how to handle this situation! He then opened his eyes to meet the eyes of the oversized, hairy infant that stood across the basin from him.

"Yes...that's it. That's *exactly* it... I'm nervous!" he exclaimed, keeping his new view of the dwarf in his mind. "I'm nervous because..." He leaned over the basin, bringing his face close to the dwarf's and whispered... *"secretly...I have always wondered if I am Michael Weaver."* He backed his face away slowly, keeping his eyes locked with the dwarf's, then sighed, shaking his head in exasperation and turned his attention back to the basin.

Infant! he thought to himself.

The broad, impudent smile on the dwarf's face had disappeared. His lips were pursed together so tightly that they appeared white and now a red heat was spreading from neck to face—so red that Mike got the impression that the dwarf's head might explode from pressure once the heat made it's way to the top.

"Ah!" the dwarf said, scowling. "You've a smart mouth, just as I thought. Well those bones I fixed for ye... I can un-fix them too!" He glowered at Mike as the steam whistled out of his ears. The thought that his sarcasm was a touch too much, it being the dwarf's home turf, crossed Mike's mind just then, but he forgot about it when the crystal clear water of the basin stirred and his attention was fully transfixed on the tube. The root-like tube quivered, sending slight ripples radiating out from their source, each ripple softly dying out before it could reach the edge of the basin. Then there was a small gurgled pop and the deep red pellet of blood was released back into the water.

Mike would never admit this to the dwarf, and he hoped it wasn't outwardly visible, but when he saw that small red dot, he felt a wave of relief wash over him. The dwarf, how-ever, was visibly disappointed. Perhaps he felt robbed of the opportunity to administer the discipline given to those who dare enter the Dwarf Kingdom and then lie about who they are. Clearly this had been a potential "once in a life time opportunity" for the dwarf that had been snatched from him. Mike rolled his eyes heavenward and stood up.

"Well…" he said, standing up to his full height now and stretching out his lower back, "now what?"

He looked down at the dwarf, who was extracting the small drop of blood from the water, using the same wand that had held it only moments ago.

"Weel," he sneered, taking a small glass vial from a nearby cupboard, slamming the door shut and whacking the wand against the vial. That little bit of drama forced the vial to spit out the blood. Then he crammed a cork into the vial and shoved it in one of his pockets.

"Done. Now we're goin' to get yer wand, so's I can be rid of yer ugly mug and get back to real work… no more babysittin!"

"I too…" Mike said, bowing dramatically, "have enjoyed my time with you!"

The dwarf let out a low growl. "Ach! Come on then, ya cheeky little…." His words became muffled as he headed out the door of the makeshift lab he'd been so proud of.

⟊

Mike couldn't believe anyone could be as miserable as that dwarf! *Grumpy!* Mike mumbled to himself and then chuck-led as he recalled an image of another dwarf, the one with the grumpy heart from Snow White and the Seven Dwarfs.

"Hey Grumpy! Wait for me!" he shouted after the dwarf, who was already at the end of the corridor and rushing around a bend.

With a few long strides, he caught up with him. The corridor was actually a tunnel, similar to the one they had taken from the cabin that led them to this *friendly* gang. The tunnel didn't appear to have been mined; rather, it looked like it had always been there—just as it was. Bright torches lined the tall walls and the crunch of well-packed earth and sand echoed off them with every footfall.

They walked in silence for a long time, it seemed to Mike anyway, and coming around another bend, he could see what he thought was sunlight at the end of the tunnel.

"Finally!" Mike said, more to himself than to the dwarf. He took in a deep breath of fresh air as they exited the tunnel—feeling like he'd been released from some sort of dark prison. He could feel the heat of the sun on his face and arms. It was only the beginning of June, but already, the temperature was well into the eighties.

"Hmpf!" The dwarf grunted, once again throwing a general look of disapproval in Mike's direction. "Get a move on, sunshine— I havna got all day!" He motioned briskly for Mike to follow him.

"Anything you say, *Grumpy!*" he mumbled, a bit too cheerfully.

"What'd you say?"

"Oh nothing!" he replied, then picked up the pace to catch up to the dwarf, who was now actually scurrying like some sort of rodent, it seemed to Mike.

Again they walked in silence, but this time Mike didn't mind. The fresh air helped immensely, but it was the awesome beauty of his surroundings that grabbed his attention. A soft but powerful hum seemed to emit from every tree, branch, flower, blade of grass—that's the sound of life itself, he thought. Bees buzzed, hovering over bright flowers sprinkled in abundance over the forest floor. Rays of sunlight penetrated the canopy of trees, each one distinct in the haze of the afternoon heat. Flowers bloomed, caught in the spotlight by the rays and light seemed to flicker off the shimmery wings of hundreds of tiny bugs flying in and out of its path. Here and there birds sang out to each other, their notes crisp and melodic. A small brook gurgled nearby accompanied by the chirping of thousands of frogs, a steady hum in the song of the forest and—if one concentrated solely on that sound—it was deafening.

Suddenly a very welcome gust of wind blew through the willow trees, causing the long, drooping branches to dance in the shimmering heat. Thousands of tiny leaves rattled together as the wind rushed through the trees, branches swaying in unison against their will. Mike stood in awe at the sight. The wind passed as quickly as it had come on and the trees resumed their lazy appearance and settled dreamily back into their slumber.

Standing there mesmerized by his surroundings, Mike was beginning to think he had been left behind and headed out at a faster clip. He hadn't heard the dwarf calling until he found himself chest to face with him. "Are ye going to stop and smell *every* flower? I havna got all day to wait on ye! Now, come wi' me!"

"Oh-KAY!" Mike commented, thinking how miserable could this dwarf be?...but he obeyed obligingly, feeling a little shiver that wasn't coming from the breezes, and letting his overactive imagination get the best of him for a moment. He quickly shook off the feeling that they were not alone.

They continued down the path, which ended abruptly. Ahead was a playful looking house set against the backdrop of a picture-perfect mountain. It looked like something straight out of a fairy-tale. Mike followed the dwarf inside and now saw that it was, in fact, not a house at all. A few strides through a simple foyer and he found himself at the entrance to a great stone hall that looked as if it had been carved out of the mountainside.

It was a massive hall. It looked as tall as the mountain was wide. It was packed with dwarves in a bustle of activity. There looked to be stations along the walls, each full with busy dwarves. A low, deep hum emanated from the massive machines and heavy carts working tirelessly mining unknown treasures from the great depths.

"Mike!" Elizabeth's voice ripped through the deep hum of noise. "Mike, over here!" Mike turned toward her shrill call—it wasn't difficult to find her—she stood at least a foot taller than any dwarf and she was leaping up and down on the spot, arms stretched high, waving frantically at Mike.

Mike barely took two strides and Elizabeth had already reached him, his father not far behind. "Mike, where *have* you been!?" She shrieked as she flung her arms around him, knocking his breath away for a second with the force. She stepped back suddenly, hands gripping his shoulders, and shook him slightly. "Well... where *have* you been? What did that awful dwarf do to you?" At that, she turned and narrowed her eyes in Grumpy's direction.

"He took my blood," he replied, amused at her dra-matics. He wondered now what they had done with the blood afterward.

"That's all?!" she said incredulously. "Why?" But before Mike could answer, his uncle had made it to them and with a slap on the back asked him if he was alright. Then he motioned him towards another dwarf.

"Michael, this eez Nori. He is Head Dvarf and vuz very good friends vit your Grandfazer."

A small, almost frail-looking dwarf compared to the first dwarves they'd met, with hand outstretched and a broad welcoming smile, took a step toward Mike. He clasped his hand firmly and shook it vigorously. "Velcome, velcome! Eet eez an honor to meet you, Michael!"

Mike couldn't help but smile—Nori's smile was infec-tious and a stark contrast to the dour-looking dwarves he had met thus far. He managed to mumble *thank-you*.

"Komm, komm, you must be very hungry…und tired!" He was pulling Mike enthusiastically through the crowded hall, beckoning Alexander, Laszlo and Elizabeth to follow. Mike's stomach grumbled loudly.

28

Dwarf Tale

That night they sat around sharing a meal and swapping stories. Nori had requested that his guests sit next to him near the head of the table. Mike was feeling very relaxed and to his joy he noticed that his father, uncle and even Elizabeth, who had worn the look of a tightly wound spring since they had arrived, looked relaxed as well. At one point, Nori, who had been staring at Mike since they sat down, put his spoon down neatly beside his bowl and asked Mike if he would like to know how he became so well acquainted with his family. Mike responded with enthusiasm— he had always loved history and his family's history was proving to be very interesting. This pleased Nori immensely.

"There eez actually *a lot* of history betveen us. Eet vuz true your great grandfazer, Mike."

For the next half hour, Mike listened intently to the story of how his great grandfather and Nori had met and the beginning of the unusual friendship that formed. It had been many, many years ago; Nori was the youngest of seven boy dwarves. His brothers picked on him constantly...not just because he was the youngest but he also was the smallest and, unfortunately, the smartest.

As Nori tells the story, "The trouble with being the smartest in the family is that it is seen as a quality of *weakness*. My older brothers weren't dumb but saw themselves more as warriors than wand deliverers (a task they saw as mundane with no promise of glory or adventure—and beneath their capabilities, so the older boys had little enthusiasm to perform this most honourable duty—delivering the wands).

Nori continued…"Dwarves were not allowed to deliver wands until they turned age 18. My second youngest brother, but by no means smaller than the rest—in fact he was the largest of the seven brothers—was due to make a Wand Delivery that night. Being as large as he was and so obviously meant for tasks of brute force—he saw the task of Wand Delivery far beneath his skill set. Size wasn't his only attribute; the art of intimidation came as naturally to him as breathing and he used it against us brothers (older or not) to get out of nearly every wand delivery.

"Being only 15, I was the only brother who had not been subjected to his *gentle persuasive* ways, at least in the area of wand delivery. As it was, though, every other brother was otherwise engaged the night of that delivery, attending a training event meant for those over the age of 20 who wished to become soldiers…which they all did. This brother had every intention of attending this event, whether welcome or not, and every intention of *not* doing the wand delivery. The only option available to him was to ask *me*. As far as he was concerned, size and age had nothing to do with delivering a wand—and, as such, moved to strike a bargain with me. A sworn to and signed statement to never harm me and provide protection from the other brothers sealed the deal and by the next evening I found myself in possession of the wand in need of delivery, trying to convince myself that, indeed, size and age had nothing to do with this task and, more importantly, that after my successful delivery, my father would see reason and be nothing short of amazed and pleased with his youngest and smallest son.

"The wand was to be delivered to a member of the Weaver family. The trip to Segesvar went without incidence...however, upon entering the city, I realized that I didn't know the city as well as I had thought and soon found myself caught in a maze of dark, unfamiliar streets—which had a distinctly sinister feel to them.

"Before I had enough time to think...or panic...two vampires advanced upon me. Perhaps they'd been watching me. Dwarves have very powerful magic of their own (some of which is not even known to human wizards), but lack of experience makes them easy prey for vampires.

"Vampires do not possess any magic, per se, and are not allowed wands, but they do possess great strength, speed and the ability to lure their prey in, even on a sole diet of chicken blood, which is all that the wizards allow them—to keep them under control. Human blood gives them a strength that is most sickening to witness. They are far more cunning and a sort of frenzy can occur. The vampires stalk the dwarves to confiscate the wands bound for delivery. Although a wand does not work properly in the hands of a vampire, it could give them enough of an edge to overpower a wizard, thus gaining the upper hand and causing more mischief.

"To my good fortune, there was a young wizard out in the streets that night: your great grandfather. He happened to be in the wrong place, but at the right time, and he heard the altercation and went to my aide.

("Just a note, dwarves and wizards generally avoid each other—your great grandfather, Daniel could never quite understand why that was, and understood even less after having the chance to get to know this young dwarf!")

"The first thing he noticed was how very young I was, or seemed to be. I was awfully small and fragile looking—not at all what he was expecting. He had always been told that a dwarf can only deliver wands at the age of eighteen, because by then they would be skilled in magic and weapons and would be much stronger... much, much stronger than this wee little dwarf standing beside him, Daniel realized. And delivering wands can be dangerous business!

"The second thing he noticed, judging by the wary and nervous glances that I was casting continuously and judging also by the fact that my entire body shook like a dying leaf in the wind desperately holding its place on the branch, was that this night likely was my first delivery— though why I was chosen, being so young, he didn't know.

"The third thing he noticed was that the wand he was to deliver was still in my possession. He let out a sigh of relief. He assumed that was what the vampires were after and was relieved that he had gotten there in time to stop them.

"At that, I stood up so fast that at first Daniel didn't know what was happening.

"'I, I h-have to...I, I mean...th-thank-you, *thank you*... truly! B-but I, I..., oh dear,' I stammered. With my back against the wall, shoulders slumped forward, I drew the wand out from under my jacket and looked at it hopelessly. Then I sighed. 'I'm late...and lost...and I'm... ahem, *afraid!*'"

"Well, in short, Daniel took pity on me and offered to help me deliver the wand. Things moved quickly after that—Daniel led me to the home where the wand was to be delivered, waited while I handed over the wand, and then brought me safely to the outskirts of town. Daniel waited there with me until the sun came up, both of us agreeing that travel through the forest at night was not safe. The next morning, Daniel led me to safety using the same tunnel that Mike's Uncle Laszlo had sent him through." Nori took a breath and slumped back in his chair.

As he continued the story, a bright shade of red was taking up temporary residence on Nori's neck and face. He went on to explain just where his existence lay: slightly lower than the lowest man on the totem pole. He talked of the general hierarchy of his family—a highly regarded and respected family at that. It went something like this: his father, the head of the family, of course, then his mother, the one who allowed his father to believe that he came first and the one who Nori was certain *actually* held first place, then his oldest brother, who was in training for first place and was frequently reminded by his mother that he was nowhere near obtaining that position owing to the fact that he often showed about as much maturity as the family dog! The eldest brother was followed by seven more brothers, Nori, as mentioned, being the youngest. He was, compared to his brothers, a very tiny dwarf indeed. All of his brothers, his father and even his mother were at least half a foot taller than most, and were solid from head to toe.

Nori was probably a foot shorter than the second youngest brother. Oh, of course, his father and mother had encouraged him by stating that he was still young yet and he would be just as tall and strong as his brothers some day, but he could sense their doubt as much as his own. It wasn't all bad, though— he may not have been big in size but he possessed an intelligence that far outweighed the collective intelligence of his entire family and a wisdom that was only equal to that of their current leader, Alfrigg the Great...it would take his family a bit longer to see that though.

That night, after that delivery, Nori and Daniel spoke until the sun came up—that was all it took for a lifelong friendship to be struck. Moreover, Daniel offered to continue helping Nori with his other deliveries in the city. Later, over the years, they learned much about each other's culture and, although wizards were still not allowed on the dwarf property, Daniel was welcomed, on occasion, to visit his friend. His family was grateful to him for helping their youngest become a very competent wand deliverer, but more than that, Nori quickly superseded his family's and fellow villagers' expectations of wisdom and leadership. It wasn't long after the death of the Great Alfrigg that the young dwarf was made the honorary head of the dwarf clan and was crowned The Great Wand Deliverer and has remained so until this day.

Mike thanked him for the great bit of history.

⌒〰〰⌒

The next morning Mike was woken abruptly by Grumpy banging on his door. "Alright, alright!" he shouted before the door came off its hinges.

"Nori's requested yer highness's presence...now!" he grumbled—daring Mike to disobey.

Mike was escorted to the same hall in which he had been introduced to Nori yesterday. Grumpy deposited Mike on an empty workbench. "Sit!" he commanded, pointing at the bench. Mike sat down obediently.

"Now what?" Mike dared to ask, giving Nori a facetious smile.

"*Now...*" Grumpy said in a long-suffering sort of voice, "ye wait! An' don't go pokin' about causin' trouble!" he added, with a look suggestive of "I dare you to try me." Mike replied to this unspoken dare with a smile that said "You wish!"

Grumpy's eyes narrowed and his face broke into a malicious grin. "I do."

The look on Mike's face must have given him the impression that Grumpy'd won that unspoken conversation. He threw his head back, laughing so hard he had to hold his stomach and walked away, leaving Mike baffled in his wake.

Mike passed the next few minutes contemplating the depths of Grumpy's malicious personality and observing the bustle of activity. At first it seemed chaotic—a mess of noise and motion—but the longer he watched, he realized that everything was running in perfect order, like a well-timed piece...it was hypnotizing. His thoughts were interrupted by a cheerful voice.

"Guten morgen, Michael!"

"Oh!" Startled, Mike stood abruptly. A bright and cheerful-looking dwarf stood beaming up at him. Mike stretched his hand out in greeting to the dwarf. "G-good morning!" he stammered. The cheerful dwarf seemed not to notice and Mike was glad of it. He hadn't let go of Mike's hand and was beaming up at him like he had just met his own personal hero. Mike was just beginning to feel awkward when the dwarf snapped out of his state of reverence.

"Oh—forgif me—I am...eet...eet eez such an honor to meet you!" he shook his hand vigorously once more.

"Und…und now I must take you to Nori," he added quickly, pulling Mike by the hand. He looked back as if to confirm that Mike was still attached to his hand. He gave him a broad smile that showed the immense pride he felt in having been given this task. "He eez vaiting for you."

Mike gave him an awkward smile, not quite feeling his celebrity status, but amused none-the-less.

They came to Nori's work bench, which, Mike noticed, was truly a chaotic mess. His escort cleared his throat loudly and drew himself up to his full height. Nori was sitting with his head bent intently over his bench.

Mike wondered secretly just how old Nori was. He certainly didn't look the age he ought to be. Mike did a quick calculation—he knew that his great grandfather was born in 1883…Nori said that he was a year younger than GGF…that would mean Nori was….

"One hundred und sirty-five!" Nori stated matter of factly, finishing Mike's thought. His face was turned down, eyes squinting through his spectacles, which rested on the end of his nose, as he tinkered with a small device on his work bench. Mike wore a look of puzzled astonishment. Nori gave a chuckle. He abandoned the small device and turned his gaze to Mike. Holding one side of his spectacles between his thumb and forefinger, resting them perfectly atop the ball at the tip of his nose, he peered over them, looking up at Mike. "You sink loudly, mein kleiner Sohn. Das ist gut—very gut for zee 'Great Dragon rider'!"

*Ooookay…*Mike thought to himself, amused that he had referred to him as 'kleiner sohn' (little son), when he stood, easily, two and half feet taller than the dwarf. *Not sure I* *understood all of what he just said, but he's smiling—a lot—so I'm going to take that as a good sign.*

"You remind me of your great grandfazer," Nori stated simply. He had returned to his intense examination of a colorful cube, which he was holding in front of him, level with his spectacles—twisting it from side to side, inspecting it carefully from its different angles. "Much taller, of course, und much better lookink." He gave a small chuckle, then sat thoughtfully for a moment, staring into the distance. Shaking his head from side to side, unconsciously adjusting his spectacles so they sat perfectly in that permanent groove left from years of wear, he chuckled then turned his gaze back to the cube. He held it up level with his eyes and said, "Ya...*much* better lookink!"

Mike, who had been watching Nori with interest and amusement, crouched next to him where he sat in front of his workbench. "What are you looking for?" he asked, pointing at the cube.

"I don't know," he said, scrutinizing the object in question, then giving a sideways glance over his spectacles at Mike. "I don't know vat *it* is."

"May I?" Mike gestured with his hand.

"Ya—of course!" Happily, he handed Mike the object. "You sink you know vat it eez und vat you must do vit it?" He leaned in close as Mike began fiddling with it.

"Oh, yes. I know what it is." He began a series of twisting movements. The tip of his tongue peeking out between pressed lips, a mannerism suggestive of full concentration. He spoke again, without looking at Nori, focusing only on each movement. "Everyone knows...ahem..." he cleared his throat, realizing his error, and gave Nori a quick apologetic look, then continued. "I mean…many people grew up with one of these. It's a puzzle, a… *twisty* puzzle." He twisted the cube back and forth in demonstration. "See?"

"Ah, ein puzzle!" Nori exclaimed, fascinated.

A small audience started to gather around Mike, watching intently as he deftly manipulated the cube's variously colored sides. The dwarves murmured amongst themselves.

Some were fascinated and others not so much, but mostly they were relieved. One dwarf mumbled, "Thank God! Nori's been staring at that thing for a week!" And another, "I was ready to knock him over the head with it if he asked me one more time for my opinion!" Mike kept his laughter on the inside.

Thinking that his audience was likely to be more intrigued with the history of the odd object than its clearly unimpressive purpose, he began, "It's called The Rubik's Cube—named after it's inventor, Alexander Rubik."

"Rubik? Zat is Hungarian, no?" Nori asked.

"Yes, Rubik came up with this in 1974," he said. "The beauty of the Rubik's Cube is that when you look at a scrambled one, you know exactly what you need to do without instruction. Yet without instruction it is almost impossible to solve, making it one of the most infuriating and engaging inventions ever conceived." He smiled.

Mike noticed the looks of pride that suddenly popped, here and there, on the many faces of his audience members. He had struck gold!

"Yes. Rubik was a sculptor and professor of architecture in Budapest…(he paused for effect) "He worked at the Academy of Applied Arts and Crafts…*in Budapest*. He once said, 'If you are curious, you'll find the puzzles around you. If you are determined, you will solve them.' I think he was right."

At that, he gained another round of impressed looks. It wasn't only that Erno Rubik had been Hungarian—after all, there were dwarves from Austria (like Nori), and Scotland (like Grumpy) and perhaps elsewhere, but...more than being from a most excellent and worthy heritage, Mr. Rubik was also a sculptor *and* an architect...two things the dwarves held in high regard. The cube itself was nothing more than a piece of colorful plastic...*unnatural*... unheard of and regarded with contempt by the dwarves (Nori excluded) and had only been created for the purpose of fun and a testing of one's puzzle-solving skills. A quick glance at his audience told Mike everything he needed to know about what the dwarves thought of "fun" (Grumpy *definitely* included), and now the inventor had gained their eternal respect.

With a final twist here and another there—Mike completed the puzzle.

"Ta-*da!*" He held it up for all to admire, clearly impressed with himself...his audience, not so much.

Mike let out a sigh, shoulders dropping as he did so. "It's finished," he said, irritated that an explanation was even necessary. "The object of the puzzle is to scramble the colors and then restore them so that each side is a solid color again," he explained, in a long-suffering sort of voice, then added, "It's considered to be the world's best selling toy!" The dawning of realization that Mike expected, at what "best-selling toy" meant, never happened and Mike resigned himself to that fact.

"Here..." he said, handing it back to Nori. "you can also use it to club somebody over the head with!" The audience responded with praise to that helpful tip.

The crowd that had gathered for the Rubik demonstration slowly disbursed, leaving only Nori and Mike again. "Come vis me, mein kleiner sohn." Nori tugged at Mike's shirt, gesturing with his other toward the back of the great hall. Mike followed obediently behind him, trying hard not to pass him with every step. They turned to the left down a narrow corridor and then down another, another, and possibly two more. Mike couldn't be sure...he was too focused on the ceiling, which seemed to drop inches with every turn, forcing him to crouch further down after each turn. The last turn brought them to a short corridor that came to an abrupt end, but, where a wall of rock should have been was a wall covered in a twisted mess of roots. Thick, ancient gnarly roots, sturdy, established roots and young, green pliable, all woven intricately together in a purposeful mess.

Mike stretched his cramped leg muscles in the small clearing in front the wall of roots.

"Only a few vizards haff ever seen zees vault—your great grandfazer vuz vun of zem—but only the outside. You are zee first to see zee inside!"

Mike wasn't sure what to expect, but watched on sure to be fascinated. Nori stepped forward and stood before the massive wall of roots. He folded his hands and bowed his head. He was completely still and silent. Mike stayed quiet, not wanting to disturb Nori, on the off chance that he was simply saying a prayer. They were at a dead-end—perhaps Nori had taken a wrong turn and was asking God to help him remember where he needed to go...he was very old, after all.

The stillness was becoming awkward and Mike began to think that not only was Nori lost, but that he had fallen asleep while praying. He reached out, intending to tap Nori on the shoulder and get his attention, but then thought that might startle him, and withdrew his hand. He decided asking would be gentler. He opened his mouth to speak, but before he could utter one syllable, Nori sprang to life. "Ah-ha!" he exclaimed with a triumphant smile on his face, startling Mike so badly that he leapt three feet in the air and smacked his head on the ceiling.

Nori didn't appear to notice what had happened to Mike or what he was currently doing to resolve the incident. He stepped toward the root-covered wall and placed his hand on a large gnarled knot. Mike was rubbing his head where a large lump was forming rapidly, but watched on, despite the searing pain in his head, wanting to know the outcome of Nori's sudden realization and what holding a gnarled old root had to do with it.

Nori stepped back from the wall and released his hold on the root. Suddenly all the roots were in motion, weaving in and out of each other. There was so much movement that Mike couldn't make sense of it, but within a few seconds he could see a pattern forming—the wall of tangles roots had transformed into two massive doors. The roots had woven themselves into the shape of a tree, one on each door, that reminded Mike of the typical image of the tree of life—roots that grew deep and wide supporting a thick sturdy trunk opening up into thousands of branches that made the full and broad canopy. The sound of wood splitting cut through the air, startling both Mike and Nori. With a sound like mountains being moved, both doors opened slowly—heavy rock scraping against the stone floor, causing the entire space they were in to vibrate.

Mike was speechless. He looked down at Nori and they exchanged a look of awesome appreciation.

"It eez quvite somzing, eezn't it?" Nori asked Mike, not taking his eyes off the doors. "Like I said, before; Very few vizards haff ever seen zees vault."

They looked on in silence as the doors continued to open slowly. Mike wasn't sure what to expect when the doors were fully open, but what he saw when they finally were, definitely wasn't it. The space inside was dark and damp and completely empty, save for one small item standing alone in the centre of the room—a tree, a small leafless tree that stood about six feet tall. It's size alone would make it a young tree, but it looked as old and sturdy as the tree of life itself.

"Oh…ah…that's it?" Mike asked trying not to sound unimpressed. "Ah…I mean—that's it? Wow!" he recovered quickly, trying to sound impressed. Nori saw right through it and laughed instead.

"You are good boy—very good manners. Your fazer should be very proud." He patted Mike on the arm. "Don't vorry, eet's not zupposed to look impressive, eet's zupposed to look forgotten. Eet vould be very difficult indeed for za vrong person…or zing, to find zis vault or even open eet, but if zay did zen vun look at zis dead tree und zay would realize zis vaz za vrong vault."

"Oh…well that makes sense. So…what are *we* supposed to see then?" Mike asked, thinking that perhaps he was the wrong person to be looking in the vault because all he could see was a dead tree.

"A dead tree," said Nori matter-of-factly.

"Oh," was all Mike could manage. Nori laughed.

"Komm, let us take a closer look." He took Mike by the arm and led him into the dark vault.

He whispered a few words and shone his lantern around. The lantern's light grew brighter. Mike could see the whole vault now. It wasn't very big, maybe the size of a large kitchen, and completely empty—just the tree.

Mike was waiting for something magical to happen, waiting for Nori to speak and something amazing to happen. He did speak but it wasn't what Mike expected: "Gif me your hand, Michael." Without waiting for Mike to comply, he took his hand and, with a surprising amount of force, managed to pull him forward, prick the tip of his finger and squeeze a drop of blood that fell to the base of the tree.

"Ow!" He freed his hand from Nori's grip and sucked the tip of his finger defensively. "How many more times will you need to do *that?*" he asked holding his wounded finger, defensively.

Nori laughed. "You vill live. Now vatch," he said as he pointed to the tree.

Fingertip in mouth, still nursing his wound, Mike watched as the blood soaked into the bark. Thin veins of it ran up the trunk and disappeared into the branches. Mike wasn't sure what to expect, but he watched the base of the tree closely, expecting black goo to gush out.

A small noise of wonder from Nori brought Mike's attention back and he turned his attention on what Nori was admiring. A single branch was sprouting leaves; they were so green that they almost glowed in comparison to the dark surroundings and the grey dead branches of the rest of the tree. It took only a minute for the leaves to mature and without ceremony, turn yellow and begin to rot. Mike felt let down by the whole process and was just about to say so when the base of the branch began to turn silver, then slowly the silver ran up the entire branch covering it right to the tip. As it passed the leaves, each one dropped, disintegrating into dust upon landing. What was left behind was a single branch of pure silver.

"Is that..." Mike started.

"Ja, mein kleiner Sohn—zat eez your vand," Nori said, touching Mike lightly on the arm. "Eet eez almost done." Mike watched on as the process completed. Fresh bark grew around the silver, then hundreds of tiny mites appeared at the base of the tree and, in single-file fashion, crawled up the length of the trunk and onto the new branch and began to eat.

"Hey!" Mike reached forward with his hand, wanting to brush the little vermin off the branch, but Nori put his hand out to stop him.

"Eetz alright, Michael" he said calmly, "zis eez supposed to happen." Mike backed away, feeling doubtful and kept a sharp eye on the vermin as they devoured the branch. Nori smiled to himself, amused by Mike's defensive behavior. The two of them watched on as the mites chewed fastidiously on the branch. Even though Nori had reassured him that this was all part of the plan, Mike was beginning to wonder if there would soon be anything left of the branch.

But, as fast as they had come, they were gone. Nori stepped forward and plucked the branch from the tree and, holding the lantern close to his hand, held it out for Mike to see. Mike stepped in closer and bent low over Nori's hand to get a good look at the wand. It was beautiful! The wood was no longer fresh and young, it looked old, like petrified wood. Mike could make out the shape of two dragons, long and slender, wrapped around the length of the wand, intertwined with one another—leaving gaps of wood, making the center visible. Mike remembered Grumpy saying that all wands were filled with silver, but what Mike could see looked more like bone. He gave Nori a questioning look. "Is that...*bone?*"

"Ja, very gut, Michael, very gut!" Nori gave Mike a look that said he was sincerely impressed with his accurate observation. "Dragon bone, to be precise!"

"Dragon bone... what...why?!" Mike asked, clearly startled. Unconsciously he took a step back, putting a little more distance between himself and the wand.

"Michael, you know zat every vizard family has a tree, for zair vands—*ja?*"

"Umm, yes. But what does that have to do with the dragon bone?" he asked, eyeballing the wand skeptically.

"Vell, Michael, it is said zat zis tree grew here from za blood of zee great Dragon. Michael...zeir eez only vun vand zat vill come from zis tree und only vun vizard zat can claim it."

Mike gave a sideways look at the tree, thinking it ought to look more impressive.

"Michael," Nori said gently. Stepping toward Mike, he took a firm grip on his hand and placed the wand in it and held it there until Mike closed his fingers around it. "Zis vand eez only meant for you...zair eez no uzzair who can claim eet." Mike let out a long, slow breath. Stepping back, Nori gave him a reassuring pat on the arm.

Then a feeling a little bit like panic gripped Mike at the sudden realization of what he held in his hand. He wanted to toss it down, but found he couldn't. Instead he stood frozen to the spot, hand gripped tightly around the wand. Slowly he turned his gaze from the wand to Nori, eyes wide.

"Wh'…what if I can't control it? What if it just…*reacts*… to me?" Mike's imagination was taking his thoughts in a dangerous direction, where there was blinding light, explosions and loss of limbs. He shuddered and Nori laughed.

"Michael—your vand does not haff a mind of eetz own. True, eet eez a conductor of your emotions, but eet eez not a 'loose cannon,' as you vould say. Eet takes much practice to kontrol your vand…und also time…vich vee don't haf a lot of. You see, every vizard receives their vand ven zay are four years old und haff much time to learn. But you, meine kleiner Sohn…vell, vee haff much vork to do. Komm, Michael, let the learning begin." He smiled warmly at Mike and motioned for him to follow as he headed out of the vault and back into the tunnel.

Staring down at the wand he held gingerly in his hand, he followed Nori out of the vault. He turned to look back at the tree and saw that it was once more nothing remarkable, even the dry leaves that had fallen to the ground had disappeared. As always, he found himself awestruck…he doubted that he would ever see any of this as normal. He tightened his grip on the wand and continued after Nori with the sound of large stone being dragged across the floor vibrating off the tunnel walls.

29

"I Feel Like I'm Five Again."

It had only been since that morning that Mike had received his wand, but it felt like he had been training physically for days. He sunk down, exhausted, onto his bed, reflecting on the events of the day, his father's snoring filling the silence in their room and his uncles from the room next door. Mike spared a brief humorous, thought to Elizabeth…she was likely scolding her father to no success.

Mike was the last one to go to bed. Nori hadn't been joking when he said that Mike had much to learn. After the vault, Nori had brought Mike down to a room that was not unlike the room where Q would present and demonstrate James Bond's assigned weapons, only the weapons were a lot less stealthy and discreet. In this room he worked Mike for hours on the "Basics of Wand Wielding." In the beginning Mike felt silly, playing with a stick pretending to be a wizard—it was hard to imagine that he was meant to be anything more than just Michael Weaver, let alone be the Great Dragon Rider, but Nori's continued insistence that he was a natural and getting consensus from his father, uncle and Elizabeth helped make the situation seem something more like "normal"—whatever that was anymore.

Mike looked down at his wand, still in his hand. As much as it still intimidated him, he had great difficulty letting it go, even more so after what he had learnt to do with it that day. Nori had been right, of course, his wand did not have a mind of its own and the thoughts Mike had of explosions and loss of limbs didn't happen. With more difficulty than he expected, he placed the wand down on his night stand as he lay down. He was exhausted and didn't even bother changing into his night clothes. He covered himself half heartedly with the blanket and, eyes on his wand, dozed off.

Sometime in the night he awoke abruptly from a bad dream. He couldn't recall the dream at all, just that he had felt vulnerable and lacking. Without thinking, he reached over and grabbed the wand from the bedside table and tucked it safely under his pillow and fell back asleep immediately, with his hand wrapped securely around his wand. The rest of the night passed without incident and Mike's dreams were filled with images of him as a child dancing and waving a stick around—playing "magic" with his friends.

When morning came, Mike found that he was alone in the room. His father had left a note on the bedside table that read: *Mike, I hope you slept well. I know you went to sleep very late last night, so I let you sleep in. Meet us in the great hall for breakfast. You won't want to miss it—Laszlo Basci reminded me that dwarf's have a reputation for their extravagant meals! Love, Apa P.S. Don't forget your wand— you'll be training with Nori again this morning.*

"Hmpf!" Mike scoffed, thinking it highly unlikely that he could forget the wand ever again. He had woken up with it in his hand.

The tantalizing smell of fried bacon rode in on the breeze through the open window and settled on Mike like a magic spell. Without knowing how he had gotten there, Mike found himself in the washroom, washing, brushing and styling mechanically and at a speed that seemed determined by his grumbling stomach. He was out the door and approaching the great hall within minutes. It always amazed Mike…and his father, how quickly a teenage boy could move when motivated by hunger. There was no magic involved here, just the need to pacify his hunger.

Mike stood before two massive doors, intricately carved with scenes of great dwarf gatherings that spanned hundreds of years—so he had been told by Nori the night before. He placed a single hand on one of the doors as he had been told to do the night before…and the two huge doors opened on their own. No sooner had he entered when the young dwarf, who had been his escort to Nori yesterday, burst through a small group that had gathered near the door.

"Ah! Guten morgen, Michael! Komm, komm, I vill take you to your fazer und your oncle." He grabbed Mike's hand and dragged him through the crowded hall. They passed by several tables piled high with food and dwarves seated snuggly onto the benches that lined each side.

"Here vee are!" the dwarf said enthusiastically, coming to a sudden stop and presenting Mike to his spot on the bench. Mike sat down beside his father and greeted everyone with a polite "Good morning." Quickly, before tucking into the mountain of food on his plate.

"Did you remember to bring your wand?" His father asked. Patting his chest near his heart, he replied, mouth full of food, "Rit hrrr, Aba."

"Ah…good…I think?" He gave Mike a dubious look but Mike nodded his head in confirmation and pulled his wand out enough for his father to see it, then placed it back securely in his jacket pocket. Mike's father laughed and patted him on the back. "Good boy. Enjoy your breakfast." Mike smiled in return, not wanting to risk speaking and food pouring out of the corners of his mouth. Elizabeth, who was sitting on the other side of Mike, tried to suppress a giggle.

Stomachs filled to bursting, they left the great hall and made their way back to the Bond Room. It was another long day of training on the art of wand mastery and it took Mike the first couple of hours not to feel silly. But he got the hang of it soon enough and felt more confident.

The next week passed much the same. In between extravagant meals, story-telling by night, hours of practice during the day, there wasn't much time for anything but sleep. Learning to use his wand properly and the numerous spells involved was more exhausting than Mike could have ever imagined. But on the fourth day of training Mike did something that amazed him and everyone else, except Nori, who had said he'd known it from the start. Mike couldn't help but smile, remembering how Nori had jumped up in sheer delight, clapping his hands. "Ausgezeichnet, Michael! Ausgezeichnet! I knew you ver capable of zees!"

It had been an accident with an excellent outcome. Mike had been practicing a fairly difficult spell. It was one of the "Weaver" spells. The objective was to throw a spell that would ensnare the recipient or object much like a spider would spin its web around its prey. Mike had been trying over and over again for the better part of an hour. The word was simple: *spin!* —but it wasn't meant to be spoken, necessarily, it was meant to be felt as you pointed the wand at the intended target. After several unsuccessful attempts, Mike's pride was bruised heavily. The training had been going so well and Nori continually praised Mike's progress—why were things going wrong now? If he was a "natural" then why couldn't he do this spell?

"This is so stupid! I feel like I'm five again!" Mike slammed his hand and wand down on the table. He turned and made to walk out the door, he needed fresh air, leaving behind a room full of astonished faces. He was almost out the door when his pride got the best of him, forcing him to turn around and, as he stormed back inside and, suddenly, without thinking, he closed his eyes and flung both his hands at the object he had been trying the spell on.

"Aaarrrgh!" The objects in question: two tall brass candle sticks, clanged loudly as the web spun around them tightly, snapping them together forcefully, causing them to fall to the floor with a loud thud.

For a moment the room was silent and Mike didn't want to open his eyes, but then everyone erupted into applause and Nori was bouncing up and down, joyfully shouting, "Ausgezeichnet!"

Mike opened his eyes and saw the candlesticks, woven tightly together, lying on the floor.

"Whoa!' Elizabeth said, stepping to Mike's side. "That… was…amazing!" she shrieked. "Do you know what you just did?" her voice was still shrill. Mike hadn't a clue. He was just so happy it had worked. He looked down at his hands and realized his wand wasn't in them.

"Mike?" Elizabeth was tugging at his sleeve. She had said his name several times, when Mike finally heard her and tore his gaze from his hands and looked at her.

"Mike, you made the spell work…without your wand… without speaking the spell!" She looked at him, eyes wide, waiting for him to acknowledge how amazing it was. He didn't. She tried again. "It's rare, Mike…*really* rare!" It finally dawned on Mike that he had performed the spell entirely on his own. He looked down at his hands again. "Whoa!"

"Ya…*Whoa* is right!" Elizabeth beamed.

That had been an amazing day and Mike had managed to do the same again with a few other "Weaver" spells throughout the rest of the week. Now he lay in bed—wide awake, unable to sleep. This was his last night and all the events of the last week played over and over in his head. Mike and his family had gotten to know the dwarves well during their stay and had forged great friendships with some of them too. Mike realized that he was going to miss them all, especially Nori. He was pretty sure that his father was going to miss them all as well. During Mike's training and every following evening the dwarves would take Alexander to what Mike could only describe as a Wizard's spa. Mike wasn't sure of the details and his father would…or possibly only *could*…tell him very little, but his forgetfulness and his tendency to withdraw seemed to have improved substantially. His behavior was similar to the times when Laszlo Basci would come to visit. Whatever it was that they had done for his father, Mike was very grateful.

His thoughts turned to the next day. He was equal parts excited and nervous. Excited for the journey and the chance to cure his father. But now that he had a wand and some ability he was nervous about using it in an uncontrolled environment. His mind filled with images of himself performing great spells with and without his wand and engaging in battle like his Uncle's, Elizabeth and his cousins had often had against the werewolves…and slowly his thoughts became his dreams as he drifted off to sleep.

30

The God's Chair

This is it, finally, the last leg of our journey, Mike thought to himself. They had just passed through the final hidden passage leaving the dwarf kingdom.

Mike turned to thank the dwarf escort they had been given when he realised that they had gone, but he was certain he had just heard Kerlak, the leader of the escort, remind him:

"No matter how large your enemy may seem, they will all have a weakness and, to find it, yeh must not let your fear and anger blind you."

Well, those were great words of advice, but now he had no one to thank. He shouted a "Thank you!" back in the direction from where they had just come. Suddenly a gust of wind kicked up the leaves from the forest floor and sent them dancing through the air. Mike watched, no longer surprised at *anything*, as the leaves circled about him, starting at his feet and spiralling up his body, and as they did so he could hear the sweet playful sound of a child's laughter. Mesmerized by the sound, he could only stand there and watch as the leaves began to dance faster. At first their movements seemed random, but slowly a recognisable form took shape. As the final leaves fell into place, Mike carefully looked at the form from top to bottom.

"*No way…!*" he said to himself more than to the others. "Kerlak?" he asked cautiously, still staring at the figure.

"You're welcome," it replied happily, startling Mike and causing him to jump backwards.

The two stared at each other for a moment and then they both burst out laughing. The others joined in too, but then…with a gust of wind…the leafy Kerlak was whisked away, his laughter carried on the wind.

"That was *brilliant!*" Mike exclaimed as their group started up the trail.

"You say that about everything, Mike," Elizabeth said, laughing.

"Well, that's because it *is* brilliant—*all of it!*" he exclaimed, waving his hand around.

Despite warnings from the dwarves that this journey might be the hardest leg of the trip yet, Mike was comforted by the fact that everyone's mood seemed hopeful. Even his father was smiling and had been since their farewell breakfast. He didn't know the details yet, but he knew that the dwarves had performed a difficult and rare spell on his father to give him optimum clarity for the journey. Lacsi Bacsi had performed long and difficult spells to provide temporary clarity many times, but Mike guessed that it was nothing compared to what the dwarves had done. His father had been with the dwarves for the entire day. He had not been at dinner last night either and Mike hadn't seen him again until this morning's breakfast.

The dwarves had warned them that there would be deterrents the closer they came to the well. The forest was laced with all sorts of magic: some from wizards who sought to preserve the secret of the well, and other magic that had always been there since the power of the well was discovered. They knew little about what to watch for, but one thing was always on their mind—how well Alexander was doing.

The journey proved quite difficult, the terrain being steep and rough. Much of the forest was travelled by humans, so their group had to "blaze" their own trail to go unseen. They had to be careful to stay out of the public eye. Mike couldn't imagine that just anybody travelled up there, as they would either have to possess some skill in rock climbing or be a wizard to scale the craggy terrain. He found himself tempted to use his wand and his new knowledge of spells, but refrained when he realised that he was actually quite good at negotiating the rocks and steep hills. His father had often commented on his sure-footedness, but he was surprised at how well he could climb. Elizabeth and Laszlo struggled, but his father was moving surprisingly well.

They continued on like this for what seemed hours and by midday they had come to a small clearing, a meadow scattered with delicate bright yellow and purple flowers. It was bordered by the forest and just big enough to capture the height of the afternoon sun. It had been only a few moments before Elizabeth suggested that this was the perfect place for a short rest. At first the others disagreed, saying it was important to press on while they still had daylight on their side—yet no one moved from where they were standing. It was a strange sensation, Mike noted; he too felt the need to press on, telling himself that this was a dangerous place to stop. It irritated him that Elizabeth had even suggested a rest. *Is she nuts?* he thought, but instead said:

"*What?* This is a terrible place to stop! We're totally exposed—out in the open."

Everyone nodded or mumbled in agreement, even Elizabeth.

Still no one moved.

Mike scanned their surroundings; there was nothing there to hide them. He looked down at the ground, which appeared cold and damp, and in between the green grass grew flowers and weeds with firm sharp stems. His face twisted in disgust when he noticed insects of all shapes and sizes crawling and climbing in between the blades of grass, yet the desire to lie down in this most inhospitable environment was overwhelming. Everything seemed to happen in slow motion as one by one they settled themselves into the grass, which to Mike's surprise felt warm and soft. Even though they'd agreed that stopping for too long wasn't a good idea, they were unable to fight the weight of their eyelids and the heaviness in their bones.

It seemed to Mike that the sweet smell of the flowers was covering him like a warm blanket, easing his mind as if he hadn't a care in the world. He still had a lingering feeling that this nap wasn't right, yet he couldn't care less. Then he thought he heard someone telling him he must not fall asleep, but the desire for a bit of shut-eye became so overwhelming he dismissed the warning and finally closed his eyes, as did everyone else...

The warm, thick feather duvet was the perfect weight, just enough to keep Mike cozy and feeling protected. He couldn't remember ever having slept on a more comfortable mattress. It hugged his body firmly and yet the touch was as light as a feather pillow. It was like lying in an endless pit of cotton balls. The warmth and comfort of the mattress was so inviting that he couldn't resist squirming and shifting to move himself deeper into it, feeling safe. It was a perfect moment and he wanted it to last forever.

He tried to recall why he was here and what he had been trying to accomplish, but it was as though a voice or many voices, were soothing him back to sleep and telling him everything was all right. At the coaxing of the voices, he snuggled himself even farther into the mattress, feeling even more secure. He thought that this might be what it felt like to sink into a giant marshmallow.

Everything felt perfect, but only for a moment—something was changing. The feelings of peace and comfort were slowly being invaded. It came on quietly, like the calm before a storm—everything seems peaceful and quiet one minute, but the fast beating of your heart tells you otherwise as you frantically scan the empty sky in search of what has made the hairs on the back of your neck bristle. Mike couldn't quite make it out, something dark and sinister, menacing and determined, and he felt that no matter how slowly it advanced, he could do nothing to stop it. It was like a shadow moving across the ground, with no barrier you could place in its path to stop it from passing over.

It arrived!

First Mike felt a dark shadow resting on his toes. He jerked his feet away instinctively and, although there was no pain, winced when he realised the shadow had not moved. Although he could not see it, for he had worked himself so deeply into the mattress that he could barely see his chest, it was an unmistakable presence that he could feel. In fact, he could feel it as it continued its torturous slow ascent across the top of his feet towards his ankles.

All feelings of peace and serenity had disappeared to be replaced with total fear and panic. He thrashed about violently, attempting to free himself of the mattress that seemed to have swallowed him whole. It had felt so wonderful before, to settle himself farther and farther into its billowy softness. Struck by a new, horrific realization, he stopped thrashing about; it wanted to suffocate him and he was helping it along with every movement!

He lay perfectly frozen, his mind racing. *What to do? What to do?* If he moved, it would happen sooner, but lying still wasn't going to stop the shadow from continuing its journey up Mike's body. Something told him that if he let it ascend to the top of his head, he wouldn't live to tell the tale!

"I'm screwed! *I'm screwed!*" he shouted into the mattress.

He wanted to pound his fists, but the mattress had closed in around him, pressing his hands too tightly to his chest, so he decided to cry instead. What did it matter now anyway? No one could see him, no one could hear him and he certainly didn't have enough air for screaming. To keep some dignity intact, he wept quietly, deep in thought. This just can't be happening to me, this can't be how it's going to end. Why? Why did I lie down? It's like a bad dream. Why did we think going to sleep here was a good idea? This is a nightmare. What's happened to everyone else, where are th—? Wait! It's like a bad dream…it's like a bad dream…it *is* a bad dream! He suddenly remembered where he was and how he had gotten there. It *was* a dream, but the impending doom and certainty of death, should he not wake up, was very real.

"Wake up! Wake up! Mike! You *have* to wake up!" he began shouting.

He stopped worrying about consuming the available air he had left; he was sure he had enough air—this was just a dream after all. A few moments of shouting proved unsuccessful; he was still in the dream and in his dream the air *was* disappearing. He felt his chest begin to tighten even more and his shouts became weaker.

"No, no, no, *no!*" he shouted in frustration, tears threatening to flow freely again. "Think, Mike, *think!*" he yelled. 'If this is just a dream, why can't I wake up?"

He tried to remain calm for just a moment, to think it through, but there was nothing, nothing but the feeling of hopelessness. The tightening in his chest and the dark shadow slowly creeping up his body, which Mike could feel had reached his thighs, told him that very dark magic was involved and it was going to kill him and the rest of the group. If there was ever a time to curse it would be now, but Mike could see how useless that would be. He had another thought. His father would have been so proud. He couldn't help but smile at the irony; his father was most likely cursing a blue streak in Hungarian right now, which could easily go on for an hour or so without repeating the same swear word twice. *That must be very satisfying*, he thought, wishing he knew Hungarian better. This made him laugh and he only momentarily thought about how much air he was wasting, but because it felt so good to laugh he decided he'd rather die laughing than full of fear. It wasn't hard to conjure up laughable memories being a sixteen-year-old boy who had recently been catapulted from his dark brooding teens into fairy tale land—and had been given a wand to boot, which he could actually use, except now…*More* irony!

Suddenly something strange began to occur; Mike felt as if his legs were getting lighter. He looked down at them, as best he could, and saw the shadow receding—it was nearly back down to his knees. Great relief encompassed him as he realised that his laughter was forcing the shadow away, but he reverted back to panic momentarily when a new thought occurred to him: *What if he runs out of things to laugh about?*

His trepidation left as quickly as it came, when out of nowhere something tickled his belly. The sensation moved from his belly to his feet then to his arms and neck, even tickling his nose as if someone was moving a feather back and forth under it. Not knowing what it was gave Mike the creeps, but the urge to laugh was stronger and it took only seconds before he could hear himself howling with laughter. He was laughing so hard that tears were streaming down his face. He grabbed his sides as they cramped from all the merriment, making him realise that he *was able* to use his arms!

The tickling stopped. Mike lay still, keeping his eyes shut, trying to determine if the shadow had passed completely. Instinctively he felt around his body, wanting to make sure he was all there and to see if he could feel whether the shadow was still there.

He was sure that to any onlooker he would appear to be an idiot, so he took a moment to silently thank Hanna's parents for not allowing Hanna to join them on this journey. Never mind that the entire journey had been perilous so far and her life would have been at risk; he was just thankful that she wasn't there to witness his vulnerable and ridiculous situation. He was only a sixteen-year-old boy after all, and few things rank more important than what a beautiful girl thinks of you. This line of thinking forced him to open his eyes and see what was really going on.

"*What the…?*" he yelled.

There before him, still and quiet, was a small row of chipmunks, all clutching an acorn with their tiny paws, staring right back at him. The one closest to Mike's face, also the largest, blinked twice adorably, turned to the other chipmunks and squeaked what Mike could only describe as a command, and with a tiny nod that said, "Our work is done here, guys!" they all scurried off. The realization that those adorable, but rather creepy little chipmunks were responsible for all the tickling dawned on Mike. He didn't even want to think about *what* had tickled his nose! A shudder ran through his body from top to bottom.

He got up from where he had been lying on the cold damp ground and checked to make sure that the others were okay. Before he saw everyone, he could hear them. *They* were all laughing. He looked down on their writhing bodies and the grim reality of what he had been thinking was confirmed; he was witnessing their bodies covered with tiny chipmunks scurrying all over them. Holding back the urge to shoo them all away immediately, Mike waited until each person showed signs of waking, then he did so, but not without a quick word of thanks. Whatever strange forces had urged them to do what they did, or maybe Mike and his family had just happened to lie down in a huge chipmunk lair, no matter; they were responsible for saving the entire group.

Although they had all endured a horrible spell, Mike was glad that they were all safe and awake. He went to help his father up, then Elizabeth and lastly Laszlo, and grimly noted to himself that everyone lay exactly where they had been standing when they all agreed that stopping there was a bad idea.

At first no one said anything. They stood there, silently observing each other and wondering whether or not they had all just had the same experience. What had tickled them to the point of waking? Only Mike knew the answer to that one.

"Well, that's just disgusting and ridiculous," Elizabeth shrieked when Mike kindly offered up the answer to her.

She looked him straight in the eyes and held his gaze, searching for the truth. She looked so serious and so absurd that Mike couldn't help but laugh.

"*Hmph!*" she pouted, then turned on her heel, grabbed her pack, flung it over her shoulder and began making her way across the meadow. Mike, his father and Laszlo just stared at each other in bewilderment. Mike looked at his uncle.

"What was that all about?"

Laszlo, clearly unaware of what had prompted his daughter's bizarre reaction, simply shrugged his shoulders.

"I have *no* idea," he replied, trying to hold back his own laughter.

Swallowing the last of his mirth, Mike called out to her.

"Elizabeth, what was th—?"

"You're lying!" she shouted, cutting Mike off in mid-question.

She didn't even turn around or stop stomping across the meadow. She simply stretched one arm up defiantly, her finger pointing in an accusatory manner up to the sky. Well, that was all it took for the three of them to burst out laughing once more.

"Werewolves, vampires, dragons…" Mike began, while gasping for breath between fits of laughing. "Those she can handle, but…but…" He could barely get these last words out he was laughing so hard now. "But *chipmunks*, they send her over the top!"

All of them were laughing so hard that they could barely breathe. Mike fell over, clutching his sides, howling over this revelation. Finally Elizabeth stopped crushing nature's beauty with the angry stomp of her feet and turned back to the group. Her expression could only be described as a mix of rage and embarrassment.

"*Apa!*" she demanded, wondering where his loyalties lay.

Laszlo became silent instantly, then, rolling his eyes, he commented woefully:

"*Oh, dear.*" He straightened himself out, cleared his throat and barked an order at the other two, loud enough for Elizabeth to hear. "Gentlemen, if you've quite finished…shall vee continue?"

Alexander and Mike stopped laughing just long enough to give Elizabeth the impression that they had heard Laszlo and had his back on this one.

"Yes *sir!*" Mike shouted, jumping to attention, giving his uncle a quick salute then quickly grabbing his pack off the ground and falling in line behind his father, who had already assumed his position behind Laszlo.

The three of them made their way to where Elizabeth stood, single file like soldiers on a march. Nobody could keep a straight face, which only enraged Elizabeth even more.

"It must be hard to admit you have a fear of small woodland creatures," Mike said thoughtfully, his father looking at him and rolling his eyes. "Especially when you're the only girl," he continued.

For a moment he felt sorry for her. He looked at her as they drew nearer and could have sworn he saw steam blowing out of her ears, making him think about what he had just said, but then he decided that he felt more sympathy for his uncle.

"We're going to have to be more careful," he warned. "Kerlak said that the magic would only get worse the *closer* we get to the well and we're not even halfway there."

♦

A few hours later, Alexander was losing his strength and Mike and Laszlo placed him gently at the foot of a large tree, making sure to keep him in the shadows. Knowing that they had nearly reached the well and judging by Alexander's current state, they didn't want to take any chances. The urge to move forwards and be done was strong, almost undeniable, however.

"We've come through so much, we can't stop now!" Elizabeth said, turning to Mike, grabbing him by the hand and yanking him up from where he was sitting beside his father.

"*Whoa!*" he exclaimed, steadying himself as she let go of his hand.

"Oh, c'mon, *let's go!*" she said, tugging impatiently at him, clearly ready to press on, and no one was moving fast enough for her.

They had barely taken two steps when Laszlo swung his arm, barring their way.

"*Vait!*"

"*Apa!*" Elizabeth exclaimed, turning on him with that all-too-familiar seething glare in her eyes.

Elizabeth elected to stay behind with Alexander, as everyone, including him, agreed that he needed a chance to recuperate. No one knew what else, if anything, lay ahead, especially now when they were so close to achieving their goal. No one knew how it would play out. Those they had asked could tell them what the water in the well could do, but no one, not even the dwarves, could explain how simple or complex the actual *drinking of the water* would be.

ᏇᎿᎦᎵᎾ

Laszlo and Mike made their way towards the edge of the small clearing, moving slowly and cautiously as they went. The anticipation of something nasty jumping out at them, more werewolves or something worse, perhaps an enchantment so dark and powerful it would be undefeatable, rested like a great burden on Mike's shoulders. He didn't realize how tense it made him until Laszlo shot him a disapproving glare.

"Oh...." Mike cleared his throat, slightly embarrassed, removing his hand from the deathly grip he unknowingly had on his uncle's arm. They carried on, Laszlo rubbing his arm where Mike had gripped it so tightly, surprised by the pain, but impressed by his nephew's strength. He knew he would need it now, for greater challenges lay ahead for Mike, which would test not only his physical strength, but also his character, much more than any wizard's he had ever known.

Laszlo let out a heavy sigh, stretched his arm towards Mike and gave him a comforting pat on his shoulder. Mike looked up and acknowledged his uncle's reassuring gesture with a smile, but he hadn't a clue what it was for and he wasn't going to ask either. He had simply accepted the fact that his relatives were all extremely emotional people and that he would continue to be hugged, kissed, pinched and cried over for a very long time to come.

Without incident, they made it through the last bit of dense, dark forest. Standing at the edge of the treeline, they could see there was a short clearing of about fifteen feet and then the edge dropped out of sight. Drawing in a deep breath, Laszlo turned to Mike.

"Dis eez eet!"

Mike made a panoramic sweep across the horizon, a view to behold. Standing at 1,300 metres up, he felt like he was on top of the world. As far as he could see in every direction, lush rolling green hills covered with deep green forest trees and vegetation formed what looked like three separate valleys. Each valley had a river that wound its way through the valley floor, cutting a line of fresh blue water between the rolling hills and often disappearing into thick patches of trees.

He could see why this was a popular destination for hikers; the view was unmatched by anything he had seen before, and having lived only an hour's drive from one of the world's largest mountain ranges, the Rockies, he had seen some of God's most breathtaking landscapes. Now he could see pristine white-capped mountains surrounded by rings of green and blue spruce varieties at the base, then thinning near the middle where the earth disappeared and gave way to massive, barren rocky peaks. Many mountains reached heights of beyond 3,000 metres and pierced the clouds. Large rivers flowed through the mountains, carving pathways through rock and valley with the fresh, icy cold water that could quench even a giant's thirst.

Thousands of deep blue and green lakes, which were so clear they mirrored the image of mountain and sky perfectly, filled valleys and crevices throughout the range. Mike had never before seen the rich, lush vegetation that covered every square inch of every rolling hill, only broken up by the different shades of deep green or shadows cast by a passing cloud across the sun. The climate was much warmer, and the fresh powerful scent of the juniper trees was a whole new experience, but—he saw no fountain.

Lost in the awe and wonder of the view, Mike jumped when Laszlo spoke.

"Mike!" his uncle said sternly, snapping his fingers in his nephew's face.

"Yes!"

Mike came back from his reverie abruptly. He had zoned out momentarily, a common characteristic of his generation, causing extreme irritation to anyone from an older generation, especially his uncle.

"Soooo, where's the fountain…and how do we get there?" Mike asked cautiously.

His uncle softened up, smiling and shaking his head. He took Mike by the arm and led him to the edge.

"Down dere," he answered, pointing downwards and still holding him protectively by the arm.

Mike looked over the edge carefully. You couldn't see it until you were standing right at the edge, but there was a three-foot drop to a huge, flat square rock, with three more just like it jutting straight out of the cliff in descending order, just like a flight of stairs! Each stair was the top of a long rectangular pillar of rock, each one lower than the next, following the slope of the mountain on which they stood. The first stair had a sheer fifty-foot drop on either side, each step thereafter being slightly shorter, but equally as vertical down both sides.

"Um…Laszlo Bacsi, are you sure this is it, because there's nothing down there, and how would we get down anyway?"

"You forget dat you are a vizard, Mike," he replied, waving his wand playfully in Mike's face. "And yes, I am very sure dat da fountain eez down dere," he said knowledgeably. "Kerlak said dat da fountain eez at da foot of da chair…and dat…" he said, pointing to the base of the rock pillars, "eez da foot of da chair."

"Yes, but what if—?" Mike started to ask.

"No vat eefs! Now, let's go get Elizabeth and your Apa… and, Mike…?"

"Yes?"

"Your apa eez going to need your help to get zsrough dis; he has become too veek and vee don't know vat vaits for us down dere."

He gave Mike a sympathetic look and a pat on the shoulder. With a heavy sigh he started back through the thick forest. Mike, feeling the weight of what his uncle had just said, looked back towards the cliff and expelled his own heavy sigh. Mimicking his uncle's thick accent he whispered to himself:

"Right…I am a vizard now. I can do dis!"

Alexander looked a lot better than he had when they had left him only a half an hour before, largely due to Elizabeth forcing him to eat and rehydrate. Anna Nani had packed heaps of food and two thermoses of tea. One thermos was quite large, which was for the whole group. There was also a smaller one that came with special instructions.

"Dis vun for Apa, ven he no valk no more," Anna Nani had instructed Mike in her best English.

He probably would have understood had she said it in Hungarian, but he didn't bother pointing that out because her efforts were so amusing.

Elizabeth's efforts were not wasted. The tea had an almost Red Bull-like effect on Alexander, so they made it back to the cliff in good time without him requiring much assistance.

Now came the task of descending.

"Vell, how *are* vee going to get down?" Laszlo asked, looking directly at Mike. "Let's see vat you have learnt."

"Oh, I see…a *test*," Mike replied with a hint of sarcasm. With a dramatic sweep of his hand, he pulled his wand out of his back pocket. "Stand back, everybody!"

He had been dying to use some of the spells he was taught by the dwarves. As dramatically as he had pulled the wand from his back pocket, he raised it straight up over his head, then brought it back down, squatting as he did so, stabbing the tip of the wand into a small patch of dirt that had gathered over years near the edge of the first stair, generating a small spark.

Nothing happened.

"Mike, you didn't say the spell," said Elizabeth, stifling a giggle.

Not moving from the position he was in, he simply shot his hand up, stopping her in mid-judgment.

"*Wait for it…*" he said, secretly not so sure that he had pulled it off and, if not, was he ever going to live down the added drama?

Beads of sweat were just starting to form when he noticed that small green shoots were starting to emerge from where the tip of his wand had pierced the dirt. They grew larger and longer, like thick green ropes, each one weaving its way in and out of the others—and before long had wound their way to the bottom of the great stone pillars. Sticky thin threads reached out from the green rope and adhered themselves to the pillars, securing the huge mass of vine.

A wave of relief and pure excitement washed over Mike. Slowly he pulled the wand from where it had pierced the earth, afraid that moving it might cause his entire efforts to disintegrate before him.

"*Yes!*" he exclaimed when he saw that the vine wasn't going anywhere.

He felt like he was five again and had just learnt to ride without training wheels. He looked up at his father, who wore a proud, but awkward, smile on his face, and Mike thought he saw the faintest hint of moisture in the corners of his eyes.

"Vell done, Mike," Laszlo said, patting him on the shoulder.

Elizabeth…? Well, she was impressed for sure. Mike could tell because she didn't have anything to say. She simply stared at the vine, then at Mike, then back at the vine. Mike elected not to ruin the moment by confirming whether she was impressed or not. He knew why she was speechless, and it wasn't like they hadn't seen him perform magic before; it was because he had cast the spell without words.

Mike's father, uncle and the dwarves had all explained that it took years of experience and practise to develop the skill of *csendben leadott varazslat*—casting silently. Even then, a mature witch or wizard did not automatically possess this skill. It was something that required a great deal of focus and quick thinking. One needed to be able to block out every other thought. Having a wand improved your aim; you simply had to point at your intended target. It was like communicating telepathically with your wand, with which you had to have an excellent relationship as with a best friend, like the bond between teenager and cellphone. There were some, very few, witches and wizards who could *cast silently*. It would be like calling, texting, emailing without your mobile—very difficult. Not having had much practise or years of experience made what Mike had just done amazing!

When Elizabeth finally came to, she asked him how he had done it. There was a distinct tone of accusation to her question, as if she was sure he must have fooled them all with a cheap trick or sleight of hand. He understood that this was difficult to accept for he had surprised himself too, so he was compassionate in his reply.

"I don't know how it happened, I...I just *felt* it," he said, flattening his palm over his heart as he spoke.

The look of disbelief was still evident on her face, but she managed to sound sincere. "Well...that was *truly amazing!*" she exclaimed, laughing and throwing her arms around him. "I am so *totally* jealous!"

Day was making its lazy transition into evening, a signal to them that they had better make their way down the massive pillars. The vines proved to be solid and easy to descend. The energy boost Alexander had received from the tea was already beginning to wear off, so Laszlo suggested that he go in front of Alexander, and Mike should follow. They landed on a smooth surface, the base of the pillars, and looked around for any sign of the fountain.

They weren't sure what they were looking for specifically, but either way there wasn't anything that resembled a fountain, just a small pool of water from the last rainfall that had collected in a shallow groove in a nearby boulder.

The view overlooking the three valleys was just as breathtaking from down there as it was from the top of the stairs. Now it was obvious to Mike, seeing from the bottom up, that the pillars they had just climbed down were one of a set of two. Another fifty feet to the right of them was another set of immense stone pillars, similar in natural design. The landscape at the base between the two pillars was slightly flat, but curved up into the mountain wall, giving it the distinct look of the seat of a huge chair, the two stone pillars on either side serving as the armrests.

"*God's chair!* I see it now!" Mike said in recognition and awe.

They were standing together, confined to the small amount of flat space at the base of the armrest. Everywhere else they could go would require serious rock climbing skills or magic, and they were sure Alexander didn't have the strength for either. Mike had made his father drink another small cup of the tea, but he knew it wouldn't last long and they didn't want to waste time because it didn't look as if they would find the fountain anytime soon.

Everyone, including Mike, was casting spells here, there and everywhere, trying to find something, anything that might lead them to or reveal the fountain. Mike slumped down on a flat boulder next to his father, Elizabeth following suit after twenty unsuccessful minutes of looking. Laszlo, being the far more experienced wizard, continued to try.

"Apa, are you *sure* that we are in the right place?" Elizabeth inquired of her father, with a hint of annoyance.

Laszlo, hands still raised in the air ready to cast another spell, stopped, turned his head towards them and spoke sternly.

"Elizabeth, I did not come all dis vay to be in da wrong place, I am certain dat vee are in da right place!"

He continued his search as if he hadn't even stopped to answer an annoying question from his daughter. Mike knew how his uncle felt about this subject, so he had known better than to voice his concerns out loud. Being silent wasn't Elizabeth's specialty.

But Mike couldn't sit still.

"Michael, we'll find it. Be patient," his father said soothingly.

"I can't, Apa. We're so close, I can feel it. I just can't *see* it!"

Mike stood up and paced the rock impatiently. He needed to do something, anything; he felt useless just standing there. He spied a small rock near his feet and decided to vent his frustration on it. He kicked it, intending to send it careening over the edge, but instead he sent it flying into a crevice between the two biggest pillars. Before disappearing into the crack it hit a small patch of mushrooms growing right near the opening.

"*Ow!*" came a small squeak.

Elizabeth, who had been watching Mike pacing then kicking the rock, giggled and chided:

"*Baby!*"

"It wasn't *me!*" Mike retorted defensively. "It came from over there."

He was pointing to the mushroom patch. Elizabeth gave him a doubtful look, which only made him more defensive. His father was also grinning now.

"You never were a good shot, Michael."

"Apa! It wasn't me! It came from over...."

Vexed to the point of having to prove himself, Mike quickly searched the ground for another stone and threw it at the mushroom patch impatiently. Thankfully he hit the small patch, saving himself further humiliation, striking a large mushroom square on the shoot causing it to uproot and topple over.

Laszlo had stopped his search and turned his attention back to the group, just in time to witness the fallen mushroom pick itself back up and transform slowly into what looked to Mike like a small garden gnome. Shaking his tiny fists he began shouting and cursing at Mike, who only understood every second word, partly due to the fact that he was shouting in Hungarian and partly because every second word was the same. Mike decided that either the gnome was a teenager or that gnomes in general must have bad mouths.

Stunned, amused and genuinely sorry, Mike leaned down, approached the gnome cautiously and offered an apology. He reached his hand out in a goodwill gesture, expecting the gnome to climb on so that he could see if he was all right. Looking warily up at Mike and the other giants who had gathered around (except Elizabeth, who had decided that this little gnome bore an uncanny resemblance to a chipmunk) and with the aid of a miniature staff, he cautiously hobbled towards Mike's hand. He stopped just before stepping onto his hand. Mike assumed that he was intimidated by their size and the number of them.

"It's OK, little guy, we won't hurt you," he said, reassuringly.

The gnome looked up at him with big innocent eyes, the cutest creature Mike had ever seen, making him wish he had never kicked the rock that hurt him. Raising his staff the gnome made to dock on Mike's hand.

"That's right, you're safe with me," Mike said coaxingly, moving his hand forwards to shorten the distance for the cute little gnome.

Suddenly the gnome's staff came smashing down on Mike's palm, piercing his flesh deeply. He yanked his staff out quickly, allowing the blood to flow freely. Astonished, Mike looked down at him and saw that those big innocent eyes had become narrow and sinister. The gnome yelled something rude back up at him, turned and scampered away like a mouse that's broken free of a cat's claws, and scurried into the crevice. The mushrooms in the patch from where he had appeared all quickly followed him inside.

Mike looked down at his hand bearing the small, but surprisingly painful, wound. Tiny thin black lines began to spread away from the wound like branches on a tree. Laszlo grabbed Mike's hand, put his finger to the wound, then touched it with his tongue. He grimaced and spat to the side.

"It's poison from a toad!"

Mike stood up, panicking now.

"What does *that* mean?"

He was angry now, for not only had the gnome humiliated him, he had poisoned him too! He yanked his hand away from his uncle, who was searching through his pack for some kind of herb, and ran to the crevice, crouched down and tried to get in as far as could. He was only able to get his head in, but that was enough.

"Get back here, you little…you little…*creep!*" he yelled, thinking there were so many more satisfying words that came to mind, but he couldn't share those out loud.

His uncle and father were shouting at him to get back, so, feeling foolish, he started to back out when he saw a ray of light fall on his hand. He followed the beam from his hand to what looked like another crevice to the left. He stayed very still and listened intently. He was sure he could hear the gnome's laughter from inside the crevice.

"Shh, I hear something!" he shouted softly to his family.

He then heard something else and strained to make it out. It sounded like gurgling at first. He listened harder— it was water! He could hear the sound of water splashing, like a small stream or waterfall trickling down a slope. He backed out of the hole as quickly as he could.

"I hear water!" he yelled. "There's light coming from inside the crevice! We have to get in there!" He was grabbing his father by both shoulders, shaking him with every word. "Apa—I—think—we've—found—it!"

Alexander and Laszlo exchanged looks of "let's try it" mixed with "could this really be it?" Alexander stepped out of Mike's grasp, raised his wand, swung it gracefully in a large semicircle and spoke.

"Nyiljon ki!" Loosely translated: "Open Sesame!"

Mike watched his father with anticipation as Laszlo rubbed a sticky paste, smelling like rotting compost, into his wound. It sent a burning sensation through his hand, making him flinch, but he was too fascinated with what was happening with the pillars to really take much notice. The crevice began to grow wider and wider until it became a large arched doorway. Mike thought it resembled the flat black doorways that the Roadrunner would use to escape from Wiley-Coyote.

Alexander motioned for them to move towards the door, so they grabbed their gear and walked in cautiously. The door went from being tall and narrow to a gaping hole that they could all fit through comfortably. Mike pointed out the shaft of light coming from the left. They stopped to listen for the water and this time it was audible enough for all of them to hear it clearly. Alexander performed the same spell, and this time the gaping hole opened up into a lush green clearing surrounded by huge weeping willows, every graceful branch covered in a soft cottony substance. Droplets of moisture caught in the cotton, glistening like diamonds from the moon's radiant light. Mike looked up and saw the biggest, brightest full moon he had ever seen.

They walked right into the clearing. The doorway shrunk back to its original size, the sound of it decreasing reminding Mike of a horror movie when the only means of escape locks itself behind you.

"This is amazing and a *little* creepy," Mike offered.

"It's beautiful..." Elizabeth said dreamily. "But I agree with Mike, something doesn't feel right."

Laszlo's and Alexander's sentiments were the same. They advanced slowly, fanning out into the clearing.

"Don't touch anyting yet," Laszlo cautioned them.

Mike and Elizabeth had gone out to the right, Alexander and Laszlo to the left. They had barely taken a few steps when Mike and Elizabeth shouted simultaneously.

"*I hear water!*"

"Mike! *Look!*"

Laszlo and Alexander rushed over to them at the mention of water, but Mike was looking at where Elizabeth's finger was pointing. To the right of them was a huge rock wall, just like the one behind them through which they had entered. It curved around a bend and there, at the base of the wall, scurrying around the bend and almost out of sight, was the small group of gnomes who had led them there.

"C'mon!"

Mike took off after the gnomes, Elizabeth close behind him.

"Wait, Mike! What about the water?" she shouted.

He was already around the bend and out of sight when his answer came.

"I can hear water over h—!" A pause. "*Whoa...!*" he exclaimed, awestruck.

Elizabeth had just rounded the bend and crashed into Mike, who had stopped abruptly, making her flustered and irritated.

"Mike! What are you...?" she questioned, not finishing her query when she realised why he had stopped so suddenly.

Alexander and Laszlo had just come around the bend. Alexander, who had experienced a sudden decline in strength, was being supported by Laszlo as they came to a standstill. The four of them stood stock-still in silence and awe. There before them was a massive stone wall that stood twice as high as the one leading around the bend, crystal clear water cascading gently over the top and all the way down into a large stone basin that looked like it had been carved out by giants.

"This is it—*the fountain!* Apa, we've found the fountain!" Mike shouted in jubilation. As he turned to hug his father, he noticed how he was slumped against Laszlo for support.

"Apa?"

Mike's heart tightened in his chest as worry took over. Instinctively and gently he took his father's free arm and placed it around his shoulders, holding him up with Laszlo's help.

"Vee have to get your fazer to da fountain *now!*"

Mike nodded in agreement, willing to accept any course of action necessary. He had never seen his father like this. He had almost no strength and looked slightly delirious, but acknowledged Mike and Laszlo's help with a weary smile and a quiet word of thanks.

Mike looked over at Elizabeth, who was walking next to her father, rummaging through their pack for Anna Nani's tea. She had been unusually quiet, but looked up at Mike and gave him a sympathetic smile. He could see that tears threatened the corners of her eyes, so decided to just nod his head in thanks. Not wanting the tears to flow, she turned her attention back to searching in the pack with a bit more vigour than necessary, producing the thermos of tea a few seconds later. Nervous and upset, she overfilled the small cup causing the hot tea to slop over the sides and onto her hands.

"*Elizabeth!*" Laszlo chided.

"Apa! I am doing my best!" she retorted, that defiant look in her eyes again.

Laszlo, knowing he couldn't beat his daughter's stubbornness, backed down and gave her a gentle pat on the shoulder.

"I know...tank-you," he said in English.

Despite the situation, Mike shook his head and smiled to himself, drawing an unimpressed but sheepish glance from Elizabeth. She tipped the cup up to her uncle's mouth, letting him drink as much as he could.

"Thank-you," he said weakly.

It had an immediate effect on him, giving him enough strength to walk with Mike's aid. Taking advantage of his boost in strength, they wasted no time getting to the fountain.

◠◡◠

The size of the fountain was impressive. The rock wall only stood about three feet high, but from its base to where they stood in front of it was about ten feet or so and it spanned another six feet from side to side. Despite the fact that the basin was full to the brim and that water from the waterfall was flowing continuously into the pool, there was no sign of any spillage. The outside edges and the ground surrounding the basin were completely dry and no visible stream led away from the basin or rock wall.

Once again Mike found himself in awe and wonder at this magic. He was sure he would never stop being amazed;

the past couple of months had been full of memorable moments, events and revelations that he wanted to remember always. It suddenly dawned on him how truly awful it would be to *know* that you have thousands of memories, but couldn't *remember* the details. His heart ached deeply—for the first time ever—over how dreadful his father's situation must be. Consumed by sympathy and a great deal of guilt, Mike placed his father gently against the wall of the basin and began to search for an obvious sign indicating how to administer the water to Alexander correctly. He circled the basin frantically, barking out commands to Elizabeth and his uncle.

"Uncle Laszlo, what *are* we looking for? *How* do we do this? C'mon, we can't waste any time!"

Noting Mike's unwarranted and sudden agitation, Laszlo sensed that he had finally grasped his father's dire condition, so did not respond in anger, but rather compassion.

"Mike, everyting eez going to be OK; vee vill find vat vee are looking for and vee vill cure your fazer."

Mike calmed down a little.

"Oh…I know. It's j-just that I don't want to run out of time." He paced back and forth looking from his father, who was leaning his head back against the rocks with his eyes shut and brow furrowed like he was trying hard to remember something, and then to Laszlo and Elizabeth. "Does he just need to drink it, splash his face in it or swim in it? Do we need to say a spell? Do we dunk him in it?" he asked, waving his hands dramatically with every question.

"I have to drink it."

"*What?*"

Mike stopped pacing and rushed to his father's side. His eyes still closed and head bent back against the cool rock wall, his father said it again.

"I have to drink it."

"Apa, are you sure? I mean…how do you know that is what you have to do?"

Alexander was so dreadfully tired, but he straightened his neck, opened his eyes and looked right at his son.

"I just *know* that's what I have to do."

Elizabeth grabbed the thermos that was on the ground with all their gear, unscrewed the cup from the top and handed it to her uncle.

"*Vait!*" Laszlo objected, reaching over to try and grab the cup before Elizabeth handed it over.

It was too late; Alexander already had the cup in his hand, but didn't drink, acknowledging his cousin's objection.

"Vait, just vait for a moment." Laszlo put his hand up and motioned to Alexander to stop. "Are you certain dat dis eez vat you need to do? How do you know? No one vuz able to tell us vat to expect, how can you be sure?"

"Laszlo, I don't know how I am supposed to do it, but I *am* certain that I need to drink it, and soon; we are running out of time."

"I can't be sure. Eet seems too easy," came Laszlo's reply. "If vee do dis da vrong vay, eet could be very bad," he added darkly.

"Maybe it's supposed to be simple. Maybe that's the trick," Elizabeth said, standing at the edge of the basin now. Reaching her hand into the water, she scooped up a small amount and let it trickle back into the pool. "It's just water, Apa, we should just try—"

"Elizabeth, *no!*" Laszlo shouted, lurching forwards trying to stop her, but again it was too late. The sound of a low rumble shook the air. Everyone froze, looking at each other and then at Elizabeth.

"Elizabeth, vat *have* you done?" her father asked ominously, but she had no time to reply.

A deafening crack resounded through the air, like a mountain splitting in two. They looked at the rock wall behind them to see that a huge piece of rock had started to split away from the wall. Knowing that an avalanche was inevitable, Mike and Laszlo grabbed Alexander, Laszlo reached with his free hand to grab Elizabeth's hand and the four of them made for the clearing to get away.

They had only taken a few steps when everything began to shake violently, throwing them to the ground. Dazed and frightened, they tried to find their footing only to be knocked down again. There was another loud crack. As if their heads were working independently from their minds, each turned to look back at where the rock had begun to split away from the wall, not one of them expecting to see what their eyes witnessed.

Terror filled Mike, and most certainly the others too, but he couldn't speak for their condition, as his eyes were fixed on what stood before him. He could not believe what he was seeing, he did not *want* to believe what he was observing. The boom of another crack filled the air as a massive chunk of the mountain separated itself completely from the remaining wall. It did not fall to the ground, but incredibly was moving independently with arms and legs, and at the top, as tall as the mountain itself, was a head!

"What…is…*that?*" Mike whispered loudly, unable to hide the terror in his voice.

Still on the ground, Laszlo motioned for them to back away. Crawling quickly, quietly and being careful not to back into one of the many cracks in the ground, he answered Mike.

"No one has ever seen one before! No one believed dey vere real…."

Laszlo's voice trailed off. Hiding behind the trunk of a huge willow and under the cover of its weeping branches, hoping, praying they hadn't been seen by "it," Mike pressed his uncle urgently for an answer.

"What…? *What* hasn't anyone seen, Laszlo Basci?"

"Yes, Apa, what is it? What do we do?" Elizabeth added in a shrill voice.

Sensing their panic and feeling completely unnerved himself, he turned to them, taking Elizabeth's hands in his, and addressed them solemnly.

"Eet eez a rock troll."

He stared at them both, waiting for their questions, knowing he didn't have many answers. They stared back, eyes wide, filled with disbelief and fear.

"What *exactly* does that mean?" Mike enquired.

Before anyone could answer, another crack rent the air, followed by a loud boom. Everyone stared in terror. With a huge step forwards, causing the ground to tremble so violently Mike was sure it would bring the whole mountain down, the rock troll separated itself completely from the wall, the pounding force of its step causing the earth to break open at its feet. A large crack formed and ran from the giant's feet, past the cowering onlookers and into the clearing, with smaller cracks branching out in all directions.

"This is bad…this is *really, really* bad!" Mike said, scrambling back against the rock wall, away from the branch-like fissure that passed only a few feet from them and, although the fissures weren't great in size, instinctively they all did the same.

Mike leaned forwards and pulled his father over to him, helping him to settle against the wall. He turned to him, shut his eyes for a moment, let out a long sigh, opened his eyes again and spoke reluctantly.

"Apa…what do we need to do?"

Alexander, giving his son a pat on the leg, drew in a deep breath and sighed as he exhaled.

"We need to *fight* it."

He was exhausted and Mike was sure he wasn't capable of even crawling out of there, let alone fighting the monster.

"Apa, *no!* It's too dangerous!" He turned to Laszlo and Elizabeth, pleading, "C'mon, we have to do *something!* This is too much for him. Can't you see we *need* to get him that water and get the hell out of here?"

"Mike, vee von't give up," his uncle offered sincerely, "but dere eezn't any magic I know dat vill destroy dis troll."

"*What?*" Mike and Elizabeth exclaimed simultaneously.

"We only have to *distract* it," Alexander said weakly.

"Your fazer eez right, vee only need to distract eet!" He was silent for a moment, thinking hard, then clapped his hands together and huddled the three of them closer. "Now listen carefully…dere aren't many spells dat vork against rock, so vee use da rock against him instead."

He looked at them individually, waiting for acknowledgment that they understood what this meant—they did. Plan A was to get back to the fountain unnoticed. Getting out from under the willow canopy was easy enough; then, still crawling to stay out of sight and because the rock troll was walking and the ground shook so violently that standing wasn't an option anyway, they made their way to the rock wall on their side of the fountain, hoping that a second troll wouldn't spring out of it. Creeping slowly and quietly they crawled along the wall. With no tree cover left they were completely exposed now and all eyes were on the troll, which was spinning its head three hundred and sixty degrees searching for what had brought it out of its long slumber.

Moving quickly while its head was turned away, they made it to the edge of the fountain. Elizabeth scrambled to get the small thermos lid out of her pocket and had just handed it to her father, who was to scoop some water up in it, but he never got the chance. Just then the troll's stone-grey eyes swept over them. It roared, letting out a deep rumble that shook the earth and mountain, making rocks fall all around them and into the fountain, sending splashes of water over the edge and onto them. Mike hoped beyond hope that that was enough to bring his father's memory back, but that was asking for too much as there was no apparent change in Alexander save that he looked even more tired than a few minutes ago.

Exhausted or not, Alexander was the first to stand up and prepare. It only took the troll one small step to cover the distance between them. A flash of green sprang from the end of Alexander's wand and exploded against the massive chest of the troll. Mike was sure it was meant to have more of an effect than it did, but unfortunately it only caused the troll to stumble back a little. Laszlo, however, took advantage of the troll's momentary disorientation, dipped the cup into the fountain and quickly tipped it into Alexander's mouth, catching him off guard and causing him to splutter half the water out.

Wide-eyed they all watched, waiting to see if it worked. A few seconds passed and nothing happened except that the troll regained its footing. Alexander looked at Laszlo, disappointment in his eyes.

"I don't feel any different."

Everything happened very quickly after that. Laszlo, frustrated, dipped the cup into the fountain again, thinking that maybe Alexander needed to drink more, but Alexander raised his hand to protest, thinking they needed a different approach. Mike was watching the two of them, wondering how two experienced wizards couldn't figure this out, and Elizabeth was the only one who was watching the troll.

"Alexander Bacsi, *look out!*" she screamed, just as the troll brought the back of its boney hand down on Alexander with a loud smack that sent him sailing clear over the fountain to the other side, where he hit the ground with a bone-breaking thud.

"*Nooooo!*" Mike yelled in rage.

He tore his wand from his pocket and advanced on the troll. A deep purple blast left his wand and the outline of a huge sledgehammer appeared in the air right next to the troll's head. Mike made a sweeping motion with his wand and just as the troll noticed the hammer it came crashing into the side of its head, knocking it clear off. It dropped to the ground with a loud thud and rolled a short distance away.

Without hesitation, Mike ran over to his father while the troll searched for its head. Elizabeth shrieked praises at Mike, getting her own wand ready for battle, then with a quick sweep, she spoke the first thing that came to her mind...

"Discombobulate!"

A large bucket of giant-sized marbles emptied itself onto the ground right in the path of the fumbling troll. Laszlo crouched down next to Mike, who was already holding his father's head in his lap.

"Apa, Apa!" he shouted, shaking him. "Apa, wake up! *Please wake up!*"

Laszlo ran his wand back and forth over Alexander's body, eyes closed and murmuring words in Hungarian. Mike looked at his uncle in desperation, praying that whatever he was doing would wake his father. He looked back down at him—it didn't seem to be working. Frustration turned to despair and tears poured willingly from his eyes, stinging his cheeks as they streamed down his face.

"Apa...*please, please* wake up!" he begged. "This can't be it! This can't be how it ends!" he screamed inside his head. "Uncle...please, please help him!" he pleaded.

Laszlo looked at his nephew, his eyes full of compassion. "I vill...I vill."

Giving his eyes a quick wipe, he began again, only this time the murmurings were different. Mike looked down at his father's near-lifeless face and lovingly wiped away the tears that had fallen from his eyes onto his father's cheeks.

"Thank-you...," his father said in a weak, rasping voice.

"*It worked!* Uncle Laszlo, it worked! He's awake! *He's OK!*" Mike looked back down at his father and shouted, "You're OK, wait...*are* you okay? Are you hurt? Is anything broken?"

No immediate reply, so he asked again. "Apa? Are you OK?"

His father gave a weak laugh and, looking up at his suddenly very grown-up son, he replied, "I'm OK; no broken bones, just winded."

Relief flooded through Mike as he looked up at his uncle.

"Let's get him back to the fountain. We've got to get him back and figure this out before that troll kills us all!"

The two of them helped Alexander up and, each taking an arm, made the few steps back to the fountain. Elizabeth had successfully kept the troll at bay for those few moments, but Mike saw that it had now found and replaced its head and had noticed that they were back at the fountain. He helped Laszlo lean his father up against the fountain wall, said a quick but deeply sincere word of thanks and turned to face the troll, which was now preparing to strike Mike out of the way, like it had his father.

Mike ducked just in time to miss the troll's hand, but for such a large and awkward-looking monster it was surprisingly nimble and was already bringing its enormous hand back to grab Mike. He would not have been able to escape the troll's grasp had his uncle not struck him with a stunning spell. Mike ran through the troll's legs and, standing behind it, he began to shout, trying to divert the monster's attention away from the fountain. Mike guessed that this was the troll's entire purpose: to protect the fountain and its secrets. The thought infuriated him; he could not understand why it couldn't be available to those who *really* needed it!

His anger was good, helping him stay focused and keeping the troll away, giving his father and Laszlo time to figure out their next move. It didn't last long though, for once the troll turned its attention back to Mike it was relentless and fast. Mike used all the spells he could think of to fight back, but the troll was getting too close and had backed him into a niche in the mountain wall. Other than through its legs, Mike had nowhere to run.

One large stony hand came down on Mike's left, trying to snatch and crush him with its long rock fingers. Mike made futile attempts to stun the troll, but it seemed to have become immune to Mike's stuns already. His heart started to beat wildly and he shut his eyes awaiting his imminent doom.

It didn't come. Mike opened one eye cautiously and saw that the troll was struggling against a firey whip that Elizabeth had cast, which caught around the troll's wrist. Mike didn't have long. He considered running between the stone pillars that were the troll's legs, but there wasn't enough room to pass through, when out of the corner of his eye, he saw the troll's other hand reaching down to grab him. Its hand was caught by another firey whip, this time his Uncle had cast the spell. Mike searched frantically for an escape route, but was closed in on all sides.

Alexander was still leaning against the wall of the fountain, helplessly watching as his family kept this giant at bay, giving him time to figure this out. He was so tired and weak that it took all his efforts to stay upright against the wall. He had long kept his frustration at bay, but now it was threatening to break him down completely. He just wanted to *remember*...

He glanced up at the sky and watched the clouds as they parted, revealing an intensely bright full moon. He sighed heavily. He looked back at the pond, admiring the moon's radiant reflection in it, when he noticed a strange shape forming in the centre of the moon in the water. He expended the last of his energy and pulled himself up and leaned over the edge of the pool to take a closer look. The image became more intense; it hurt his eyes to look at it for too long, like staring at the sun, but the shape also became clearer. It was a goblet! It was as white and as pure as the moon, outlined with a thin silver line. His heart skipped a beat. *This was it!* He knew it with such an intense certainty that he plunged his hand into the water, pulled the moon-lit goblet, full to the brim, out of the fountain and drank down the purest, freshest water he had ever tasted.

From the moment the icy cold water hit his lips his mind began to fill. He could feel the water as it flowed down his throat into his stomach and every part of his being. A flood of memories came rushing back like a tidal wave, crashing relentlessly against his brain and his heart, filling him up like a dam during a flood. It was so intense he felt like he would pass out if he didn't have more. With trembling hands, afraid he might not be able to hold the goblet much longer he dipped it into the fountain again and quickly drank the water down. Not waiting for any further signs, but knowing beyond a doubt that he had to, he filled the goblet once more and drank every drop.

Suddenly, as if he had been blasted by a fireman's hose right in his chest, he was pushed against the fountain wall and a flood of memories, intellect and emotions washed over his mind, heart and spirit, keeping him pinned there, crushing him until finally he was full. The pressure was gone and he expected his body to be weak and broken, but no, he felt a renewed surge of vitality course through him. He was so aware and awake that he could feel it passing along the walls of his veins, throughout his heart and mind, like billions of pieces of information travelling the intricate circuit ways of his brain.

He looked down at the goblet; the intense light of the moon had left it. No longer adorned with the purest light, it was made of plain grey rock, smooth to the touch, but not a single sparkle to it. It had served its purpose. Alexander placed it gently back into the fountain and his heart ached as he let it go, watching it disappear down into the grey of the rock lining the fountain bed. It had given him his life back.

A cry from Mike brought him back to the present. Alexander stood up, his wand at the ready as if he had never for a moment forgotten the wizard he had been so long ago. He followed the sound of his son's cries. He could see the rock troll, so huge it was hard to miss, with its back to him, facing the rock wall opposite the wall from which it had emerged. Elizabeth and Laszlo had cast whips around the troll's wrists and now, Elizabeth, her strength unable to match the troll's, was losing the tug of war. It gave a final tug with its massive arm and sent her flying forwards, breaking the spell of the whip. Laszlo was also struggling, but was still fighting to hold the huge arm back. With one hand released, it wouldn't be long before the troll was able to break free of Laszlo's grasp too. It grabbed hold of the whip and, with the strength of both arms now, yanked itself free of Laszlo's spell as well, sending him flying.

Now the troll focused its full attention on Mike, who had not been able to find a way out from its trap. It bent its massive stone body down and with a small sweep of its hand, wrapped its powerful fingers around Mike, snatching him up off the ground. Mike cried out in pain, the troll's grip crushing his chest and the jagged edges of the rock fingers tearing through his clothes and into his skin.

Alexander had run to the aid of Elizabeth and Laszlo, helping them back onto their feet. Neither was hurt, just winded. Both were stunned to see Alexander so full of vitality.

"Alexander...h-how did you...? V-vat did you...?" Laszlo stuttered, amazed, but Alexander, holding his wand ready to strike, was already running towards the troll and didn't stop to answer.

The sound of his son's cries pierced his heart, sending a wave of panic through him and a surge of painful memories crashing over him. The memory hit him so hard he stumbled and fell to the ground. Memories of the night he and his family had been attacked thirteen years ago, forcing him and Mike into exile, flooded his mind. Images of the struggle, spells flying from wand to wand, a great fire, a dragon that lay lifeless on the ground next to him, Mike, just a baby, crying and reaching up for his mother, Alexander's wife—his beautiful wife—flashed through his head with a searing pain.

Another agonising cry from Mike pierced the air, filling Alexander's heart with rage and forcing him back to the task at hand. Shaking his head to force the memories aside, he stood up slowly, every movement with purpose.

Raising both hands into the air above his head, eyes closed, he pulled his hands back slightly, palms facing each other and spoke.

"*Disintegrate!*"

A small, bright green ball of energy began to form between his hands, growing larger and larger as it turned with increasing speed.

"*Hey!*" he shouted at the troll.

With Mike in its grip, the troll turned its massive body to face its puny attacker. The ball of energy had reached the size of a basketball. Alexander's hands gripped it tightly, pulling back slightly.

"*Catch!*" he said with black vehemence, hurling the ball forwards, hitting the troll square in the chest with such force that its whole body flew into the rock wall behind it, the green light of the ball smouldering in its chest.

The troll's massive body slid down the mountain wall, and hit the ground with an earthquake intensity, involuntarily releasing its grip on Mike, who rolled, ungracefully out of its hand without a second thought. Laszlo and Elizabeth were there and dragged him away, saving him from the cascade of rock debris falling all around the monster. Seeing that Mike was out of harm's way, Alexander took one step forwards, steadied himself and looked straight at the fallen troll.

"*Let's finish this!*"

His arms were still stretched out in front of him, directed at the smouldering green light in the troll's chest. He lowered his head and with as much power as he could muster, he pulled his arms back stretched out on either side of his body. The green ball, glowing brighter and brighter, exploded like a bomb, blowing the troll's body apart, sending chunks of rock in all directions. Bits of sticky green arms, legs, body and head hit the ground with thunderous crashes.

Exhausted, Alexander fell to his knees as jubilant cries came from behind him. He turned immediately, scrambled to his feet and stumbled to where Mike stood, supported by Laszlo and Elizabeth. He was hurt, Alexander could tell by the way he was bent over slightly and had one arm wrapped around his chest, but he was beaming from ear to ear, tears of joy streaming down his face. He hobbled forwards as his father ran to him.

"*Apa...Apa, you did it!*"

Alexander caught him in his arms, steadying him, then embracing him protectively.

"Michael, you're hurt! I am *so* sorry...."

There was a crushing feeling in his chest, tears stung his eyes and guilt filled his whole being. This was his little boy again, desperate for his father's protection. So many years he couldn't be there for his son. So many years Mike had to bear the burden of protecting him instead. He held Mike's face in his hands, really looking at him, amazed at the years of experience and wisdom his young face held. Overcome with grief, he pulled Mike back in for another fatherly hug.

"I am so sorry, Mike, so sorry. You'll never have to face anything alone again," his grip tightening; he didn't ever want to let go.

Mike winced.

"Apa...my ribs...!"

At that moment he realized that he had his father back at last. Every scratch, every bruise, every broken bone was worth it, even his father's suffocating hug. Arm in arm, they turned to Laszlo and Elizabeth, who was dabbing her eyes and sniffing noisily.

"It worked! I can't believe it…!" she exclaimed, more tears pouring out now. She ran to embrace him, nearly knocking him over. "I am *so* happy! That spell was just amazing! I never knew something like that existed!"

Alexander laughed, Elizabeth's jubilation was contagious. Laszlo was standing with them now. Placing his hands on Alexander's shoulders, they looked at each other for a long moment, at first neither saying anything, but they understood each other. They had come a long way. The journey had been long and hard, and both had waited patiently for many years for this day to come. Alexander spoke first.

"Laszlo…I…I don't know…I…I can't thank you enough. All your hard work…I know you sacrificed so much, thank you!"

Laszlo looked humbly at his older cousin; years of hard work and careful planning had come to a glorious end and he let a wave of relief wash over him.

"Eet vuz a great honour to help you zsrough dis and I vould do eet all again. I am vit you to da end!" They hugged each other, breaking their embrace with a smack on the back.

"Vee should go," Laszlo stated. "Da troll von't stay down forever." He looked back towards the crumbled desecration that was once a troll, turned back to Alexander and, with a knowing gaze, said, "Eet has been a long time since anyone has used dis magic. I have never seen eet done myself. I had almost forgotten eet existed."

"Yeah, Apa, that was amazing! I definitely want to know how to do *that*!" Mike piped up.

"I didn't *remember* that I could perform that spell myself."
Alexander laughed. "It was a *Woven Spell;* a spell that can
only be cast by a blood member of the Weaver family. Like
our family name suggests—we are *Weavers.* It is the web of
a Darwin Bark Spider, known to have the strongest web on
earth. Used on anything else, it would be permanent, but
on a Rock Troll...well...nothing is permanent." He pointed
toward a cluster of rocks, that could have been any part of
the Rock Troll, that were struggling against the sticky green
web, trying to pull themselves back together.

"Laszlo is right, the spell won't last much longer," Alexander said, hurrying them away from the troll and back to
the entrance.

With a swish of Laszlo's wand and the words "Nyiljon
ki!", once again the rock wall opened to give them passage
back to the real world.

When they emerged, night had fallen. Thinking that the
return journey would be too hard on Mike and not wanting
to risk an unnecessary encounter with any more unsavory
creatures, they elected to use the Travelling pearls to get
them back home.

Everyone took their pearls from their pockets and placed
them in between their teeth, ready to bite down on Laszlo's
command. They joined hands, holding on tightly.

"*Bondon!*" Laszlo exclaimed.

They all bit down hard on the pearls and with a great
swoosh they were sucked into the hidden space that lies
between time and place. It only took seconds in a long dark
tunnel before there was a blinding flash of light and then....

They were standing in a circle in the middle of Anna Nani's cow pasture…still holding hands. Mike leaned discreetly to the side and expelled the contents of his stomach in a practised manner. "I am never going to get used to this," he mumbled as he wiped his mouth with his sleeve. He turned back to the group.

Epilogue

Everyone laughed. Releasing hands from one another they turned in the direction of Anna Nani's home, Elizabeth and Alexander supporting Mike as they made the short trip back. Just then, without any warning, Alexander fell to his knees, holding his head between his hands, groaning in agony.

"Apa! What is it? What's wrong?"

Panicking, Mike dropped to his knees in front of his father, ignoring the stabbing pains shooting through his ribs, looking his father over for signs of injury, but finding none. His father bent his head down still holding it.

"Wait! Just give…just give me a…a moment," he said, struggling with each syllable.

Memories were rushing in so quickly he gripped the sides of his head for fear of it bursting, potentially causing him to lose precious memories that he had only just retrieved. Bits of information flashed through his mind, like fast forward on a DVD, moving from chapter to chapter, revealing only the smallest details of what you are seeing.

He saw himself flying, then a flash of blinding light, he was falling and fire seemed to be all around him, he was home then outside in a forested area, flashes of light sailing past his head. Hooded figures were advancing on him, a woman was screaming in the background, more flashes, he was firing spells back at his attackers, one fell to the ground, now he was standing over his attacker's body, hood slightly pulled back revealing the ear and his neck, which was mostly covered in jet black hair. Peeking out just a little was a black mark, he couldn't quite make it out, but the memories continued to flash by. His wife was standing before him, her face was so beautiful and full of so much sorrow, tears were streaming down her face; he was reaching out to touch her face, but she was out of reach. Mike was in his arms, crying out for his mother, he was shouting out to her too. There was another blinding flash of light then a searing pain in his chest, then he and Mike were being sucked into a portal. The last thing he saw as the portal door closed was his wife being dragged away by the hooded figures. She was calling out to him, but he couldn't hear and then the door was shut with a bang.

The images stopped and Alexander slumped to the ground, exhausted.

"Apa?"

Mike reached out to help his father up, Laszlo and Elizabeth supporting him to a standing position. They helped him over to a small bubbling stream that ran through Anna Nani's property, helping him to kneel down. He reached into the water and splashed his face several times. The water was cold and fresh, it felt good and the pressure in his head began to subside. Elizabeth handed her uncle a small towel, which she procured from her bag. As she patted his face dry he gave a muffled, "Kosci."

Mike knelt down beside his father on the bank of the stream.

"Apa, what just happened?"

Alexander looked at his son, once more taken by surprise at the wisdom that lay behind his eyes, yet his face was so young.

"It's my memories, Mike. I thought they had all returned when I drank from the fountain. I felt so full and whole again." He leaned over and placed his hand on his son's shoulder. "Just now though…*those* memories…they were of our last night here, the battle that sent us into exile."

"What?" Mike asked in anticipation, wishing Hanna were there. No one had ever told or could ever confirm what really happened that night, not until now. Alexander stood up, pulling Mike up with him.

"This same flash of memories hit me earlier, just before I cast my spell on the troll. Only this time there was more and the images were clearer. There is something there I am meant to figure out, like the missing piece of a puzzle, I think."

Mike was anxious to know what his father had remembered—Laszlo and Elizabeth too, especially Laszlo. He had been the one who had tried to piece together the events of that night for so many years, to help his cousin, but so many questions were still unanswered.

"Alexander, please, you *must* tell us vat you saw," Laszlo begged.

"Yes, yes, absolutely, you're right, Laszlo. I saw a mark, a tattoo or something, on the neck of one of my attackers. It was shaped like a crescent moon, deep red in colour."

"Abaddon!" Laszlo said with loathing.

"What does that mean?" Mike asked, eyes wide and anxious to know every detail.

He couldn't believe it. After all these years, he would finally know what happened to them and why. What would cause someone to attack their family, resulting in his mother's death and their thirteen-year exile?

"Da Order of da Blood Moon, dat's vat it means."

"The Order of the Blood Moon…?" Mike repeated. "Who are *they*?"

"Vampires!" Laszlo spat the word out with disgust. "Da lowest of all creatures! Vee should have known!"

"Vampires! *What*?" Mike exclaimed, horrified.

"Oh no…*oh no*!" Elizabeth said, her hand up to her mouth, shaking her head.

"Mike…." Alexander said quietly, but with urgency.

"Yes, Apa?" Mike responded immediately, hearing the intensity in his father's voice.

"There's something else…" He paused, looking hard at his son, then continued. "I saw your mother."

"You did *what*…? What did you…?" Mike asked cautiously, unable to finish the questions, not sure if he was ready to hear the answers.

Alexander looked at his son, his cousin and his niece. He was so grateful to have them there; each had sacrificed so much to help him. He drew them close, so that they were arm in arm in a circle.

"That last image…" he began, "was of your mother. She was being dragged away."

Mike could feel rage welling up inside him as he imagined his mother's broken body being dragged away by these foul creatures, wretched lifeless demons!

"Michael!" his father said, shaking him, seeing the sudden change that had come over his son's face.

"*What*?" Mike snapped back, turning away from the circle, not wanting to deal with it in front of everyone, just wanting to be alone with his anger. Even Hanna would not have been able to comfort him.

"There's more," his father said patiently, grabbing him by the arm, trying to turn him back.

"I don't want to hear anymore!" Mike yelled, yanking his arm out of his father's grip and starting to walk away.

Knowing there was no use in forcing him back, Alexander called after him instead.

"*She was alive!*"

Mike stopped dead in his tracks. Elizabeth gasped, and Laszlo muttered something in Hungarian that sounded like shock.

"She was *alive!*" Alexander repeated. "In this vision, she was calling out to us. I saw her, Michael." Alexander hastened to his son's side, gently turning him to face him. "I saw her, Mike."

Mike couldn't look up at his father, tears streaming down his cheeks, and despite the pain in his ribs he held his father tightly.

"You *saw* her? You *really* saw *her?*"

"I did, Mike, it was her, and she was alive," Alexander said, full of compassion.

Pulling back slightly from his embrace, Mike was thoughtful for a moment then hesitated, unsure of whether he should ask his next question.

"Do you believe…." There was a long pause. He was so afraid of the answer that he could barely voice the question. "Do you believe she is *still* alive?"

"I don't know." Alexander replied, his voice sounding distant. Thoughts swirled around in Alexander's mind at a dizzying pace, then stopped abruptly on a single thought.

He looked at his son, his eyes and voice full of determination. "I don't know, but I know we *have* to find out and I know where we can start."

Acknowledgments

With special thanks…

To my husband Erno—not one single word of this story would have been written without your amazing love and support.

To my daughter, Timea, and my son, Mihaly, for filling my life with immense joy.

To Tamara Dever and her amazing team at TLC Graphics for faithfully using their incredible talents, support and guidance.

To my gifted editor Barbara Munson for making order out of the chaos of my words and giving each of them a home in this story… and for teaching me the proper use of an ellipsis…

To my family and friends for your encouragement and support…and for not tiring of me being busy "because I have to finish this book."

About the Author

E.C. Varga grew up in western Canada underneath the big sky in the land wedged between prairies of endless horizons and the mighty heights of the Rocky Mountains. She resides there now with her husband, son and daughter. She loves music and all God's creatures great and small—many of whom reside in her yard. "Time well spent" is getting lost in a good book.